FOR TALLULAH SNOWBLOOD.
MATT

FOR CATHERINE, HOME IS BY YOUR SIDE.
CHRISTIAN

ODY-C, VOLUME ONE: OFF TO FAR ITHICAA. First printing. June 2015. Copyright © 2015 Milkfed Criminal Masterminds, Inc. & Christian Ward. All rights reserved. Published by Image Comics, Inc. Office of publication: 2001 Center Street, Sixth Floor, Berkeley, CA 94704. Originally published in single magazine form as ODY-C #1-5. "ODY-C," the ODY-C logo, and the likenesses of all characters herein are trademarks of Milkfed Criminal Masterminds, Inc. & Christian Ward, unless otherwise noted. "Image" and the Image Comics logos are registered trademarks of Image Comics, Inc. No part of this publication may be reproduced or transmitted, in any form or by any means (except for short excerpts for journalistic or review purposes), without the express written permission of Milkfed Criminal Masterminds, Inc., Christian Ward, or Image Comics, Inc. All names, characters, events, and locales in this publication are entirely fictional. Any resemblance to actual persons (living or dead), events, or places, without satiric intent, is coincidental. Printed in the USA. For information regarding the CPSIA on this printed material call: 203-595-3636 and provide reference #RICH–620772. For international rights, contact: foreignlicensing@imagecomics.com. ISBN: 978-1-63215-376-0.

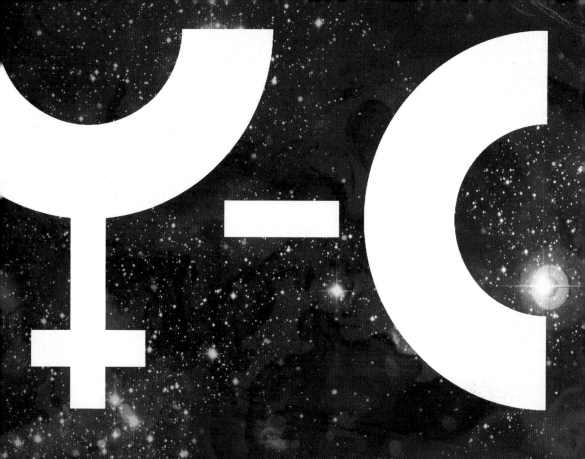

VOL 1 - OFF TO FAR ITHICAA

STORY - MATT FRACTION
ART & COLORS - CHRISTIAN WARD

LETTERING - CHRIS ELIOPOULOS
FLATS - DEE CUNNIFFE

EDITOR - LAUREN SANKOVITCH

DESIGN - CHRISTIAN WARD & DREW GILL

ODY-C CREATED BY MATT FRACTION AND CHRISTIAN WARD

SING IN US, MUSE
OF ODYSSIA
WITCHJACK AND WANDERER
HOMEWARD BOUND
WARLESS AT LAST

1

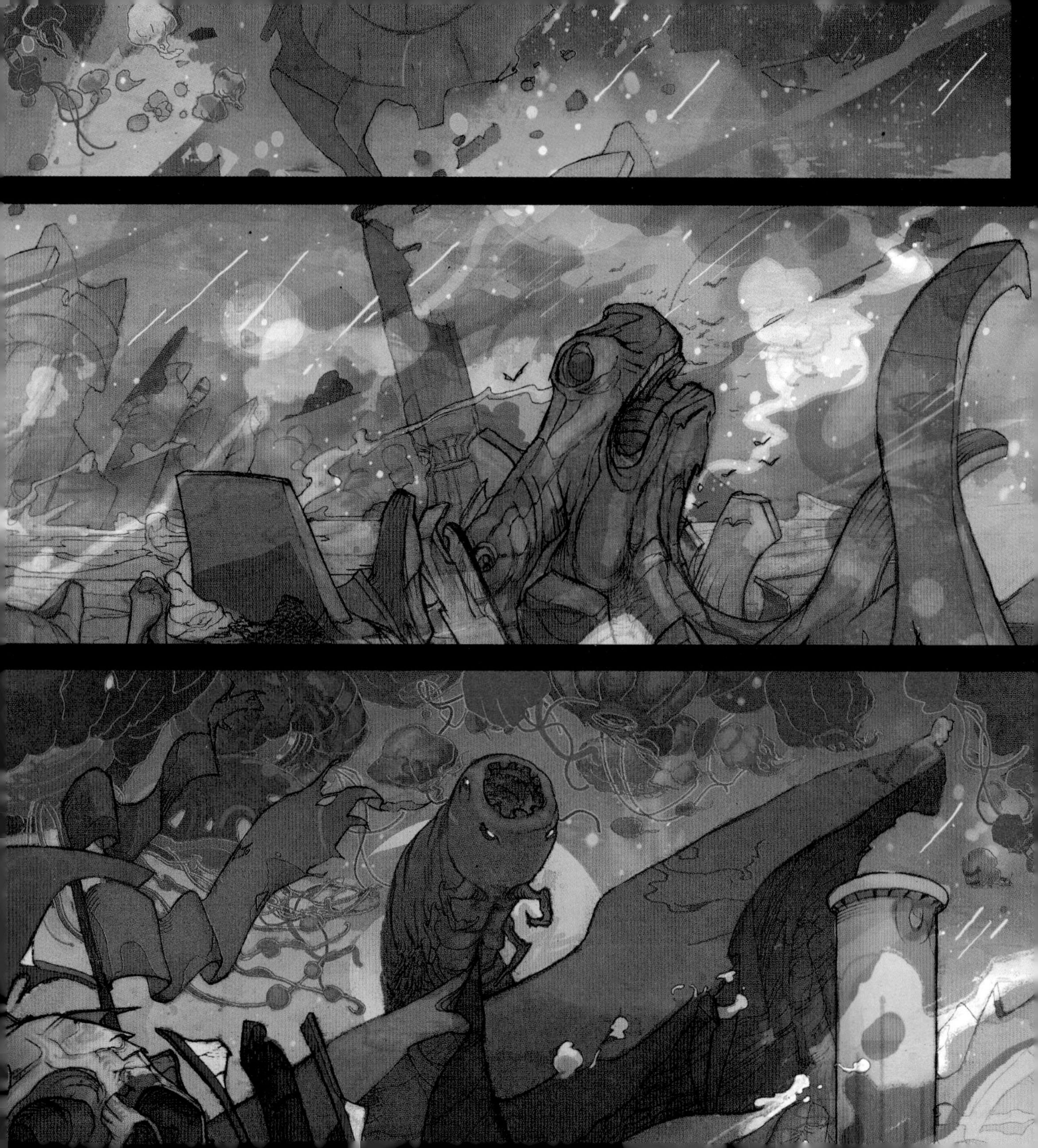

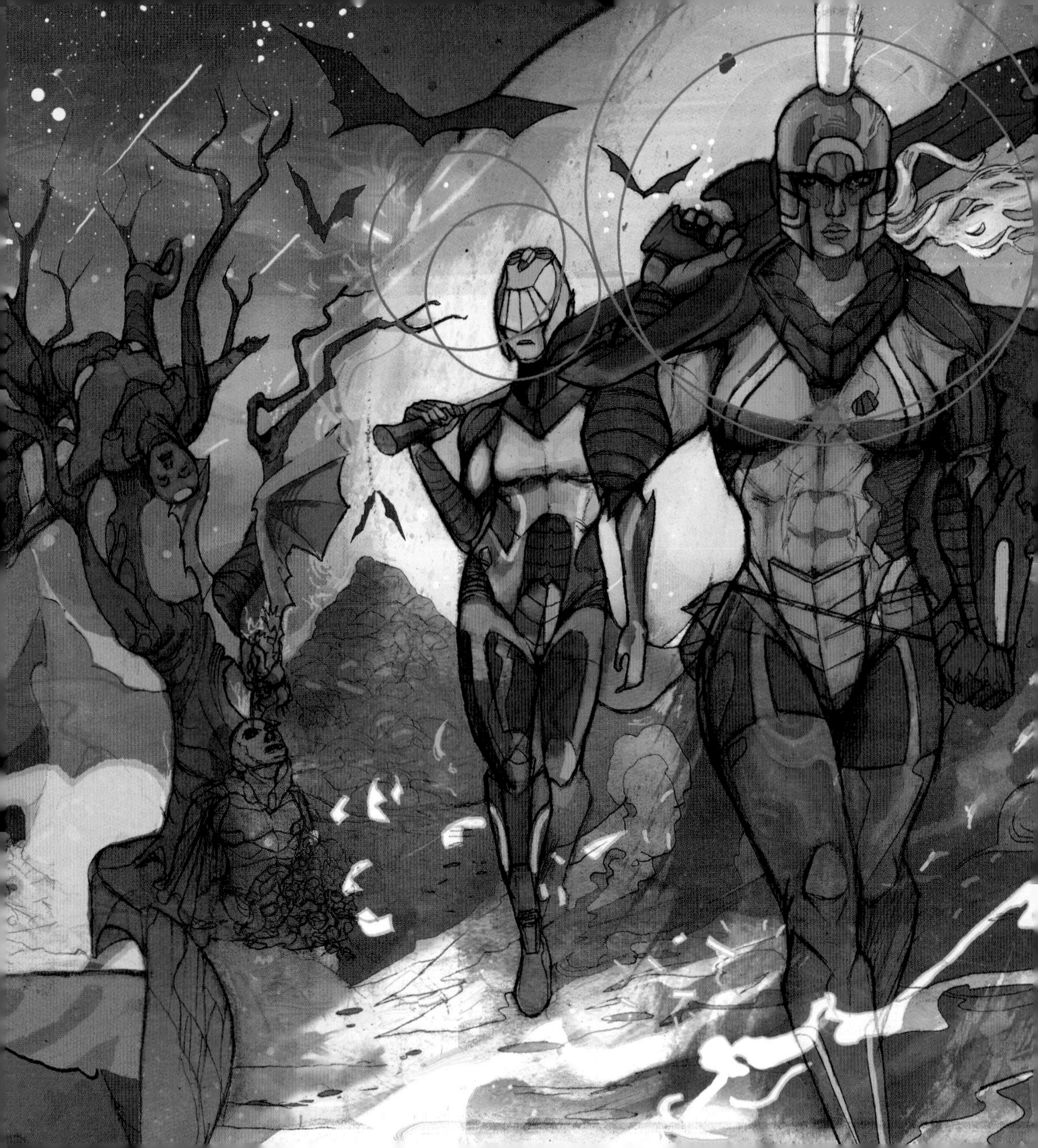

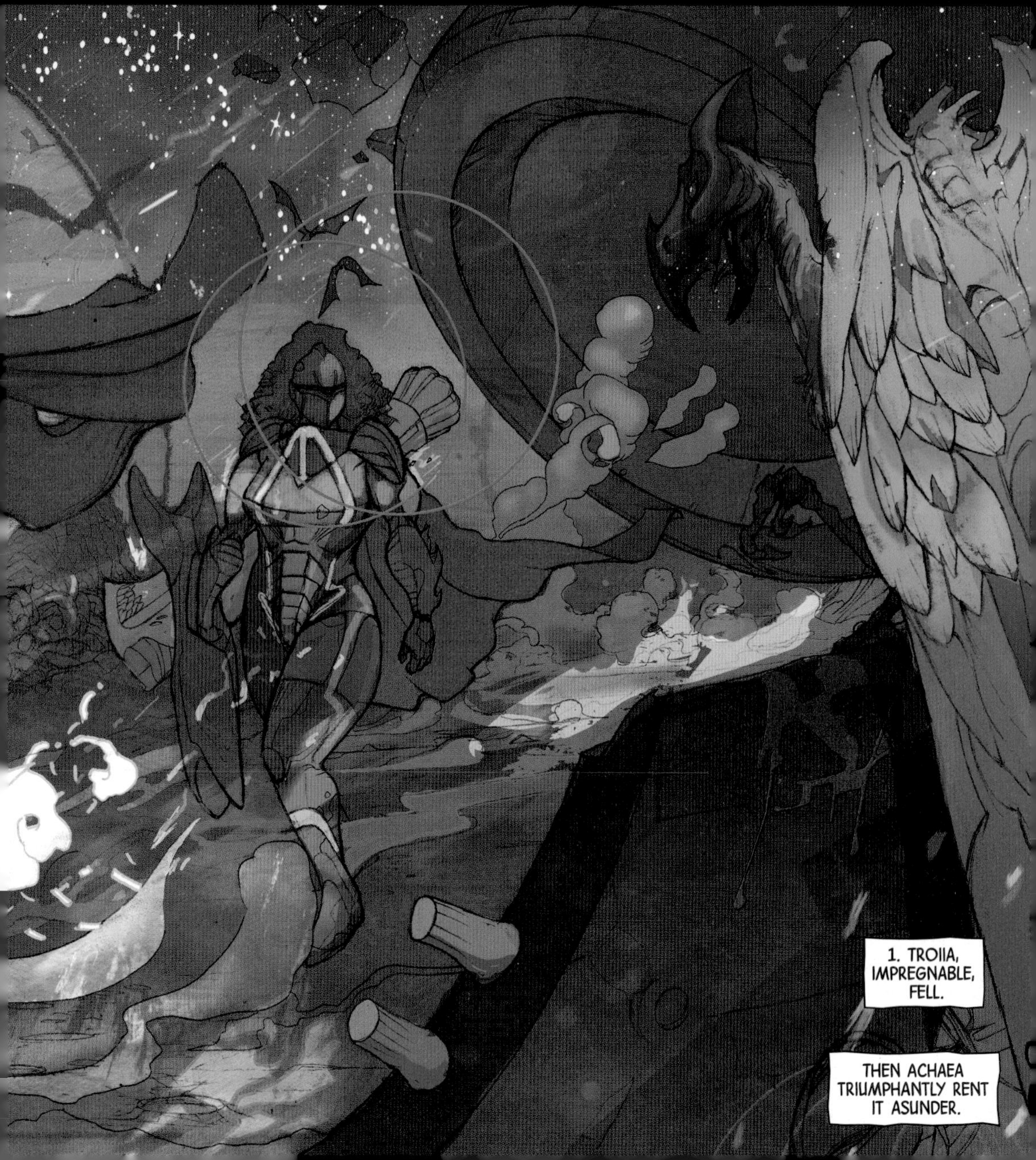
1. TROIIA, IMPREGNABLE, FELL.
THEN ACHAEA TRIUMPHANTLY RENT IT ASUNDER.

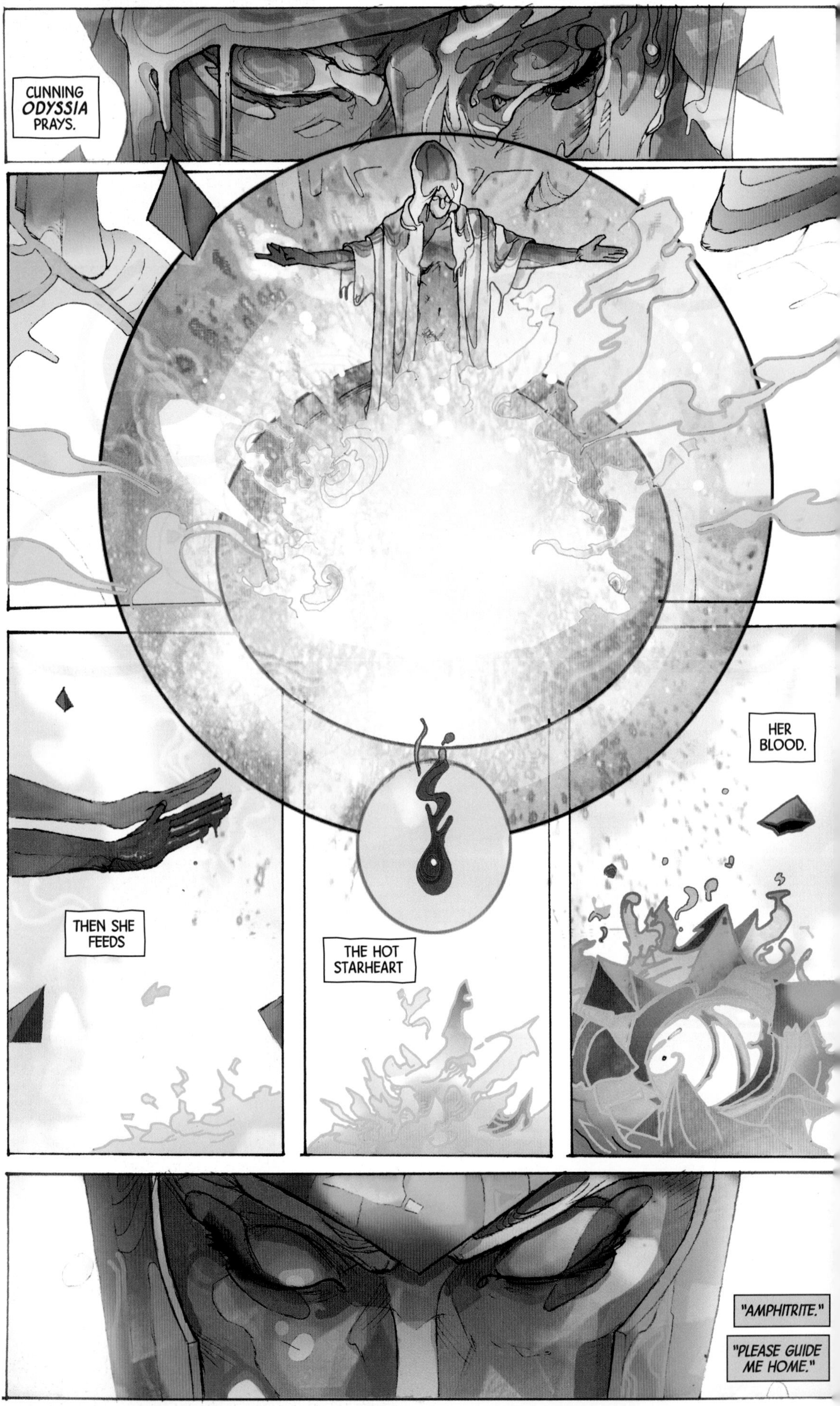

CUNNING ODYSSIA PRAYS.
THEN SHE FEEDS
THE HOT STARHEART
HER BLOOD.
"AMPHITRITE."
"PLEASE GUIDE ME HOME."

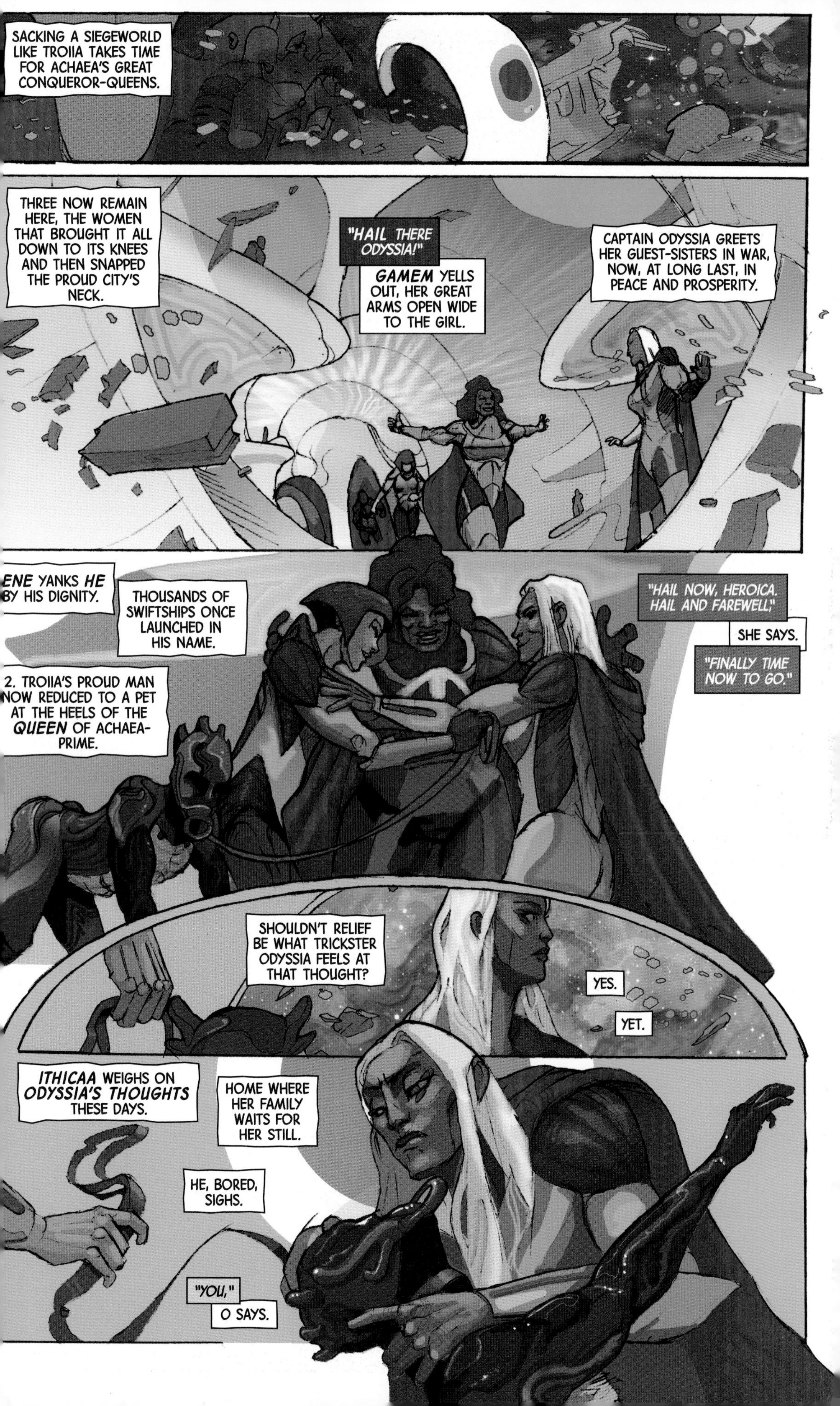
SACKING A SIEGEWORLD LIKE TROIIA TAKES TIME FOR ACHAEA'S GREAT CONQUEROR-QUEENS.
THREE NOW REMAIN HERE, THE WOMEN THAT BROUGHT IT ALL DOWN TO ITS KNEES AND THEN SNAPPED THE PROUD CITY'S NECK.
"HAIL THERE ODYSSIA!"
GAMEM YELLS OUT, HER GREAT ARMS OPEN WIDE TO THE GIRL.
CAPTAIN ODYSSIA GREETS HER GUEST-SISTERS IN WAR, NOW, AT LONG LAST, IN PEACE AND PROSPERITY.
ENE YANKS HE BY HIS DIGNITY.
THOUSANDS OF SWIFTSHIPS ONCE LAUNCHED IN HIS NAME.
2. TROIIA'S PROUD MAN NOW REDUCED TO A PET AT THE HEELS OF THE QUEEN OF ACHAEA-PRIME.
"HAIL NOW, HEROICA. HAIL AND FAREWELL,"
SHE SAYS.
"FINALLY TIME NOW TO GO."
SHOULDN'T RELIEF BE WHAT TRICKSTER ODYSSIA FEELS AT THAT THOUGHT?
YES.
YET.
ITHICAA WEIGHS ON ODYSSIA'S THOUGHTS THESE DAYS.
HOME WHERE HER FAMILY WAITS FOR HER STILL.
HE, BORED, SIGHS.
"YOU,"
O SAYS.

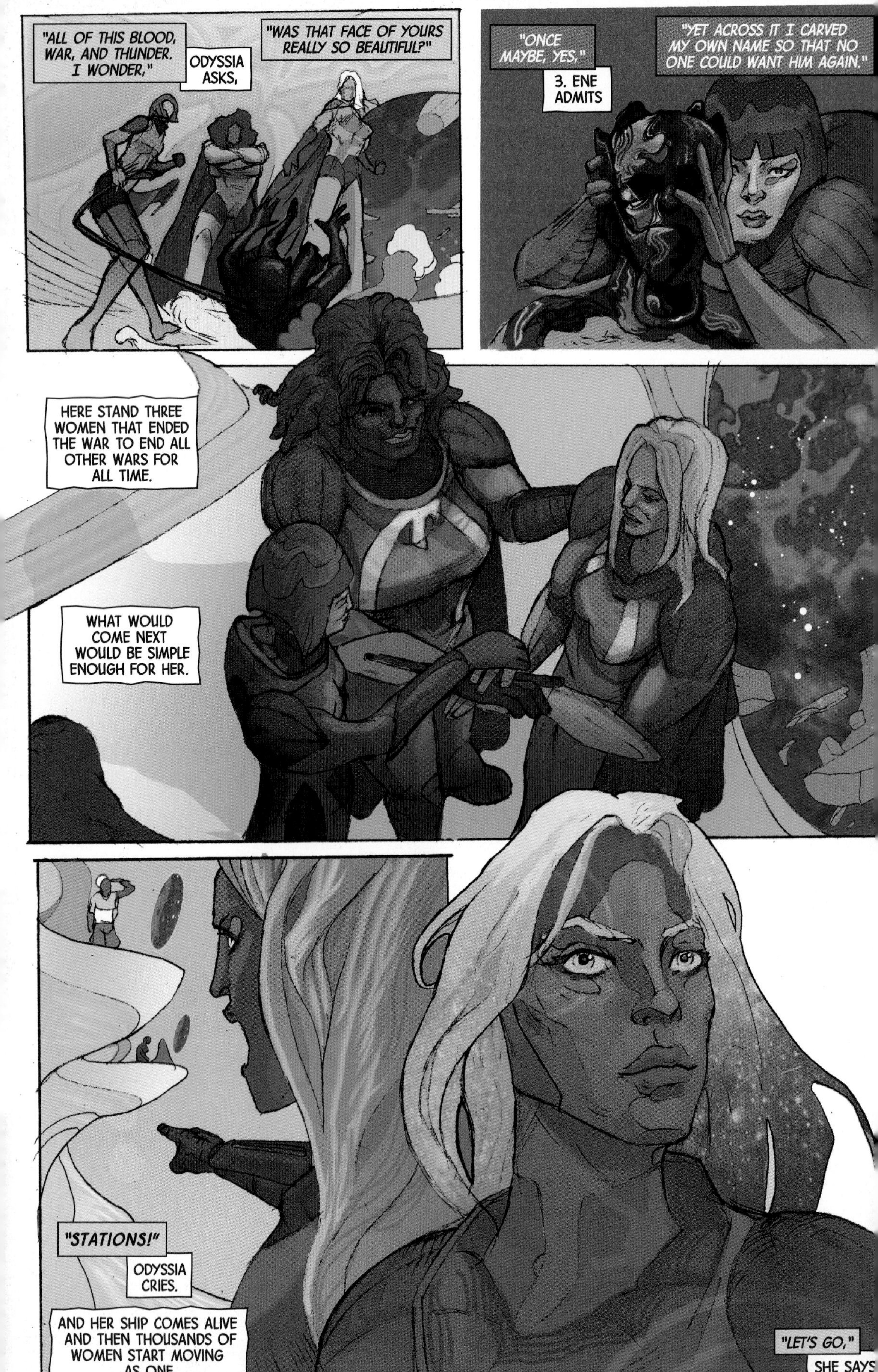
"ALL OF THIS BLOOD, WAR, AND THUNDER. I WONDER,"
ODYSSIA ASKS,
"WAS THAT FACE OF YOURS REALLY SO BEAUTIFUL?"
"ONCE MAYBE, YES,"
3. ENE ADMITS
"YET ACROSS IT I CARVED MY OWN NAME SO THAT NO ONE COULD WANT HIM AGAIN."
HERE STAND THREE WOMEN THAT ENDED THE WAR TO END ALL OTHER WARS FOR ALL TIME.
WHAT WOULD COME NEXT WOULD BE SIMPLE ENOUGH FOR HER.
"STATIONS!"
ODYSSIA CRIES.
AND HER SHIP COMES ALIVE AND THEN THOUSANDS OF WOMEN START MOVING AS ONE.
"LET'S GO,"
SHE SAYS

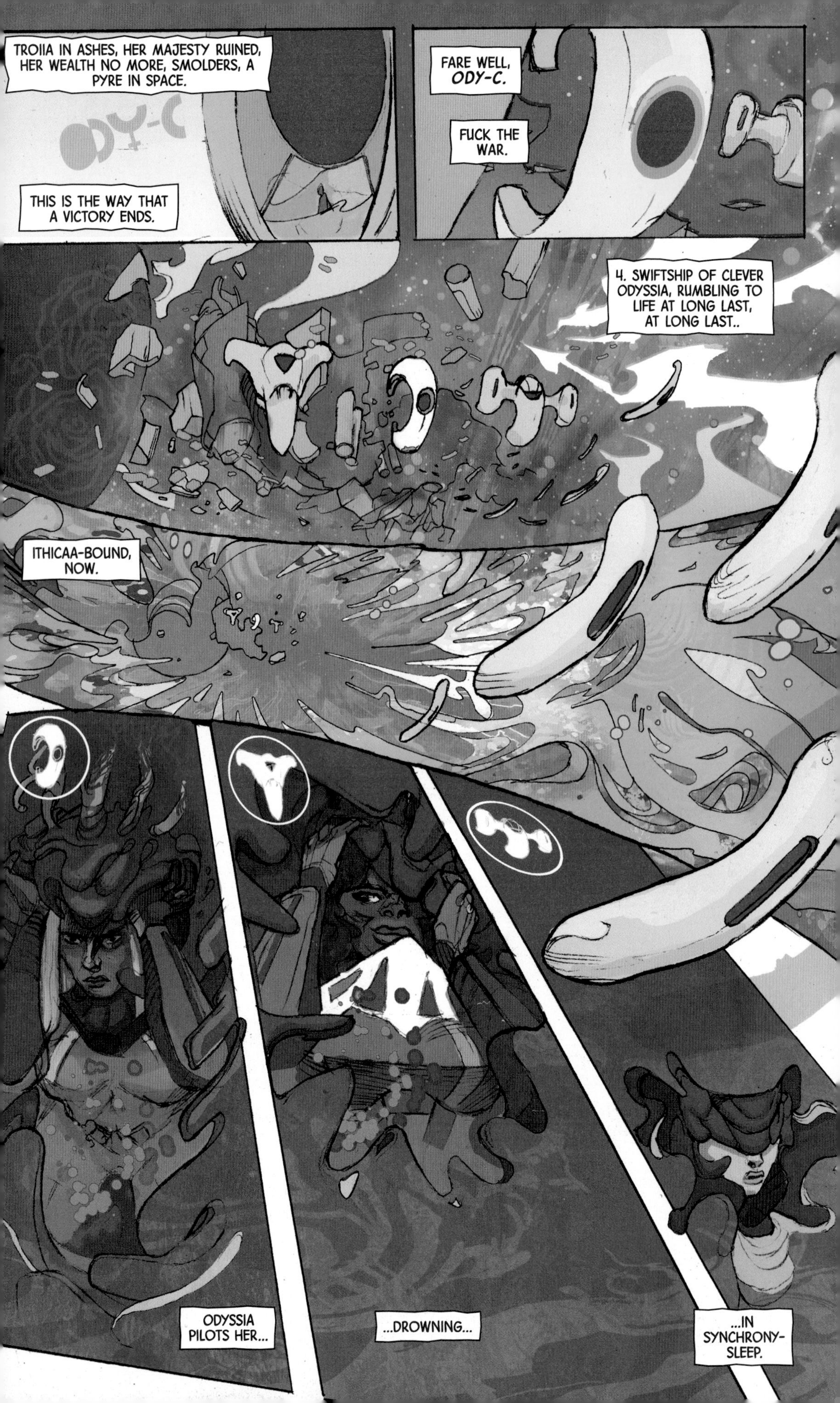

TROIIA IN ASHES, HER MAJESTY RUINED, HER WEALTH NO MORE, SMOLDERS, A PYRE IN SPACE.
ODY-C
THIS IS THE WAY THAT A VICTORY ENDS.
FARE WELL, ODY-C.
FUCK THE WAR.
4. SWIFTSHIP OF CLEVER ODYSSIA, RUMBLING TO LIFE AT LONG LAST, AT LONG LAST..
ITHICAA-BOUND, NOW.
ODYSSIA PILOTS HER...
...DROWNING...
...IN SYNCHRONY-SLEEP.

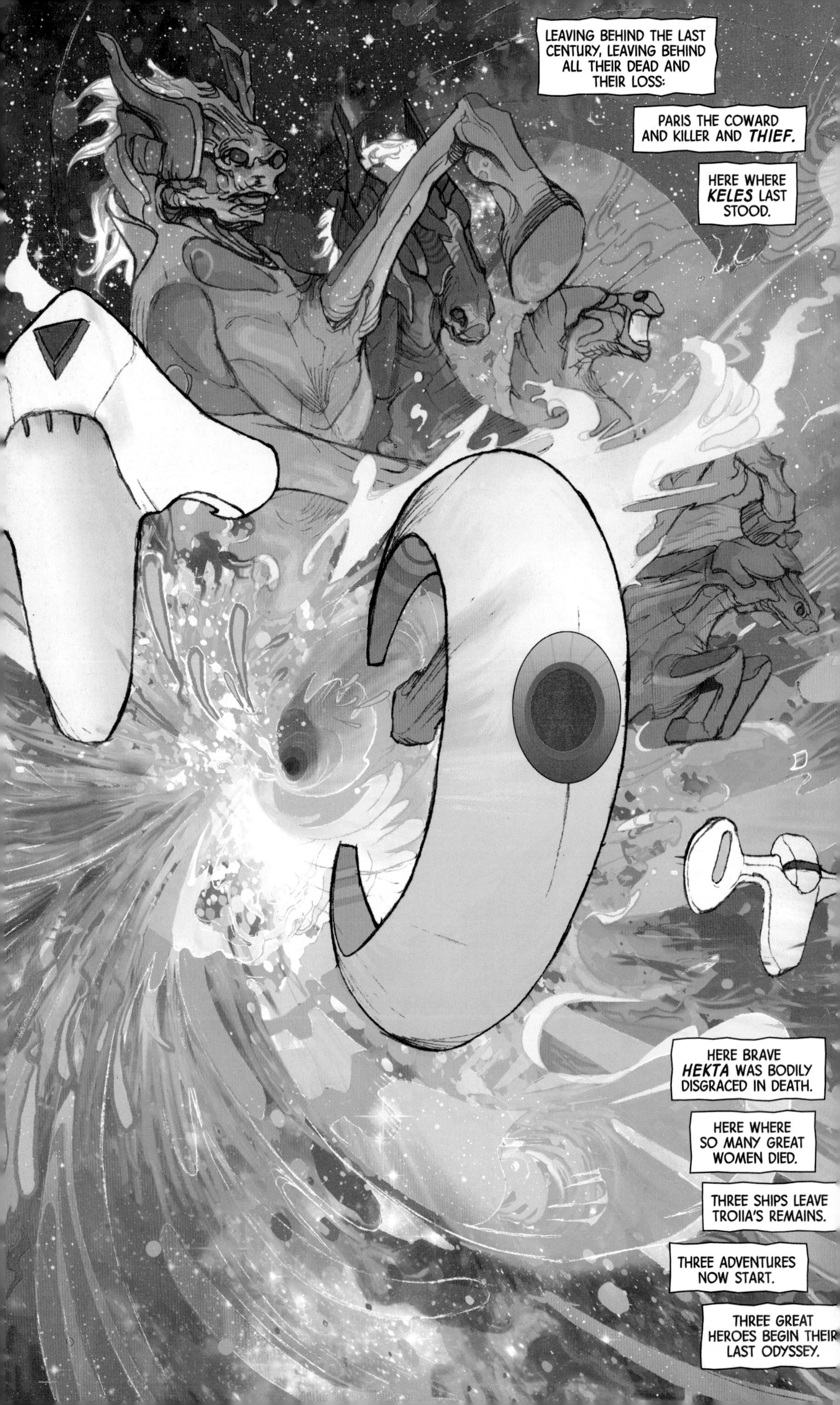
LEAVING BEHIND THE LAST CENTURY, LEAVING BEHIND ALL THEIR DEAD AND THEIR LOSS:
PARIS THE COWARD AND KILLER AND *THIEF.*
HERE WHERE *KELES* LAST STOOD.
HERE BRAVE *HEKTA* WAS BODILY DISGRACED IN DEATH.
HERE WHERE SO MANY GREAT WOMEN DIED.
THREE SHIPS LEAVE TROIIA'S REMAINS.
THREE ADVENTURES NOW START.
THREE GREAT HEROES BEGIN THEIR LAST ODYSSEY.

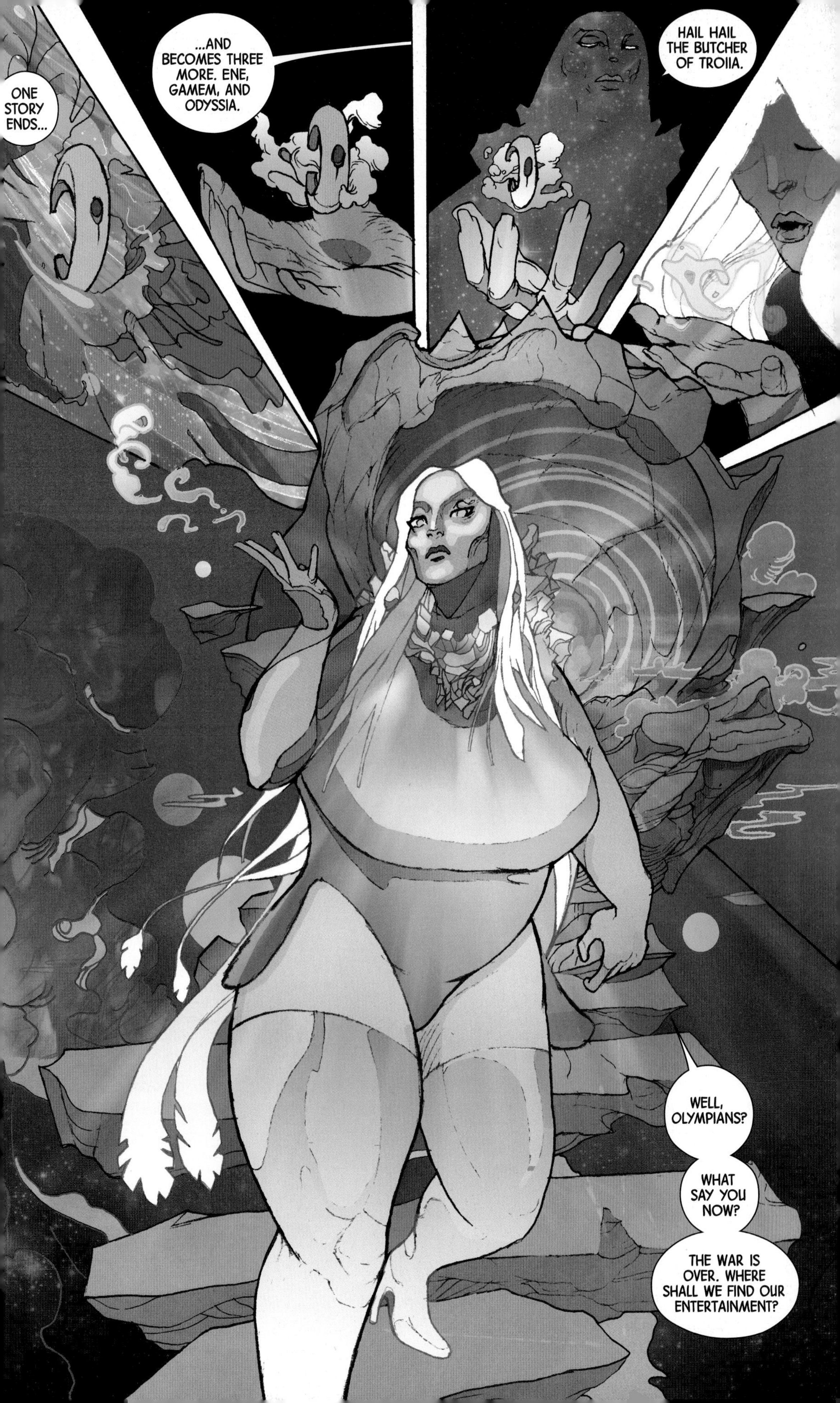

ONE STORY ENDS...
...AND BECOMES THREE MORE. ENE, GAMEM, AND ODYSSIA.
HAIL HAIL THE BUTCHER OF TROIIA.
WELL, OLYMPIANS?
WHAT SAY YOU NOW?
THE WAR IS OVER. WHERE SHALL WE FIND OUR ENTERTAINMENT?

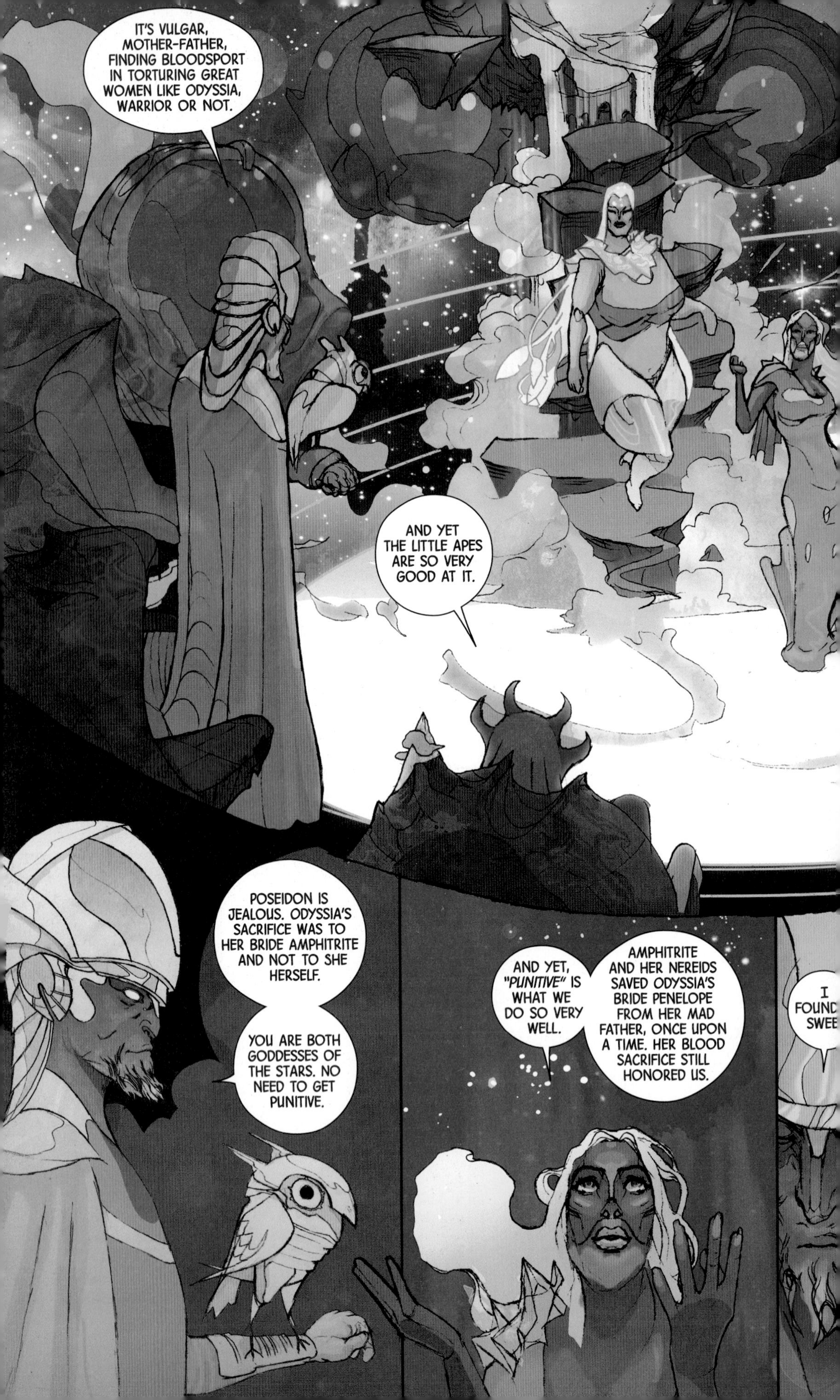
IT'S VULGAR, MOTHER-FATHER, FINDING BLOODSPORT IN TORTURING GREAT WOMEN LIKE ODYSSIA, WARRIOR OR NOT.
AND YET THE LITTLE APES ARE SO VERY GOOD AT IT.
POSEIDON IS JEALOUS. ODYSSIA'S SACRIFICE WAS TO HER BRIDE AMPHITRITE AND NOT TO SHE HERSELF.
YOU ARE BOTH GODDESSES OF THE STARS. NO NEED TO GET PUNITIVE.
AND YET, "PUNITIVE" IS WHAT WE DO SO VERY WELL.
AMPHITRITE AND HER NEREIDS SAVED ODYSSIA'S BRIDE PENELOPE FROM HER MAD FATHER, ONCE UPON A TIME. HER BLOOD SACRIFICE STILL HONORED US.

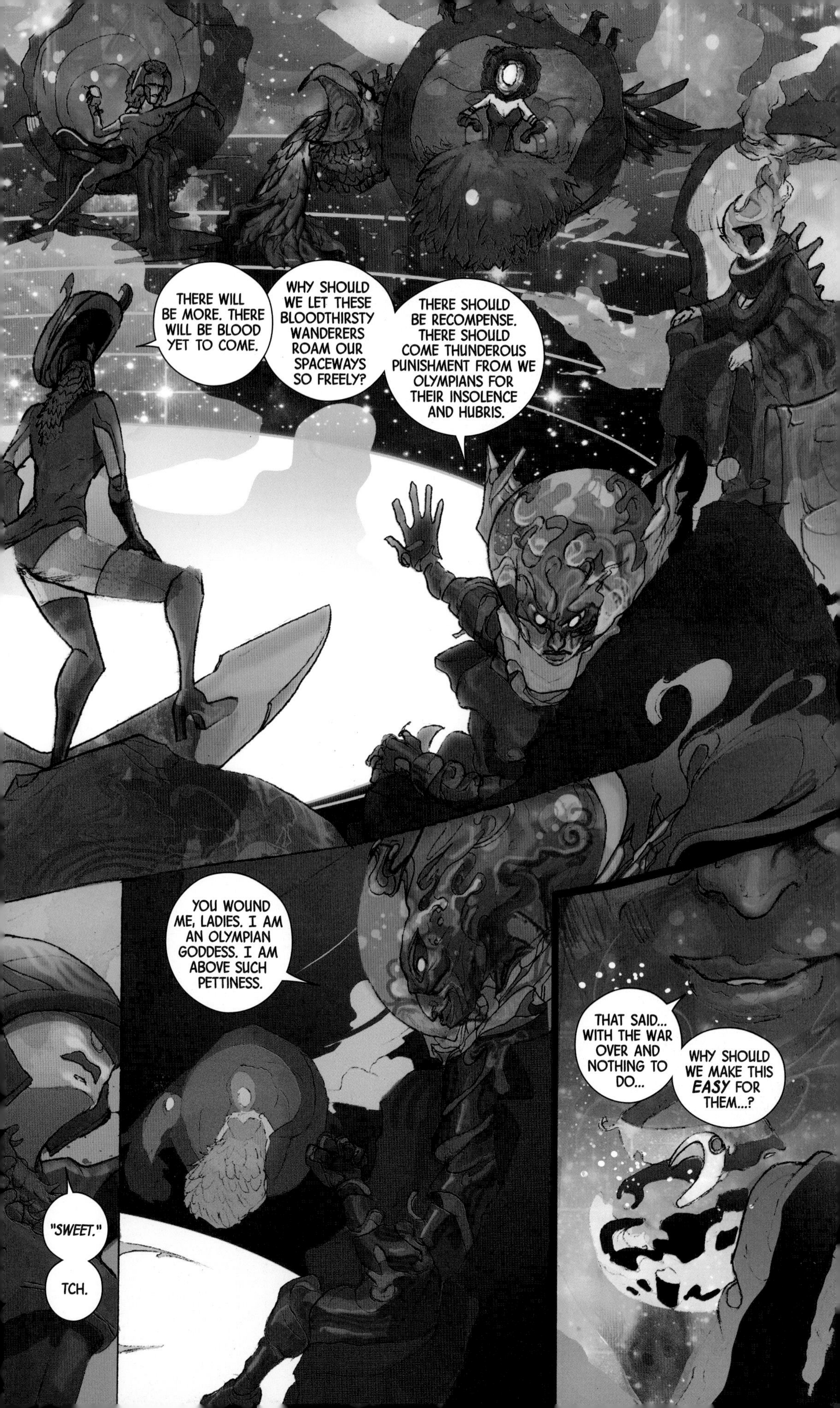
THERE WILL BE MORE. THERE WILL BE BLOOD YET TO COME.
WHY SHOULD WE LET THESE BLOODTHIRSTY WANDERERS ROAM OUR SPACEWAYS SO FREELY?
THERE SHOULD BE RECOMPENSE. THERE SHOULD COME THUNDEROUS PUNISHMENT FROM WE OLYMPIANS FOR THEIR INSOLENCE AND HUBRIS.
YOU WOUND ME, LADIES. I AM AN OLYMPIAN GODDESS. I AM ABOVE SUCH PETTINESS.
"SWEET."
TCH.
THAT SAID... WITH THE WAR OVER AND NOTHING TO DO...
WHY SHOULD WE MAKE THIS *EASY* FOR THEM...?

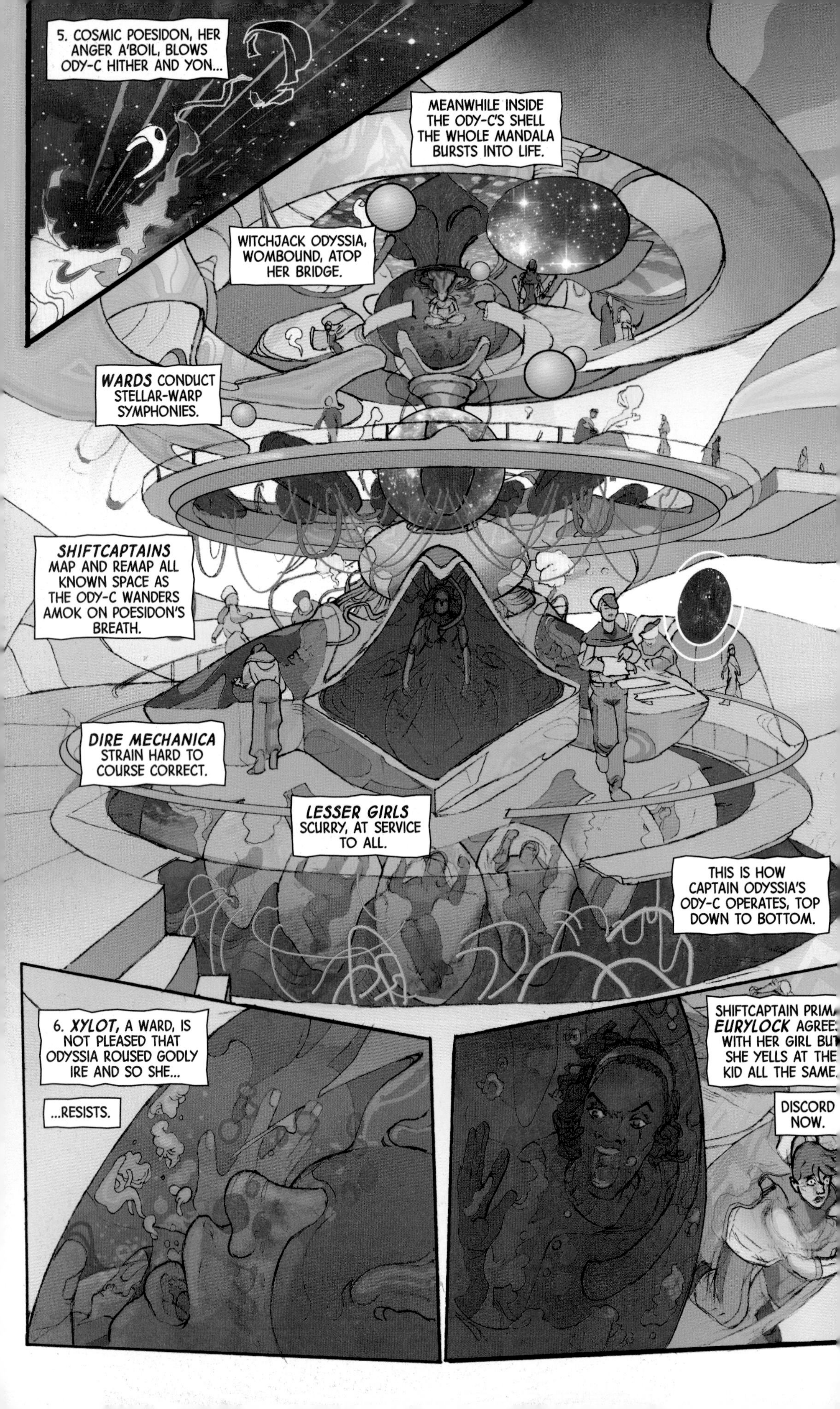
5. COSMIC POESIDON, HER ANGER A'BOIL, BLOWS ODY-C HITHER AND YON...
MEANWHILE INSIDE THE ODY-C'S SHELL THE WHOLE MANDALA BURSTS INTO LIFE.
WITCHJACK ODYSSIA, WOMBOUND, ATOP HER BRIDGE.
WARDS CONDUCT STELLAR-WARP SYMPHONIES.
SHIFTCAPTAINS MAP AND REMAP ALL KNOWN SPACE AS THE ODY-C WANDERS AMOK ON POESIDON'S BREATH.
DIRE MECHANICA STRAIN HARD TO COURSE CORRECT.
LESSER GIRLS SCURRY, AT SERVICE TO ALL.
THIS IS HOW CAPTAIN ODYSSIA'S ODY-C OPERATES, TOP DOWN TO BOTTOM.
6. XYLOT, A WARD, IS NOT PLEASED THAT ODYSSIA ROUSED GODLY IRE AND SO SHE...
...RESISTS.
SHIFTCAPTAIN PRIMA EURYLOCK AGREES WITH HER GIRL BUT SHE YELLS AT THE KID ALL THE SAME.
DISCORD NOW.

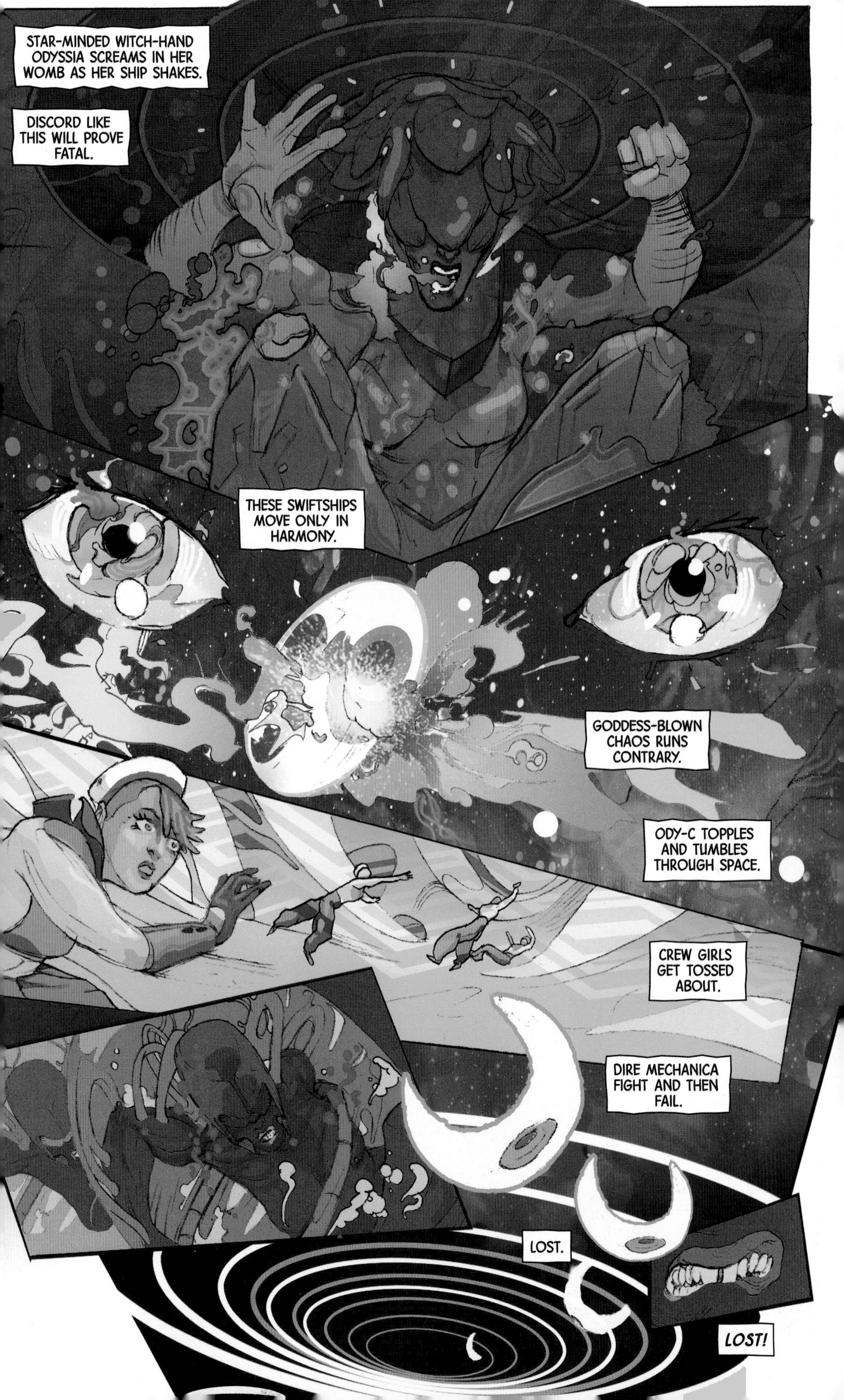

STAR-MINDED WITCH-HAND ODYSSIA SCREAMS IN HER WOMB AS HER SHIP SHAKES.
DISCORD LIKE THIS WILL PROVE FATAL.
THESE SWIFTSHIPS MOVE ONLY IN HARMONY.
GODDESS-BLOWN CHAOS RUNS CONTRARY.
ODY-C TOPPLES AND TUMBLES THROUGH SPACE.
CREW GIRLS GET TOSSED ABOUT.
DIRE MECHANICA FIGHT AND THEN FAIL.
LOST.
LOST!

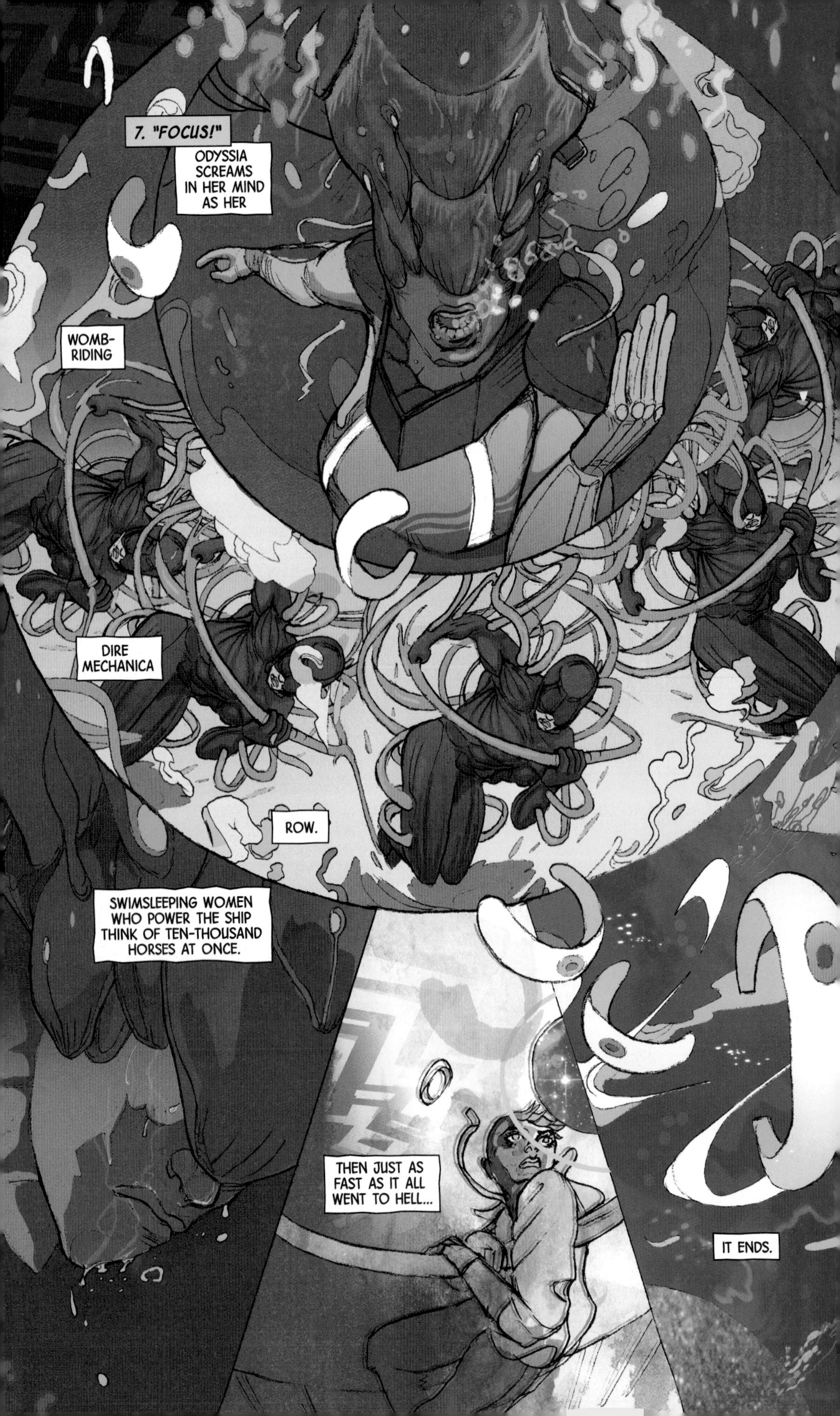
7. "FOCUS!"
ODYSSIA SCREAMS IN HER MIND AS HER
WOMB-RIDING
DIRE MECHANICA
ROW.
SWIMSLEEPING WOMEN WHO POWER THE SHIP THINK OF TEN-THOUSAND HORSES AT ONCE.
THEN JUST AS FAST AS IT ALL WENT TO HELL...
IT ENDS.

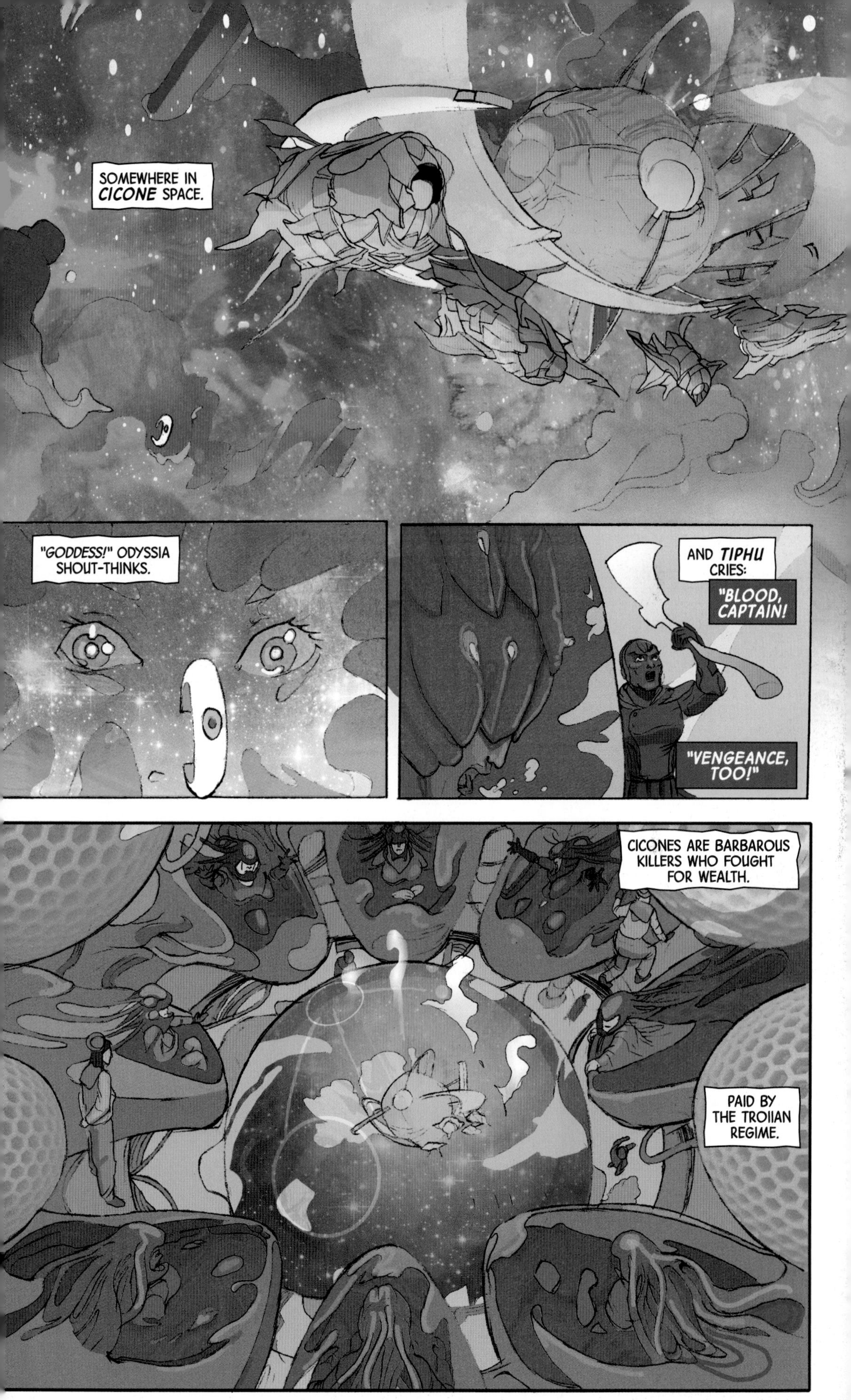
SOMEWHERE IN *CICONE* SPACE.
"*GODDESS!*" ODYSSIA SHOUT-THINKS.
AND *TIPHU* CRIES:
"*BLOOD, CAPTAIN!*
"*VENGEANCE, TOO!*"
CICONES ARE BARBAROUS KILLERS WHO FOUGHT FOR WEALTH.
PAID BY THE TROIIAN REGIME.

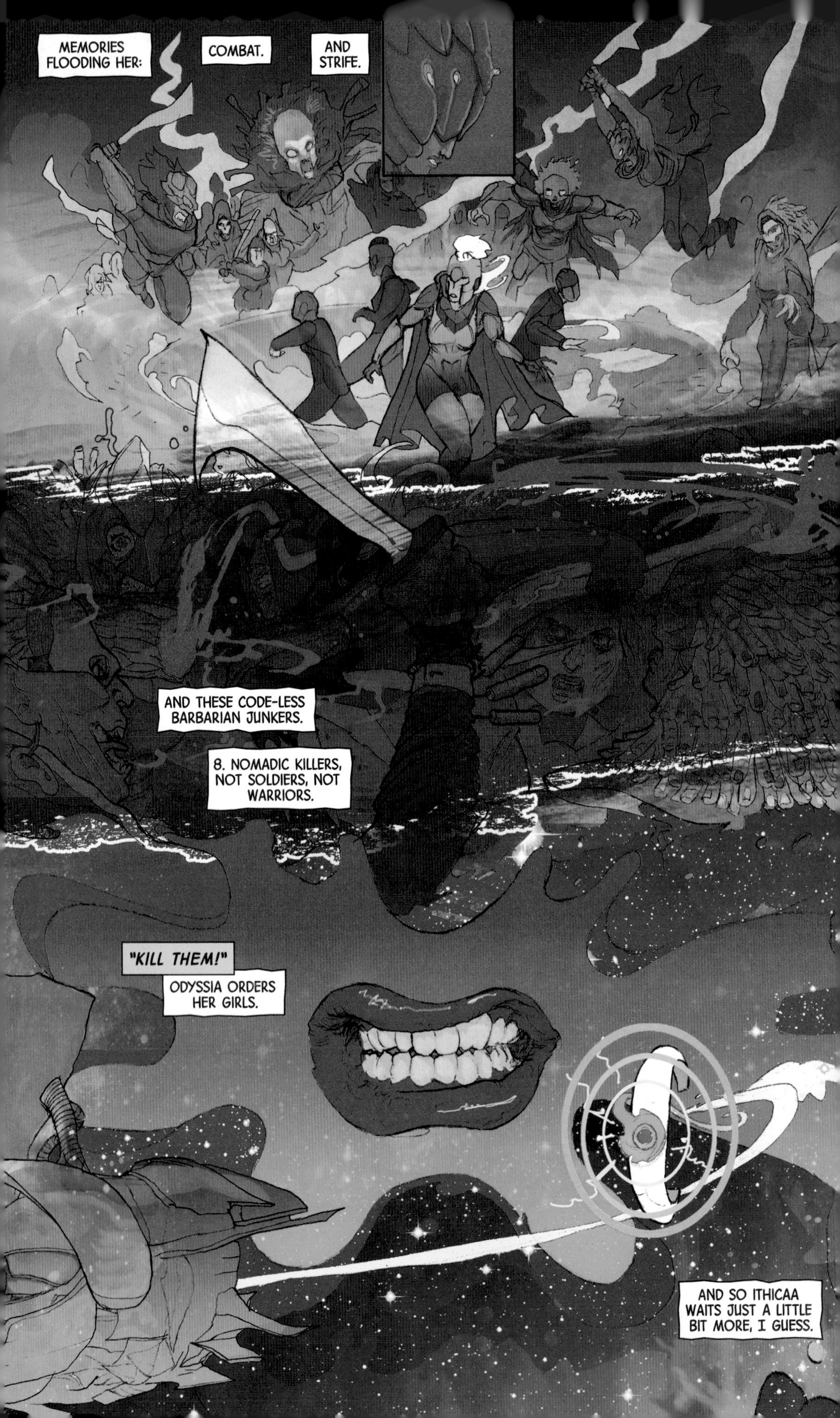
MEMORIES FLOODING HER:
COMBAT.
AND STRIFE.
AND THESE CODE-LESS BARBARIAN JUNKERS.
8. NOMADIC KILLERS, NOT SOLDIERS, NOT WARRIORS.
"KILL THEM!"
ODYSSIA ORDERS HER GIRLS.
AND SO ITHICAA WAITS JUST A LITTLE BIT MORE, I GUESS.

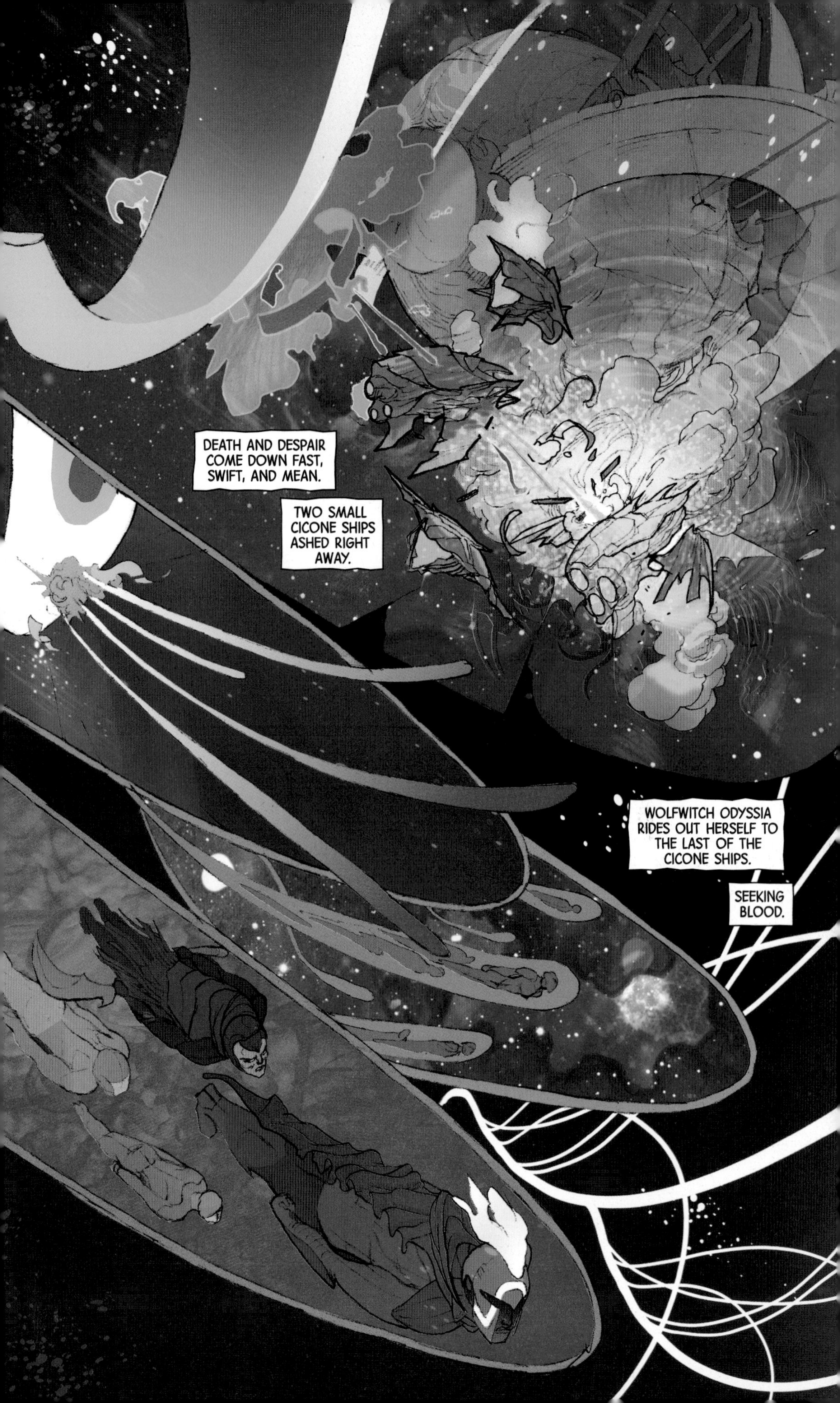
DEATH AND DESPAIR COME DOWN FAST, SWIFT, AND MEAN.
TWO SMALL CICONE SHIPS ASHED RIGHT AWAY.
WOLFWITCH ODYSSIA RIDES OUT HERSELF TO THE LAST OF THE CICONE SHIPS.
SEEKING BLOOD.

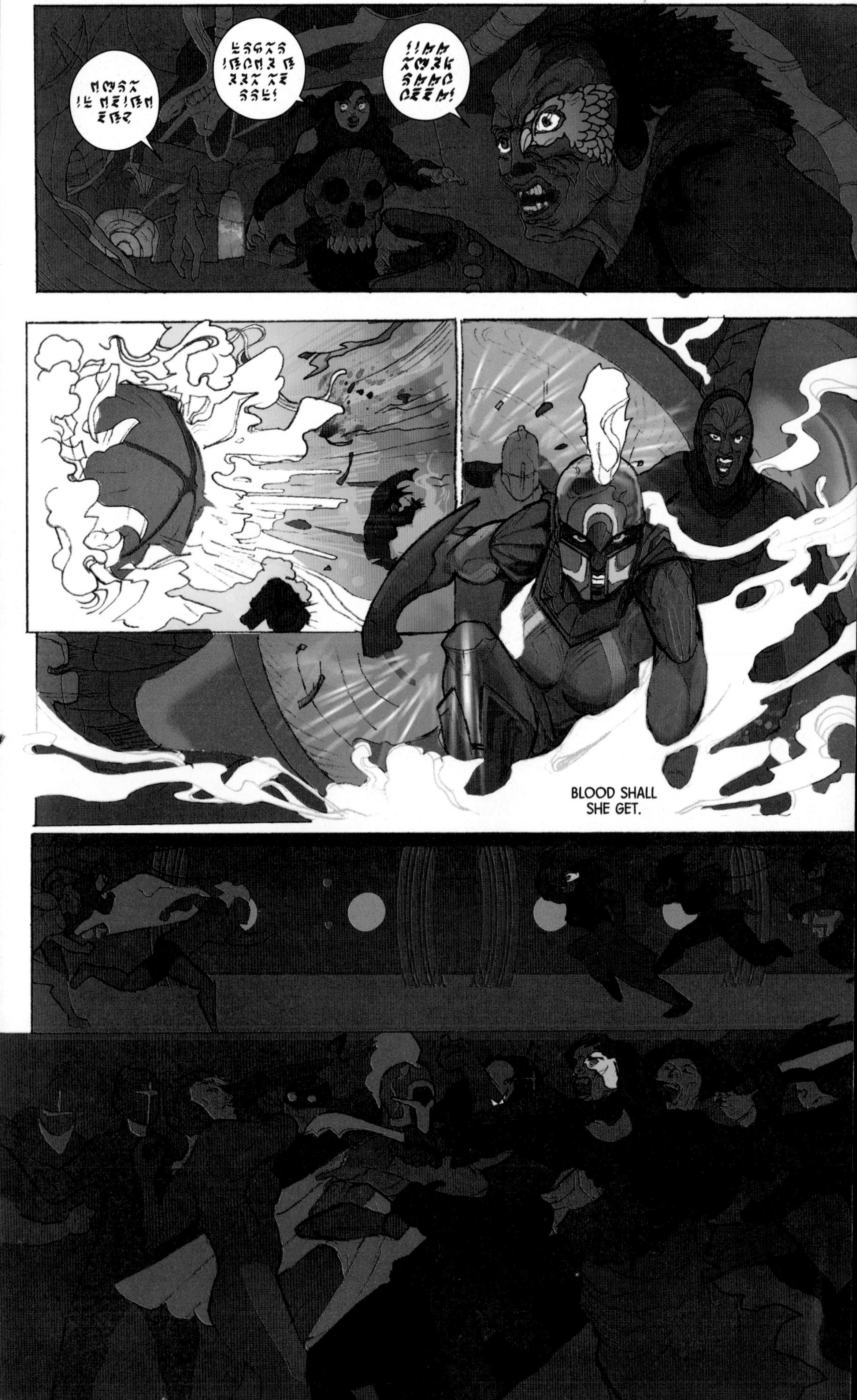
BLOOD SHALL SHE GET.

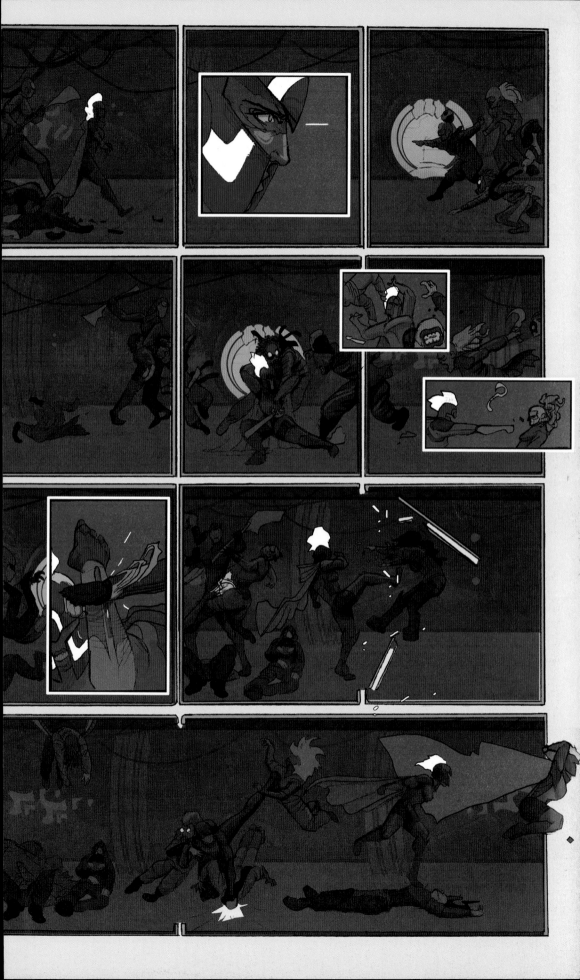

AND THUS MURDEROUS WOLFHEART ODYSSIA SETTLES UP.

AND THEN:

"WARRIOR QUEENS!"

THEIR ODYSSIA BELLOWS OUT.

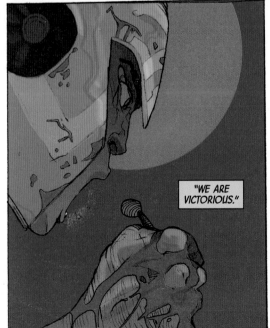

"WE ARE VICTORIOUS."

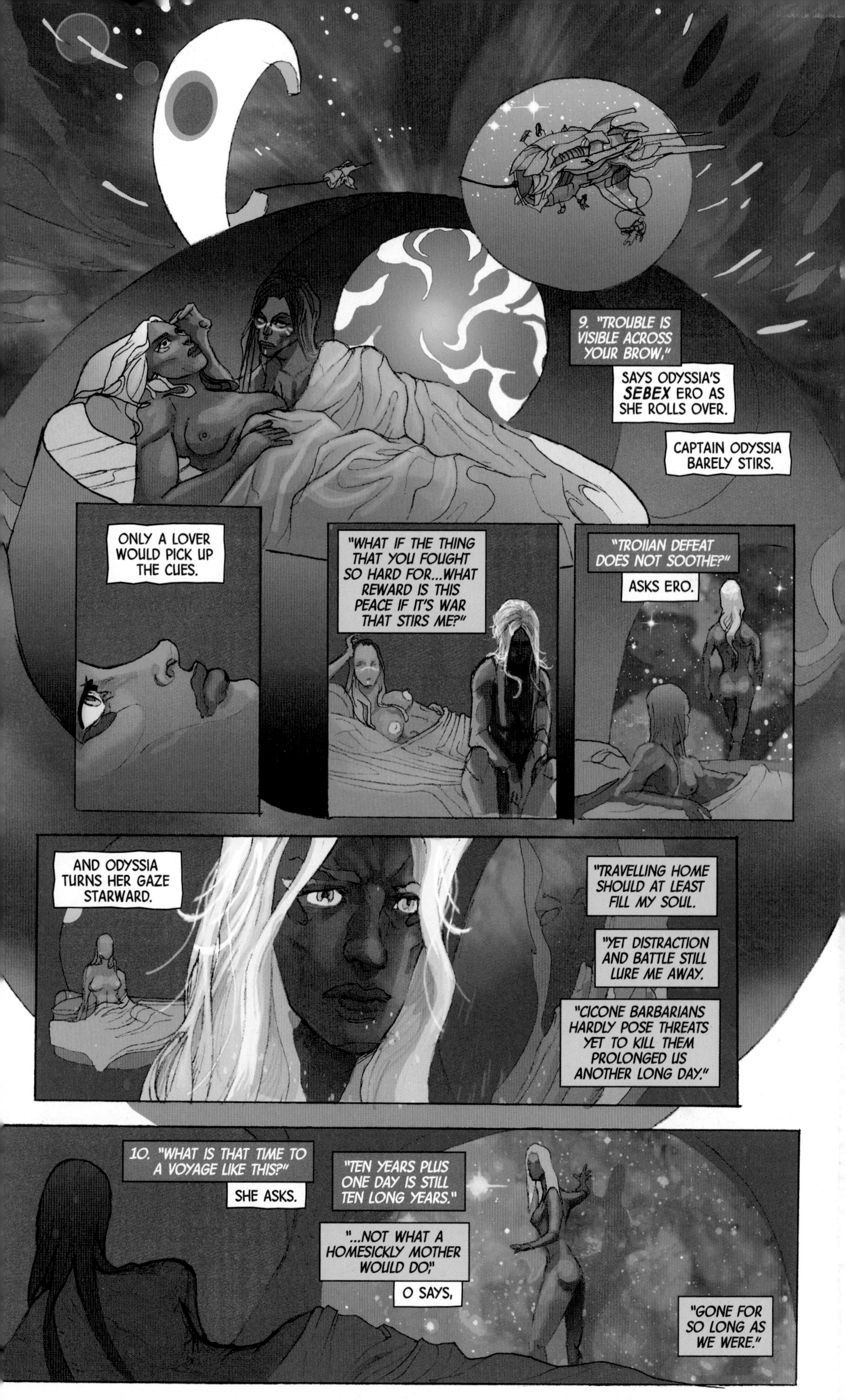
9. "TROUBLE IS VISIBLE ACROSS YOUR BROW,"
SAYS ODYSSIA'S SEBEX ERO AS SHE ROLLS OVER.
CAPTAIN ODYSSIA BARELY STIRS.
ONLY A LOVER WOULD PICK UP THE CUES.
"WHAT IF THE THING THAT YOU FOUGHT SO HARD FOR...WHAT REWARD IS THIS PEACE IF IT'S WAR THAT STIRS ME?"
"TROIIAN DEFEAT DOES NOT SOOTHE?"
ASKS ERO.
AND ODYSSIA TURNS HER GAZE STARWARD.
"TRAVELLING HOME SHOULD AT LEAST FILL MY SOUL.
"YET DISTRACTION AND BATTLE STILL LURE ME AWAY.
"CICONE BARBARIANS HARDLY POSE THREATS YET TO KILL THEM PROLONGED US ANOTHER LONG DAY."
10. "WHAT IS THAT TIME TO A VOYAGE LIKE THIS?"
SHE ASKS.
"TEN YEARS PLUS ONE DAY IS STILL TEN LONG YEARS."
"...NOT WHAT A HOMESICKLY MOTHER WOULD DO,"
O SAYS,
"GONE FOR SO LONG AS WE WERE."

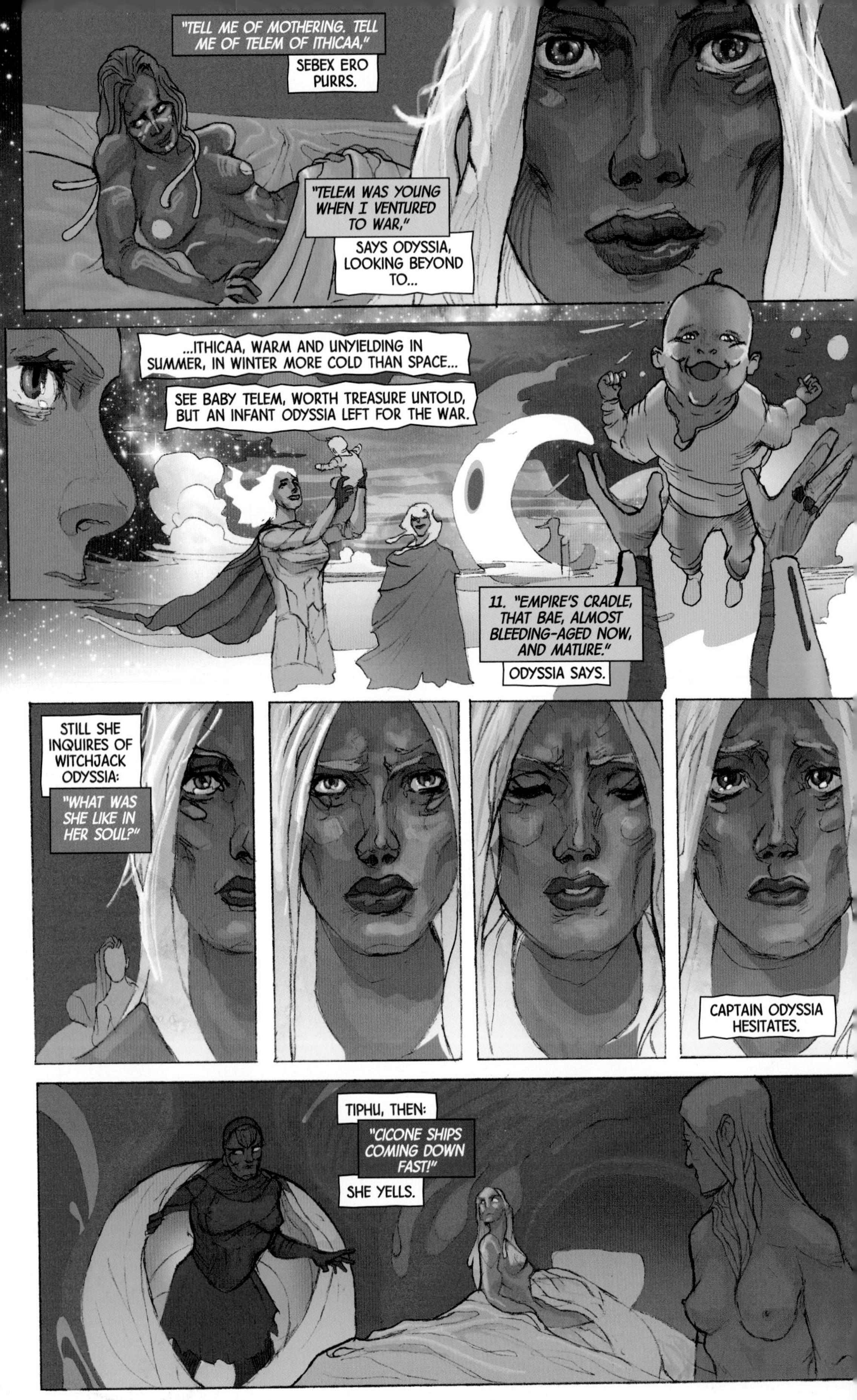
"TELL ME OF MOTHERING. TELL ME OF TELEM OF ITHICAA,"
SEBEX ERO PURRS.
"TELEM WAS YOUNG WHEN I VENTURED TO WAR,"
SAYS ODYSSIA, LOOKING BEYOND TO...
...ITHICAA, WARM AND UNYIELDING IN SUMMER, IN WINTER MORE COLD THAN SPACE...
SEE BABY TELEM, WORTH TREASURE UNTOLD, BUT AN INFANT ODYSSIA LEFT FOR THE WAR.
11. "EMPIRE'S CRADLE, THAT BAE, ALMOST BLEEDING-AGED NOW, AND MATURE."
ODYSSIA SAYS.
STILL SHE INQUIRES OF WITCHJACK ODYSSIA:
"WHAT WAS SHE LIKE IN HER SOUL?"
CAPTAIN ODYSSIA HESITATES.
TIPHU, THEN:
"CICONE SHIPS COMING DOWN FAST!"
SHE YELLS.

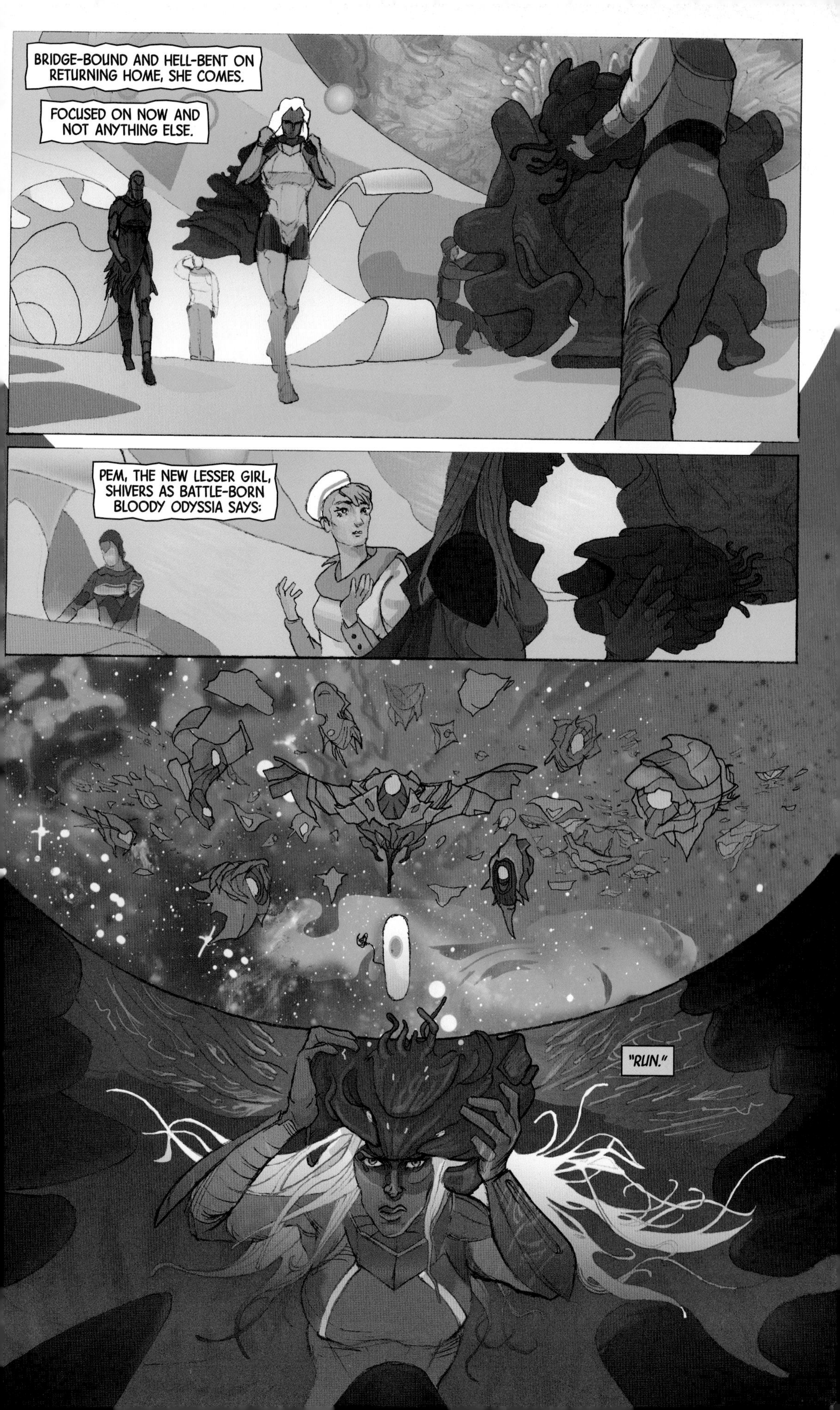
BRIDGE-BOUND AND HELL-BENT ON RETURNING HOME, SHE COMES.
FOCUSED ON NOW AND NOT ANYTHING ELSE.
PEM, THE NEW LESSER GIRL, SHIVERS AS BATTLE-BORN BLOODY ODYSSIA SAYS:
"RUN."

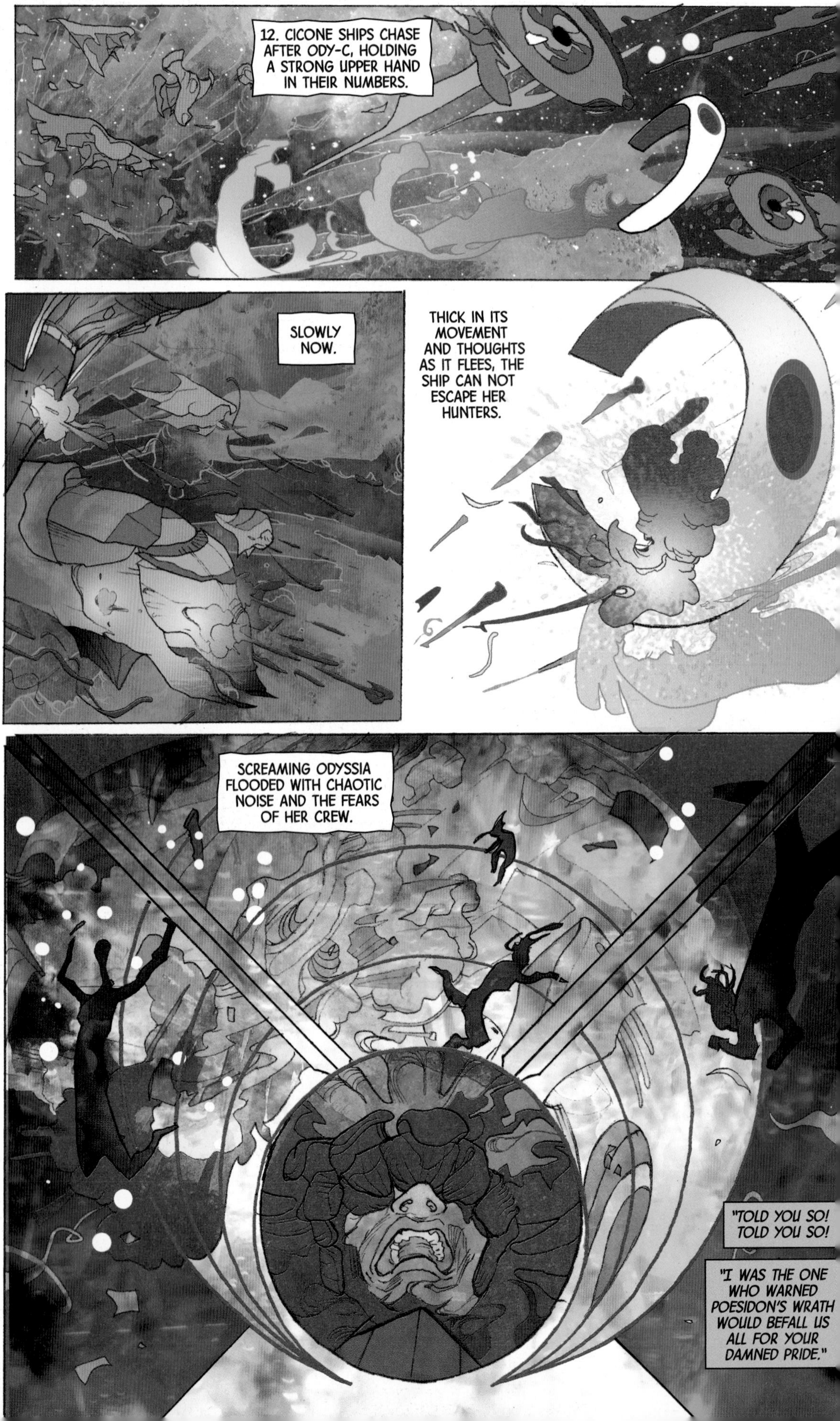
12. CICONE SHIPS CHASE AFTER ODY-C, HOLDING A STRONG UPPER HAND IN THEIR NUMBERS.
SLOWLY NOW.
THICK IN ITS MOVEMENT AND THOUGHTS AS IT FLEES, THE SHIP CAN NOT ESCAPE HER HUNTERS.
SCREAMING ODYSSIA FLOODED WITH CHAOTIC NOISE AND THE FEARS OF HER CREW.
"TOLD YOU SO! TOLD YOU SO!
"I WAS THE ONE WHO WARNED POESIDON'S WRATH WOULD BEFALL US ALL FOR YOUR DAMNED PRIDE."

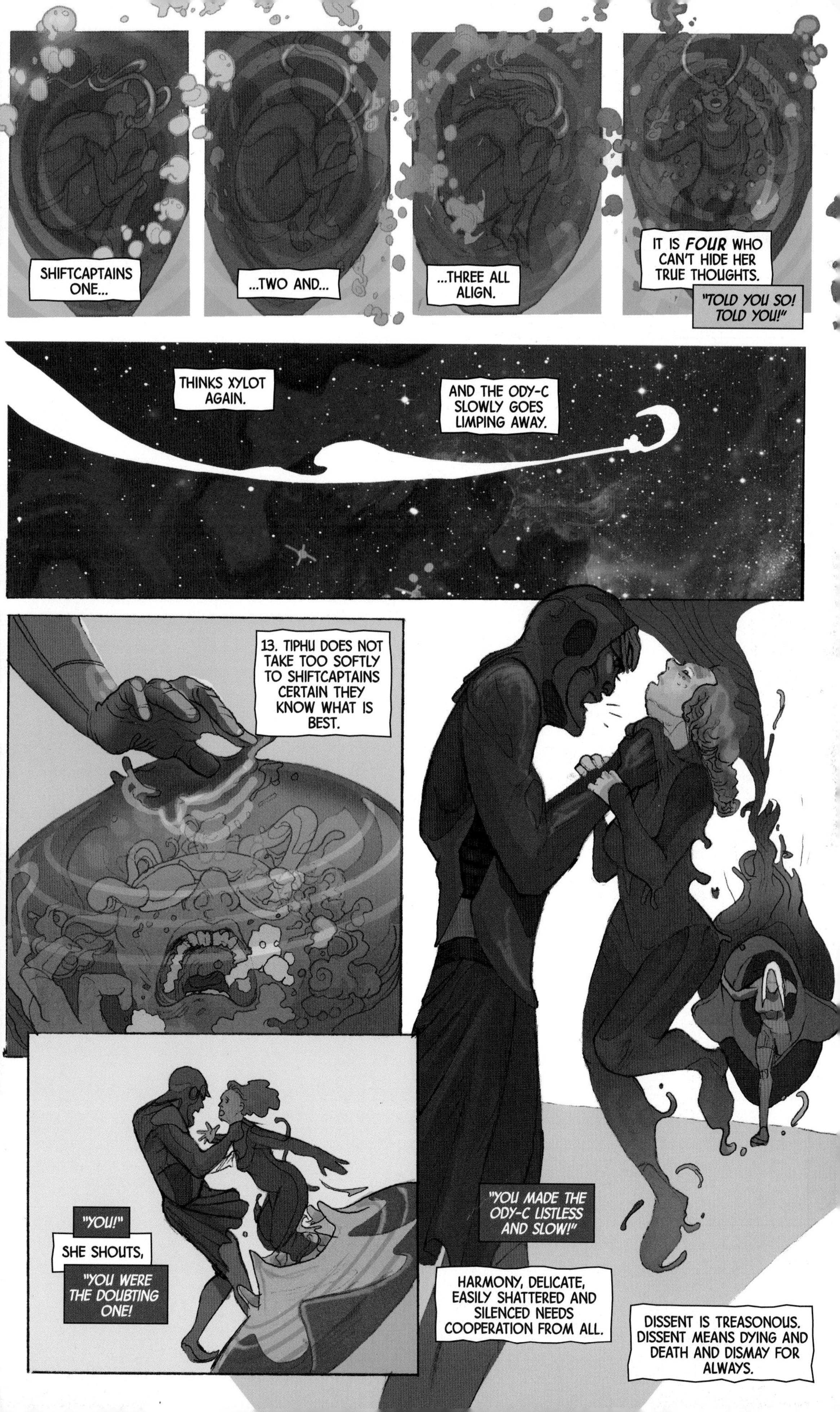

SHIFTCAPTAINS ONE...
...TWO AND...
...THREE ALL ALIGN.
IT IS *FOUR* WHO CAN'T HIDE HER TRUE THOUGHTS.
"TOLD YOU SO! TOLD YOU!"
THINKS XYLOT AGAIN.
AND THE ODY-C SLOWLY GOES LIMPING AWAY.
13. TIPHU DOES NOT TAKE TOO SOFTLY TO SHIFTCAPTAINS CERTAIN THEY KNOW WHAT IS BEST.
"YOU!"
SHE SHOUTS,
"YOU WERE THE DOUBTING ONE!
"YOU MADE THE ODY-C LISTLESS AND SLOW!"
HARMONY, DELICATE, EASILY SHATTERED AND SILENCED NEEDS COOPERATION FROM ALL.
DISSENT IS TREASONOUS. DISSENT MEANS DYING AND DEATH AND DISMAY FOR ALWAYS.

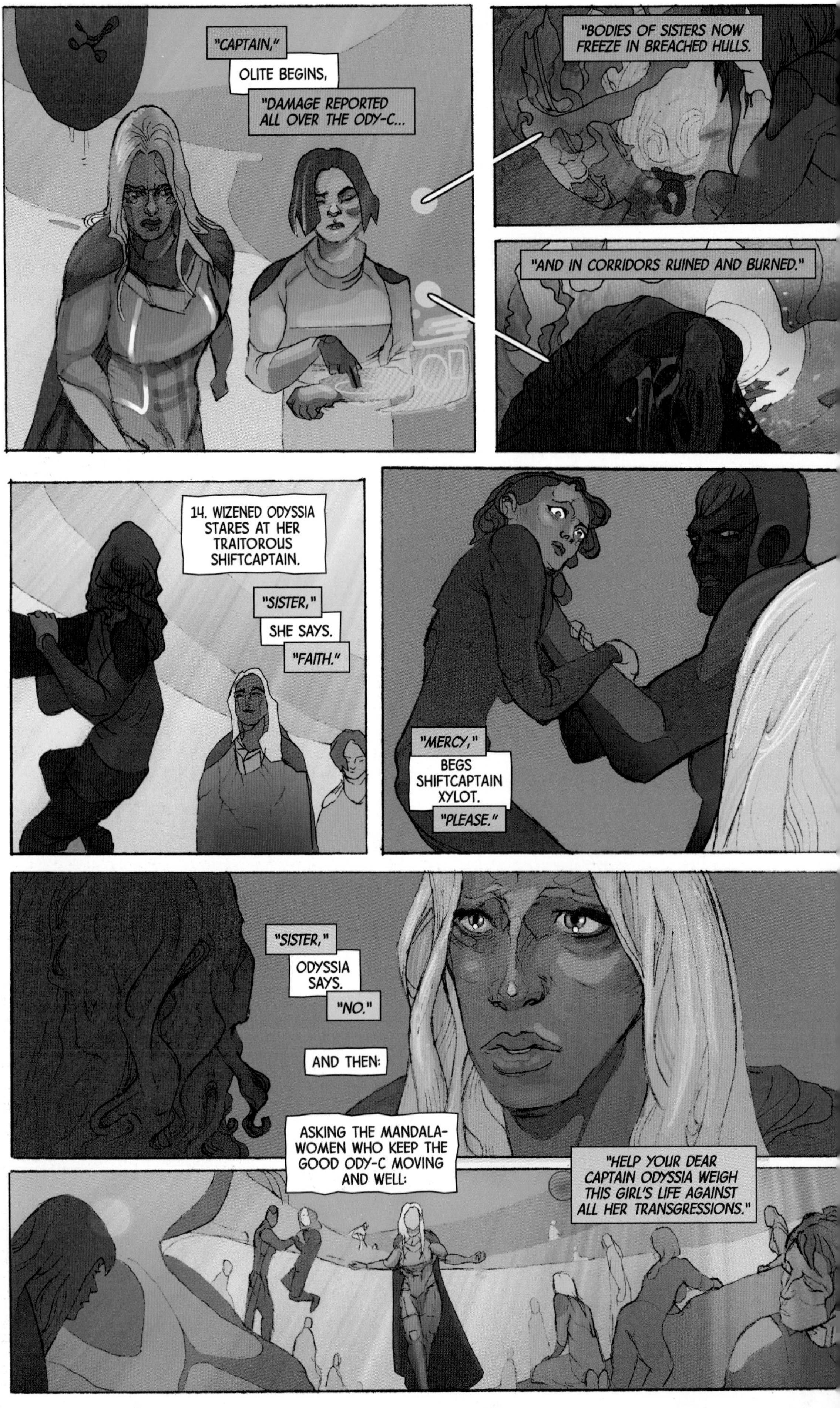
"CAPTAIN,"
OLITE BEGINS,
"DAMAGE REPORTED ALL OVER THE ODY-C...
"BODIES OF SISTERS NOW FREEZE IN BREACHED HULLS.
"AND IN CORRIDORS RUINED AND BURNED."
14. WIZENED ODYSSIA STARES AT HER TRAITOROUS SHIFTCAPTAIN.
"SISTER,"
SHE SAYS.
"FAITH."
"MERCY,"
BEGS SHIFTCAPTAIN XYLOT.
"PLEASE."
"SISTER,"
ODYSSIA SAYS.
"NO."
AND THEN:
ASKING THE MANDALA-WOMEN WHO KEEP THE GOOD ODY-C MOVING AND WELL:
"HELP YOUR DEAR CAPTAIN ODYSSIA WEIGH THIS GIRL'S LIFE AGAINST ALL HER TRANSGRESSIONS."

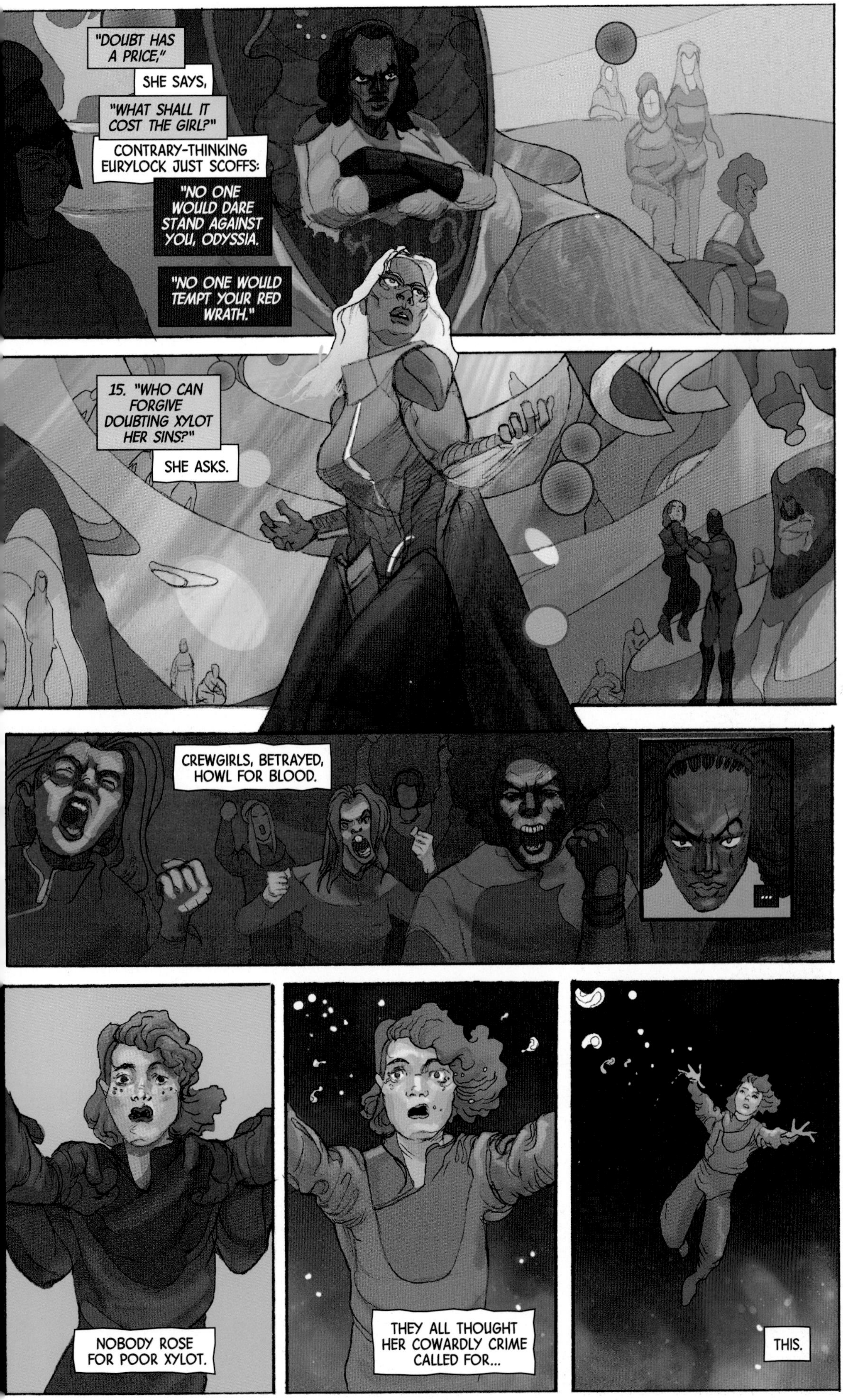
"DOUBT HAS A PRICE,"
SHE SAYS,
"WHAT SHALL IT COST THE GIRL?"
CONTRARY-THINKING EURYLOCK JUST SCOFFS:
"NO ONE WOULD DARE STAND AGAINST YOU, ODYSSIA.
"NO ONE WOULD TEMPT YOUR RED WRATH."
15. "WHO CAN FORGIVE DOUBTING XYLOT HER SINS?"
SHE ASKS.
CREWGIRLS, BETRAYED, HOWL FOR BLOOD.
NOBODY ROSE FOR POOR XYLOT.
THEY ALL THOUGHT HER COWARDLY CRIME CALLED FOR...
THIS.

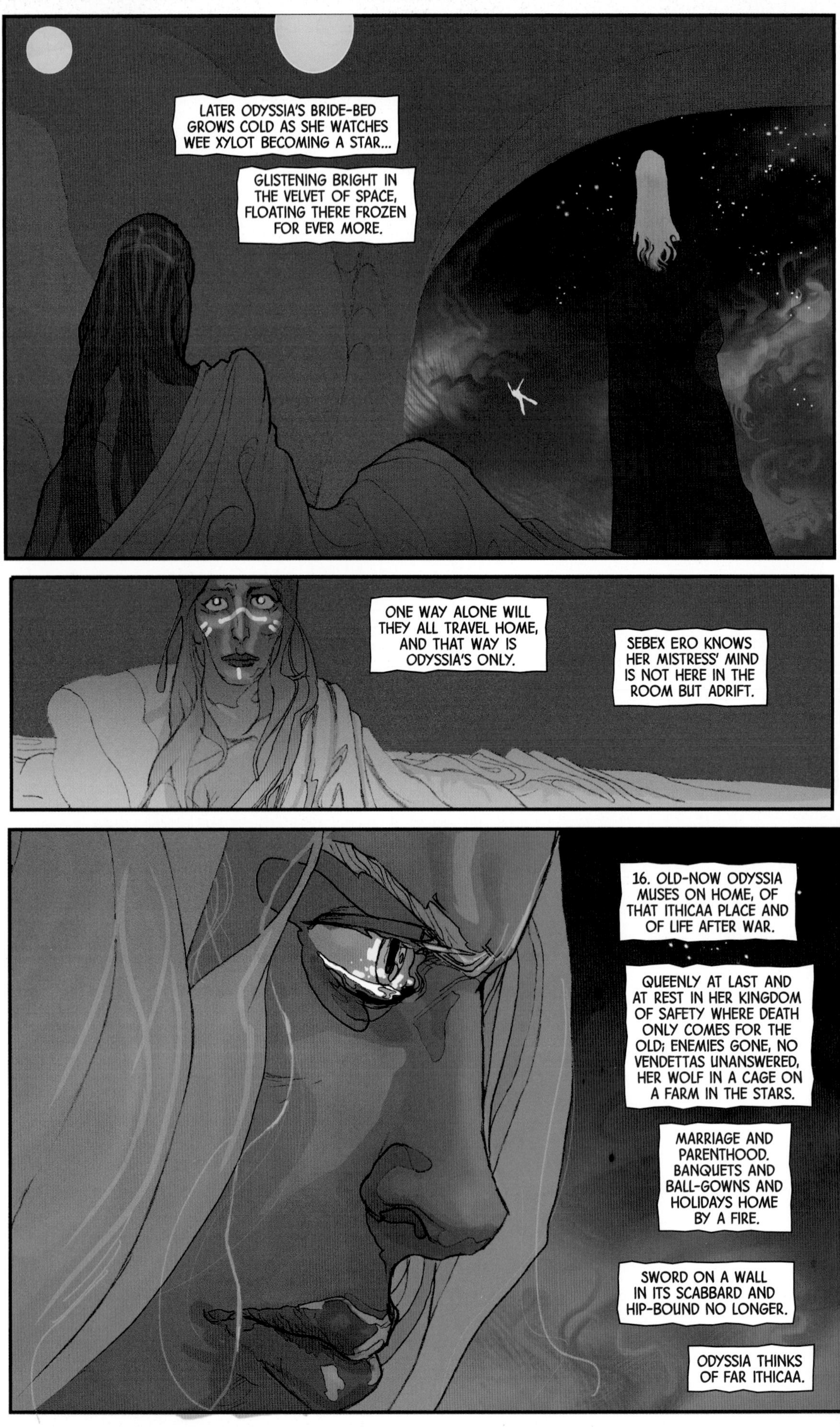
LATER ODYSSIA'S BRIDE-BED GROWS COLD AS SHE WATCHES WEE XYLOT BECOMING A STAR...
GLISTENING BRIGHT IN THE VELVET OF SPACE, FLOATING THERE FROZEN FOR EVER MORE.
ONE WAY ALONE WILL THEY ALL TRAVEL HOME, AND THAT WAY IS ODYSSIA'S ONLY.
SEBEX ERO KNOWS HER MISTRESS' MIND IS NOT HERE IN THE ROOM BUT ADRIFT.
16. OLD-NOW ODYSSIA MUSES ON HOME, OF THAT ITHICAA PLACE AND OF LIFE AFTER WAR.
QUEENLY AT LAST AND AT REST IN HER KINGDOM OF SAFETY WHERE DEATH ONLY COMES FOR THE OLD; ENEMIES GONE, NO VENDETTAS UNANSWERED, HER WOLF IN A CAGE ON A FARM IN THE STARS.
MARRIAGE AND PARENTHOOD. BANQUETS AND BALL-GOWNS AND HOLIDAYS HOME BY A FIRE.
SWORD ON A WALL IN ITS SCABBARD AND HIP-BOUND NO LONGER.
ODYSSIA THINKS OF FAR ITHICAA.

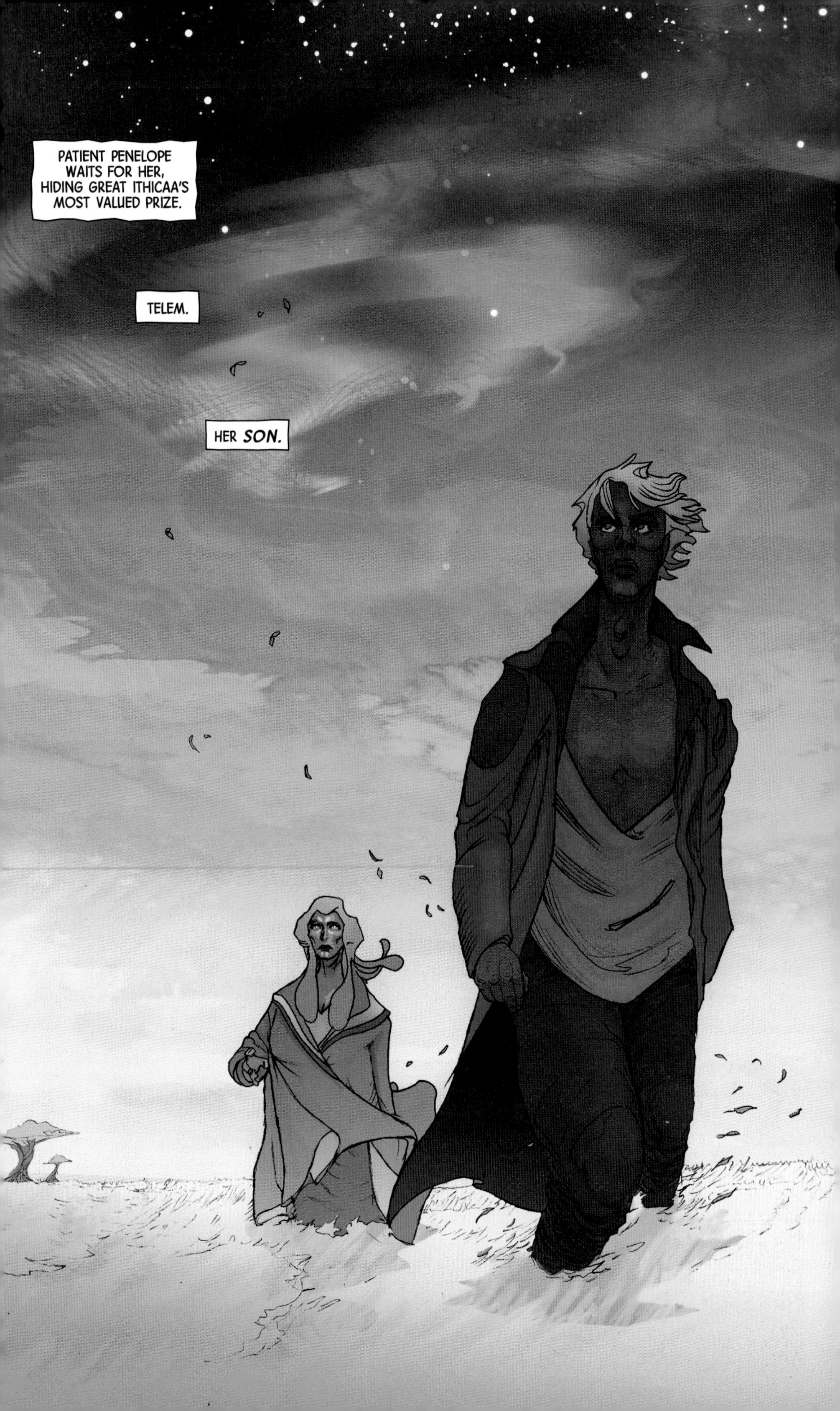
PATIENT PENELOPE WAITS FOR HER, HIDING GREAT ITHICAA'S MOST VALUED PRIZE.
TELEM.
HER *SON.*

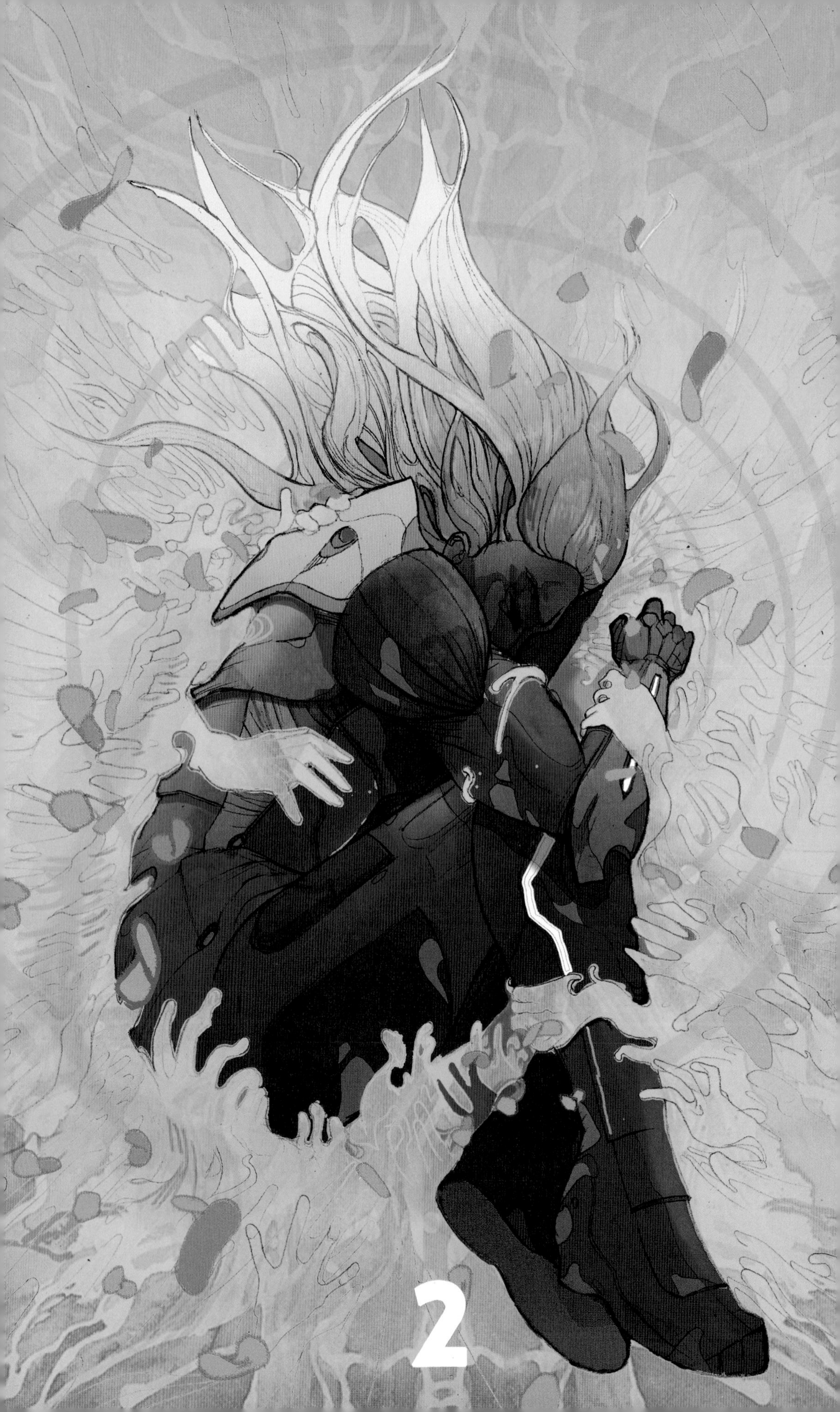

2

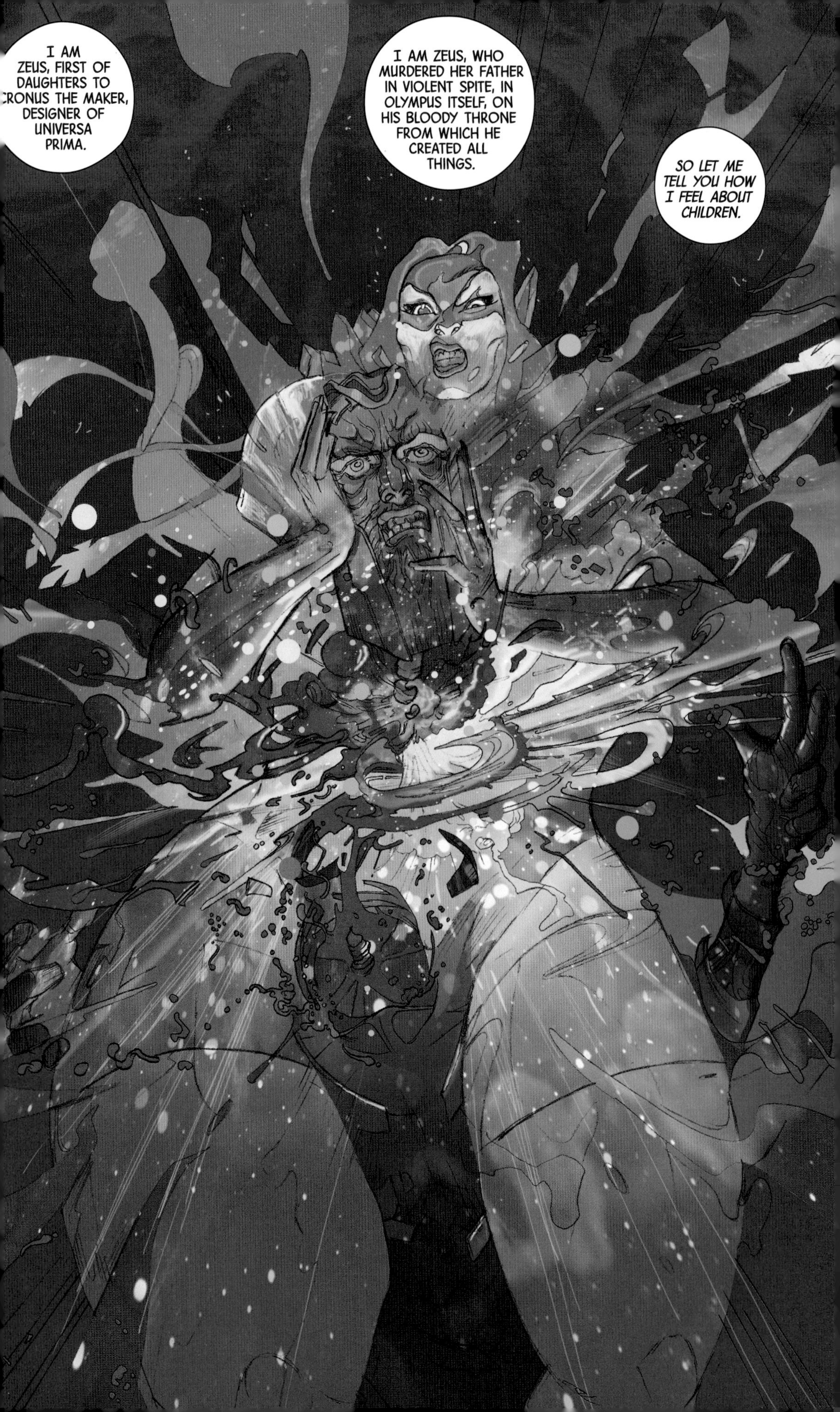
I AM ZEUS, FIRST OF DAUGHTERS TO CRONUS THE MAKER, DESIGNER OF UNIVERSA PRIMA.
I AM ZEUS, WHO MURDERED HER FATHER IN VIOLENT SPITE, IN OLYMPUS ITSELF, ON HIS BLOODY THRONE FROM WHICH HE CREATED ALL THINGS.
SO LET ME TELL YOU HOW I FEEL ABOUT CHILDREN.

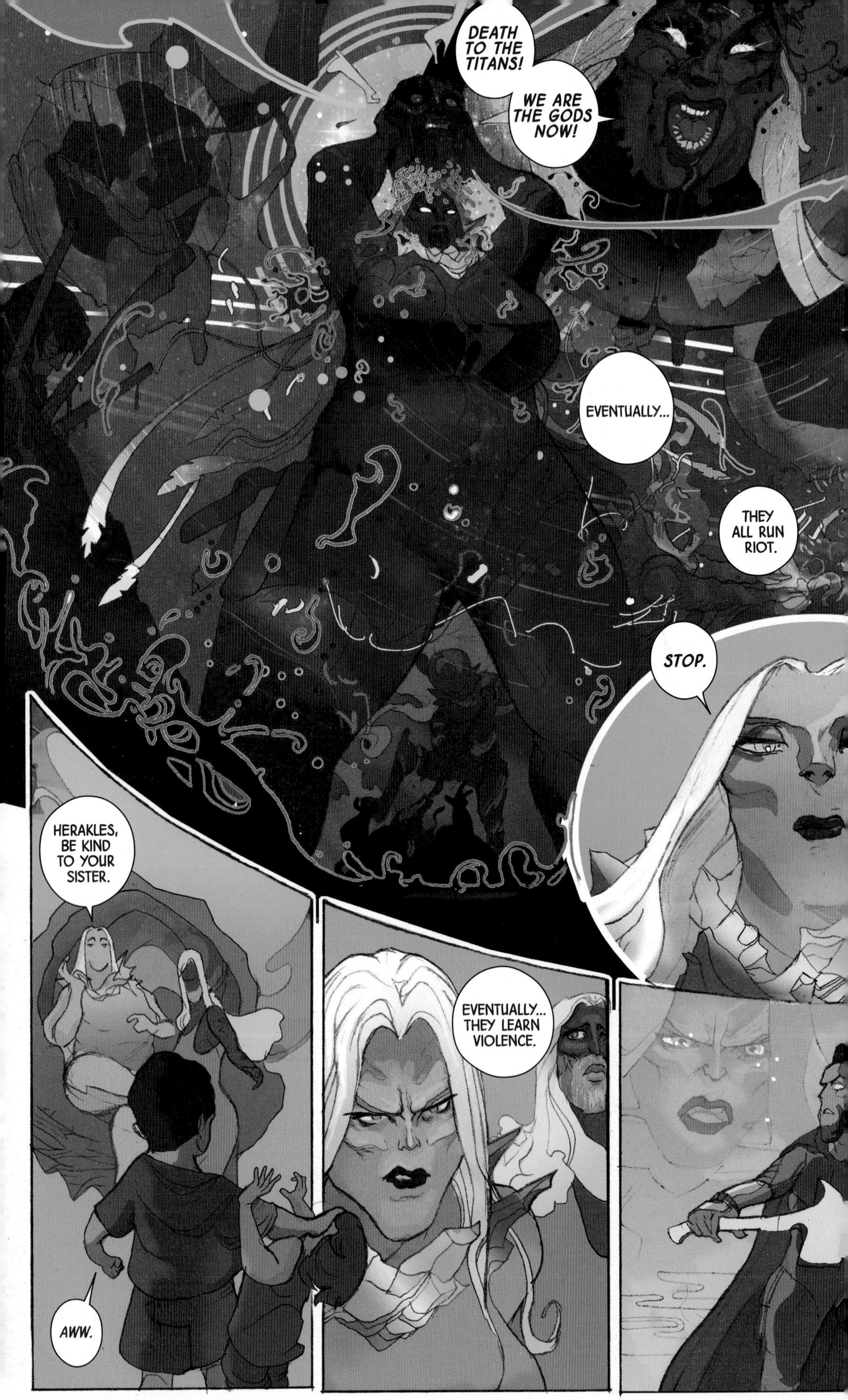
DEATH TO THE TITANS!
WE ARE THE GODS NOW!
EVENTUALLY...
THEY ALL RUN RIOT.
STOP.
HERAKLES, BE KIND TO YOUR SISTER.
AWW.
EVENTUALLY... THEY LEARN VIOLENCE.

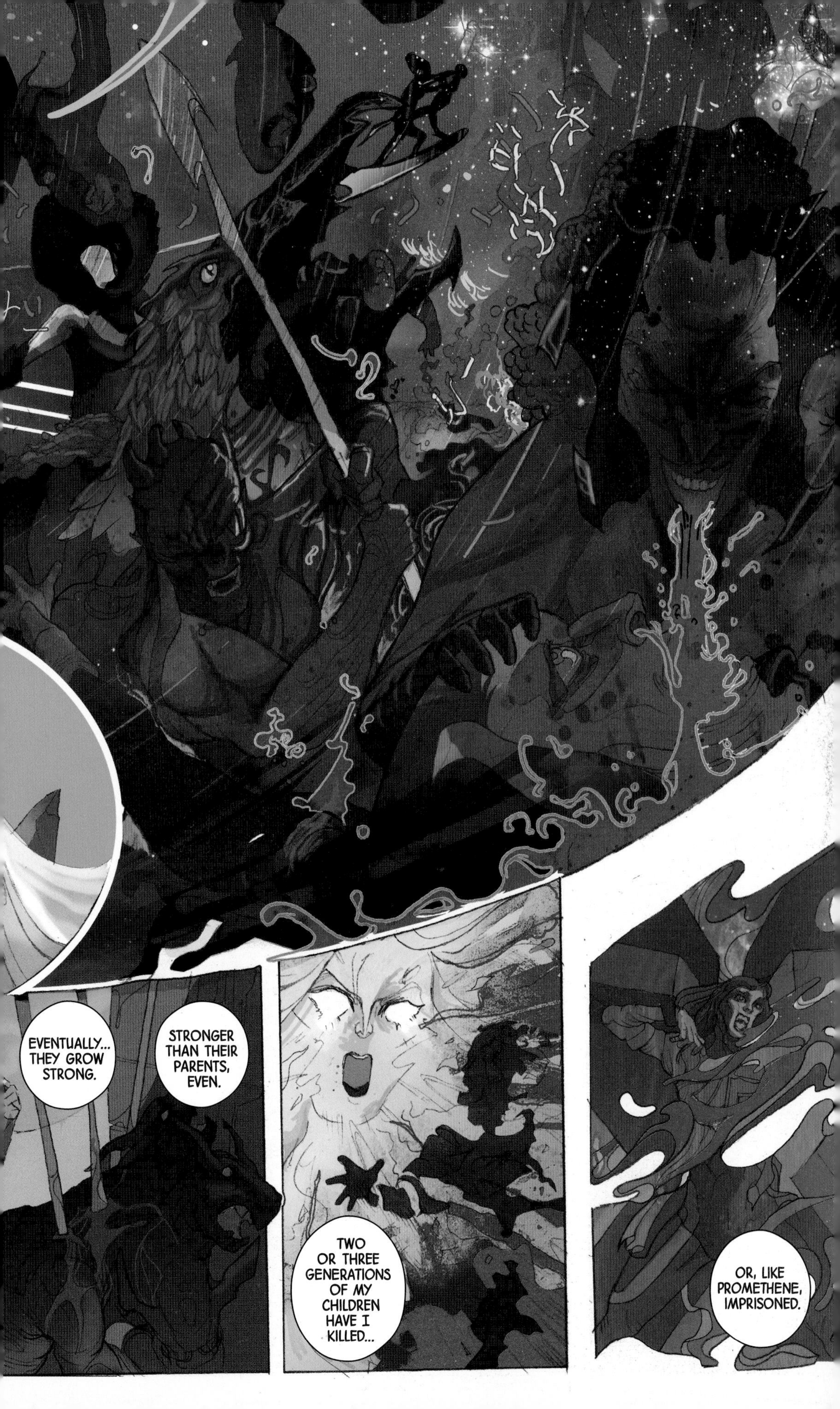
EVENTUALLY... THEY GROW STRONG.
STRONGER THAN THEIR PARENTS, EVEN.
TWO OR THREE GENERATIONS OF MY CHILDREN HAVE I KILLED...
OR, LIKE PROMETHENE, IMPRISONED.

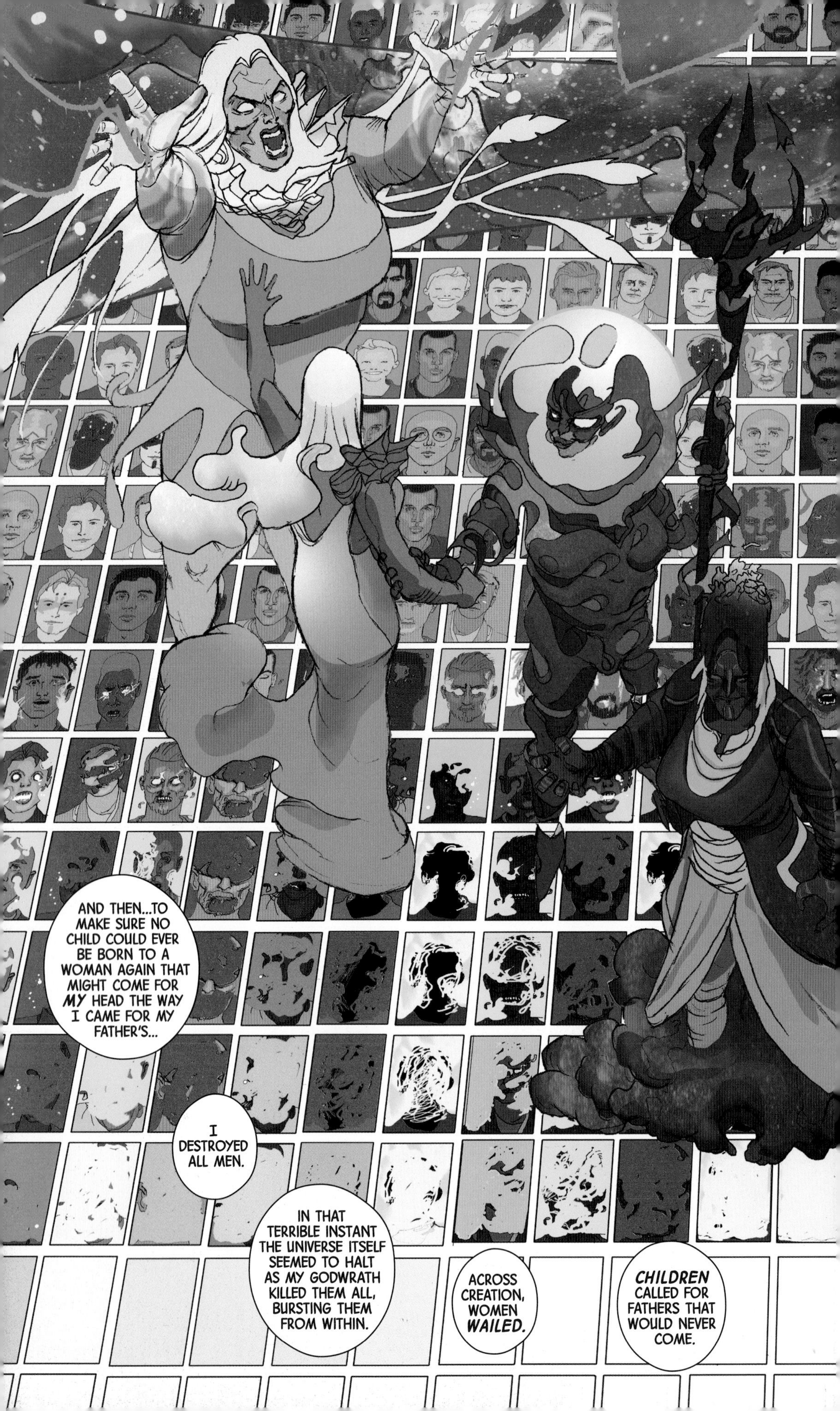
AND THEN...TO MAKE SURE NO CHILD COULD EVER BE BORN TO A WOMAN AGAIN THAT MIGHT COME FOR *MY* HEAD THE WAY I CAME FOR MY FATHER'S...
I DESTROYED ALL MEN.
IN THAT TERRIBLE INSTANT THE UNIVERSE ITSELF SEEMED TO HALT AS MY GODWRATH KILLED THEM ALL, BURSTING THEM FROM WITHIN.
ACROSS CREATION, WOMEN *WAILED.*
CHILDREN CALLED FOR FATHERS THAT WOULD NEVER COME.

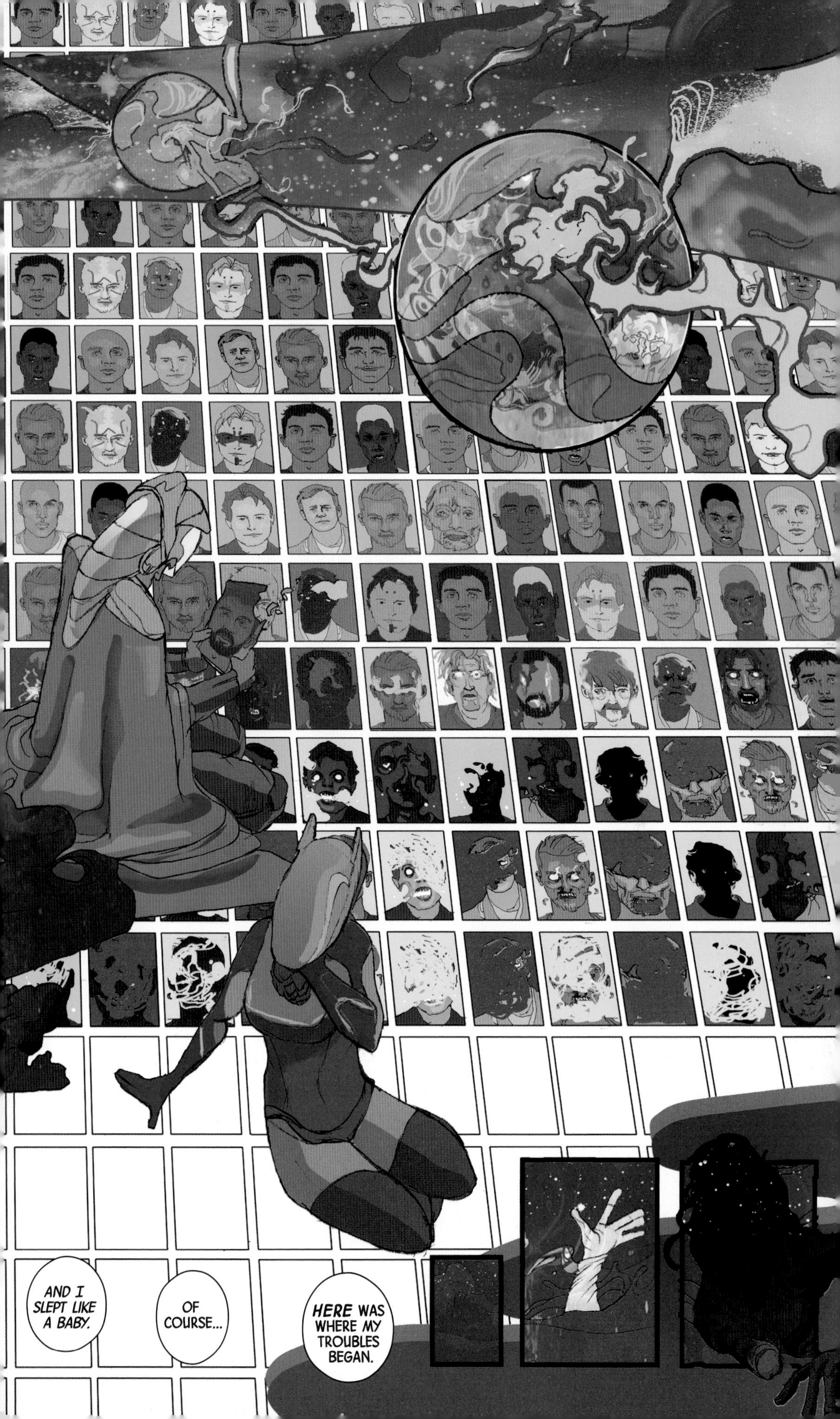
AND I SLEPT LIKE A BABY.
OF COURSE...
HERE WAS WHERE MY TROUBLES BEGAN.

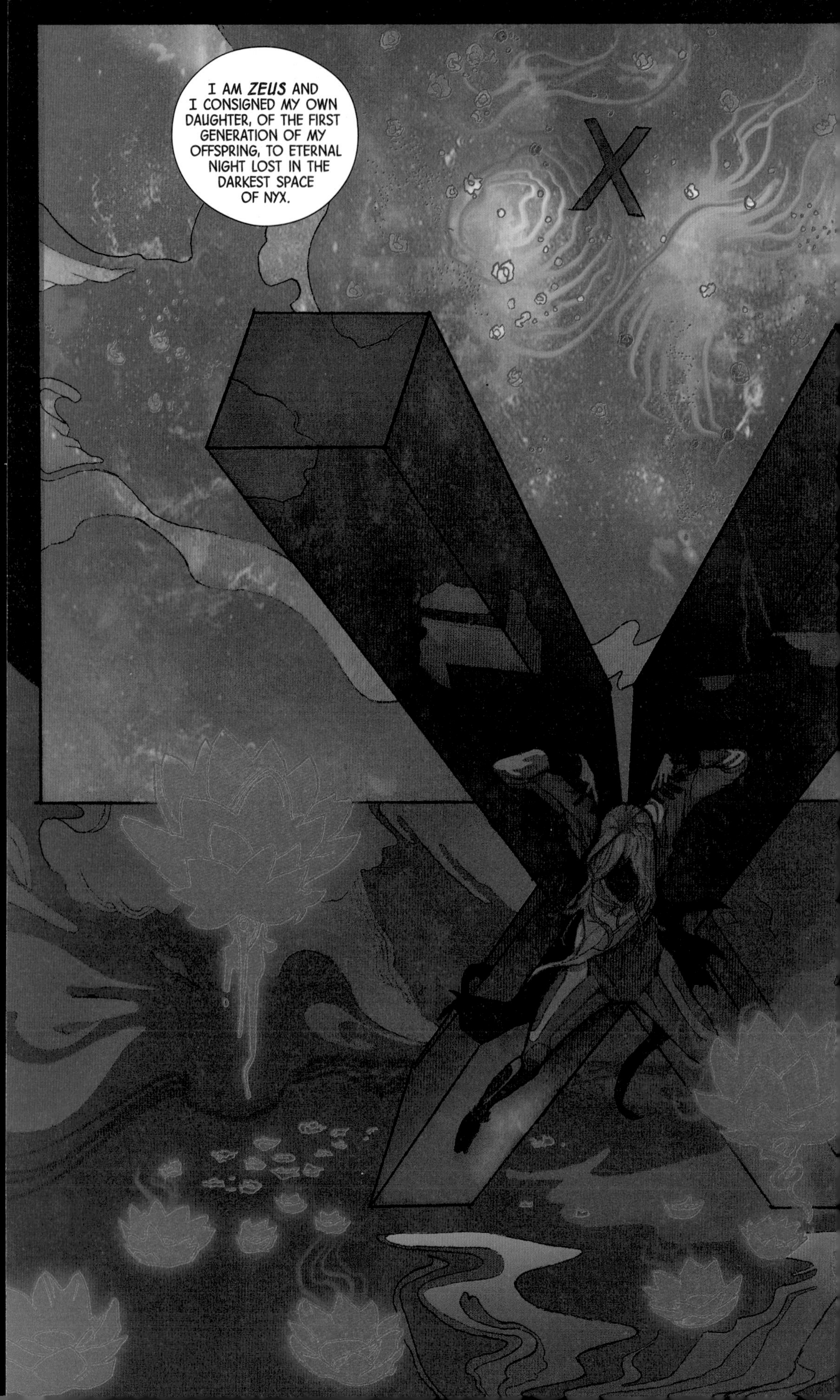
I AM ZEUS AND I CONSIGNED MY OWN DAUGHTER, OF THE FIRST GENERATION OF MY OFFSPRING, TO ETERNAL NIGHT LOST IN THE DARKEST SPACE OF NYX.

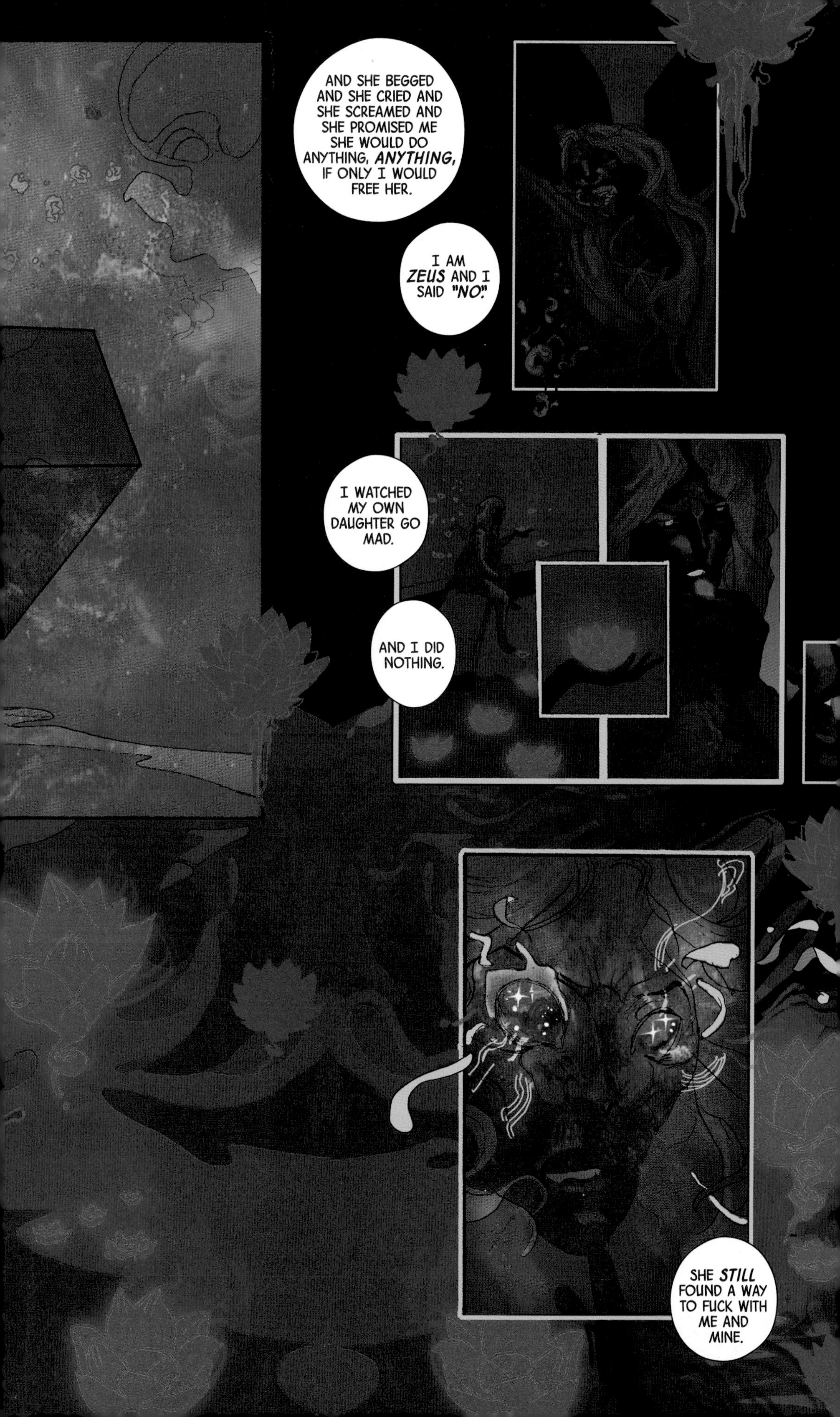
AND SHE BEGGED AND SHE CRIED AND SHE SCREAMED AND SHE PROMISED ME SHE WOULD DO ANYTHING, *ANYTHING,* IF ONLY I WOULD FREE HER.
I AM *ZEUS* AND I SAID *"NO."*
I WATCHED MY OWN DAUGHTER GO MAD.
AND I DID NOTHING.
SHE *STILL* FOUND A WAY TO FUCK WITH ME AND MINE.

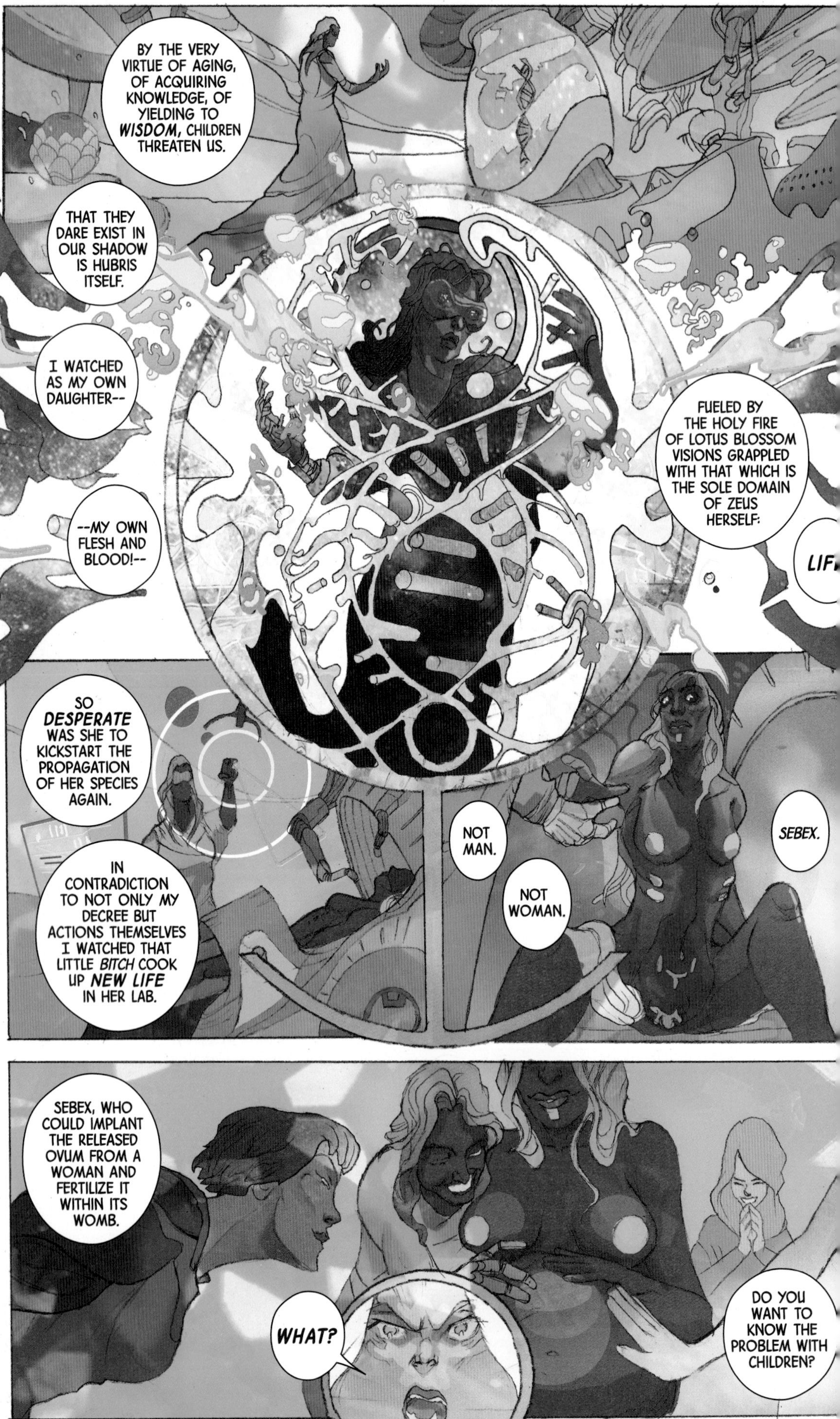
BY THE VERY VIRTUE OF AGING, OF ACQUIRING KNOWLEDGE, OF YIELDING TO *WISDOM*, CHILDREN THREATEN US.
THAT THEY DARE EXIST IN OUR SHADOW IS HUBRIS ITSELF.
I WATCHED AS MY OWN DAUGHTER--
--MY OWN FLESH AND BLOOD!--
FUELED BY THE HOLY FIRE OF LOTUS BLOSSOM VISIONS GRAPPLED WITH THAT WHICH IS THE SOLE DOMAIN OF ZEUS HERSELF:
SO *DESPERATE* WAS SHE TO KICKSTART THE PROPAGATION OF HER SPECIES AGAIN.
IN CONTRADICTION TO NOT ONLY *MY* DECREE BUT ACTIONS THEMSELVES I WATCHED THAT LITTLE *BITCH* COOK UP *NEW LIFE* IN HER LAB.
NOT MAN.
NOT WOMAN.
SEBEX.
SEBEX, WHO COULD IMPLANT THE RELEASED OVUM FROM A WOMAN AND FERTILIZE IT WITHIN ITS WOMB.
WHAT?
DO YOU WANT TO KNOW THE PROBLEM WITH CHILDREN?

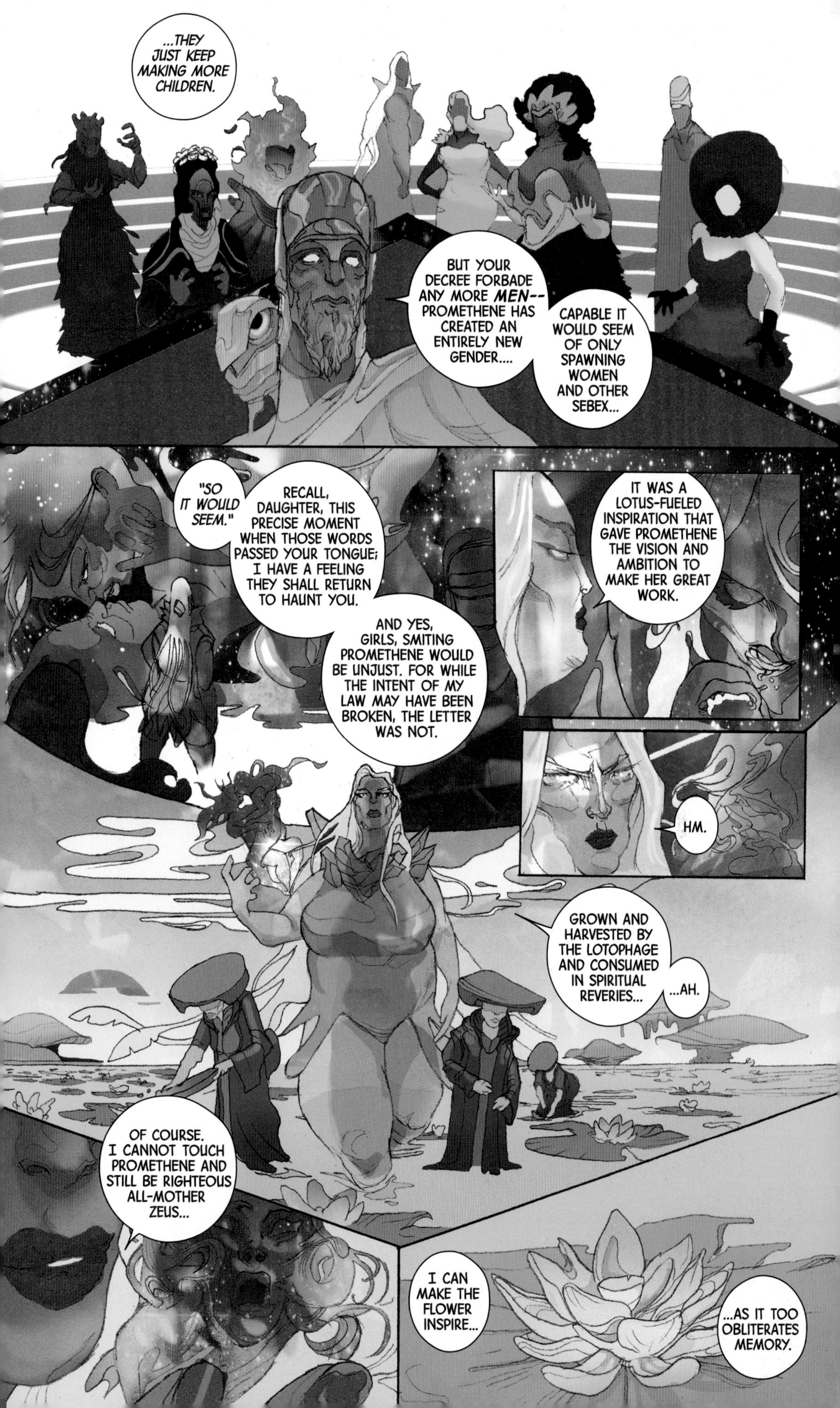
...THEY JUST KEEP MAKING MORE CHILDREN.
BUT YOUR DECREE FORBADE ANY MORE MEN-- PROMETHENE HAS CREATED AN ENTIRELY NEW GENDER....
CAPABLE IT WOULD SEEM OF ONLY SPAWNING WOMEN AND OTHER SEBEX...
"SO IT WOULD SEEM."
RECALL, DAUGHTER, THIS PRECISE MOMENT WHEN THOSE WORDS PASSED YOUR TONGUE; I HAVE A FEELING THEY SHALL RETURN TO HAUNT YOU.
AND YES, GIRLS, SMITING PROMETHENE WOULD BE UNJUST. FOR WHILE THE INTENT OF MY LAW MAY HAVE BEEN BROKEN, THE LETTER WAS NOT.
IT WAS A LOTUS-FUELED INSPIRATION THAT GAVE PROMETHENE THE VISION AND AMBITION TO MAKE HER GREAT WORK.
HM.
GROWN AND HARVESTED BY THE LOTOPHAGE AND CONSUMED IN SPIRITUAL REVERIES...
...AH.
OF COURSE. I CANNOT TOUCH PROMETHENE AND STILL BE RIGHTEOUS ALL-MOTHER ZEUS...
I CAN MAKE THE FLOWER INSPIRE...
...AS IT TOO OBLITERATES MEMORY.

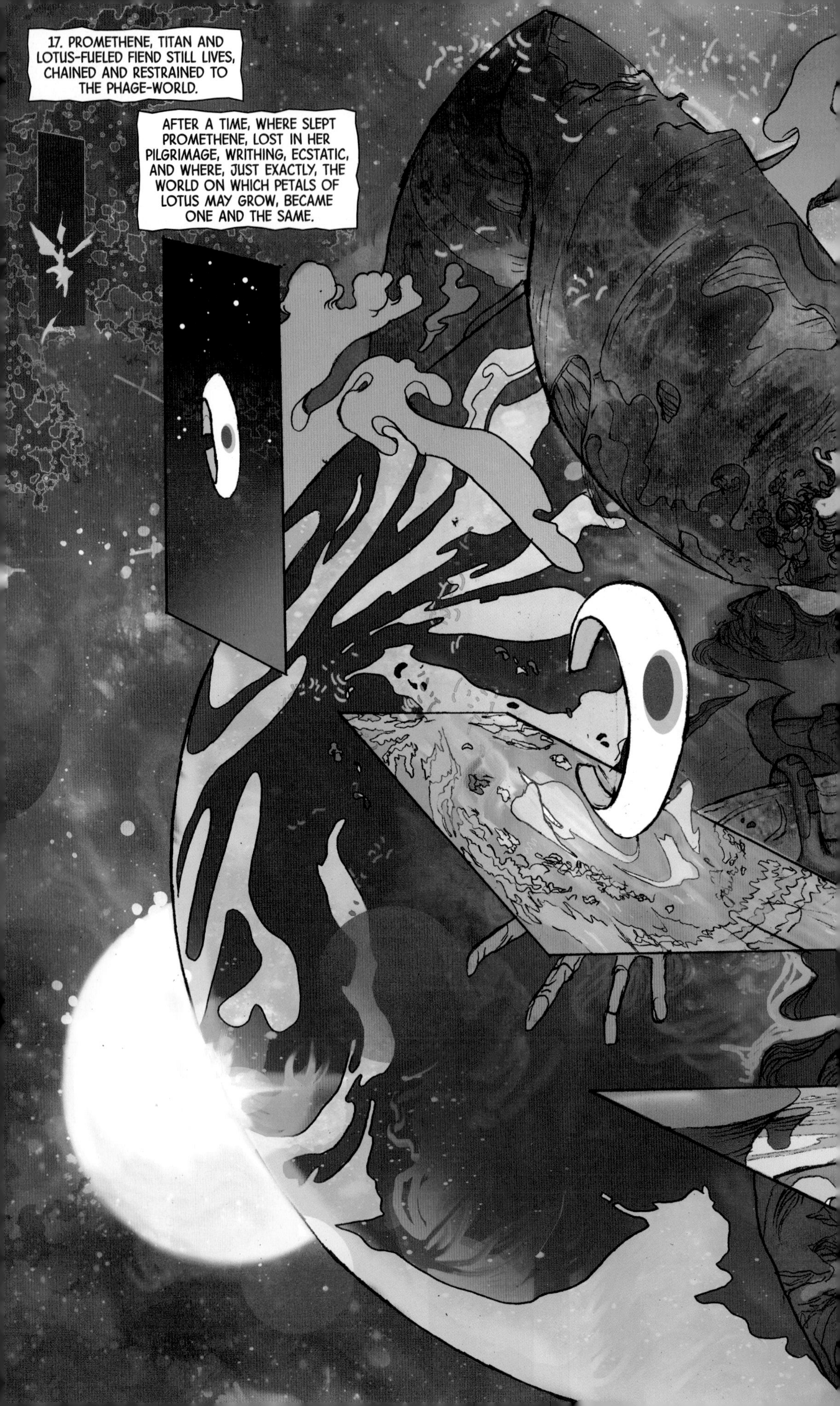
17. PROMETHENE, TITAN AND LOTUS-FUELED FIEND STILL LIVES, CHAINED AND RESTRAINED TO THE PHAGE-WORLD.
AFTER A TIME, WHERE SLEPT PROMETHENE, LOST IN HER PILGRIMAGE, WRITHING, ECSTATIC, AND WHERE, JUST EXACTLY, THE WORLD ON WHICH PETALS OF LOTUS MAY GROW, BECAME ONE AND THE SAME.

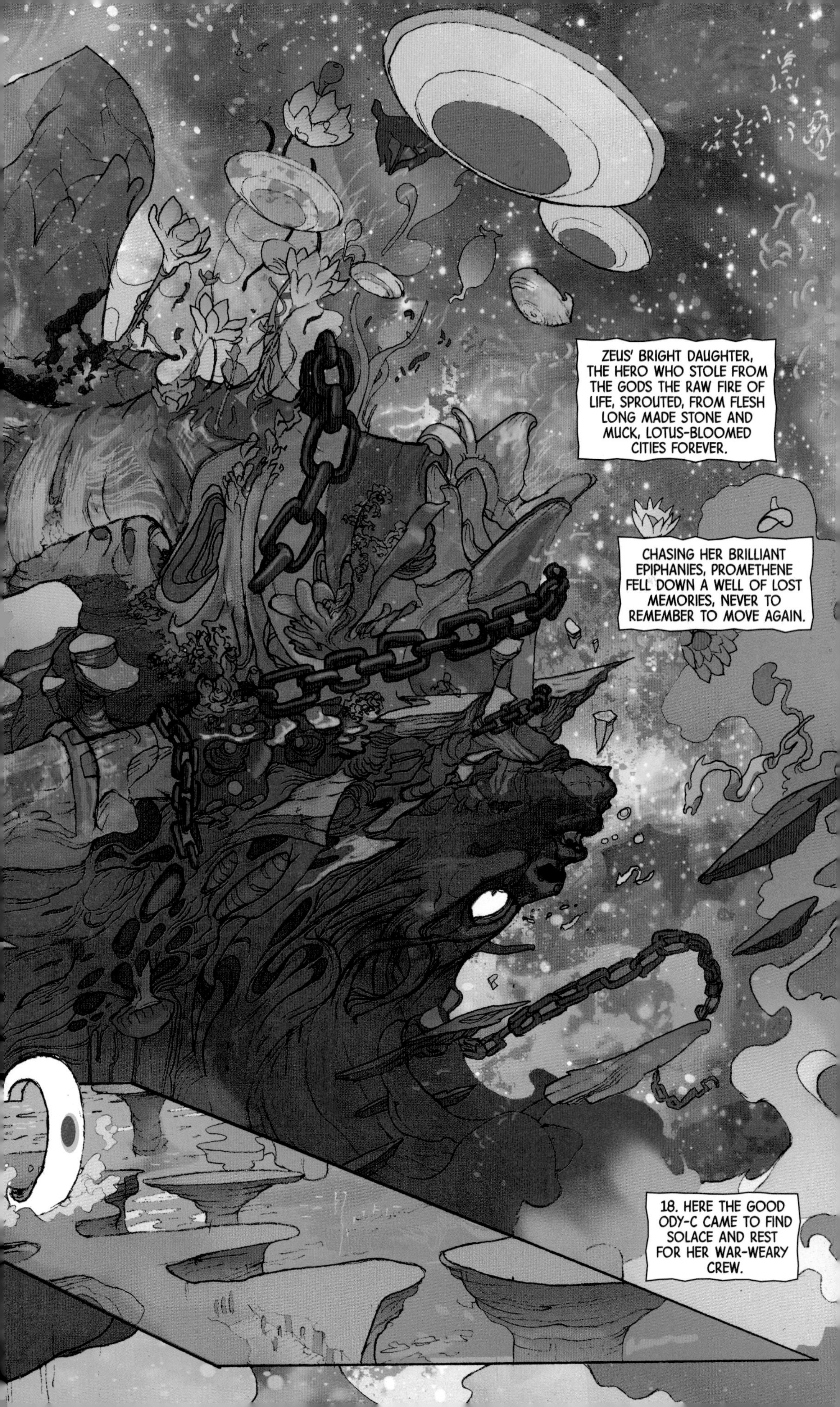
ZEUS' BRIGHT DAUGHTER, THE HERO WHO STOLE FROM THE GODS THE RAW FIRE OF LIFE, SPROUTED, FROM FLESH LONG MADE STONE AND MUCK, LOTUS-BLOOMED CITIES FOREVER.
CHASING HER BRILLIANT EPIPHANIES, PROMETHENE FELL DOWN A WELL OF LOST MEMORIES, NEVER TO REMEMBER TO MOVE AGAIN.
18. HERE THE GOOD ODY-C CAME TO FIND SOLACE AND REST FOR HER WAR-WEARY CREW.

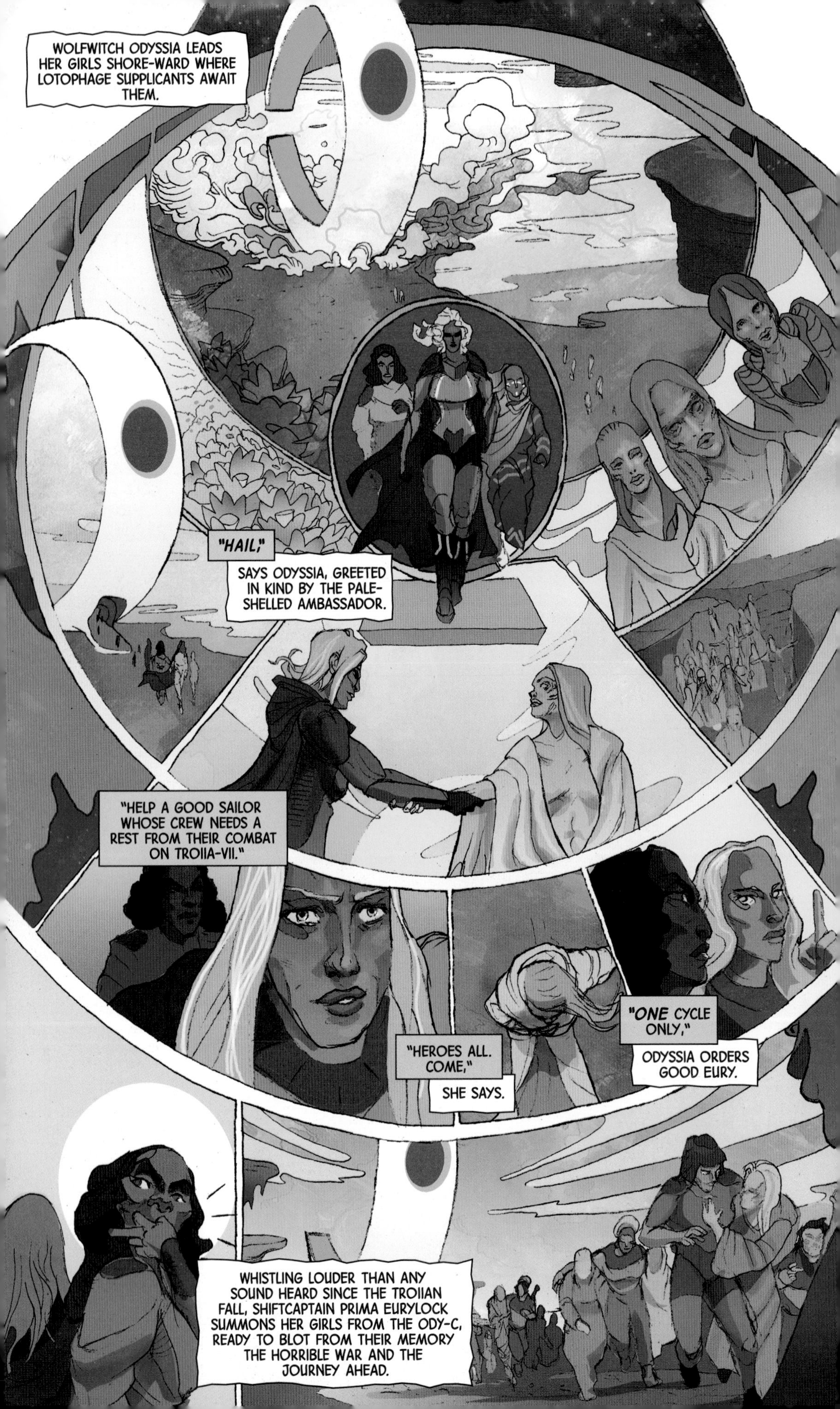

WOLFWITCH ODYSSIA LEADS HER GIRLS SHORE-WARD WHERE LOTOPHAGE SUPPLICANTS AWAIT THEM.
"HAIL,"
SAYS ODYSSIA, GREETED IN KIND BY THE PALE-SHELLED AMBASSADOR.
"HELP A GOOD SAILOR WHOSE CREW NEEDS A REST FROM THEIR COMBAT ON TROIIA-VII."
"HEROES ALL. COME,"
SHE SAYS.
"ONE CYCLE ONLY,"
ODYSSIA ORDERS GOOD EURY.
WHISTLING LOUDER THAN ANY SOUND HEARD SINCE THE TROIIAN FALL, SHIFTCAPTAIN PRIMA EURYLOCK SUMMONS HER GIRLS FROM THE ODY-C, READY TO BLOT FROM THEIR MEMORY THE HORRIBLE WAR AND THE JOURNEY AHEAD.

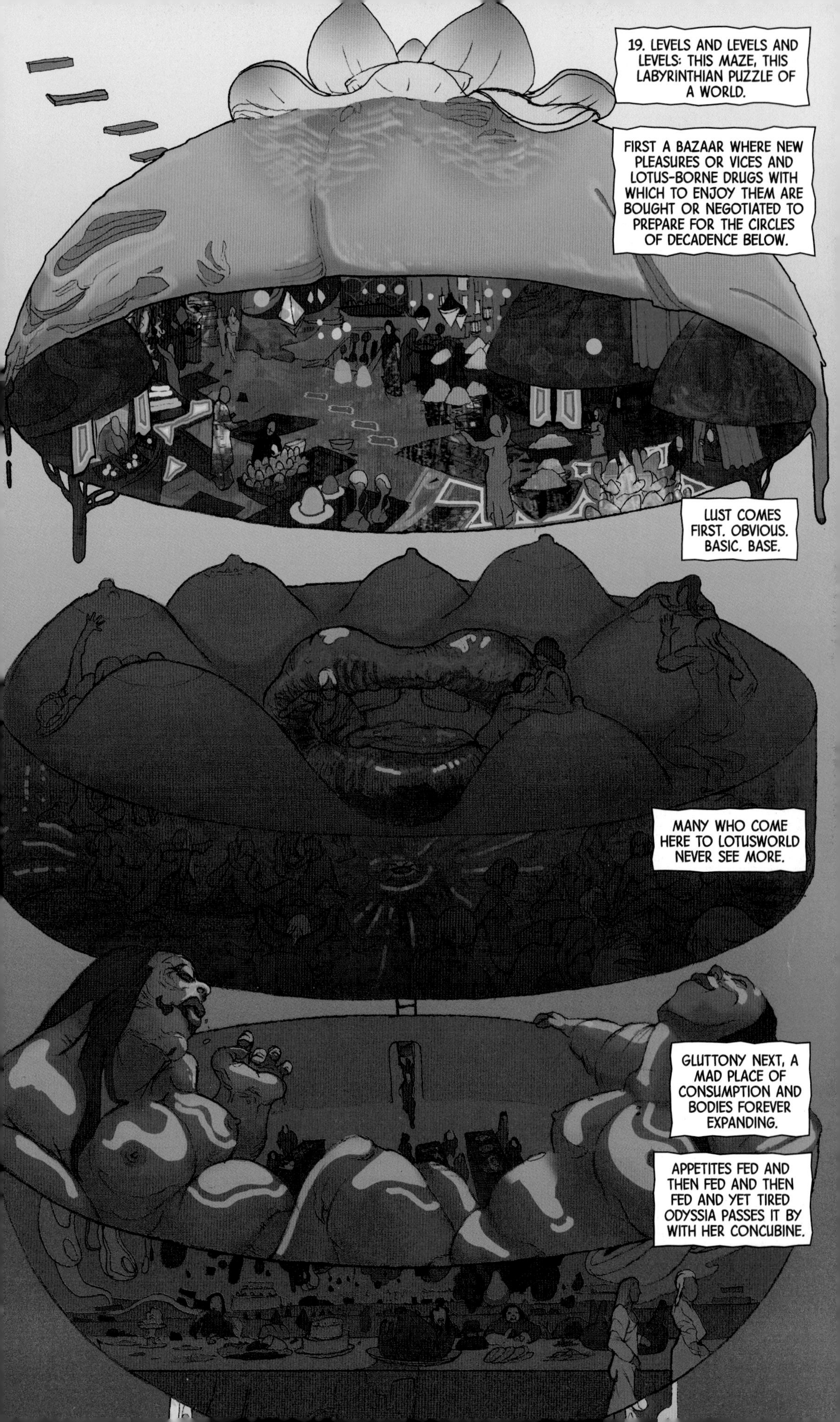
19. LEVELS AND LEVELS AND LEVELS: THIS MAZE, THIS LABYRINTHIAN PUZZLE OF A WORLD.
FIRST A BAZAAR WHERE NEW PLEASURES OR VICES AND LOTUS-BORNE DRUGS WITH WHICH TO ENJOY THEM ARE BOUGHT OR NEGOTIATED TO PREPARE FOR THE CIRCLES OF DECADENCE BELOW.
LUST COMES FIRST. OBVIOUS. BASIC. BASE.
MANY WHO COME HERE TO LOTUSWORLD NEVER SEE MORE.
GLUTTONY NEXT, A MAD PLACE OF CONSUMPTION AND BODIES FOREVER EXPANDING.
APPETITES FED AND THEN FED AND THEN FED AND YET TIRED ODYSSIA PASSES IT BY WITH HER CONCUBINE.

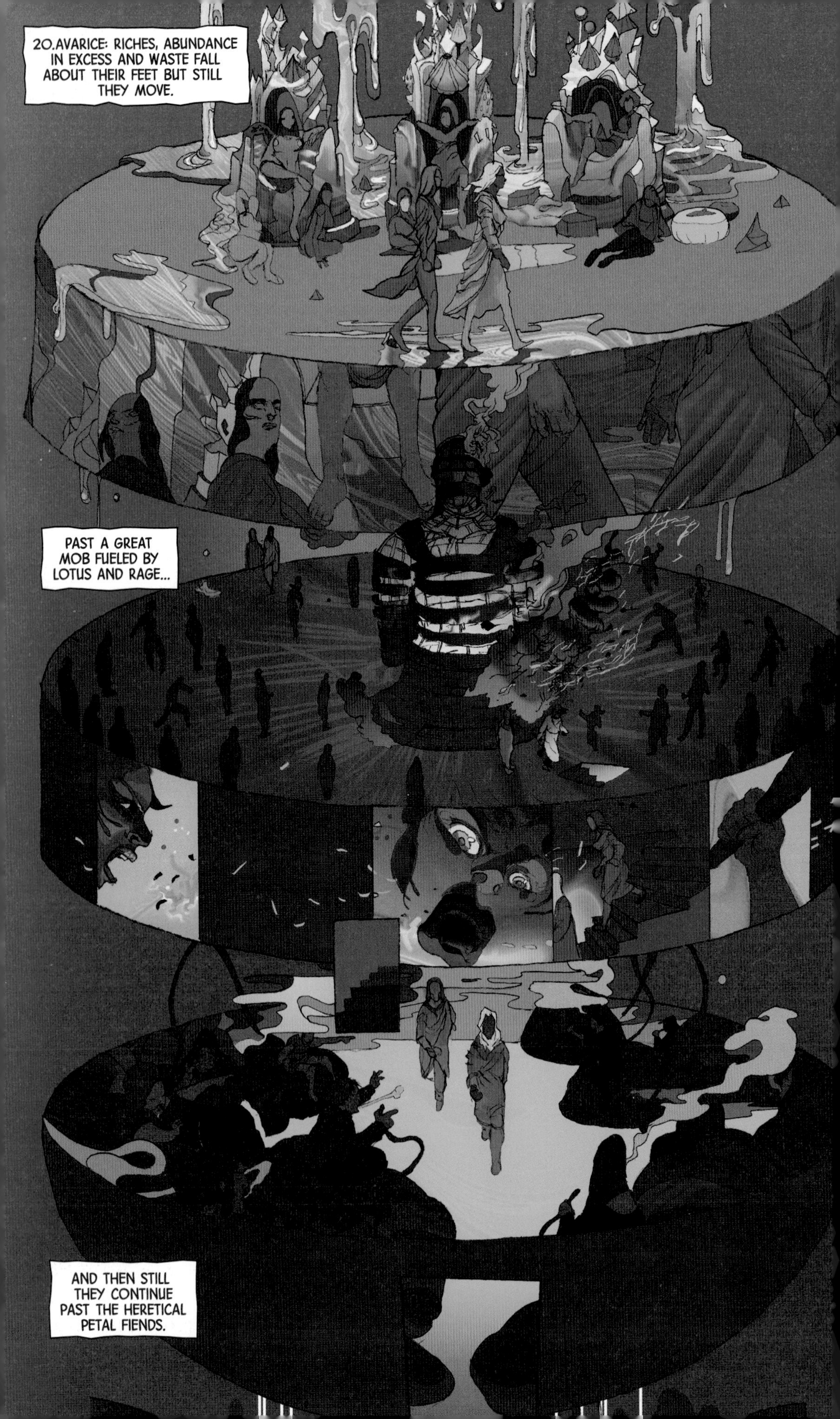
20.AVARICE: RICHES, ABUNDANCE IN EXCESS AND WASTE FALL ABOUT THEIR FEET BUT STILL THEY MOVE.
PAST A GREAT MOB FUELED BY LOTUS AND RAGE...
AND THEN STILL THEY CONTINUE PAST THE HERETICAL PETAL FIENDS.

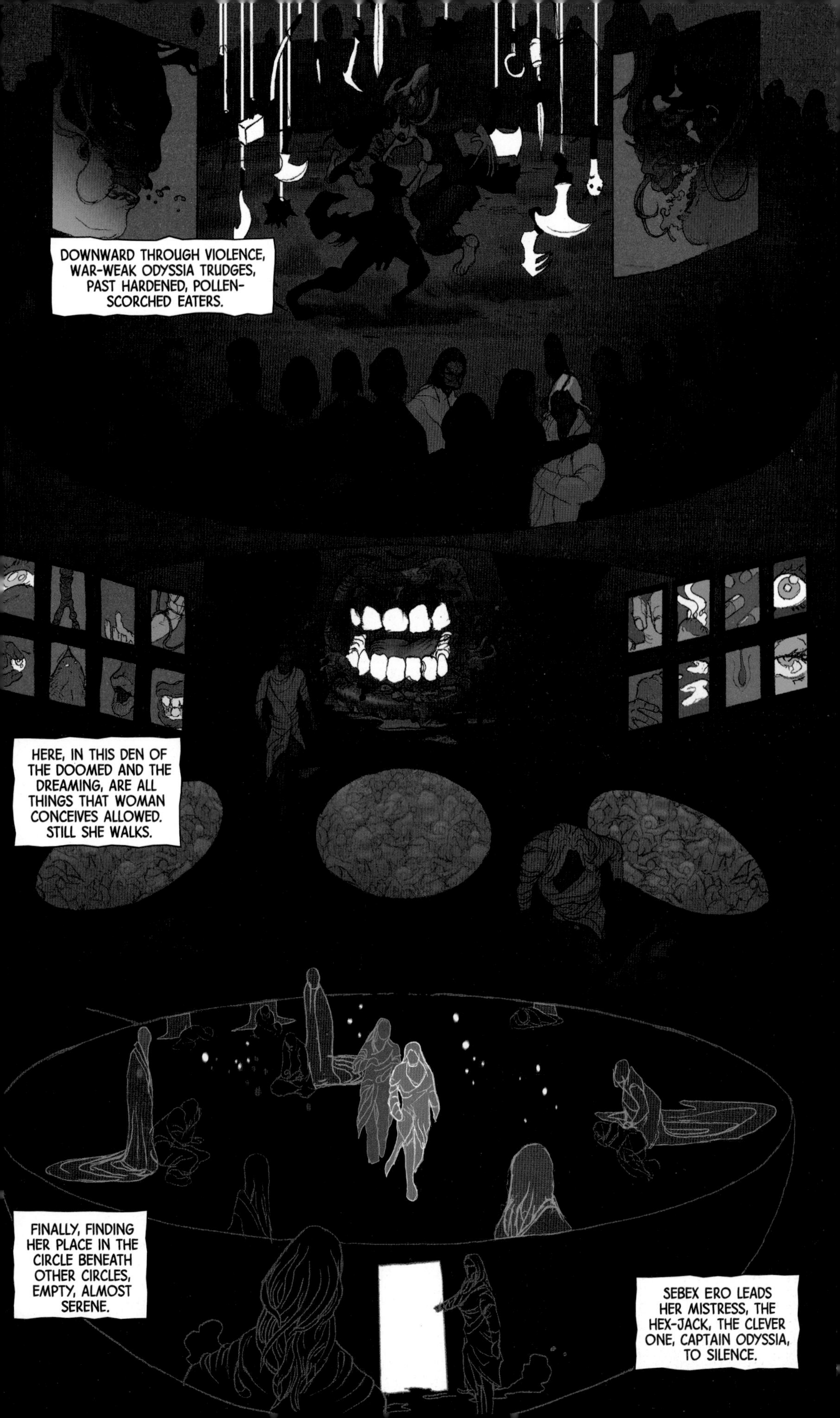
DOWNWARD THROUGH VIOLENCE, WAR-WEAK ODYSSIA TRUDGES, PAST HARDENED, POLLEN-SCORCHED EATERS.
HERE, IN THIS DEN OF THE DOOMED AND THE DREAMING, ARE ALL THINGS THAT WOMAN CONCEIVES ALLOWED. STILL SHE WALKS.
FINALLY, FINDING HER PLACE IN THE CIRCLE BENEATH OTHER CIRCLES, EMPTY, ALMOST SERENE.
SEBEX ERO LEADS HER MISTRESS, THE HEX-JACK, THE CLEVER ONE, CAPTAIN ODYSSIA, TO SILENCE.

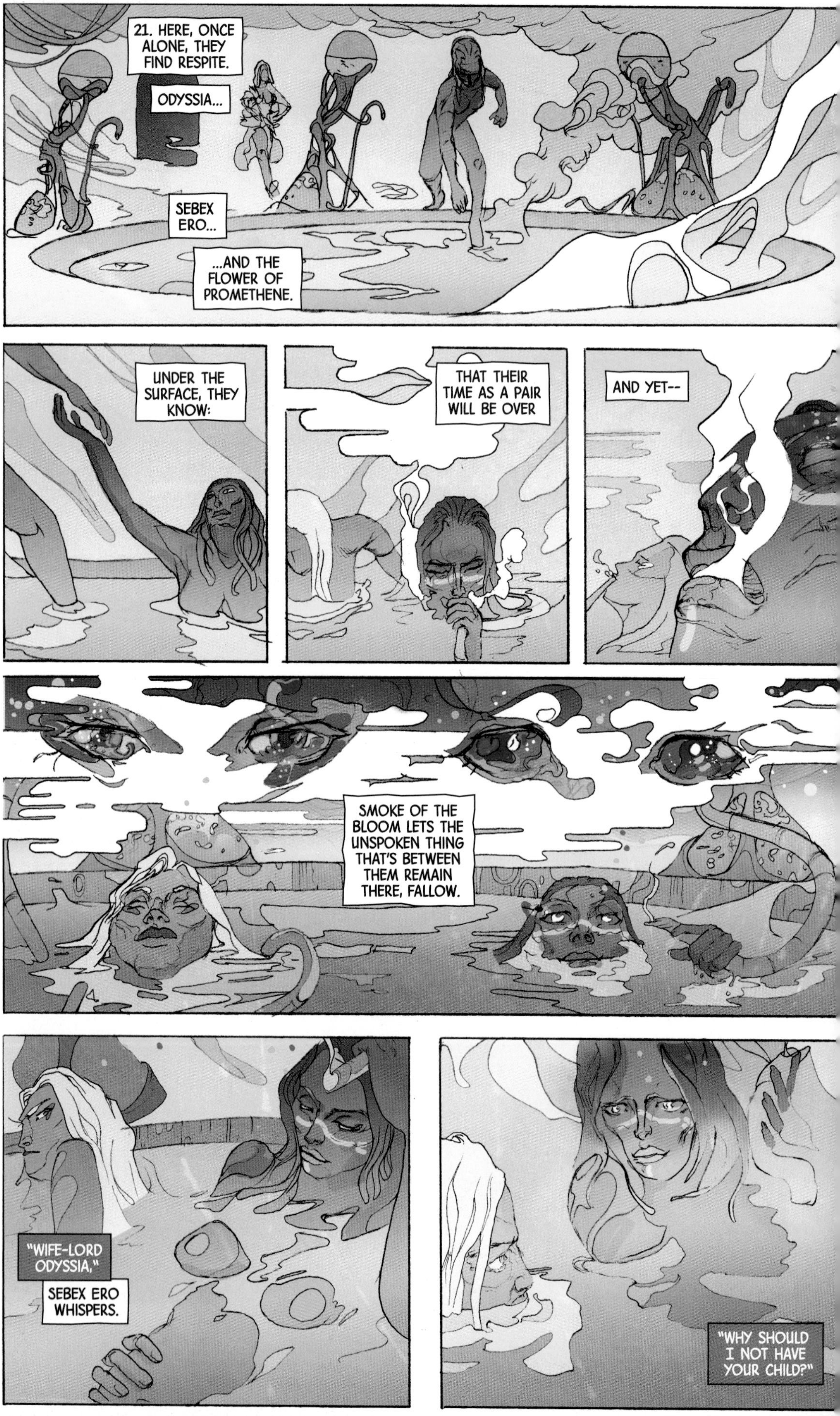
21. HERE, ONCE ALONE, THEY FIND RESPITE.
ODYSSIA...
SEBEX ERO...
...AND THE FLOWER OF PROMETHENE.
UNDER THE SURFACE, THEY KNOW:
THAT THEIR TIME AS A PAIR WILL BE OVER
AND YET--
SMOKE OF THE BLOOM LETS THE UNSPOKEN THING THAT'S BETWEEN THEM REMAIN THERE, FALLOW.
"WIFE-LORD ODYSSIA,"
SEBEX ERO WHISPERS.
"WHY SHOULD I NOT HAVE YOUR CHILD?"

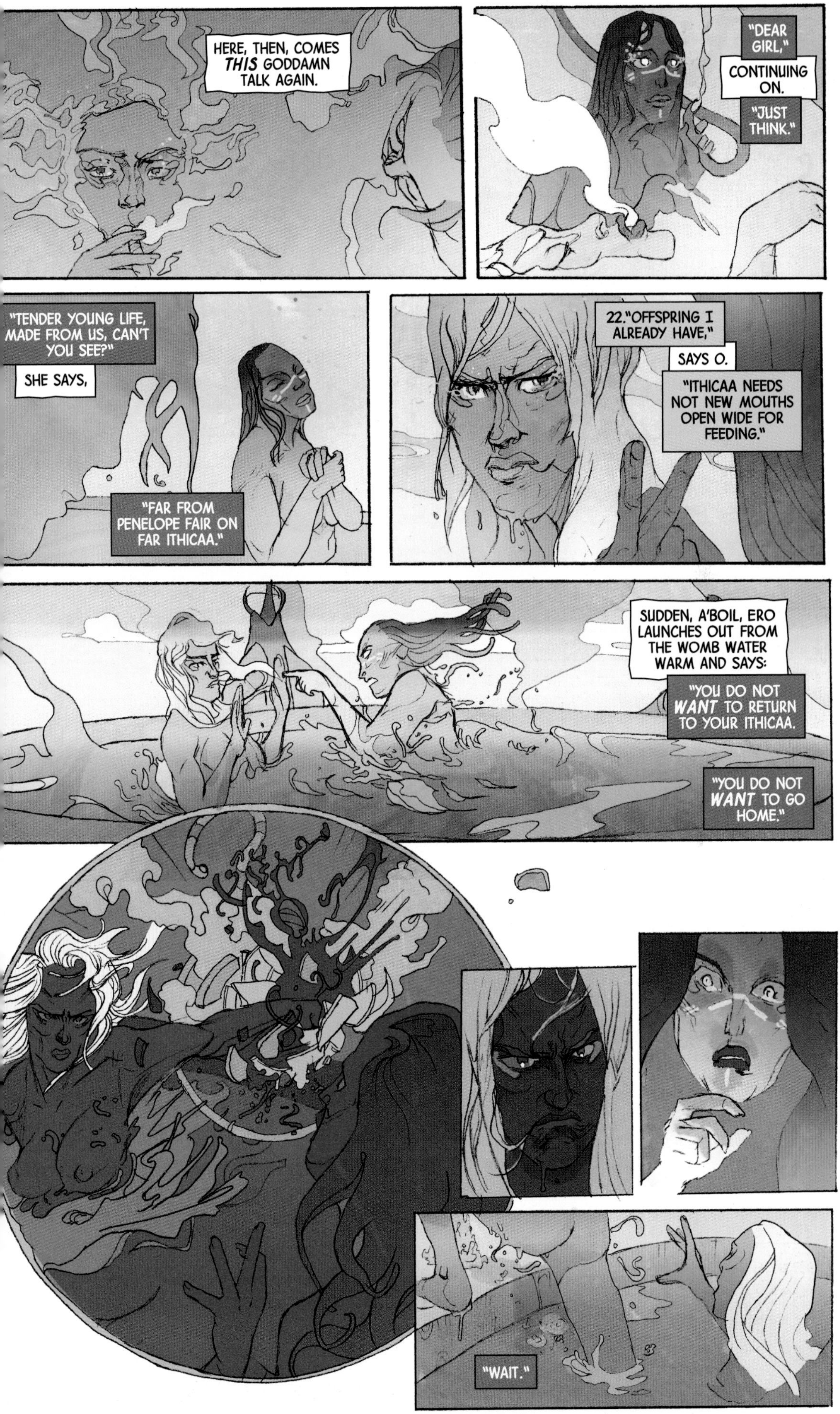

HERE, THEN, COMES *THIS* GODDAMN TALK AGAIN.
"DEAR GIRL,"
CONTINUING ON.
"JUST THINK."
"TENDER YOUNG LIFE, MADE FROM US, CAN'T YOU SEE?"
SHE SAYS,
"FAR FROM PENELOPE FAIR ON FAR ITHICAA."
22."OFFSPRING I ALREADY HAVE,"
SAYS O.
"ITHICAA NEEDS NOT NEW MOUTHS OPEN WIDE FOR FEEDING."
SUDDEN, A'BOIL, ERO LAUNCHES OUT FROM THE WOMB WATER WARM AND SAYS:
"YOU DO NOT *WANT* TO RETURN TO YOUR ITHICAA.
"YOU DO NOT *WANT* TO GO HOME."
"WAIT."

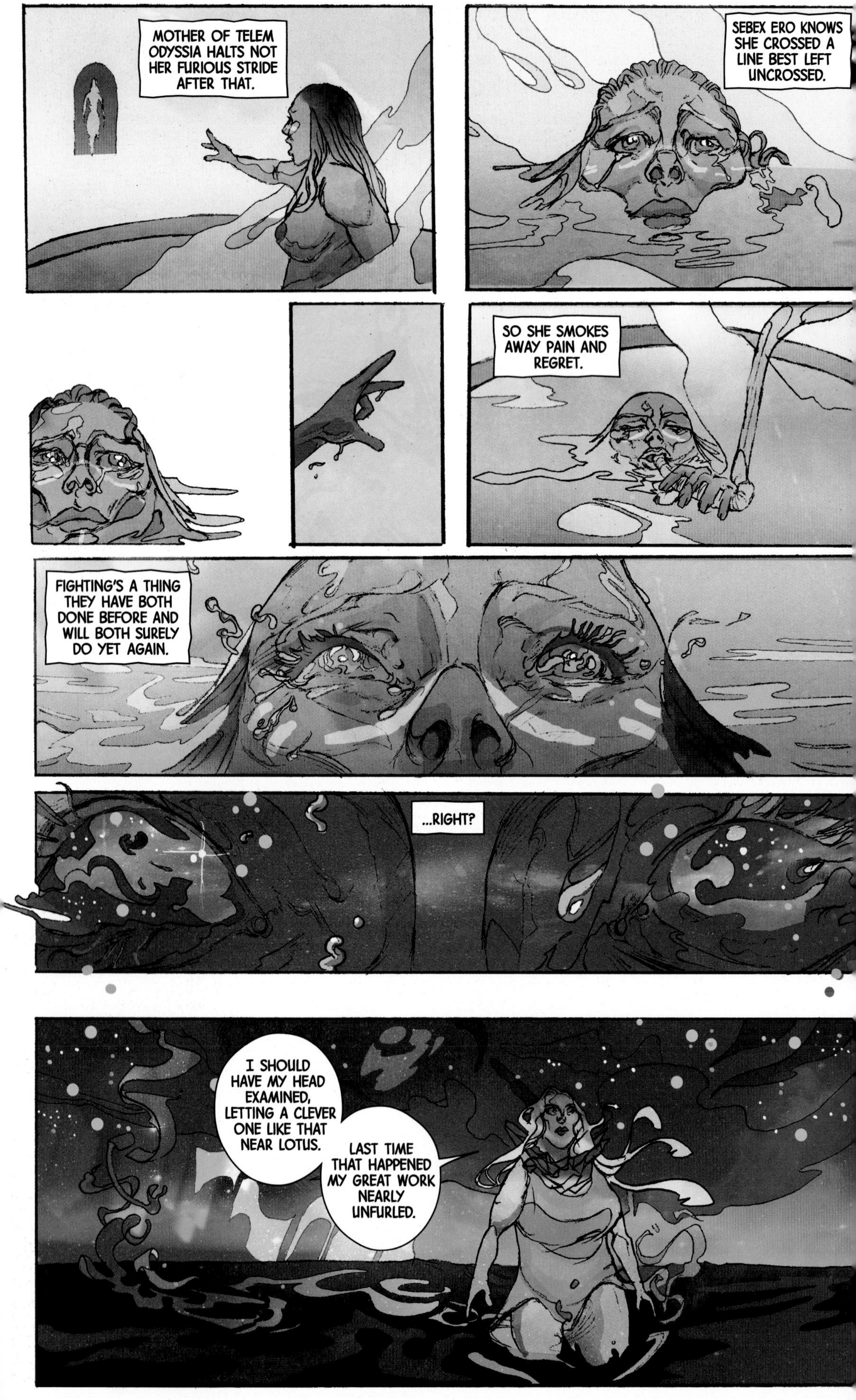
MOTHER OF TELEM ODYSSIA HALTS NOT HER FURIOUS STRIDE AFTER THAT.
SEBEX ERO KNOWS SHE CROSSED A LINE BEST LEFT UNCROSSED.
SO SHE SMOKES AWAY PAIN AND REGRET.
FIGHTING'S A THING THEY HAVE BOTH DONE BEFORE AND WILL BOTH SURELY DO YET AGAIN.
...RIGHT?
I SHOULD HAVE MY HEAD EXAMINED, LETTING A CLEVER ONE LIKE THAT NEAR LOTUS.
LAST TIME THAT HAPPENED MY GREAT WORK NEARLY UNFURLED.

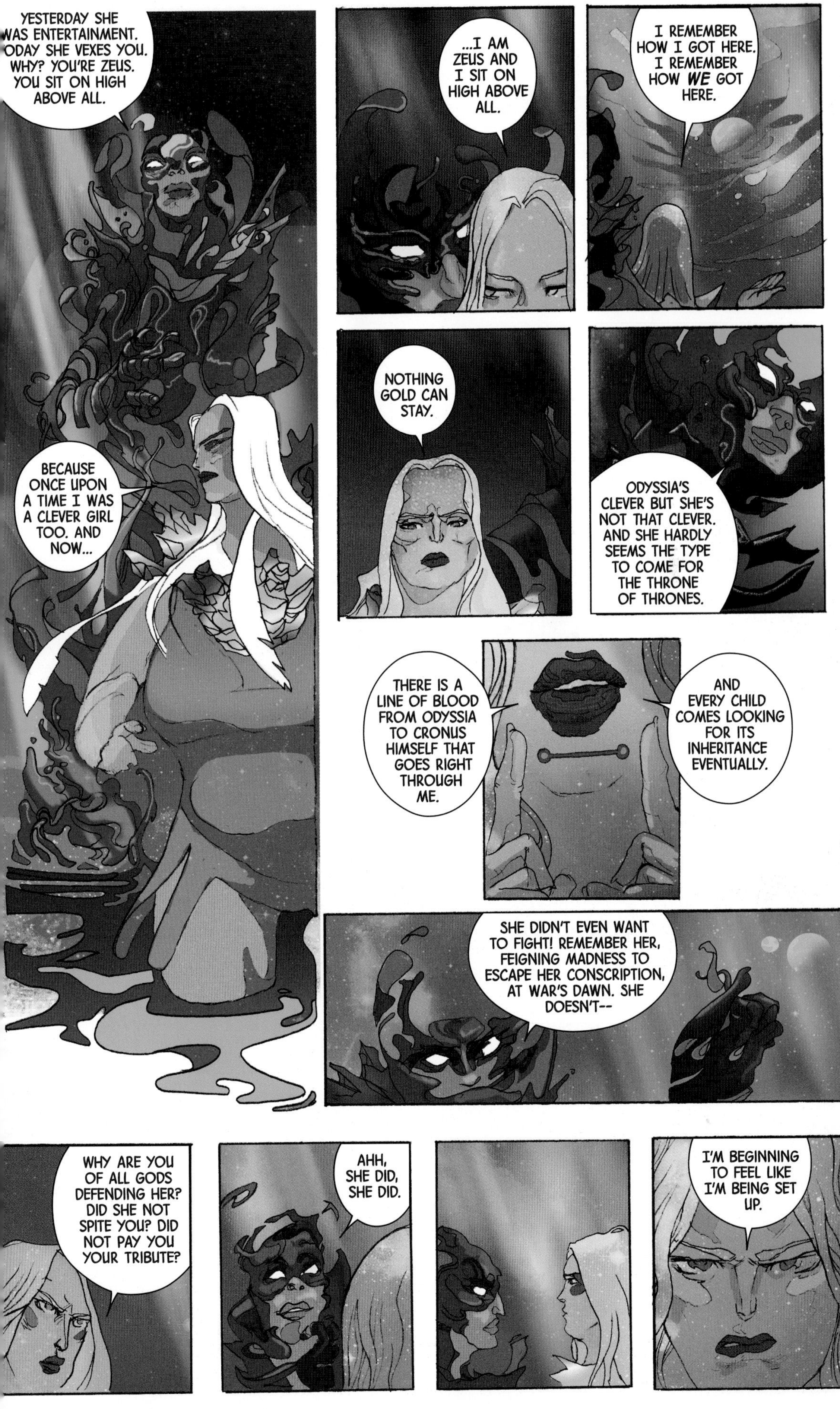

YESTERDAY SHE WAS ENTERTAINMENT. TODAY SHE VEXES YOU. WHY? YOU'RE ZEUS. YOU SIT ON HIGH ABOVE ALL.
BECAUSE ONCE UPON A TIME I WAS A CLEVER GIRL TOO. AND NOW...
...I AM ZEUS AND I SIT ON HIGH ABOVE ALL.
I REMEMBER HOW I GOT HERE. I REMEMBER HOW WE GOT HERE.
NOTHING GOLD CAN STAY.
ODYSSIA'S CLEVER BUT SHE'S NOT THAT CLEVER. AND SHE HARDLY SEEMS THE TYPE TO COME FOR THE THRONE OF THRONES.
THERE IS A LINE OF BLOOD FROM ODYSSIA TO CRONUS HIMSELF THAT GOES RIGHT THROUGH ME.
AND EVERY CHILD COMES LOOKING FOR ITS INHERITANCE EVENTUALLY.
SHE DIDN'T EVEN WANT TO FIGHT! REMEMBER HER, FEIGNING MADNESS TO ESCAPE HER CONSCRIPTION, AT WAR'S DAWN. SHE DOESN'T--
WHY ARE YOU OF ALL GODS DEFENDING HER? DID SHE NOT SPITE YOU? DID NOT PAY YOU YOUR TRIBUTE?
AHH, SHE DID, SHE DID.
I'M BEGINNING TO FEEL LIKE I'M BEING SET UP.

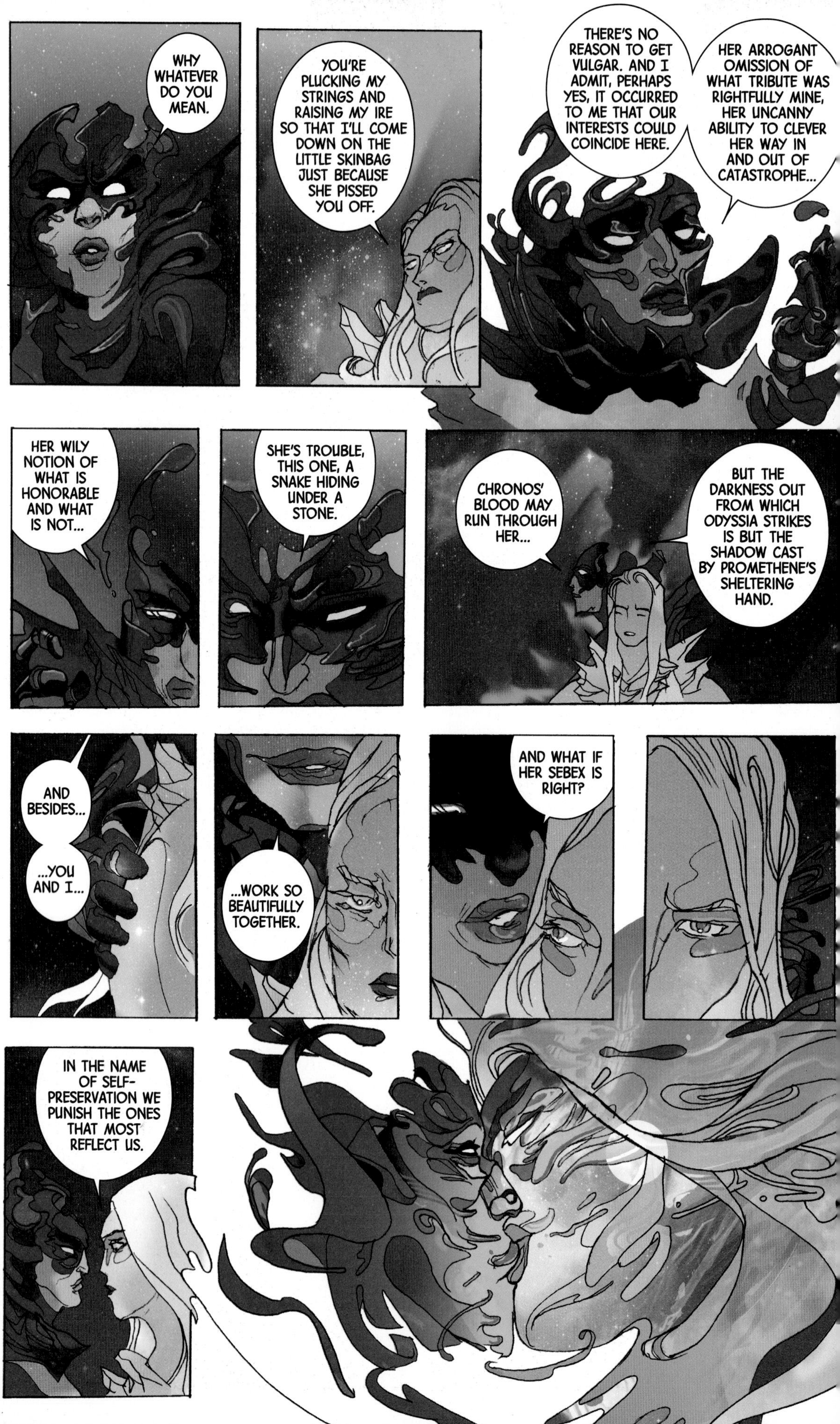
WHY WHATEVER DO YOU MEAN.
YOU'RE PLUCKING MY STRINGS AND RAISING MY IRE SO THAT I'LL COME DOWN ON THE LITTLE SKINBAG JUST BECAUSE SHE PISSED YOU OFF.
THERE'S NO REASON TO GET VULGAR. AND I ADMIT, PERHAPS YES, IT OCCURRED TO ME THAT OUR INTERESTS COULD COINCIDE HERE.
HER ARROGANT OMISSION OF WHAT TRIBUTE WAS RIGHTFULLY MINE, HER UNCANNY ABILITY TO CLEVER HER WAY IN AND OUT OF CATASTROPHE...
HER WILY NOTION OF WHAT IS HONORABLE AND WHAT IS NOT...
SHE'S TROUBLE, THIS ONE, A SNAKE HIDING UNDER A STONE.
CHRONOS' BLOOD MAY RUN THROUGH HER...
BUT THE DARKNESS OUT FROM WHICH ODYSSIA STRIKES IS BUT THE SHADOW CAST BY PROMETHENE'S SHELTERING HAND.
AND BESIDES...
...YOU AND I...
...WORK SO BEAUTIFULLY TOGETHER.
AND WHAT IF HER SEBEX IS RIGHT?
IN THE NAME OF SELF-PRESERVATION WE PUNISH THE ONES THAT MOST REFLECT US.

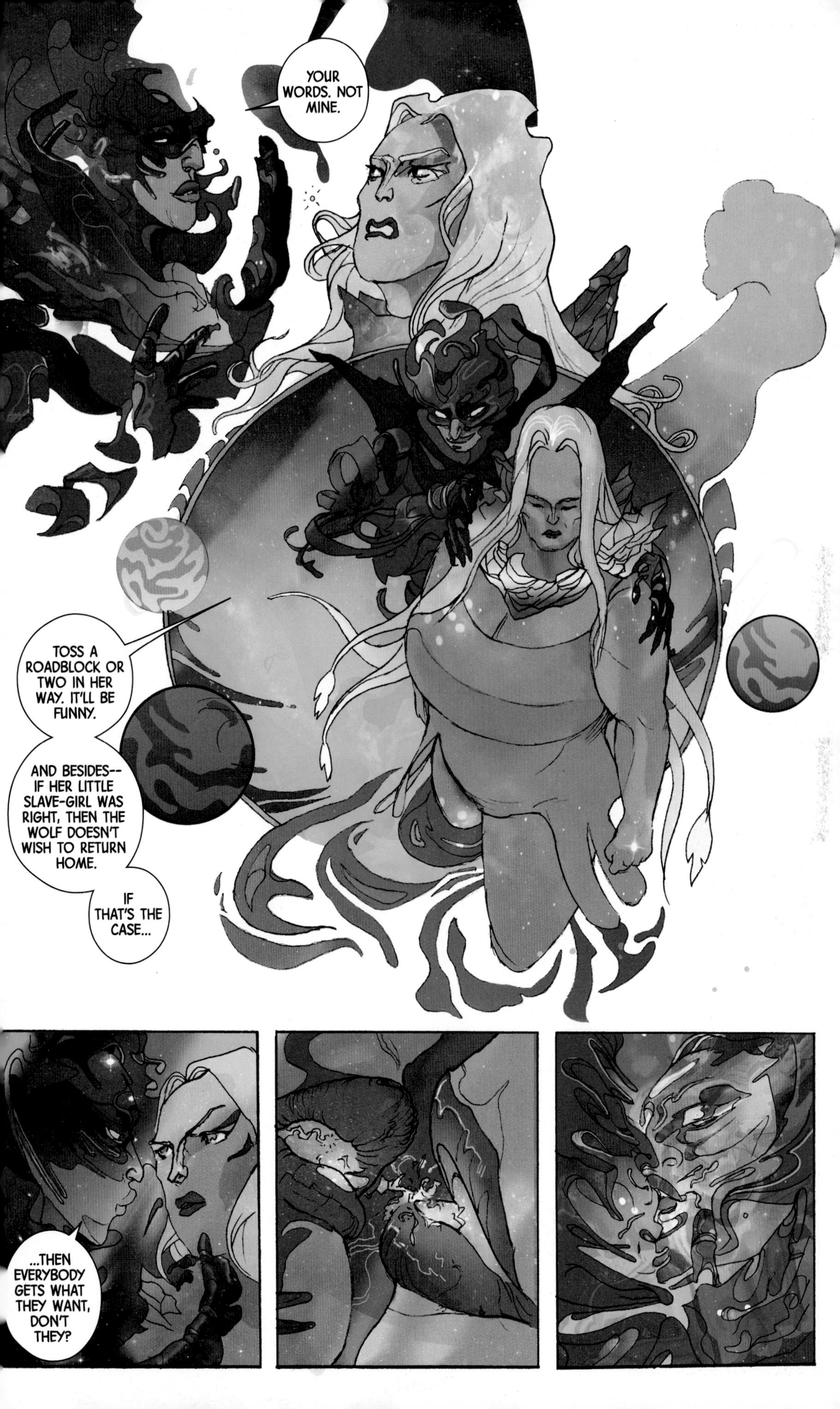
YOUR WORDS. NOT MINE.
TOSS A ROADBLOCK OR TWO IN HER WAY. IT'LL BE FUNNY.
AND BESIDES-- IF HER LITTLE SLAVE-GIRL WAS RIGHT, THEN THE WOLF DOESN'T WISH TO RETURN HOME.
IF THAT'S THE CASE...
...THEN EVERYBODY GETS WHAT THEY WANT, DON'T THEY?

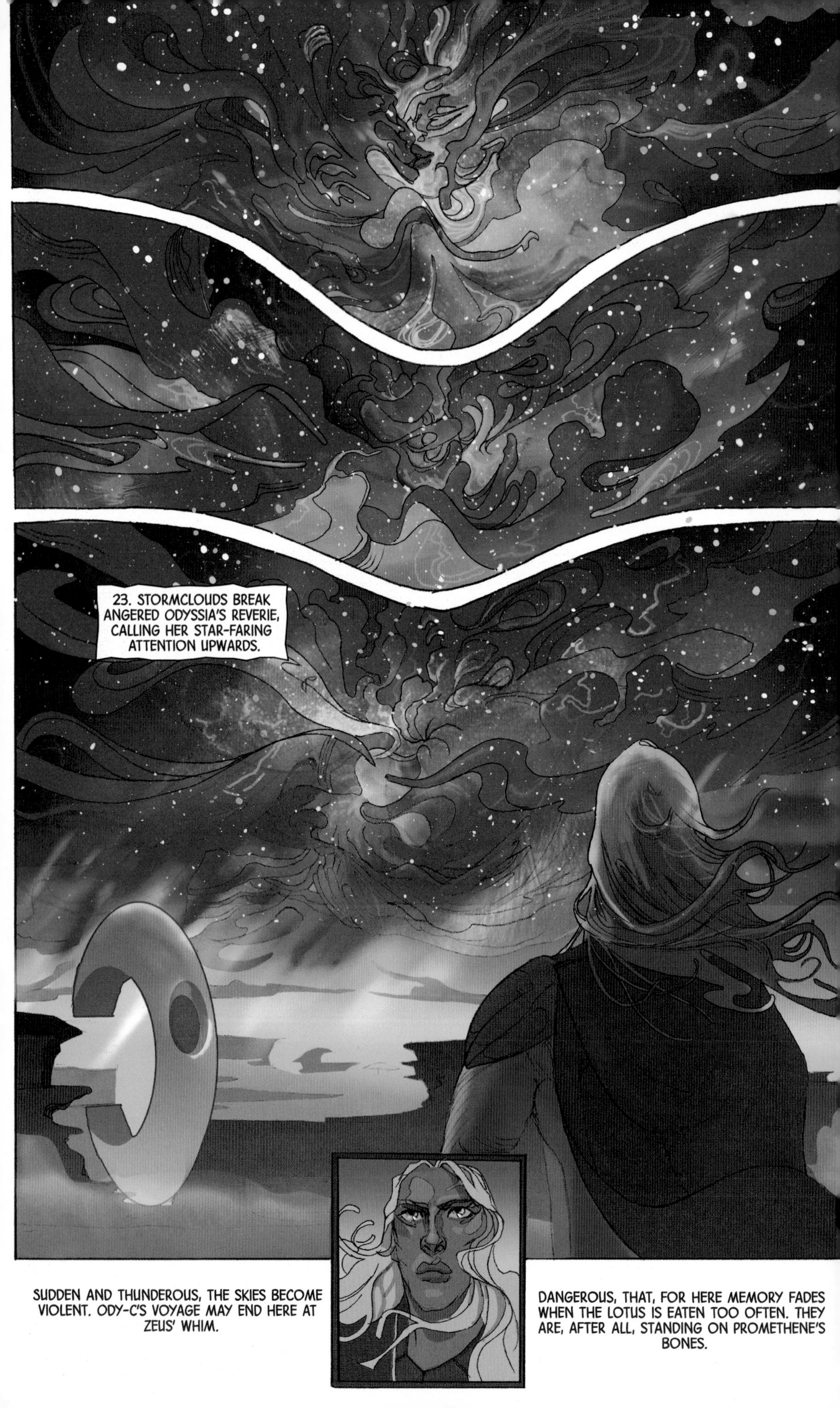
23. STORMCLOUDS BREAK ANGERED ODYSSIA'S REVERIE, CALLING HER STAR-FARING ATTENTION UPWARDS.
SUDDEN AND THUNDEROUS, THE SKIES BECOME VIOLENT. ODY-C'S VOYAGE MAY END HERE AT ZEUS' WHIM.
DANGEROUS, THAT, FOR HERE MEMORY FADES WHEN THE LOTUS IS EATEN TOO OFTEN. THEY ARE, AFTER ALL, STANDING ON PROMETHENE'S BONES.

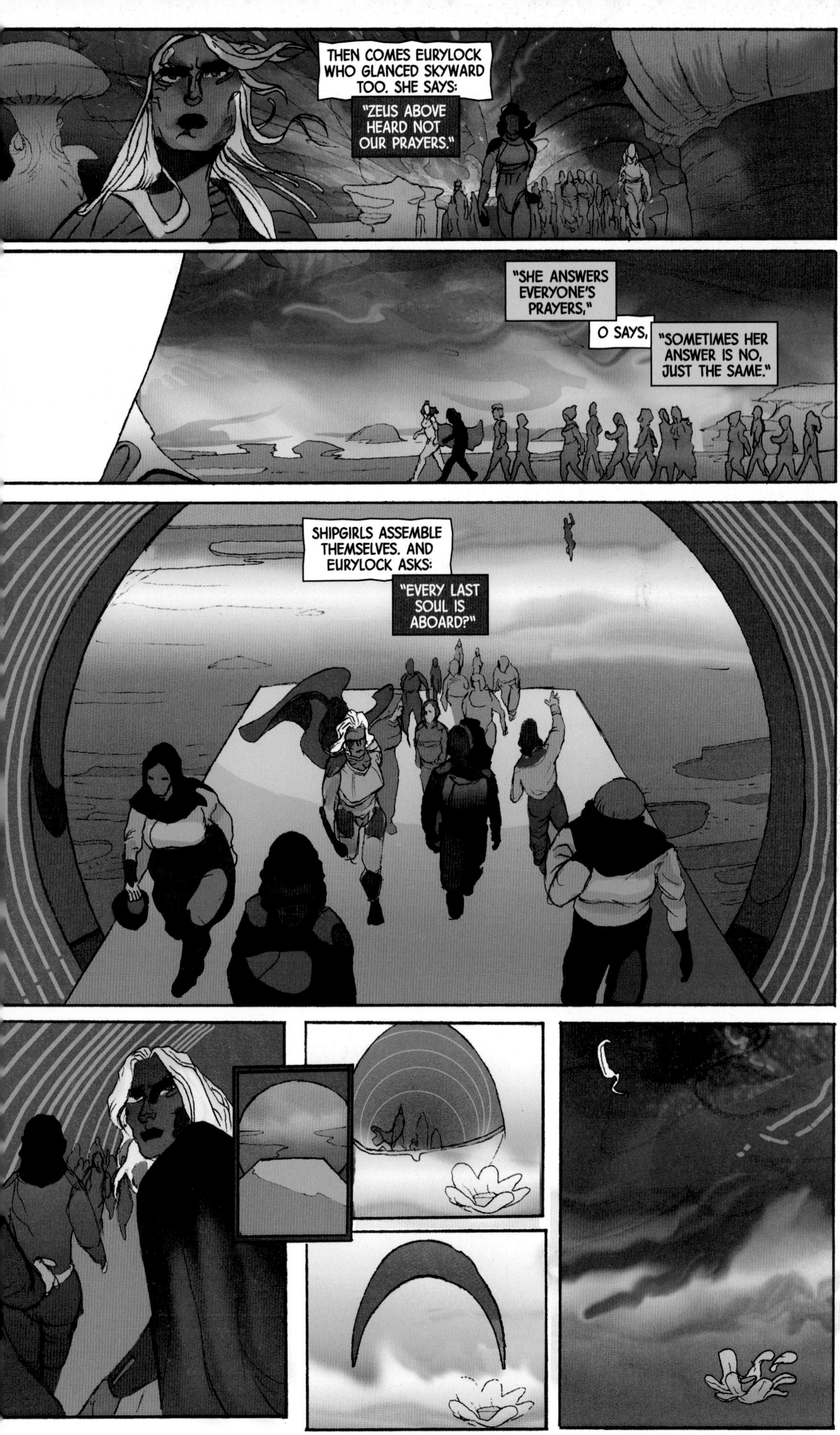
THEN COMES EURYLOCK WHO GLANCED SKYWARD TOO. SHE SAYS:
"ZEUS ABOVE HEARD NOT OUR PRAYERS."
"SHE ANSWERS EVERYONE'S PRAYERS,"
O SAYS,
"SOMETIMES HER ANSWER IS NO, JUST THE SAME."
SHIPGIRLS ASSEMBLE THEMSELVES. AND EURYLOCK ASKS:
"EVERY LAST SOUL IS ABOARD?"

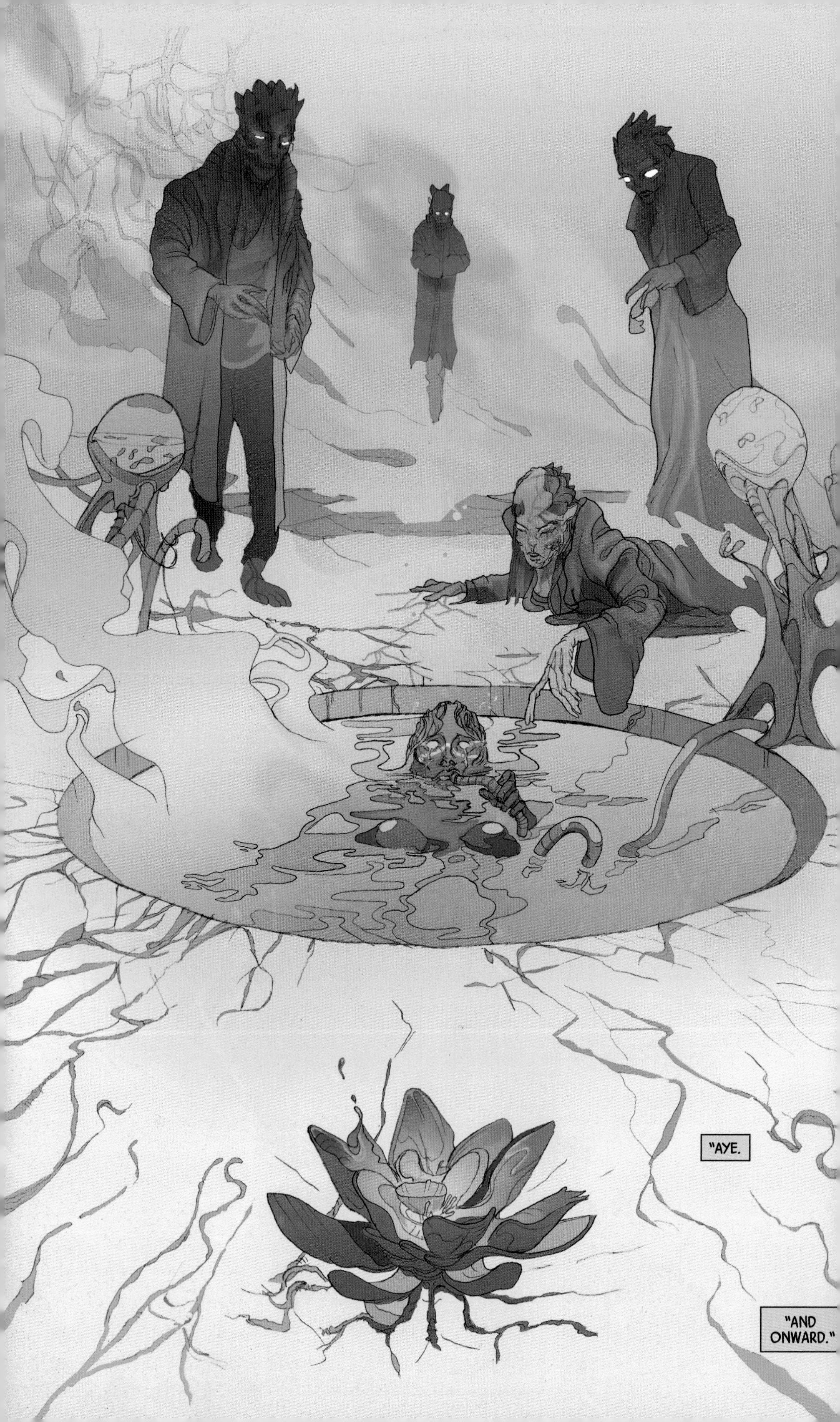
"AYE.
"AND ONWARD."

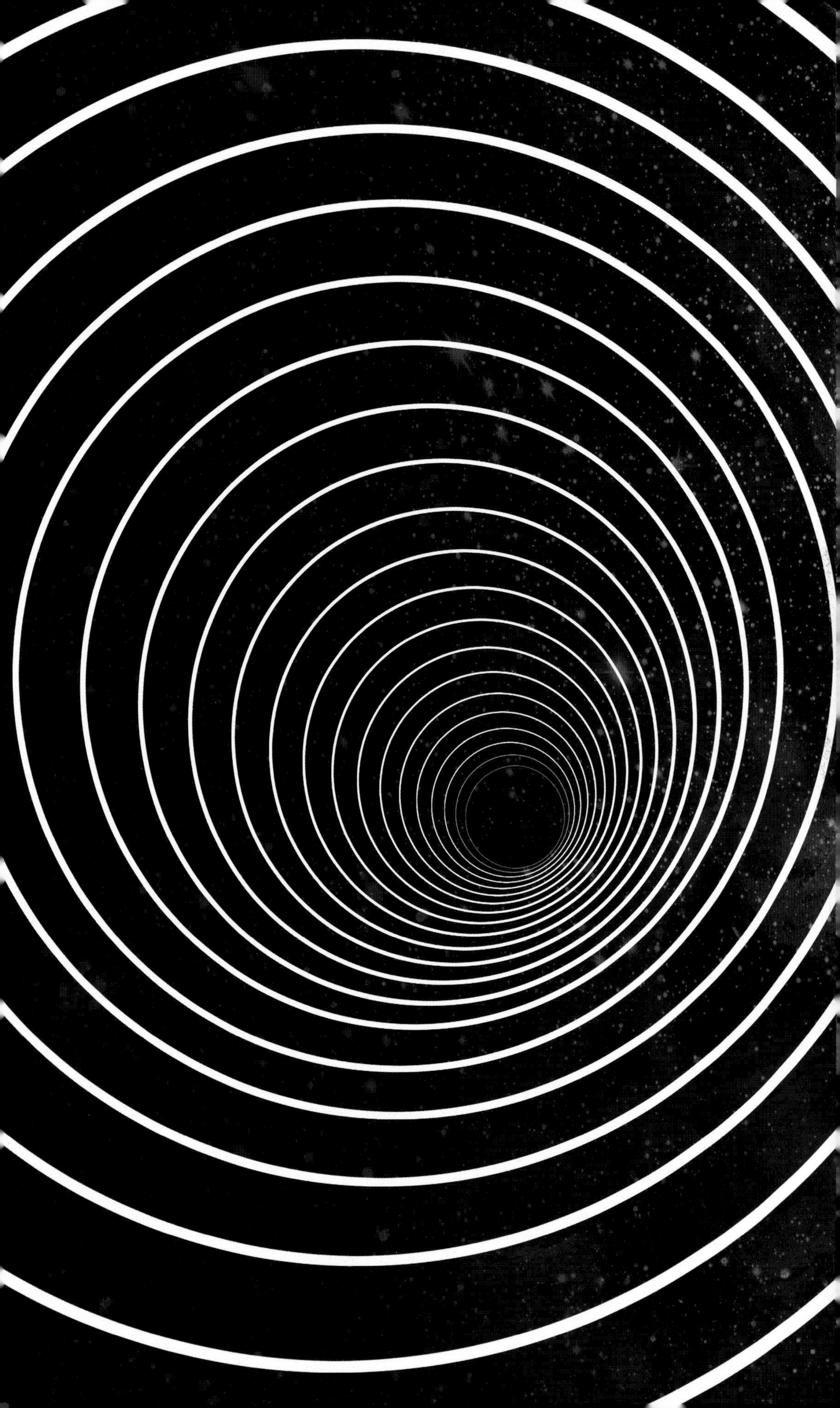

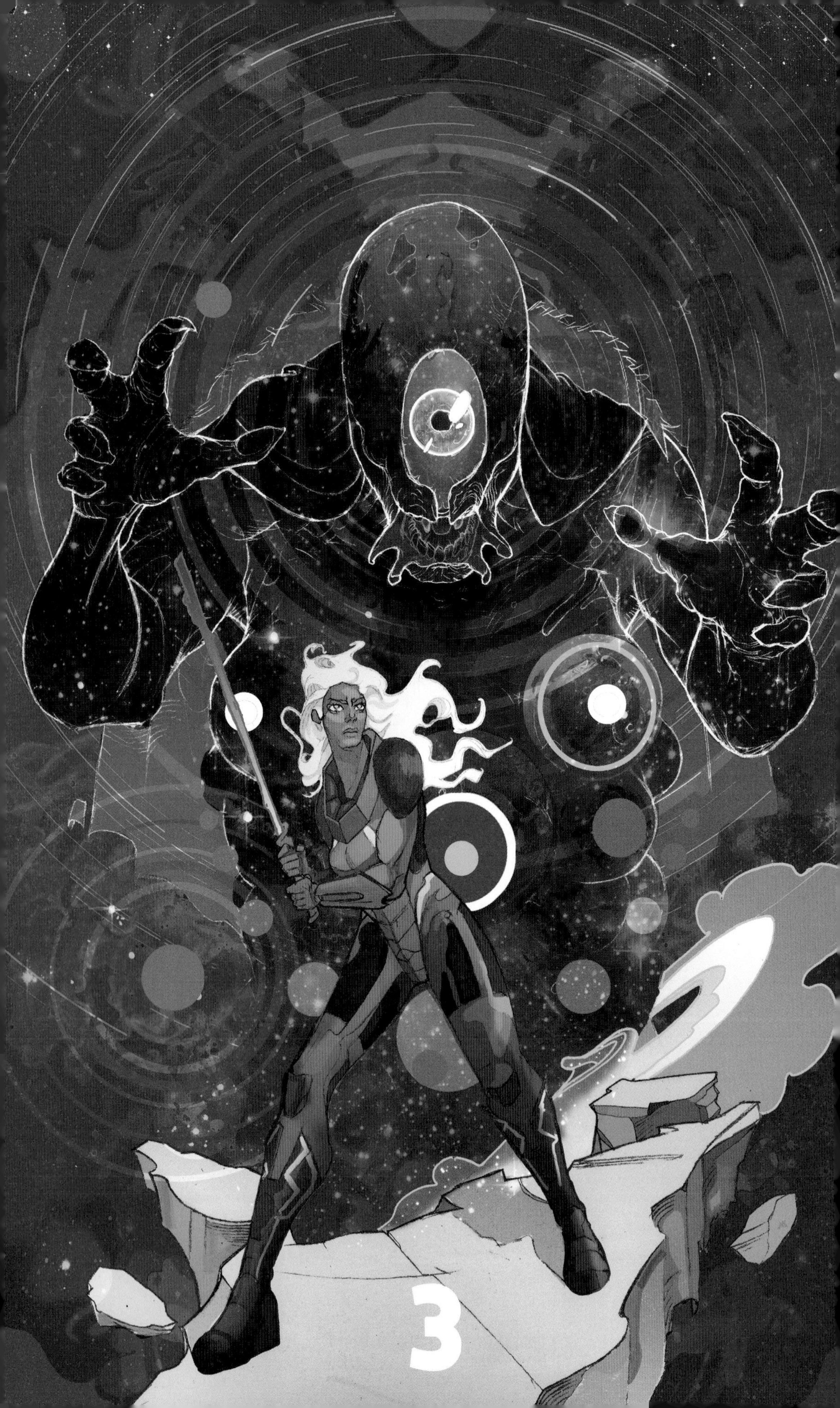
3

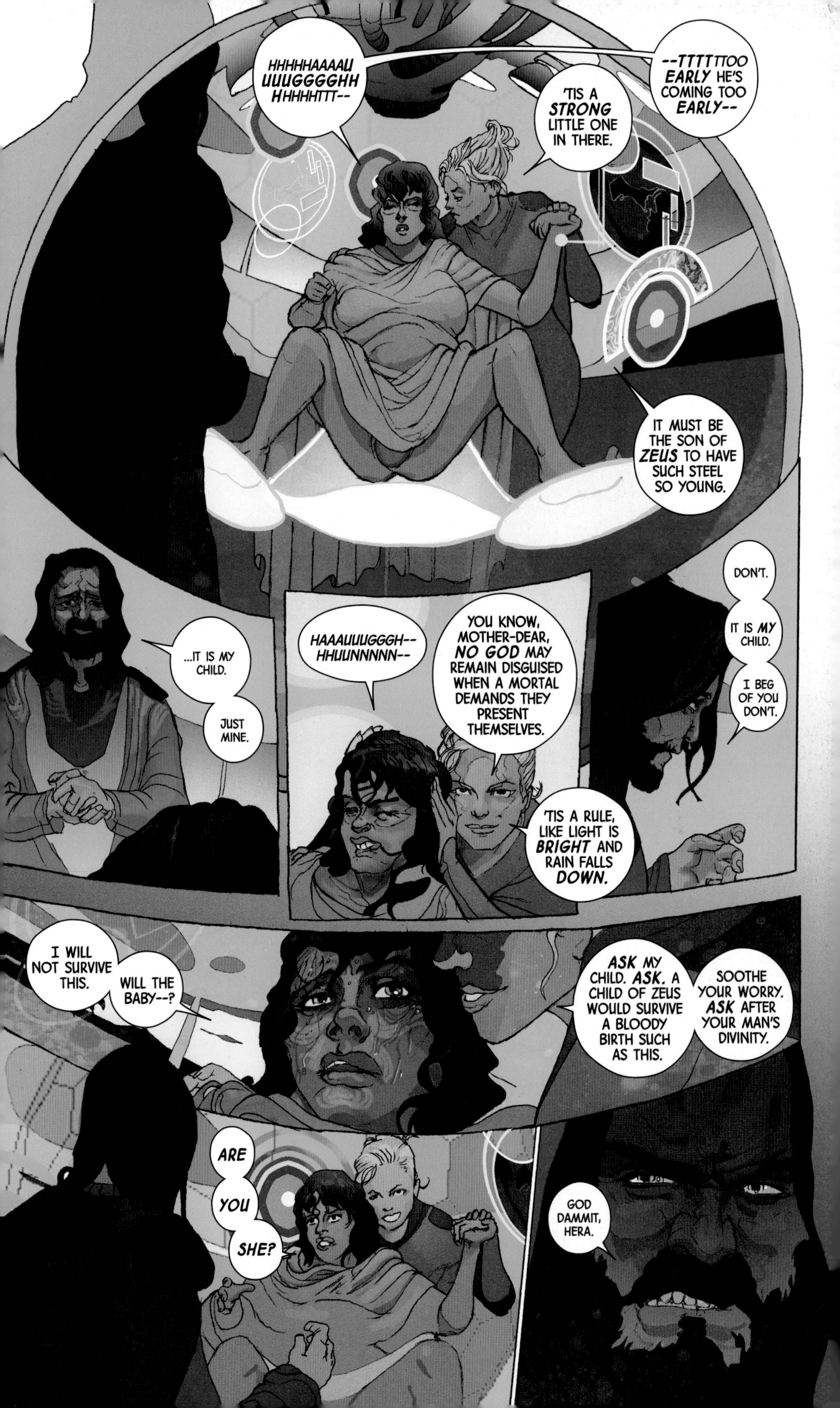
HHHHHAAAAU UUUGGGGHH HHHHHTTT--
--TTTTTTOO EARLY HE'S COMING TOO EARLY--
'TIS A STRONG LITTLE ONE IN THERE.
IT MUST BE THE SON OF ZEUS TO HAVE SUCH STEEL SO YOUNG.
...IT IS MY CHILD.
JUST MINE.
HAAAUUUGGGH-- HHUUNNNNN--
YOU KNOW, MOTHER-DEAR, NO GOD MAY REMAIN DISGUISED WHEN A MORTAL DEMANDS THEY PRESENT THEMSELVES.
'TIS A RULE, LIKE LIGHT IS BRIGHT AND RAIN FALLS DOWN.
DON'T.
IT IS MY CHILD.
I BEG OF YOU DON'T.
I WILL NOT SURVIVE THIS.
WILL THE BABY--?
ASK MY CHILD. ASK. A CHILD OF ZEUS WOULD SURVIVE A BLOODY BIRTH SUCH AS THIS.
SOOTHE YOUR WORRY. ASK AFTER YOUR MAN'S DIVINITY.
ARE
YOU
SHE?
GOD DAMMIT, HERA.

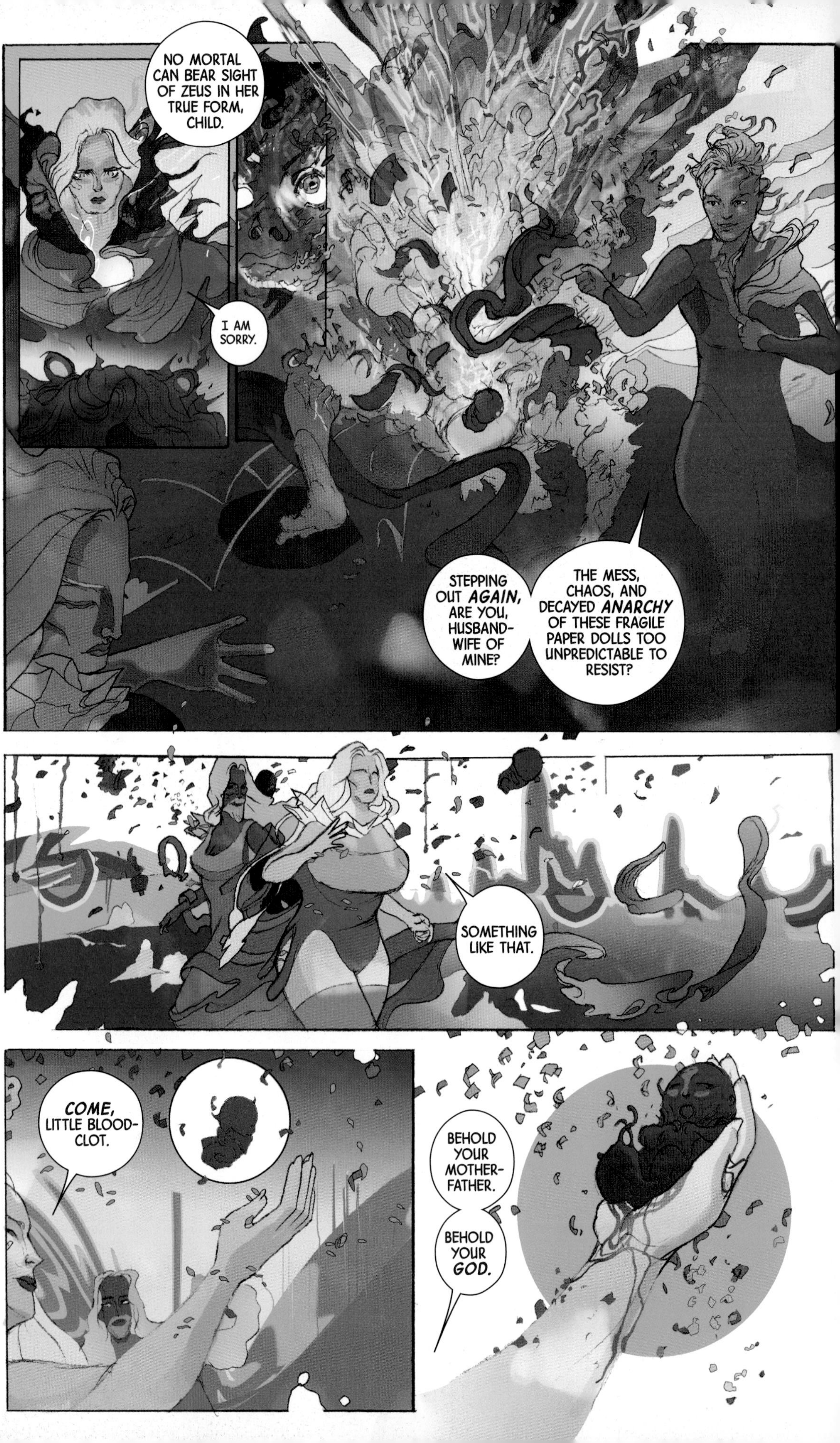
NO MORTAL CAN BEAR SIGHT OF ZEUS IN HER TRUE FORM, CHILD.
I AM SORRY.
STEPPING OUT *AGAIN*, ARE YOU, HUSBAND-WIFE OF MINE?
THE MESS, CHAOS, AND DECAYED *ANARCHY* OF THESE FRAGILE PAPER DOLLS TOO UNPREDICTABLE TO RESIST?
SOMETHING LIKE THAT.
COME, LITTLE BLOOD-CLOT.
BEHOLD YOUR MOTHER-FATHER.
BEHOLD YOUR *GOD*.

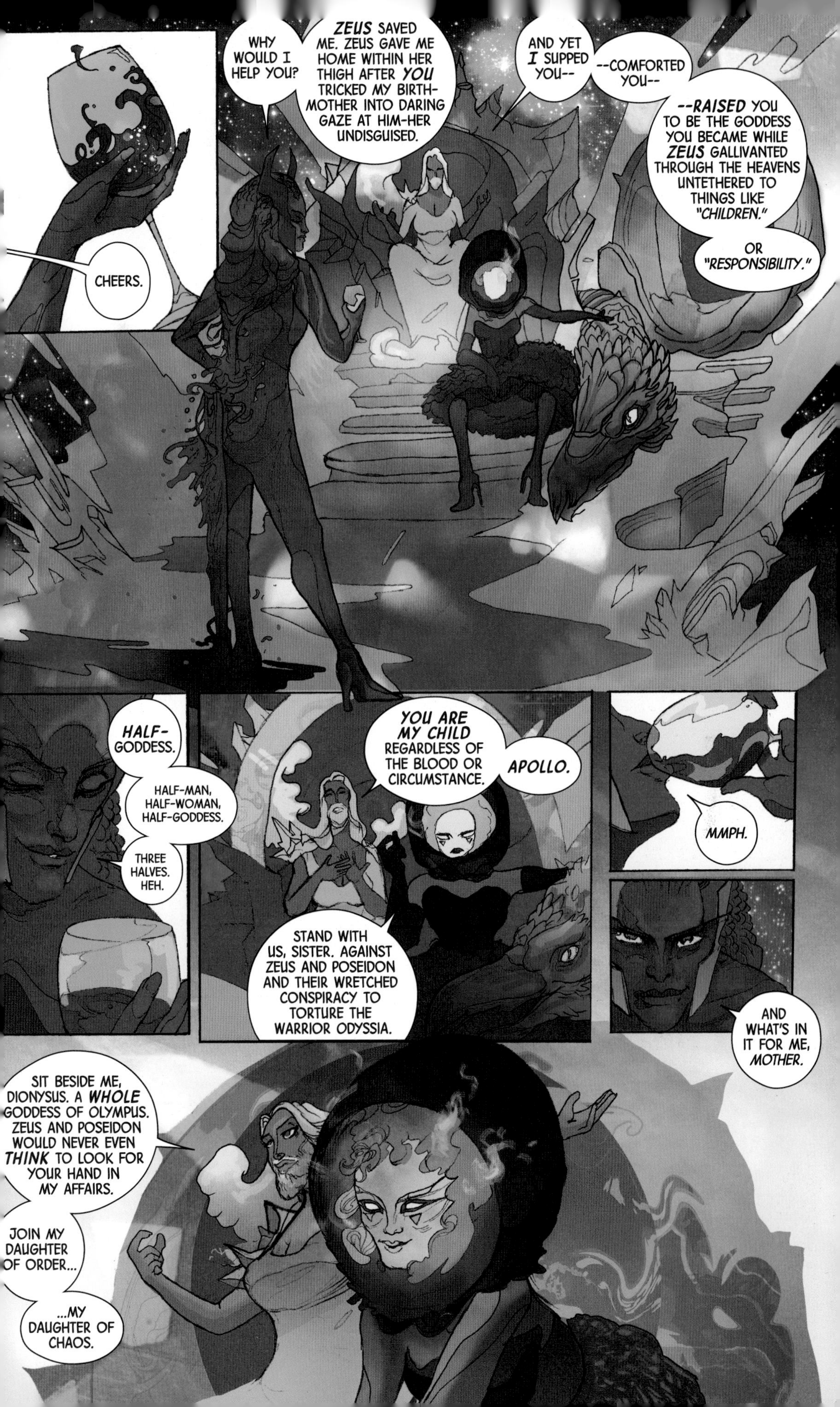

CHEERS.
WHY WOULD I HELP YOU?
ZEUS SAVED ME. ZEUS GAVE ME HOME WITHIN HER THIGH AFTER YOU TRICKED MY BIRTH-MOTHER INTO DARING GAZE AT HIM-HER UNDISGUISED.
AND YET I SUPPED YOU--
--COMFORTED YOU--
--RAISED YOU TO BE THE GODDESS YOU BECAME WHILE ZEUS GALLIVANTED THROUGH THE HEAVENS UNTETHERED TO THINGS LIKE "CHILDREN."
OR "RESPONSIBILITY."
HALF-GODDESS.
HALF-MAN, HALF-WOMAN, HALF-GODDESS.
THREE HALVES. HEH.
YOU ARE MY CHILD REGARDLESS OF THE BLOOD OR CIRCUMSTANCE.
APOLLO.
STAND WITH US, SISTER. AGAINST ZEUS AND POSEIDON AND THEIR WRETCHED CONSPIRACY TO TORTURE THE WARRIOR ODYSSIA.
MMPH.
AND WHAT'S IN IT FOR ME, MOTHER.
SIT BESIDE ME, DIONYSUS. A WHOLE GODDESS OF OLYMPUS. ZEUS AND POSEIDON WOULD NEVER EVEN THINK TO LOOK FOR YOUR HAND IN MY AFFAIRS.
JOIN MY DAUGHTER OF ORDER...
...MY DAUGHTER OF CHAOS.

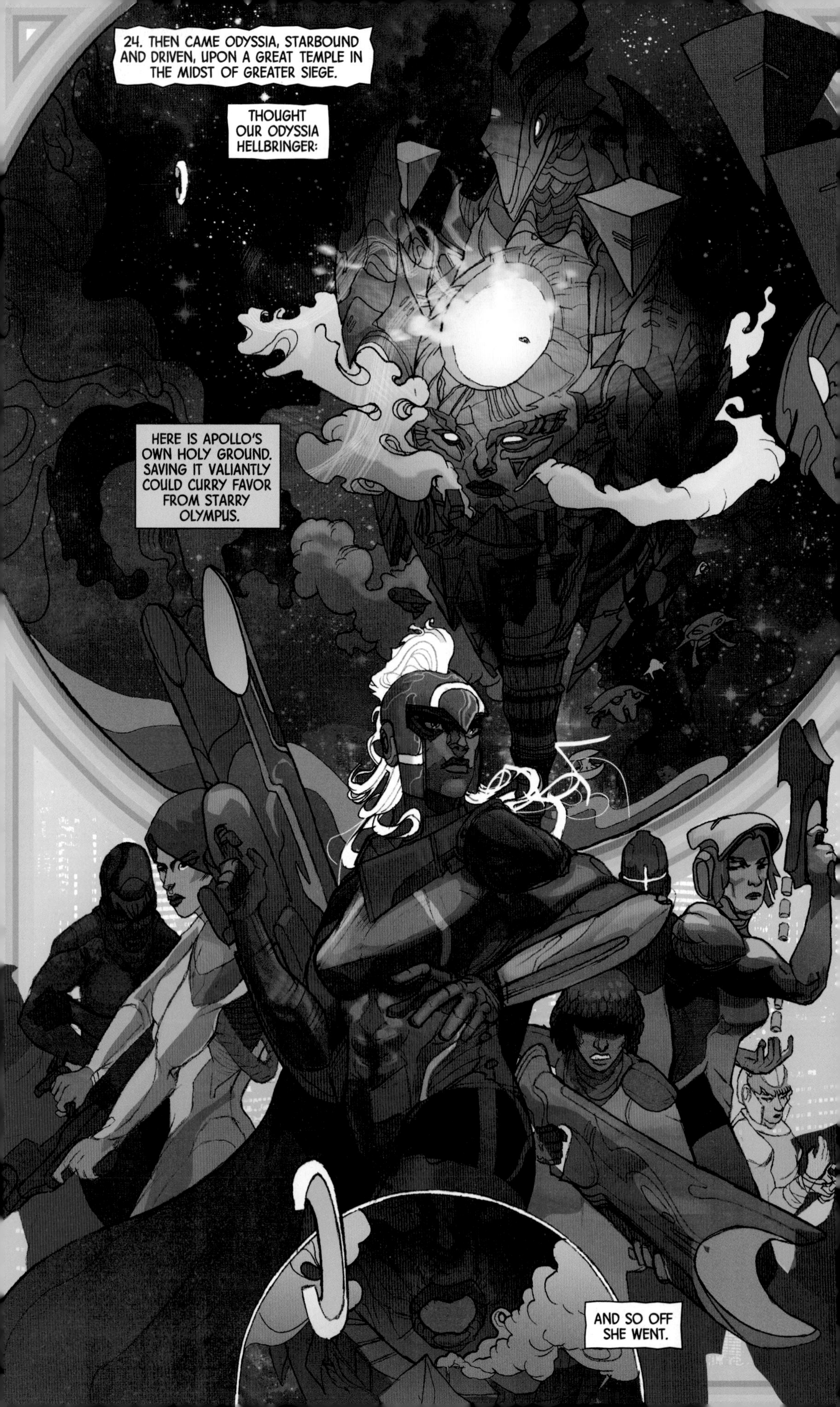
24. THEN CAME ODYSSIA, STARBOUND AND DRIVEN, UPON A GREAT TEMPLE IN THE MIDST OF GREATER SIEGE.
THOUGHT OUR ODYSSIA HELLBRINGER:
HERE IS APOLLO'S OWN HOLY GROUND. SAVING IT VALIANTLY COULD CURRY FAVOR FROM STARRY OLYMPUS.
AND SO OFF SHE WENT.

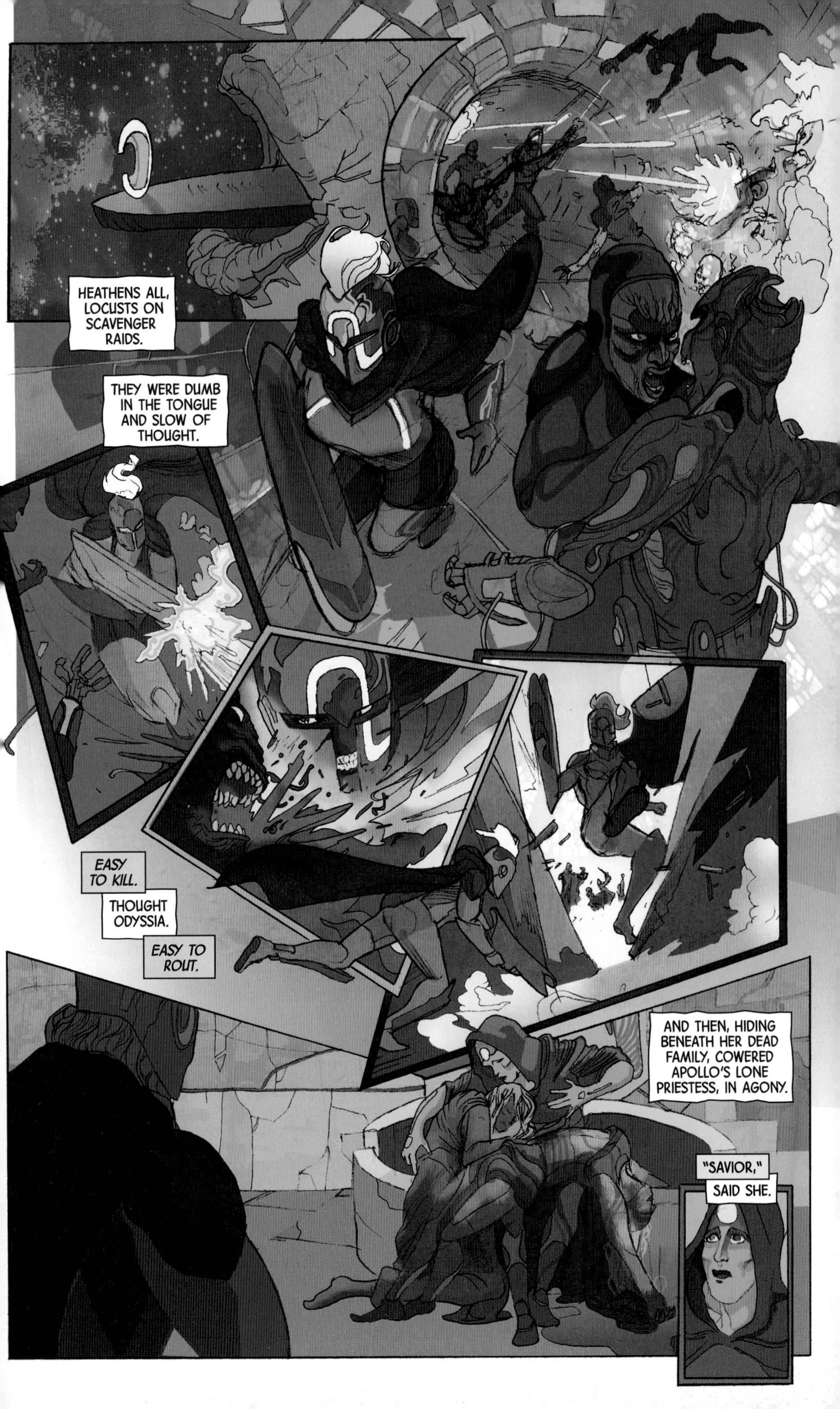
HEATHENS ALL, LOCUSTS ON SCAVENGER RAIDS.
THEY WERE DUMB IN THE TONGUE AND SLOW OF THOUGHT.
EASY TO KILL.
THOUGHT ODYSSIA.
EASY TO ROUT.
AND THEN, HIDING BENEATH HER DEAD FAMILY, COWERED APOLLO'S LONE PRIESTESS, IN AGONY.
"SAVIOR,"
SAID SHE.

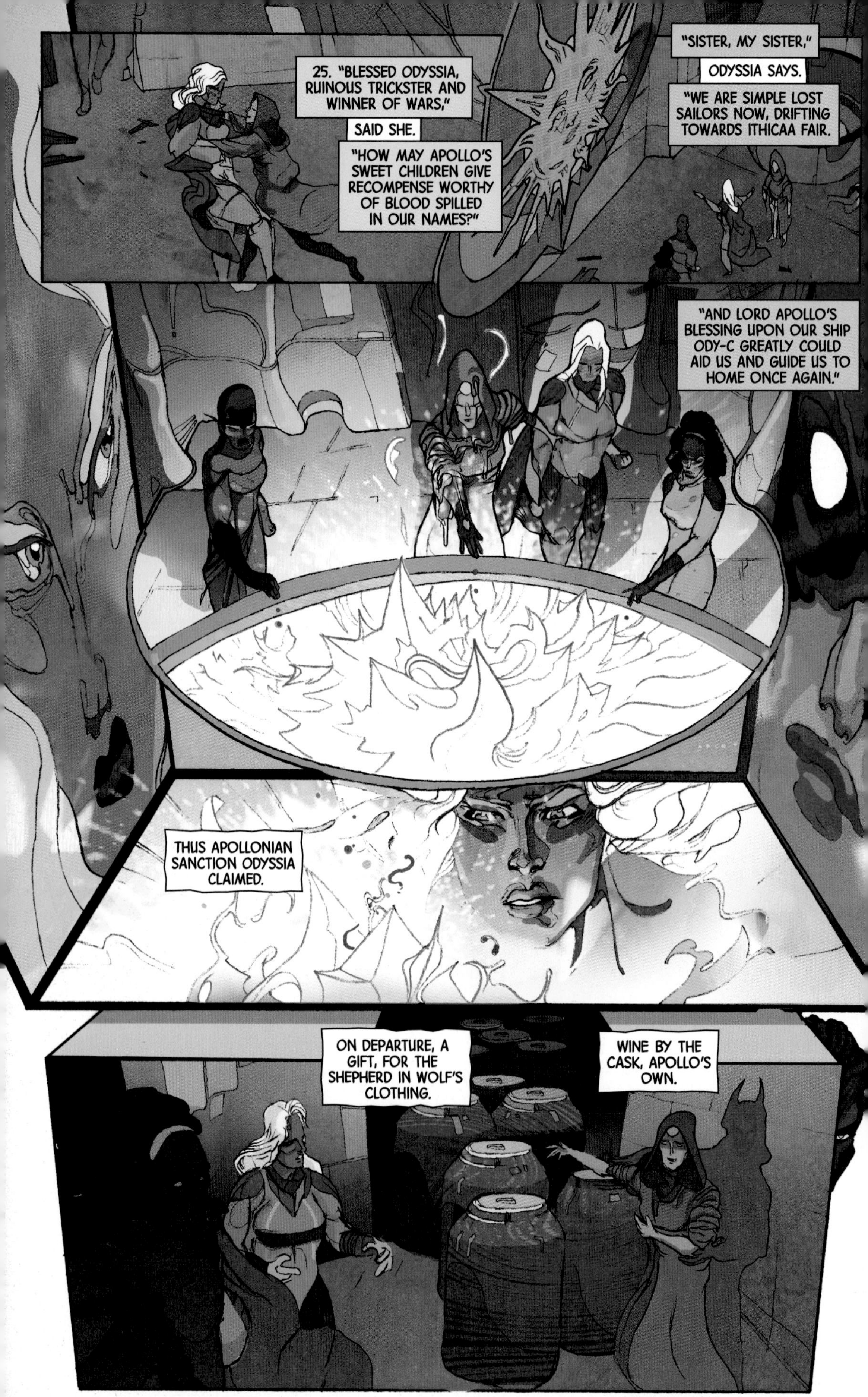
25. "BLESSED ODYSSIA, RUINOUS TRICKSTER AND WINNER OF WARS,"
SAID SHE.
"HOW MAY APOLLO'S SWEET CHILDREN GIVE RECOMPENSE WORTHY OF BLOOD SPILLED IN OUR NAMES?"
"SISTER, MY SISTER,"
ODYSSIA SAYS.
"WE ARE SIMPLE LOST SAILORS NOW, DRIFTING TOWARDS ITHICAA FAIR.
"AND LORD APOLLO'S BLESSING UPON OUR SHIP ODY-C GREATLY COULD AID US AND GUIDE US TO HOME ONCE AGAIN."
THUS APOLLONIAN SANCTION ODYSSIA CLAIMED.
ON DEPARTURE, A GIFT, FOR THE SHEPHERD IN WOLF'S CLOTHING.
WINE BY THE CASK, APOLLO'S OWN.

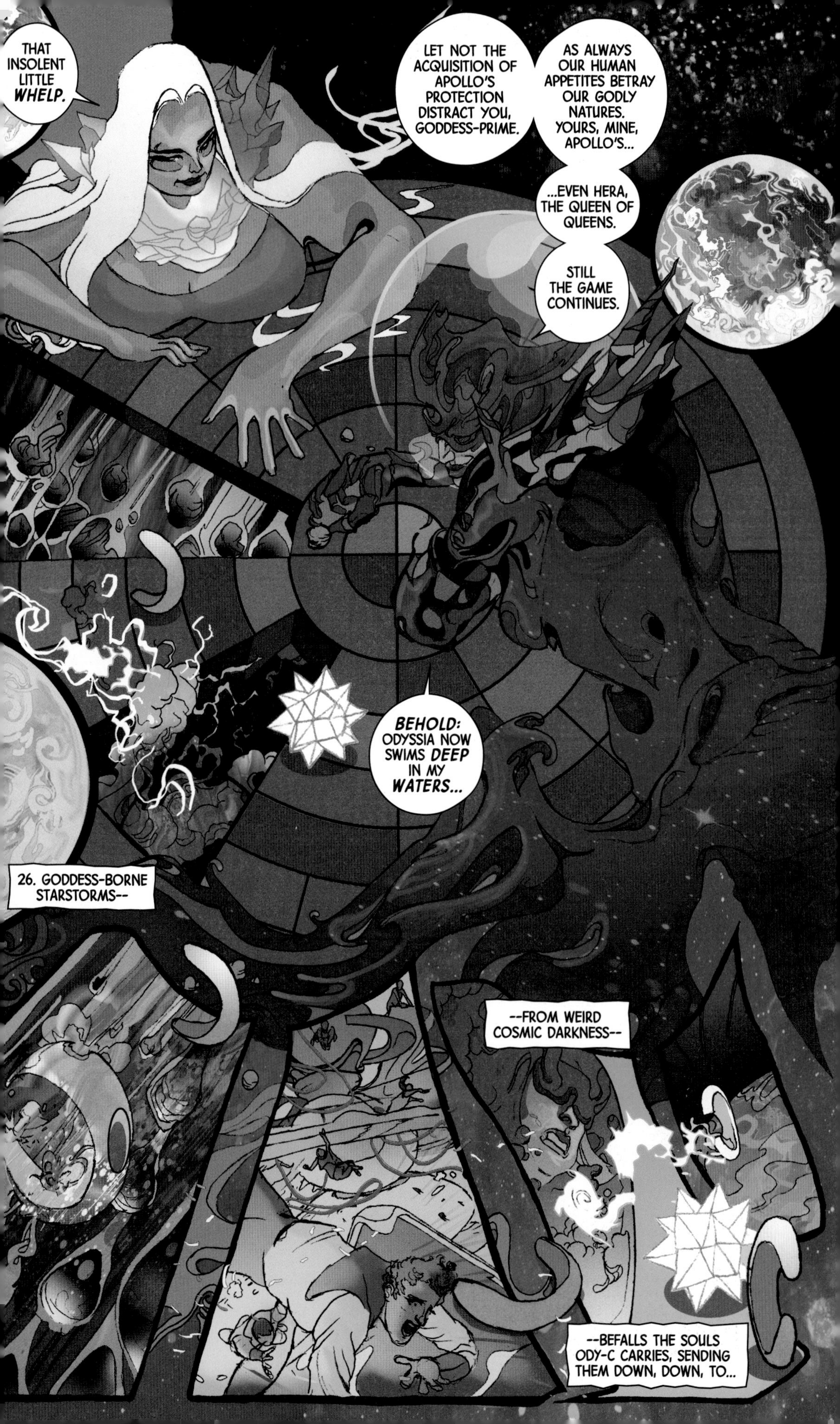

THAT INSOLENT LITTLE *WHELP.*
LET NOT THE ACQUISITION OF APOLLO'S PROTECTION DISTRACT YOU, GODDESS-PRIME.
AS ALWAYS OUR HUMAN APPETITES BETRAY OUR GODLY NATURES. YOURS, MINE, APOLLO'S...
...EVEN HERA, THE QUEEN OF QUEENS.
STILL THE GAME CONTINUES.
BEHOLD: ODYSSIA NOW SWIMS *DEEP* IN MY *WATERS...*
26. GODDESS-BORNE STARSTORMS--
--FROM WEIRD COSMIC DARKNESS--
--BEFALLS THE SOULS ODY-C CARRIES, SENDING THEM DOWN, DOWN, TO...

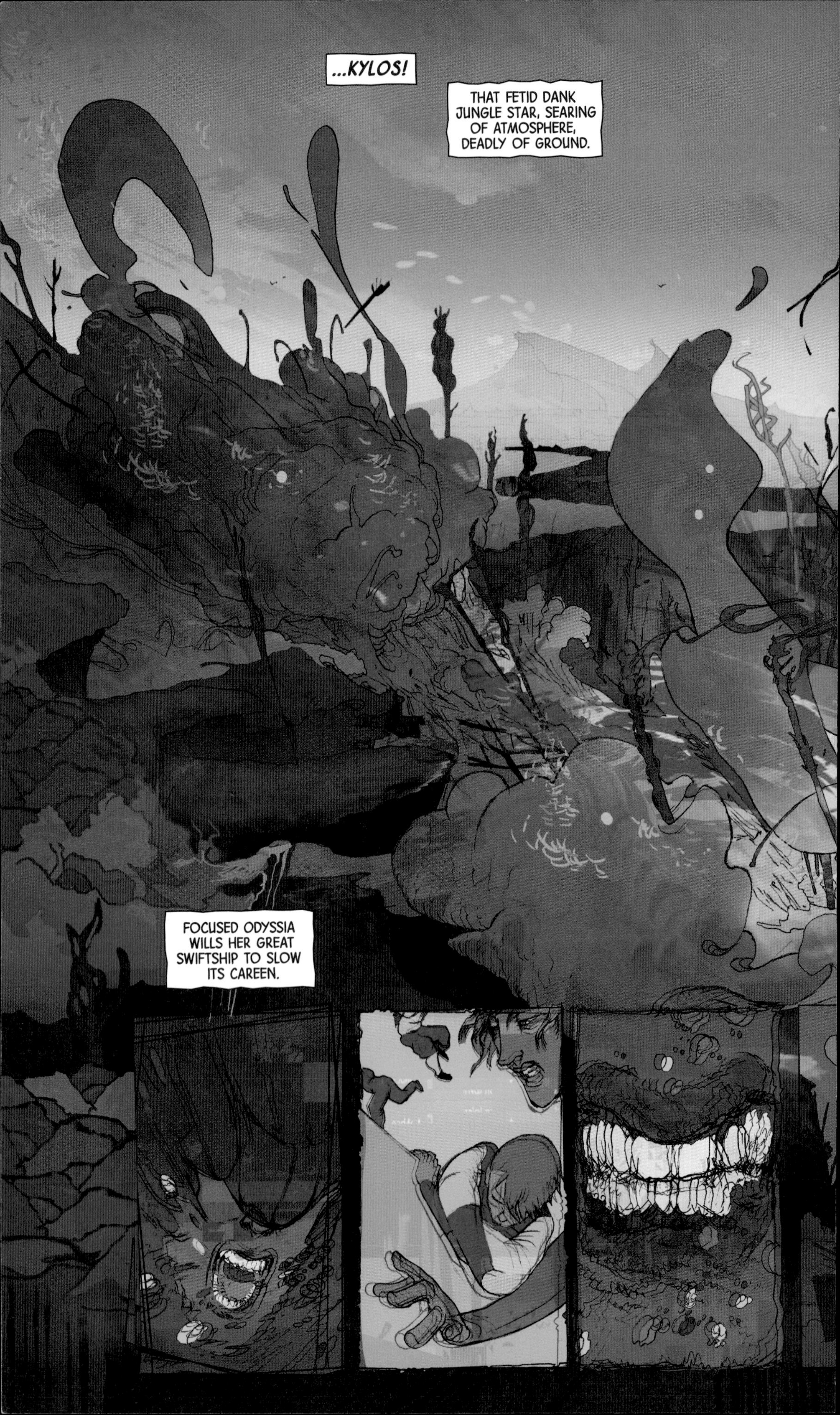
...KYLOS!
THAT FETID DANK JUNGLE STAR, SEARING OF ATMOSPHERE, DEADLY OF GROUND.
FOCUSED ODYSSIA WILLS HER GREAT SWIFTSHIP TO SLOW ITS CAREEN.

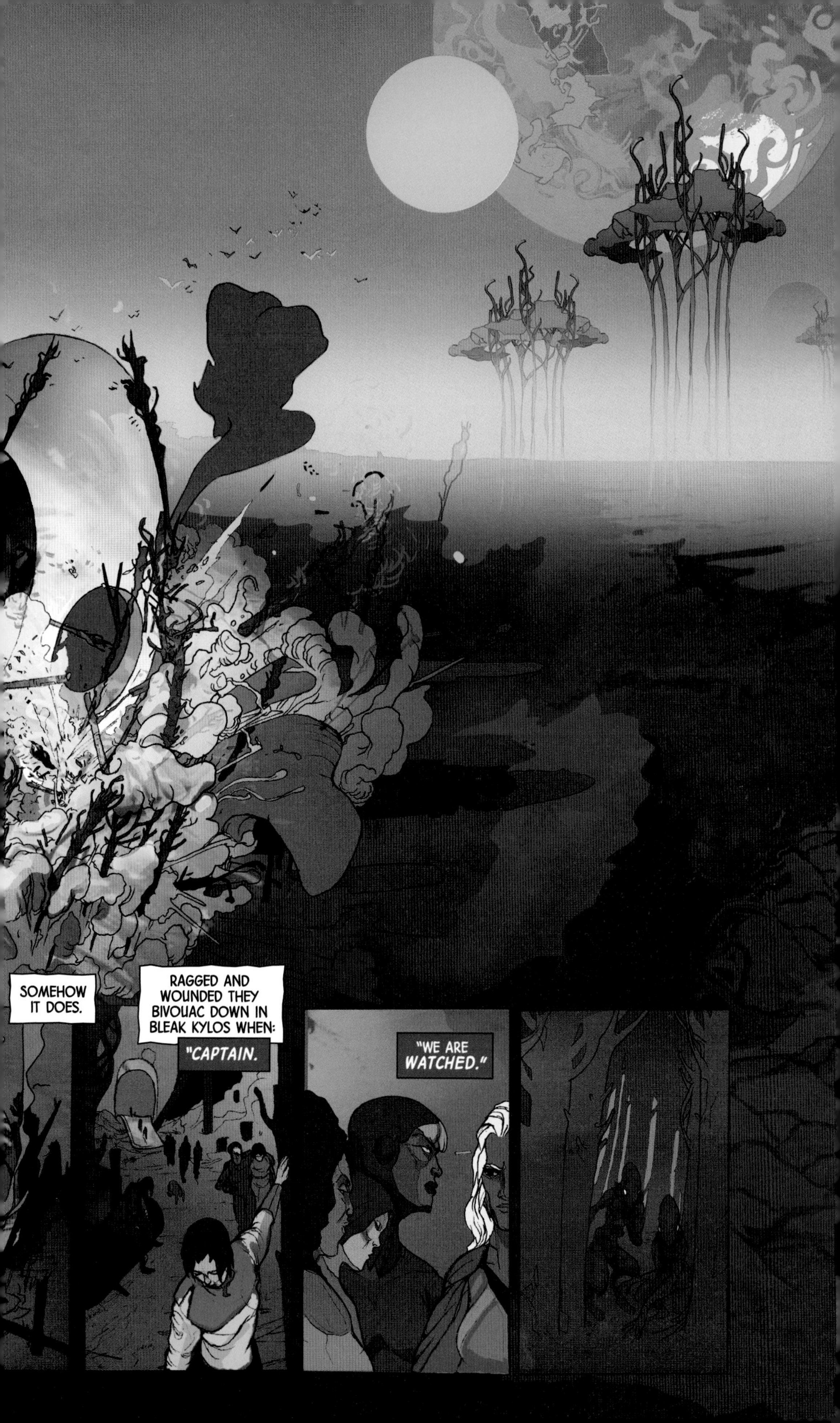

SOMEHOW IT DOES.
RAGGED AND WOUNDED THEY BIVOUAC DOWN IN BLEAK KYLOS WHEN:
"CAPTAIN.
"WE ARE WATCHED."

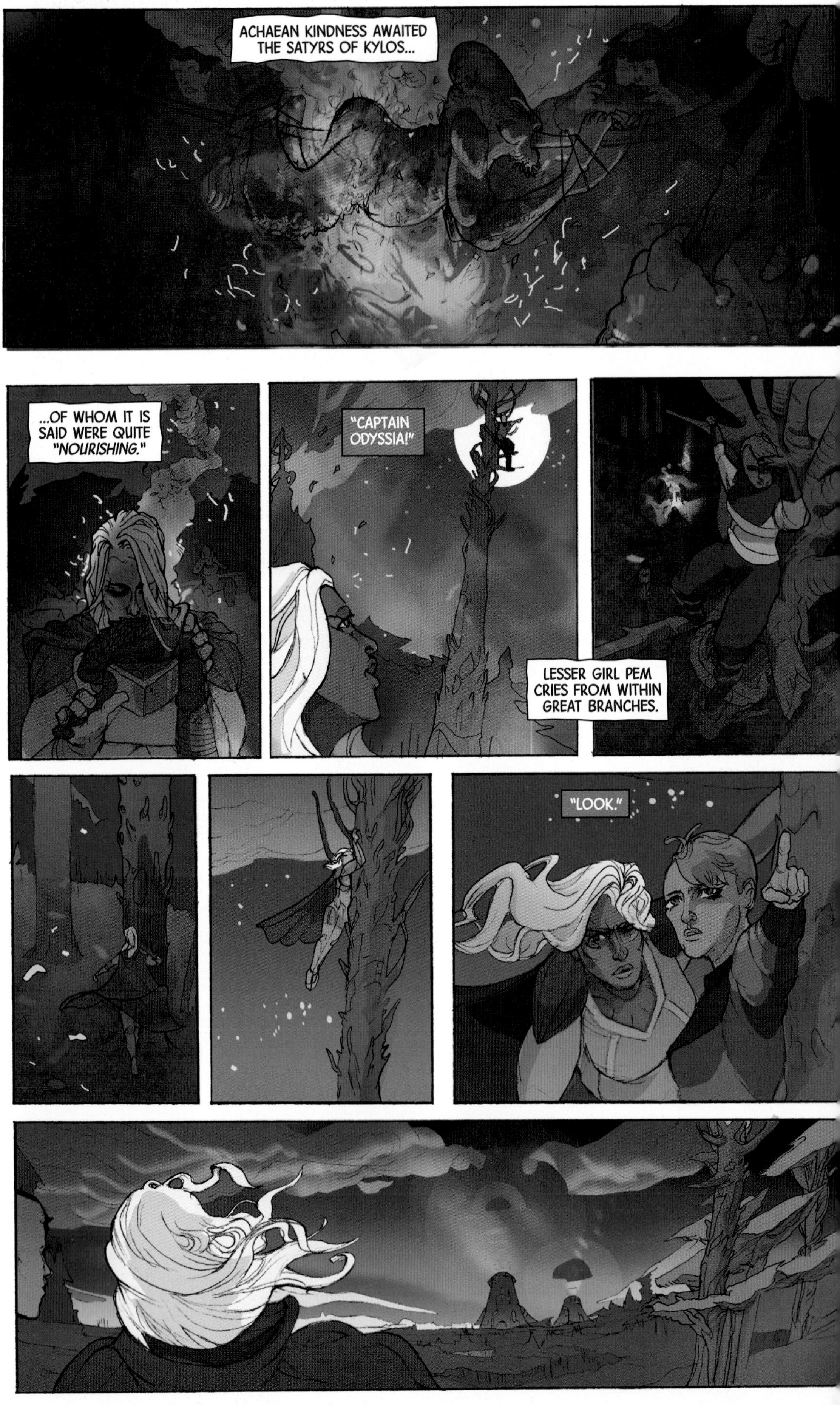
ACHAEAN KINDNESS AWAITED THE SATYRS OF KYLOS...
...OF WHOM IT IS SAID WERE QUITE "NOURISHING."
"CAPTAIN ODYSSIA!"
LESSER GIRL PEM CRIES FROM WITHIN GREAT BRANCHES.
"LOOK."

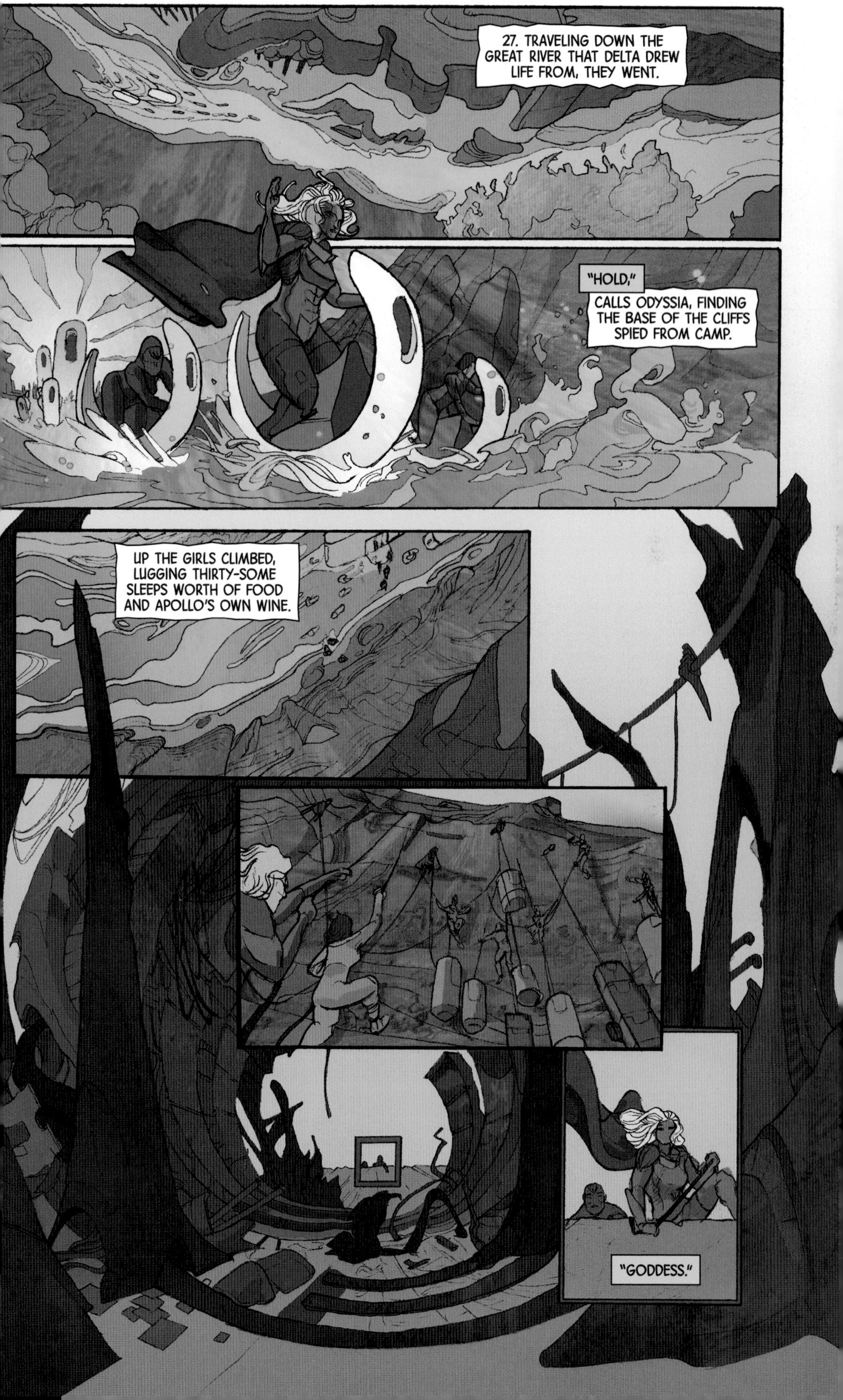
27. TRAVELING DOWN THE GREAT RIVER THAT DELTA DREW LIFE FROM, THEY WENT.
"HOLD,"
CALLS ODYSSIA, FINDING THE BASE OF THE CLIFFS SPIED FROM CAMP.
UP THE GIRLS CLIMBED, LUGGING THIRTY-SOME SLEEPS WORTH OF FOOD AND APOLLO'S OWN WINE.
"GODDESS."

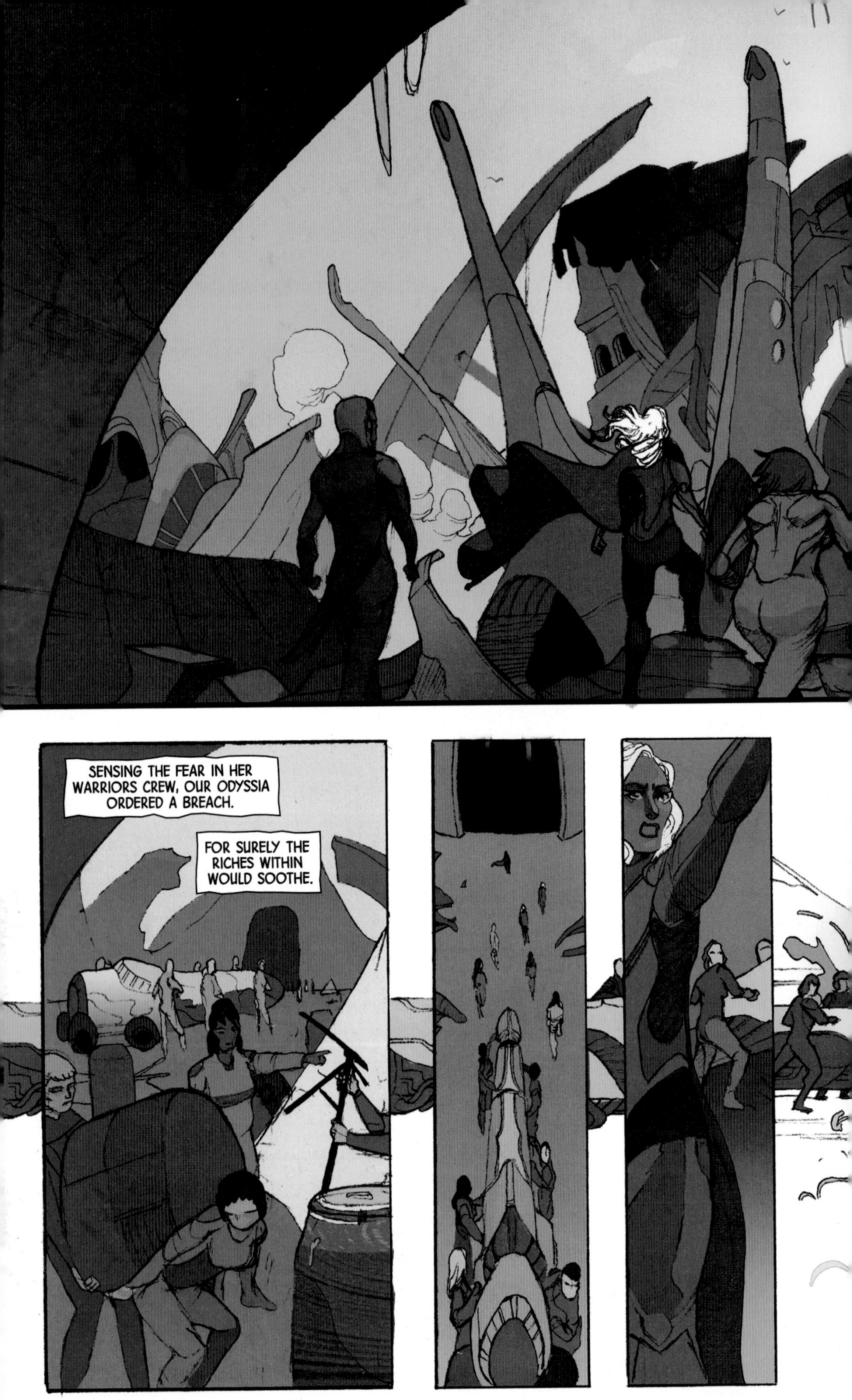
SENSING THE FEAR IN HER WARRIORS CREW, OUR ODYSSIA ORDERED A BREACH.
FOR SURELY THE RICHES WITHIN WOULD SOOTHE.

EVERYTHING FOUND ATOP DWARFED THE ACHAEANS.

THE *WOLF* SMELLED PLUNDER FOR TAKING.

"CAPTAIN!"

THE GIRLS OF THE ODY-C BEGGED.

"WHAT *THING* NEEDS A FRONT *DOOR* SO LARGE?"

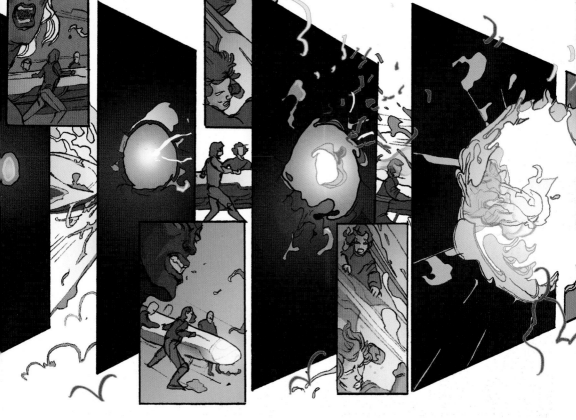

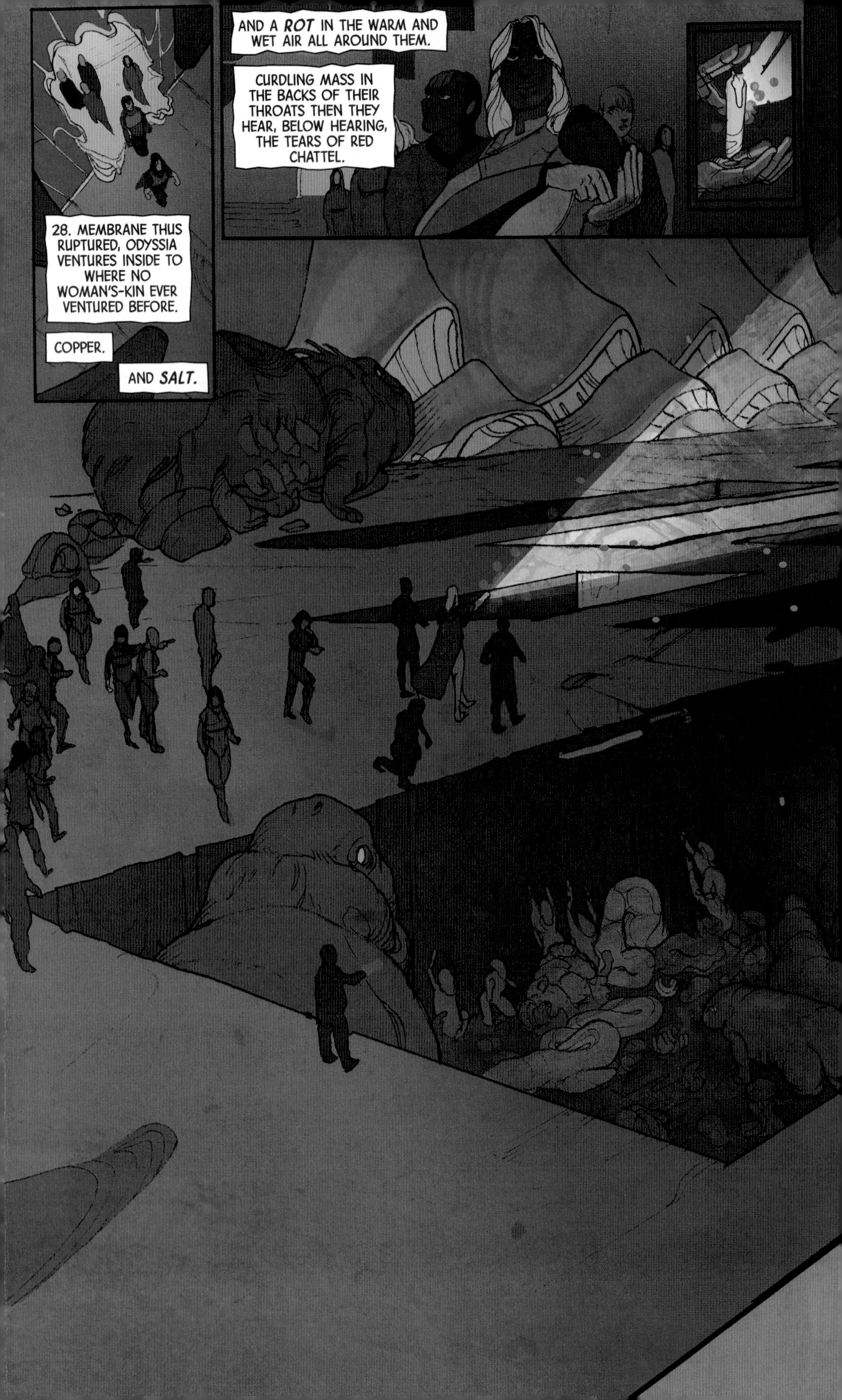
AND A *ROT* IN THE WARM AND WET AIR ALL AROUND THEM.
CURDLING MASS IN THE BACKS OF THEIR THROATS THEN THEY HEAR, BELOW HEARING, THE TEARS OF RED CHATTEL.
28. MEMBRANE THUS RUPTURED, ODYSSIA VENTURES INSIDE TO WHERE NO WOMAN'S-KIN EVER VENTURED BEFORE.
COPPER.
AND *SALT.*

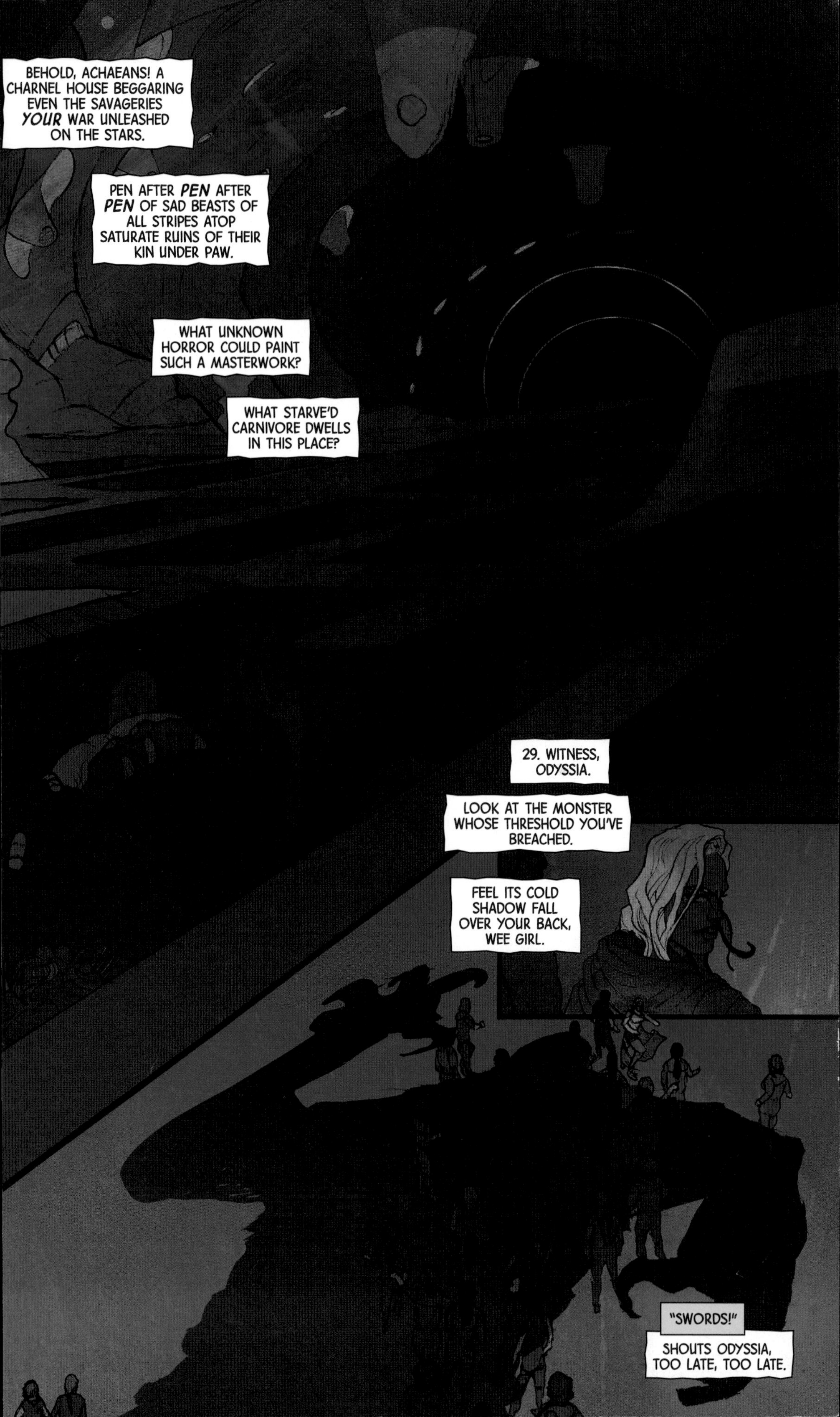
BEHOLD, ACHAEANS! A CHARNEL HOUSE BEGGARING EVEN THE SAVAGERIES *YOUR* WAR UNLEASHED ON THE STARS.
PEN AFTER *PEN* AFTER *PEN* OF SAD BEASTS OF ALL STRIPES ATOP SATURATE RUINS OF THEIR KIN UNDER PAW.
WHAT UNKNOWN HORROR COULD PAINT SUCH A MASTERWORK?
WHAT STARVE'D CARNIVORE DWELLS IN THIS PLACE?
29. WITNESS, ODYSSIA.
LOOK AT THE MONSTER WHOSE THRESHOLD YOU'VE BREACHED.
FEEL ITS COLD SHADOW FALL OVER YOUR BACK, WEE GIRL.
"SWORDS!"
SHOUTS ODYSSIA, TOO LATE, TOO LATE.

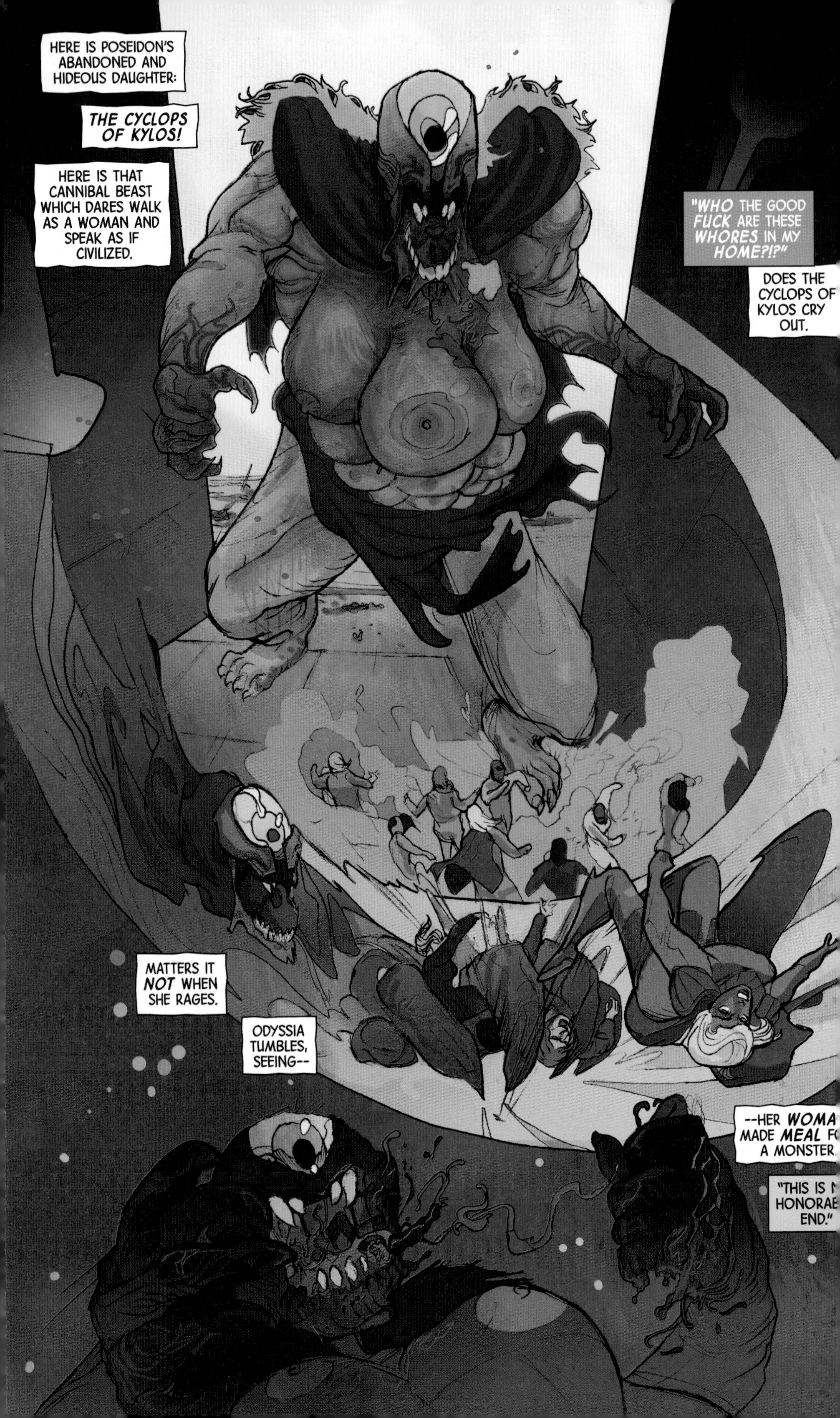
HERE IS POSEIDON'S ABANDONED AND HIDEOUS DAUGHTER:
THE CYCLOPS OF KYLOS!
HERE IS THAT CANNIBAL BEAST WHICH DARES WALK AS A WOMAN AND SPEAK AS IF CIVILIZED.
"*WHO* THE GOOD *FUCK* ARE THESE *WHORES* IN MY *HOME?!?*"
DOES THE CYCLOPS OF KYLOS CRY OUT.
MATTERS IT *NOT* WHEN SHE RAGES.
ODYSSIA TUMBLES, SEEING--
--HER *WOMA* MADE *MEAL* F A MONSTER.
"THIS IS HONORA END."

30. NEVER BEFORE HAD ODYSSIA KNOWN SUCH A BEAST BUT FOR STORIES AND FABLES HER MOTHER WOULD TELL BY THE FIRE.

MOTHER ANTICLEA, HOME STILL IN ITHICAA, LAST SHE HAD HEARD.

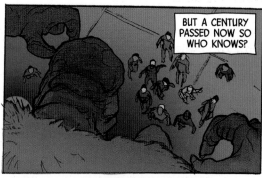

BUT A CENTURY PASSED NOW SO WHO KNOWS?

ELDERLY MOTHERS ARE NOT BUILT TO LAST EVEN IN PASTORAL ITHICAA.

THAT BRINGS ON THOUGHTS OF HER OWN FLESH AND BLOOD, MAN-CHILD TELEM.

"BRING ME MY SWORD."

UNDER THE NECROTIC HULL OF HER FLESH THERE HIDES MEAT, AND SOFT WIRES OF TENDON, AND BONE.

ORPHANQUEEN FINDS HER WARM TARGET ONCE MORE.

"PAIN MEANS IT FEELS!

"IF IT FEELS THEN IT DIES!"

SHE RALLIES.

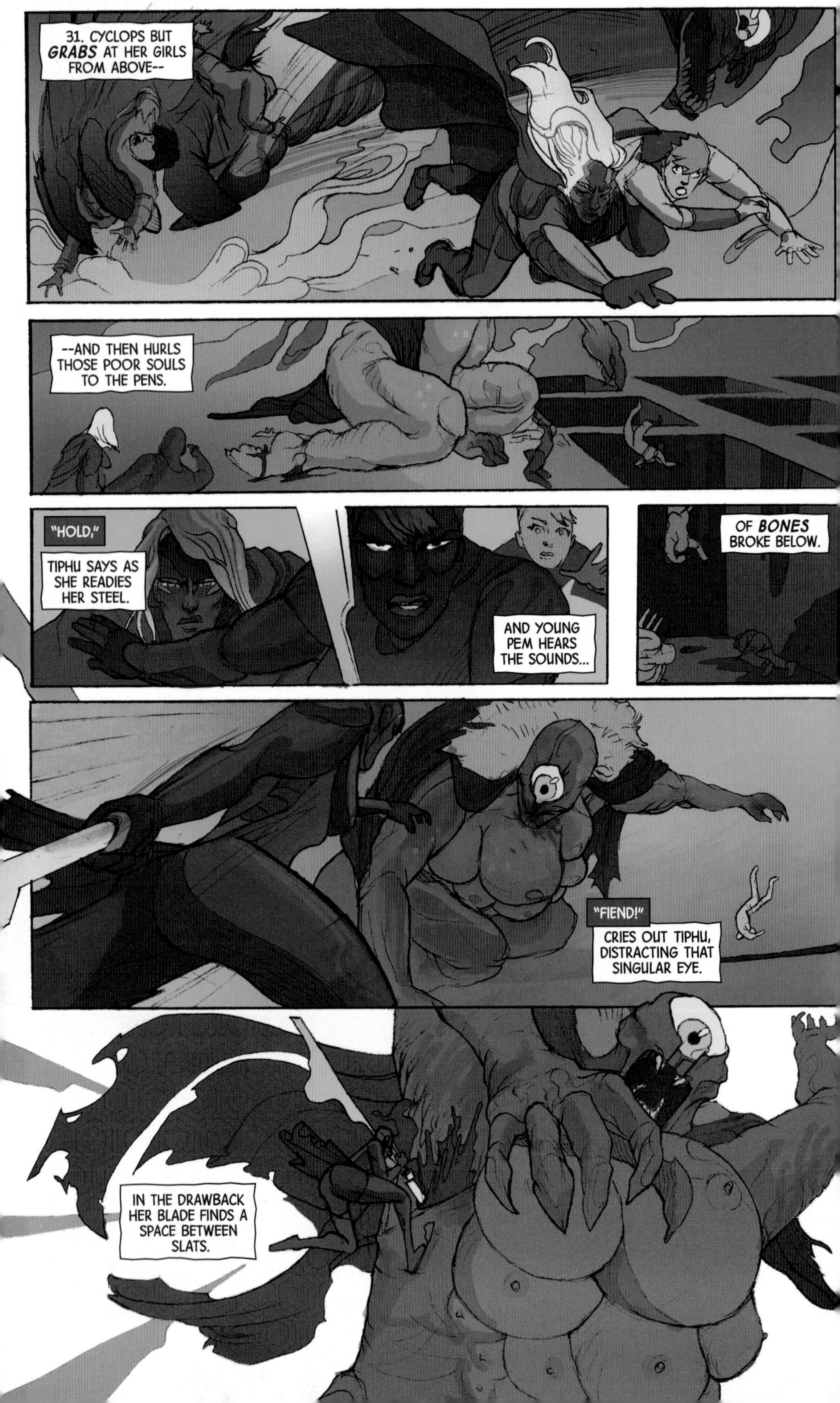

31. CYCLOPS BUT GRABS AT HER GIRLS FROM ABOVE--
--AND THEN HURLS THOSE POOR SOULS TO THE PENS.
"HOLD,"
TIPHU SAYS AS SHE READIES HER STEEL.
AND YOUNG PEM HEARS THE SOUNDS...
OF BONES BROKE BELOW.
"FIEND!"
CRIES OUT TIPHU, DISTRACTING THAT SINGULAR EYE.
IN THE DRAWBACK HER BLADE FINDS A SPACE BETWEEN SLATS.

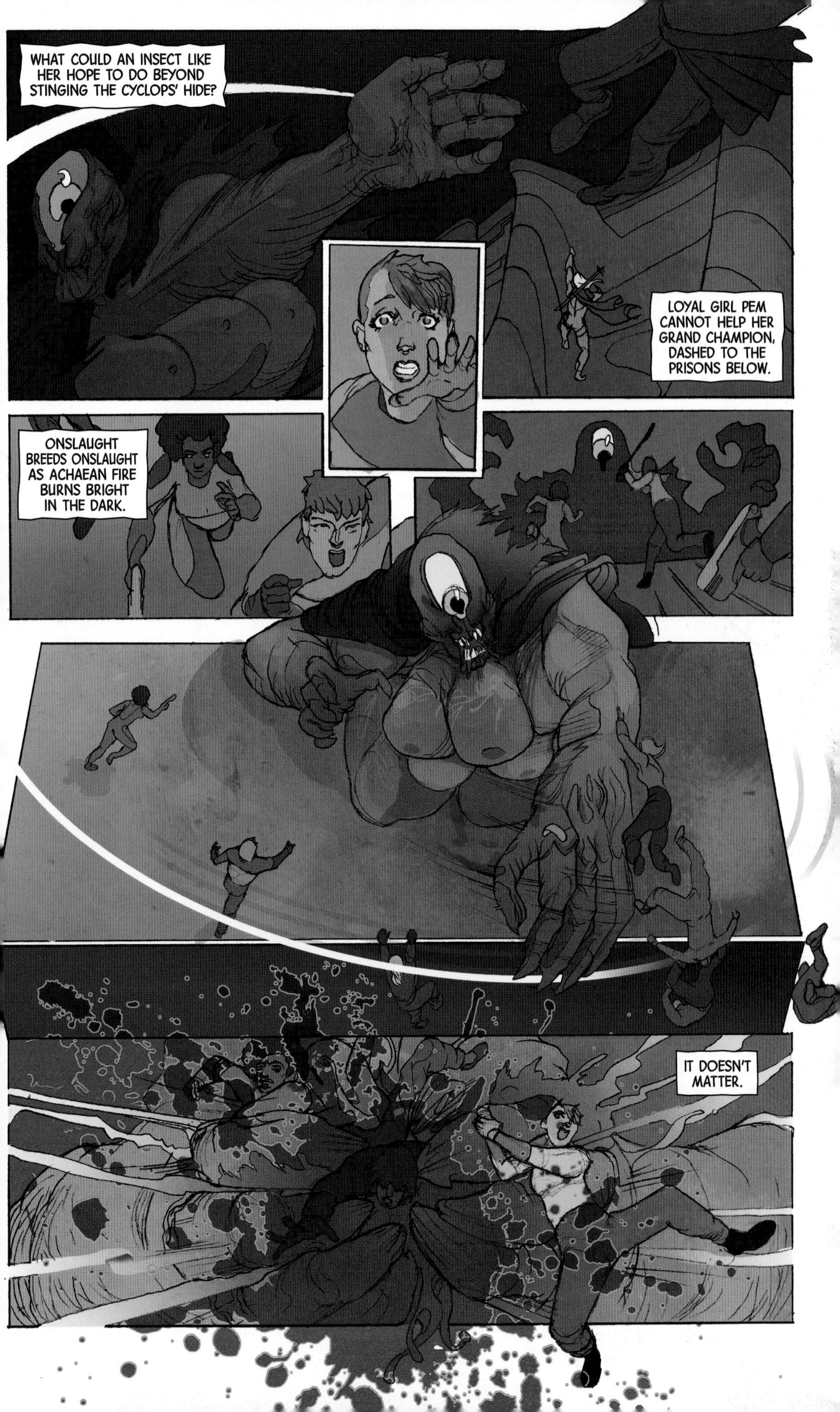

WHAT COULD AN INSECT LIKE HER HOPE TO DO BEYOND STINGING THE CYCLOPS' HIDE?
LOYAL GIRL PEM CANNOT HELP HER GRAND CHAMPION, DASHED TO THE PRISONS BELOW.
ONSLAUGHT BREEDS ONSLAUGHT AS ACHAEAN FIRE BURNS BRIGHT IN THE DARK.
IT DOESN'T MATTER.

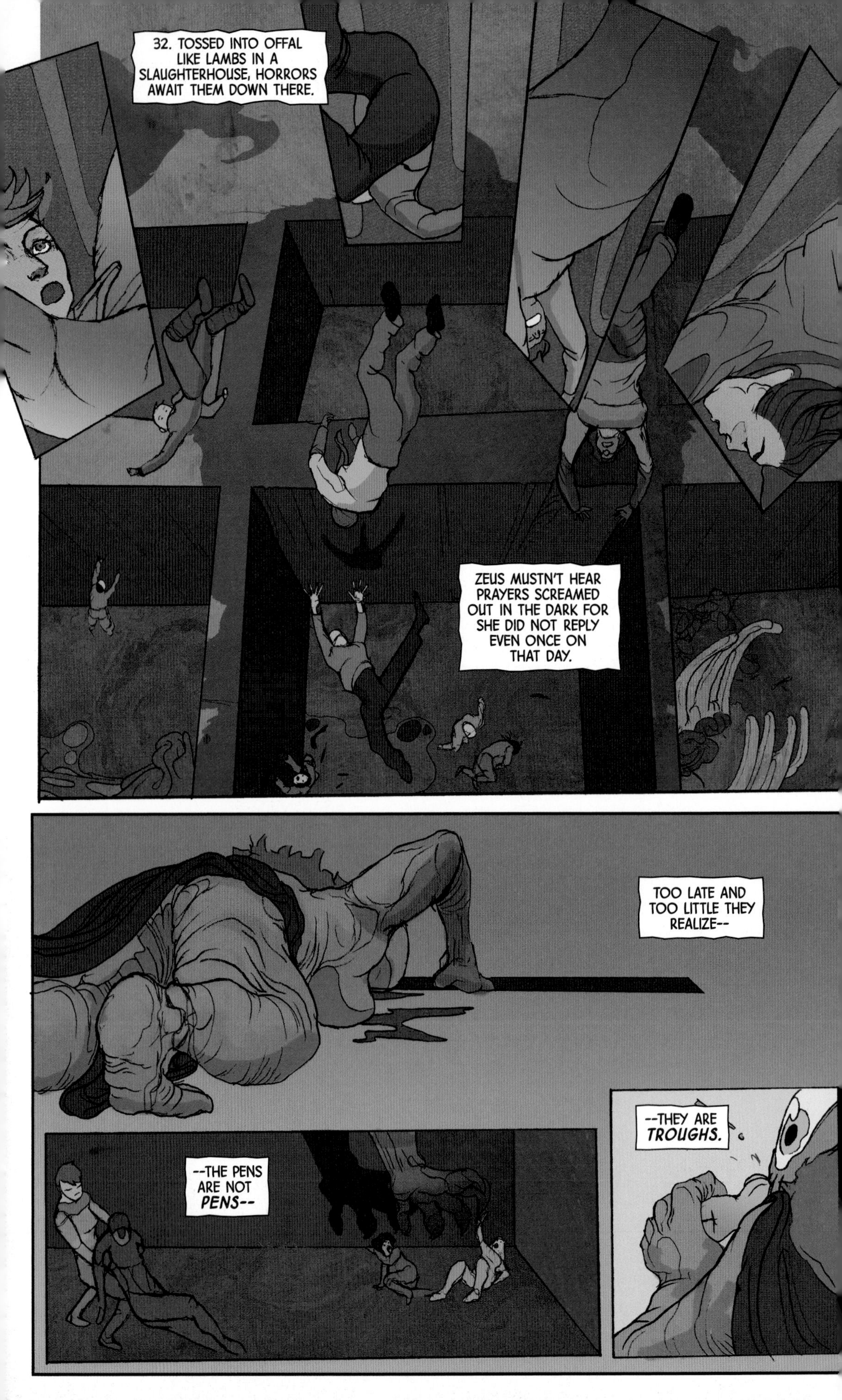

32. TOSSED INTO OFFAL LIKE LAMBS IN A SLAUGHTERHOUSE, HORRORS AWAIT THEM DOWN THERE.
ZEUS MUSTN'T HEAR PRAYERS SCREAMED OUT IN THE DARK FOR SHE DID NOT REPLY EVEN ONCE ON THAT DAY.
TOO LATE AND TOO LITTLE THEY REALIZE--
--THE PENS ARE NOT *PENS*--
--THEY ARE *TROUGHS.*

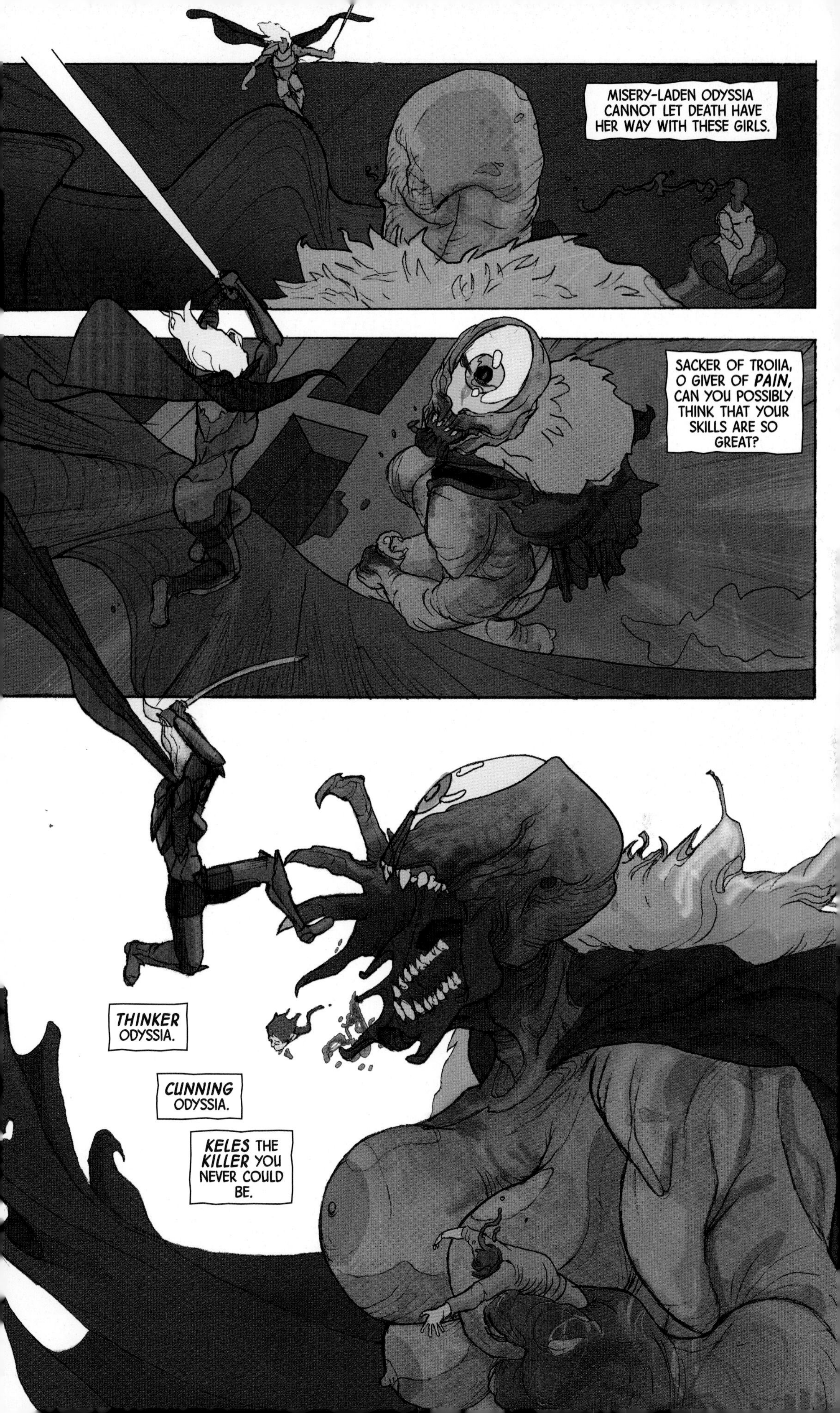
MISERY-LADEN ODYSSIA CANNOT LET DEATH HAVE HER WAY WITH THESE GIRLS.
SACKER OF TROIIA, O GIVER OF PAIN, CAN YOU POSSIBLY THINK THAT YOUR SKILLS ARE SO GREAT?
THINKER ODYSSIA.
CUNNING ODYSSIA.
KELES THE KILLER YOU NEVER COULD BE.

SEE?

33. DOWN IN THE RUINOUS PILES OF VISCERA ONCE HER COMMAND AND HER CREW...

...ODYSSIA RECALIBRATES.

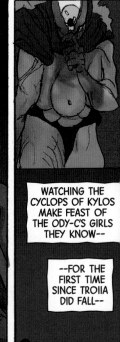

WATCHING THE CYCLOPS OF KYLOS MAKE FEAST OF THE ODY-C'S GIRLS THEY KNOW--

--FOR THE FIRST TIME SINCE TROIIA DID FALL--

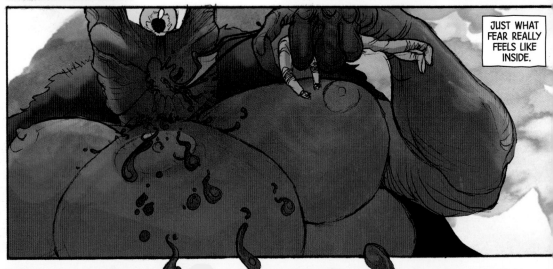

JUST WHAT FEAR REALLY FEELS LIKE INSIDE.

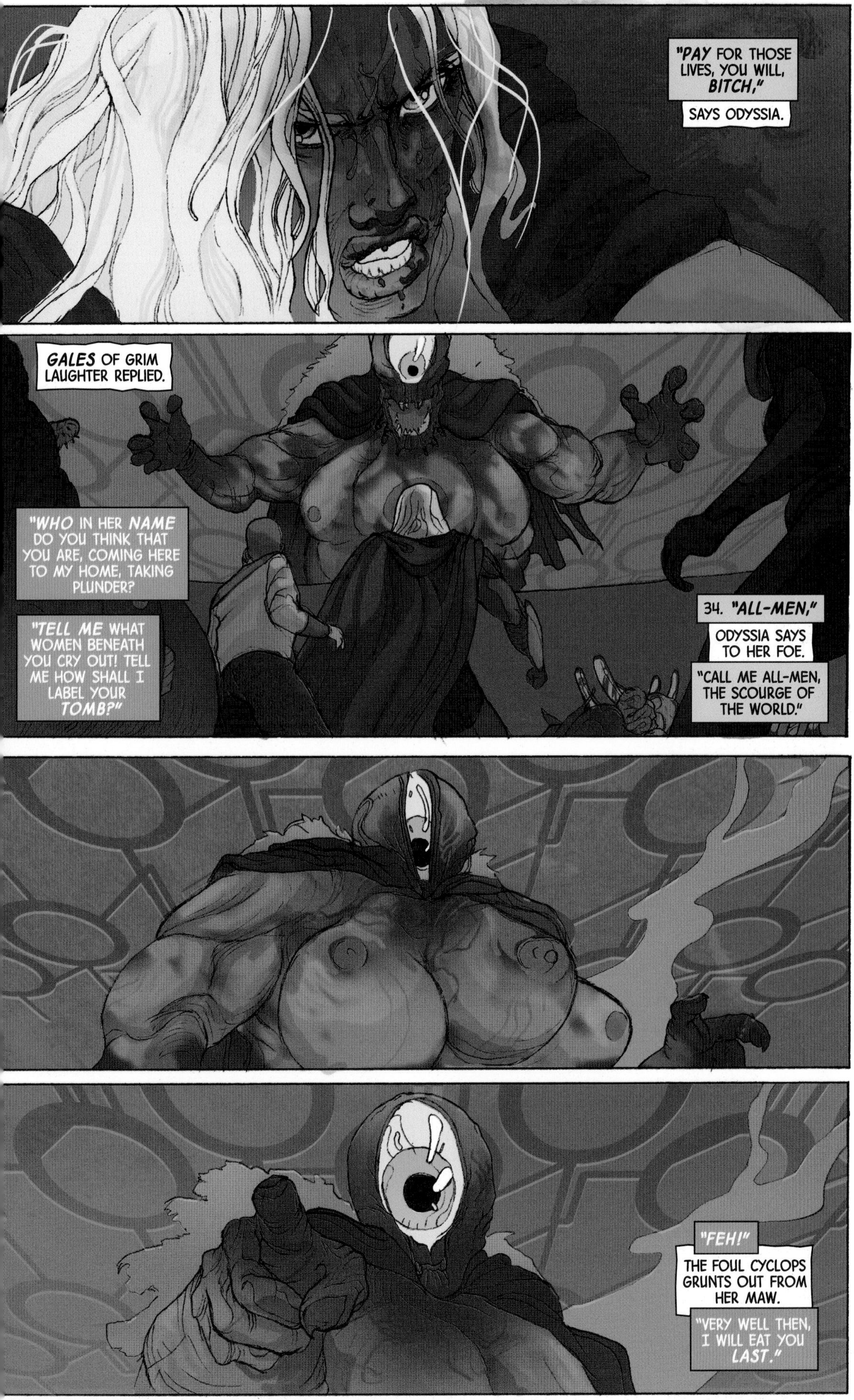
"PAY FOR THOSE LIVES, YOU WILL, BITCH,"
SAYS ODYSSIA.
GALES OF GRIM LAUGHTER REPLIED.
"WHO IN HER NAME DO YOU THINK THAT YOU ARE, COMING HERE TO MY HOME, TAKING PLUNDER?
"TELL ME WHAT WOMEN BENEATH YOU CRY OUT! TELL ME HOW SHALL I LABEL YOUR TOMB?"
34. "ALL-MEN,"
ODYSSIA SAYS TO HER FOE.
"CALL ME ALL-MEN, THE SCOURGE OF THE WORLD."
"FEH!"
THE FOUL CYCLOPS GRUNTS OUT FROM HER MAW.
"VERY WELL THEN, I WILL EAT YOU LAST."

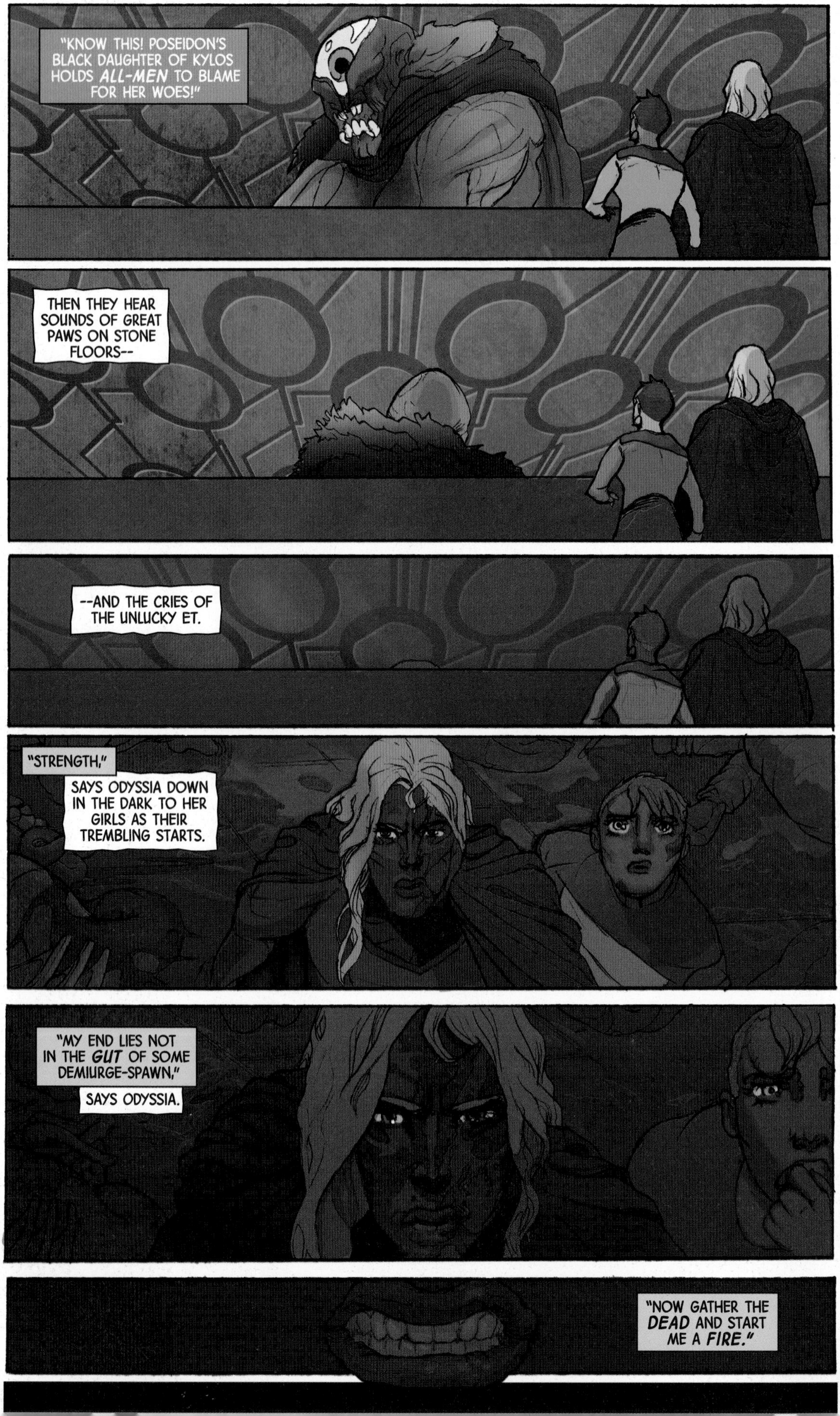
"KNOW THIS! POSEIDON'S BLACK DAUGHTER OF KYLOS HOLDS ALL-MEN TO BLAME FOR HER WOES!"
THEN THEY HEAR SOUNDS OF GREAT PAWS ON STONE FLOORS--
--AND THE CRIES OF THE UNLUCKY ET.
"STRENGTH,"
SAYS ODYSSIA DOWN IN THE DARK TO HER GIRLS AS THEIR TREMBLING STARTS.
"MY END LIES NOT IN THE GUT OF SOME DEMIURGE-SPAWN,"
SAYS ODYSSIA.
"NOW GATHER THE DEAD AND START ME A FIRE."

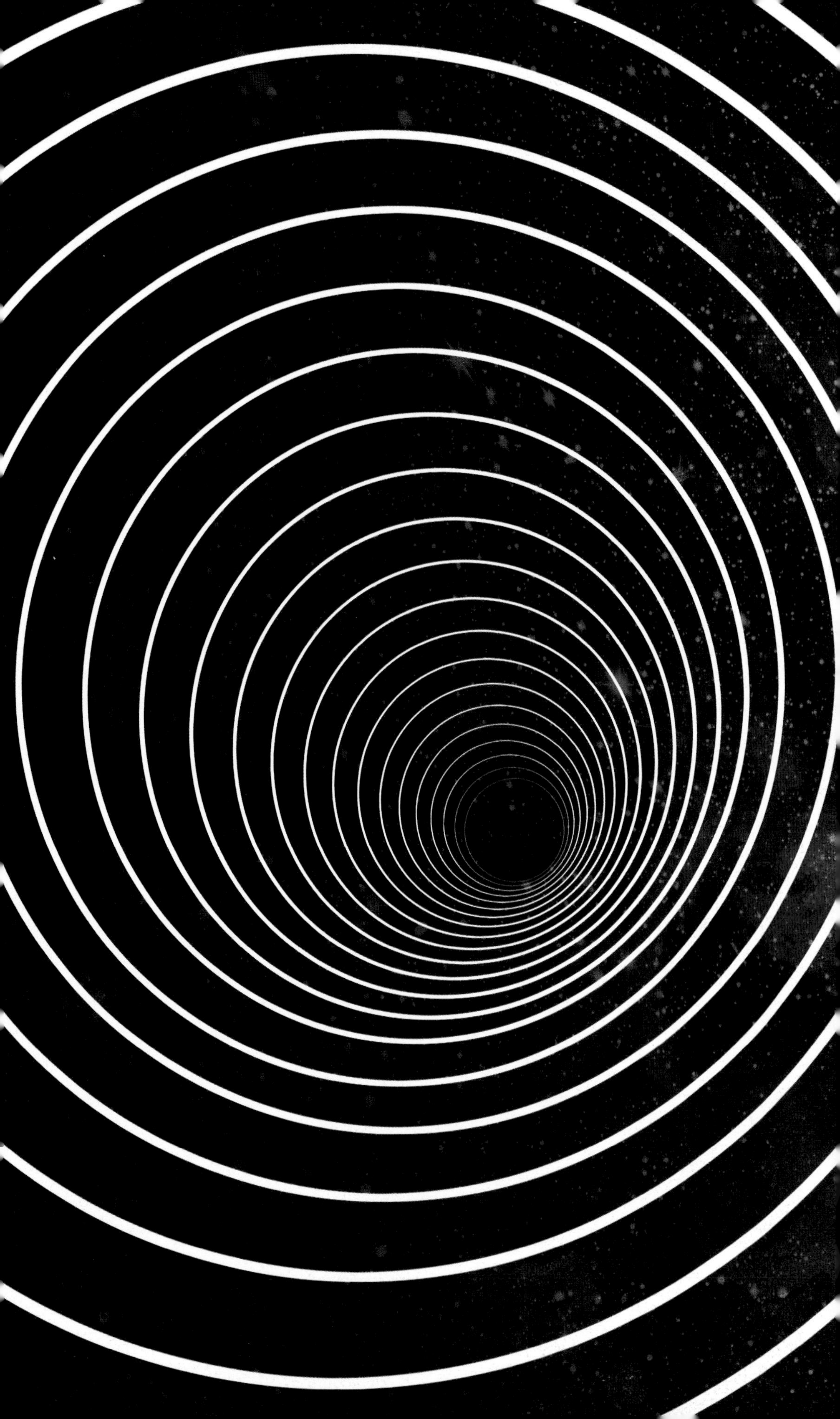

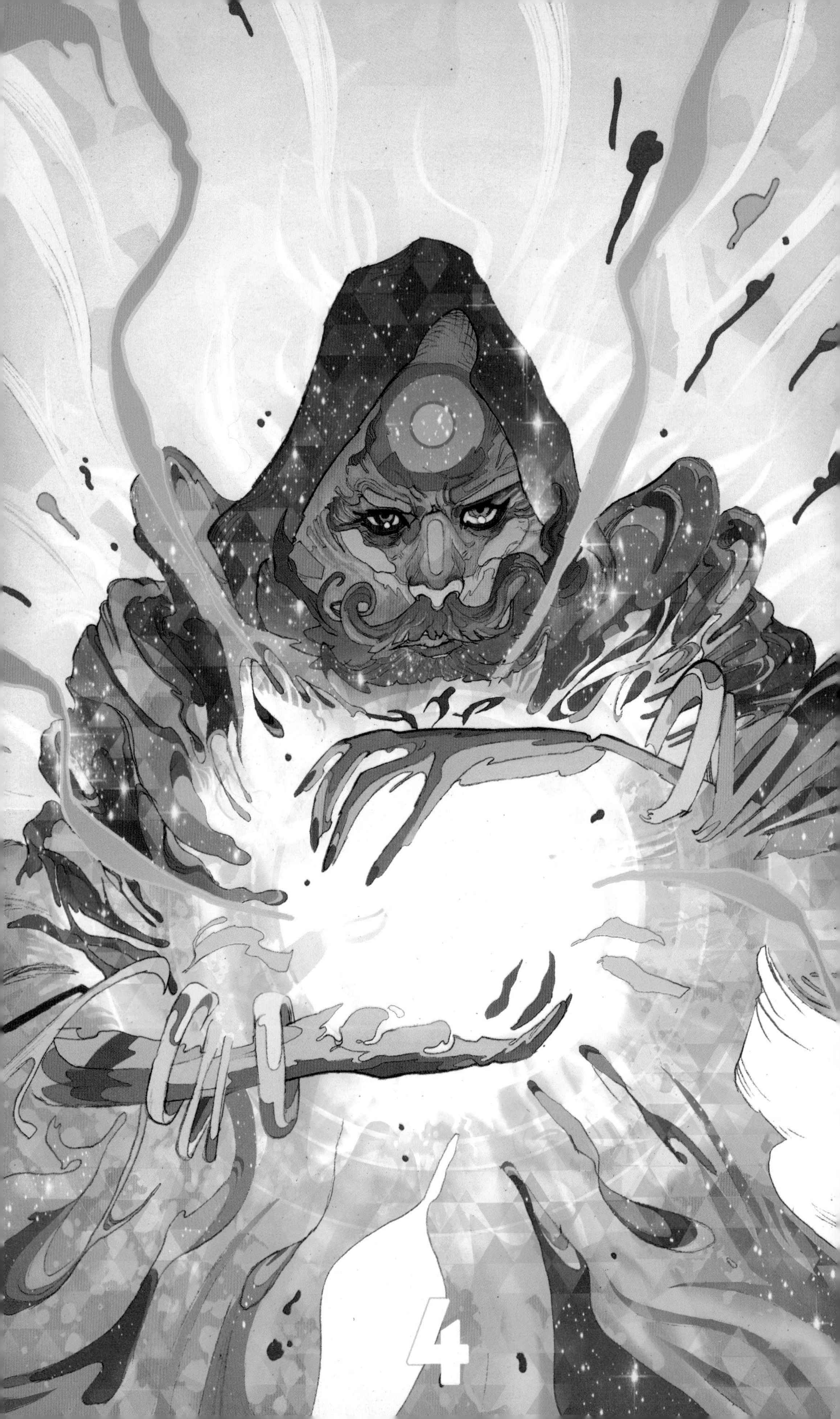
4

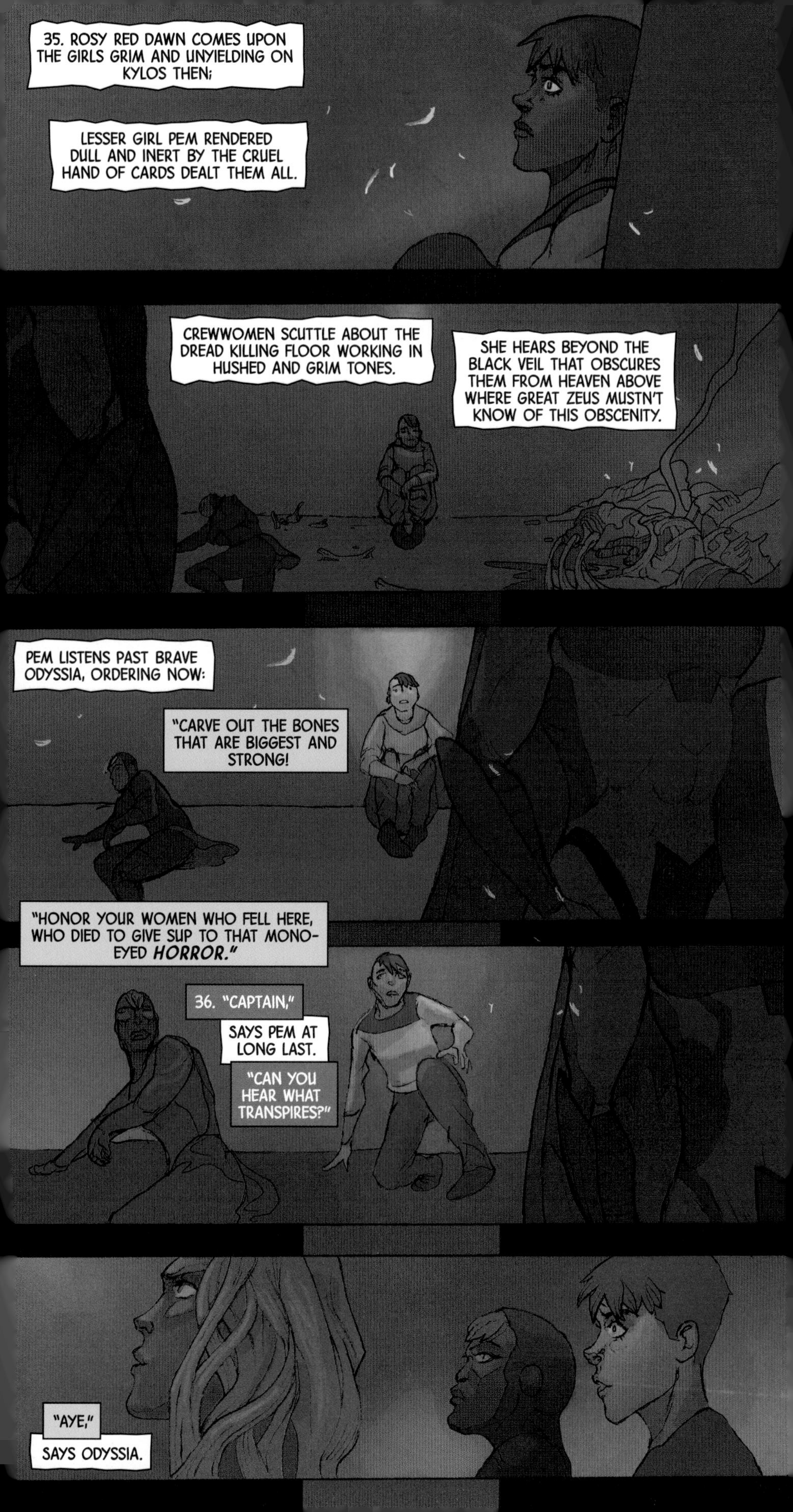
35. ROSY RED DAWN COMES UPON THE GIRLS GRIM AND UNYIELDING ON KYLOS THEN;
LESSER GIRL PEM RENDERED DULL AND INERT BY THE CRUEL HAND OF CARDS DEALT THEM ALL.
CREWWOMEN SCUTTLE ABOUT THE DREAD KILLING FLOOR WORKING IN HUSHED AND GRIM TONES.
SHE HEARS BEYOND THE BLACK VEIL THAT OBSCURES THEM FROM HEAVEN ABOVE WHERE GREAT ZEUS MUSTN'T KNOW OF THIS OBSCENITY.
PEM LISTENS PAST BRAVE ODYSSIA, ORDERING NOW:
"CARVE OUT THE BONES THAT ARE BIGGEST AND STRONG!
"HONOR YOUR WOMEN WHO FELL HERE, WHO DIED TO GIVE SUP TO THAT MONO-EYED HORROR."
36. "CAPTAIN,"
SAYS PEM AT LONG LAST.
"CAN YOU HEAR WHAT TRANSPIRES?"
"AYE,"
SAYS ODYSSIA.

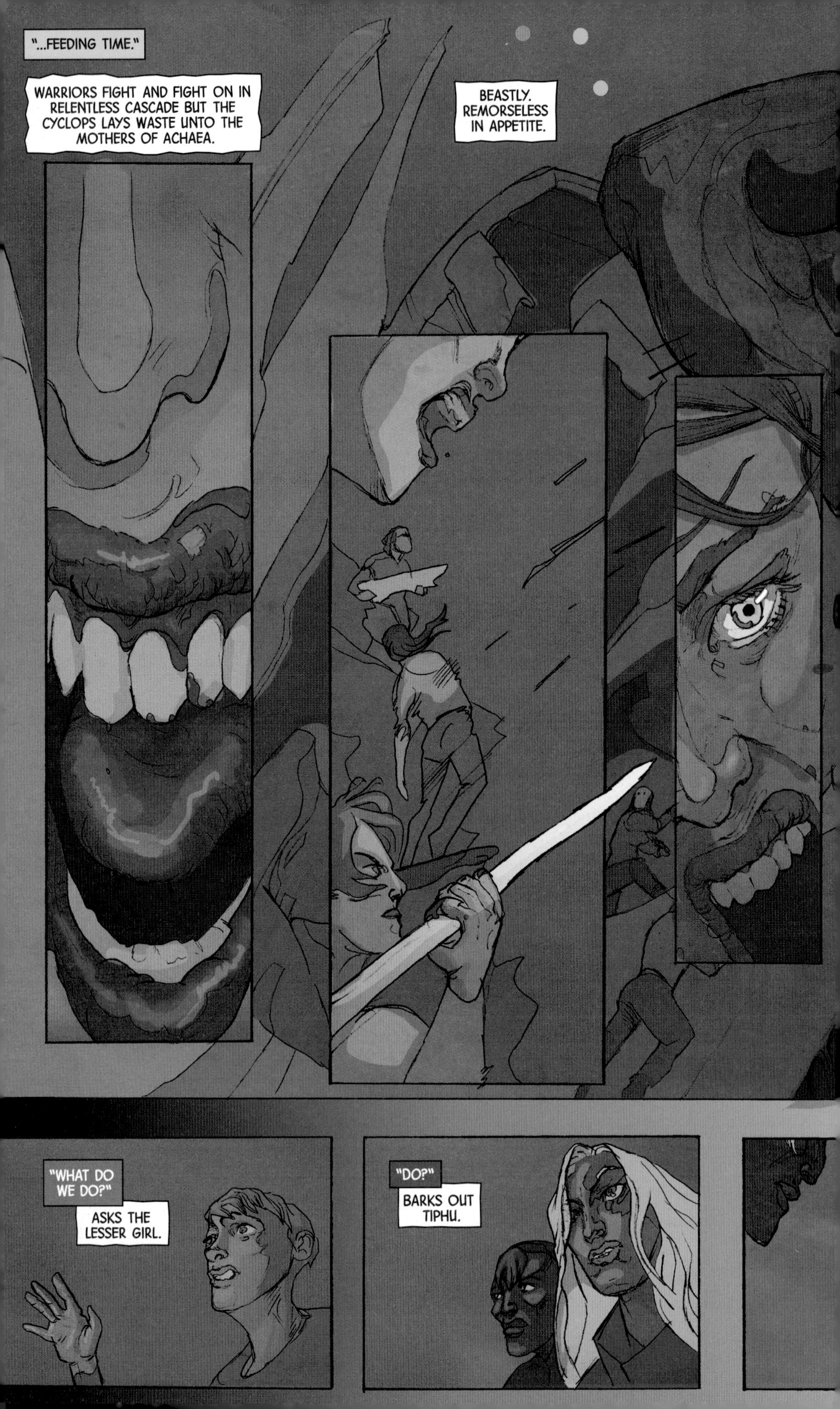
"...FEEDING TIME."
WARRIORS FIGHT AND FIGHT ON IN RELENTLESS CASCADE BUT THE CYCLOPS LAYS WASTE UNTO THE MOTHERS OF ACHAEA.
BEASTLY. REMORSELESS IN APPETITE.
"WHAT DO WE DO?"
ASKS THE LESSER GIRL.
"DO?"
BARKS OUT TIPHU.

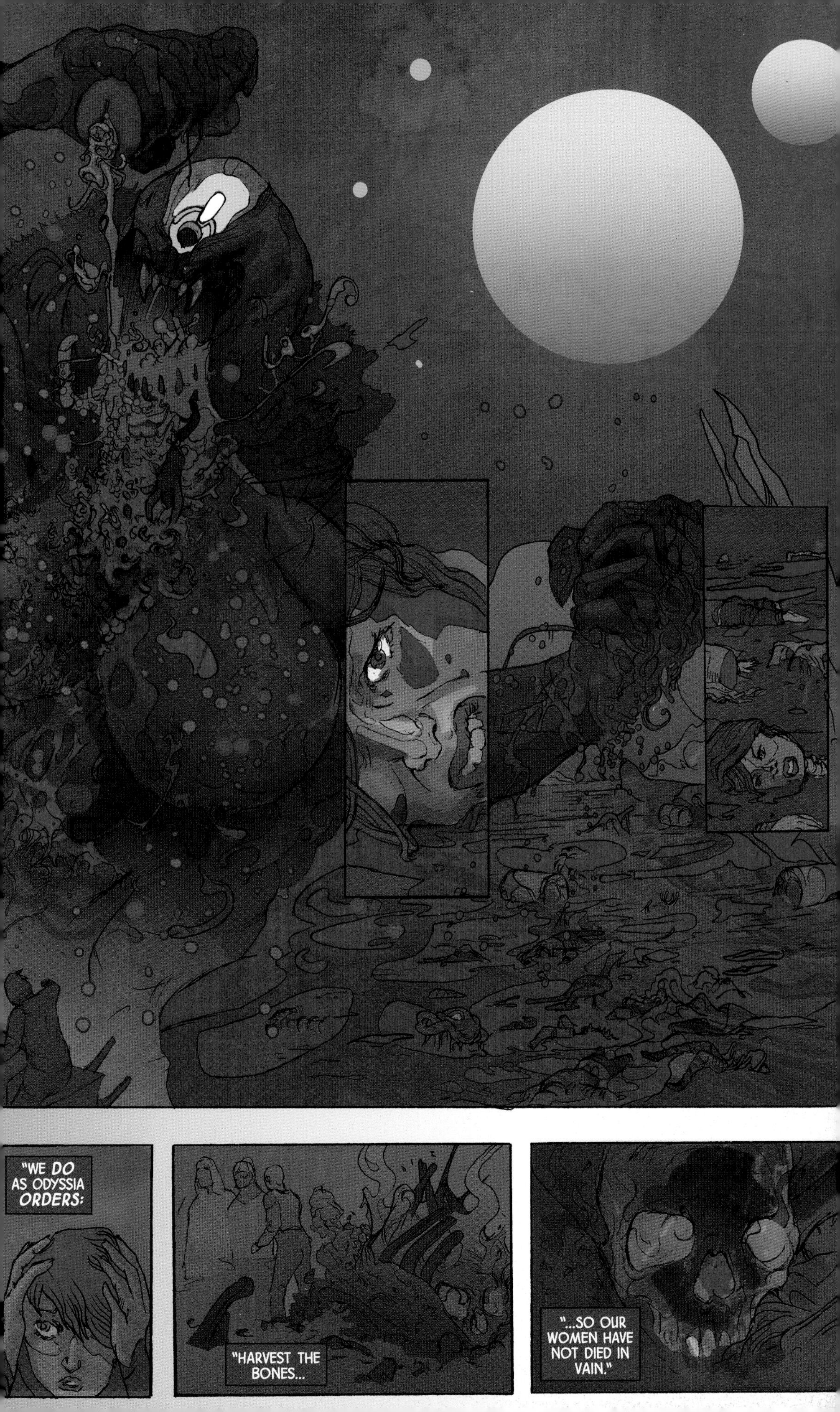
"WE DO AS ODYSSIA ORDERS:
"HARVEST THE BONES...
"...SO OUR WOMEN HAVE NOT DIED IN VAIN."

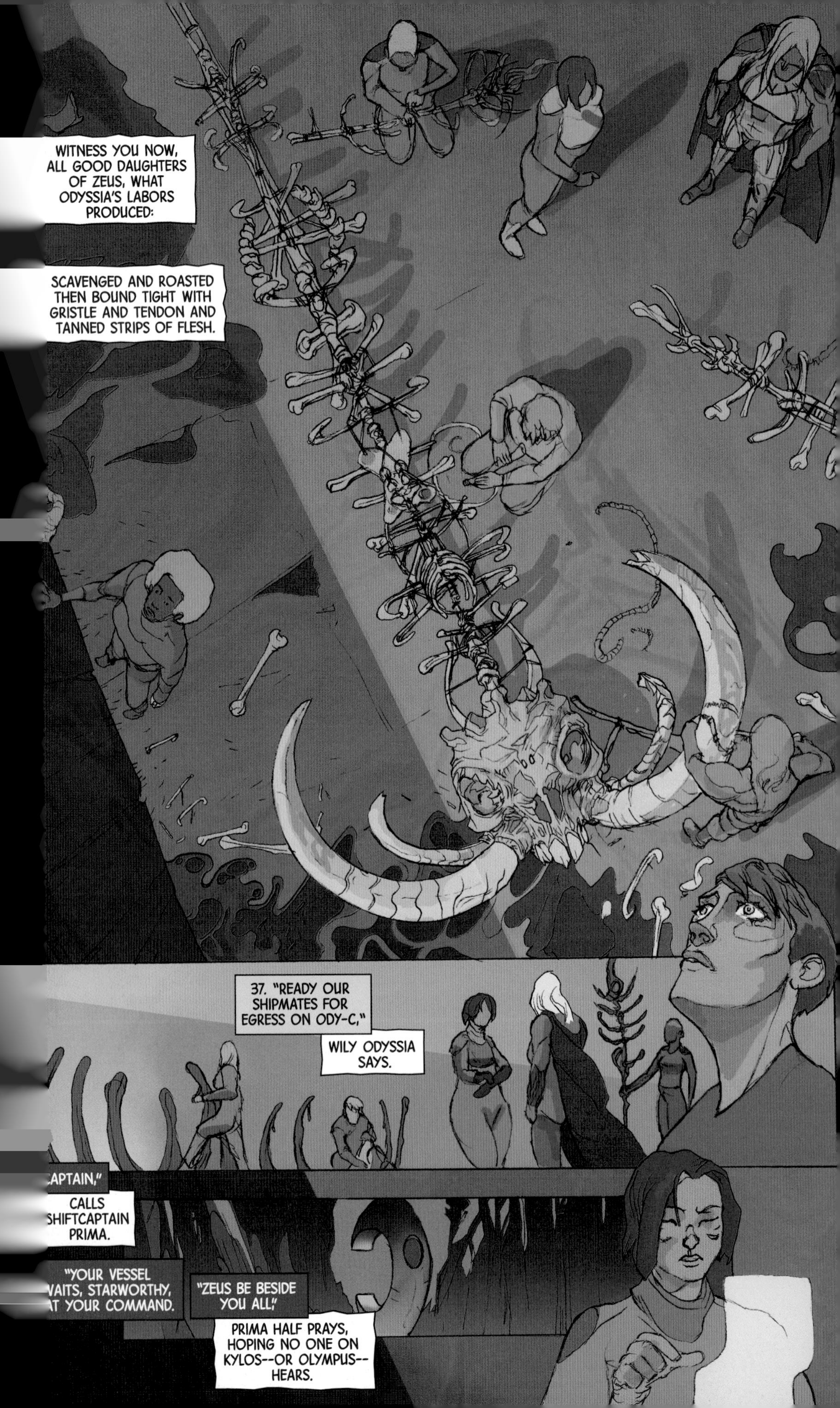
WITNESS YOU NOW, ALL GOOD DAUGHTERS OF ZEUS, WHAT ODYSSIA'S LABORS PRODUCED:
SCAVENGED AND ROASTED THEN BOUND TIGHT WITH GRISTLE AND TENDON AND TANNED STRIPS OF FLESH.
37. "READY OUR SHIPMATES FOR EGRESS ON ODY-C,"
WILY ODYSSIA SAYS.
APTAIN,"
CALLS SHIFTCAPTAIN PRIMA.
"YOUR VESSEL AITS, STARWORTHY, T YOUR COMMAND.
"ZEUS BE BESIDE YOU ALL,"
PRIMA HALF PRAYS, HOPING NO ONE ON KYLOS--OR OLYMPUS--HEARS.

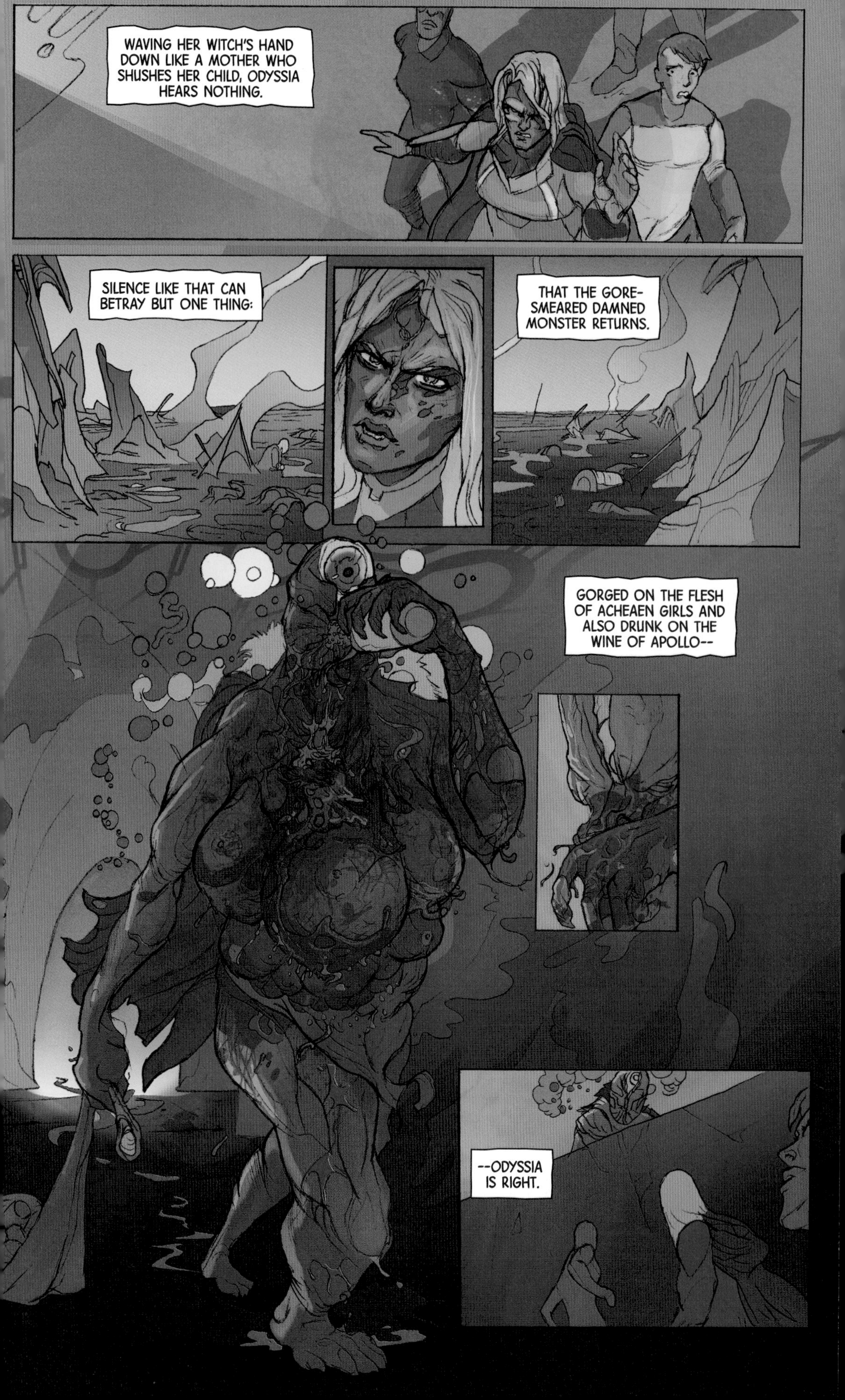
WAVING HER WITCH'S HAND DOWN LIKE A MOTHER WHO SHUSHES HER CHILD, ODYSSIA HEARS NOTHING.
SILENCE LIKE THAT CAN BETRAY BUT ONE THING:
THAT THE GORE-SMEARED DAMNED MONSTER RETURNS.
GORGED ON THE FLESH OF ACHEAEN GIRLS AND ALSO DRUNK ON THE WINE OF APOLLO--
--ODYSSIA IS RIGHT.

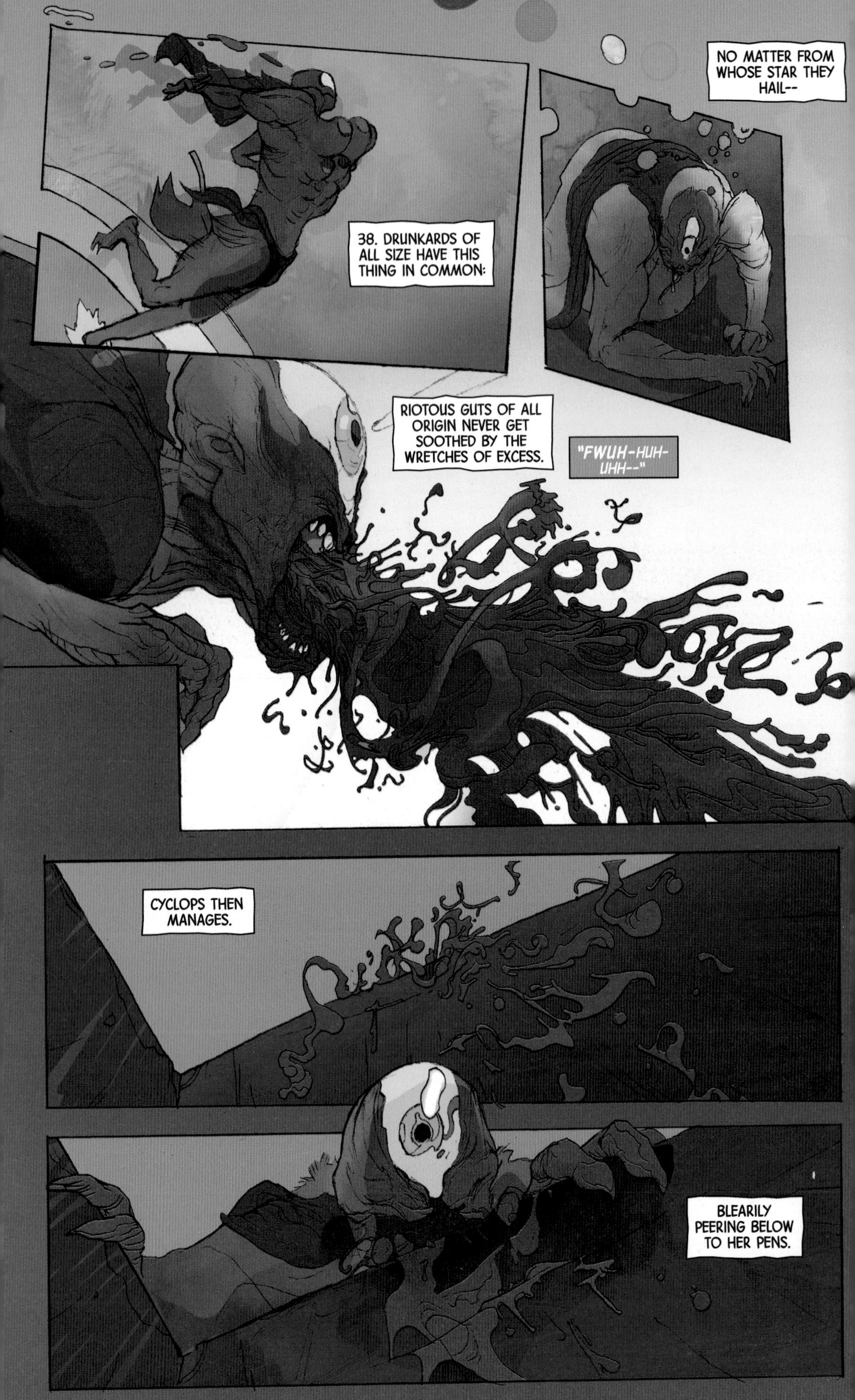
38. DRUNKARDS OF ALL SIZE HAVE THIS THING IN COMMON:
NO MATTER FROM WHOSE STAR THEY HAIL--
RIOTOUS GUTS OF ALL ORIGIN NEVER GET SOOTHED BY THE WRETCHES OF EXCESS.
"FWUH-HUH-UHH--"
CYCLOPS THEN MANAGES.
BLEARILY PEERING BELOW TO HER PENS.

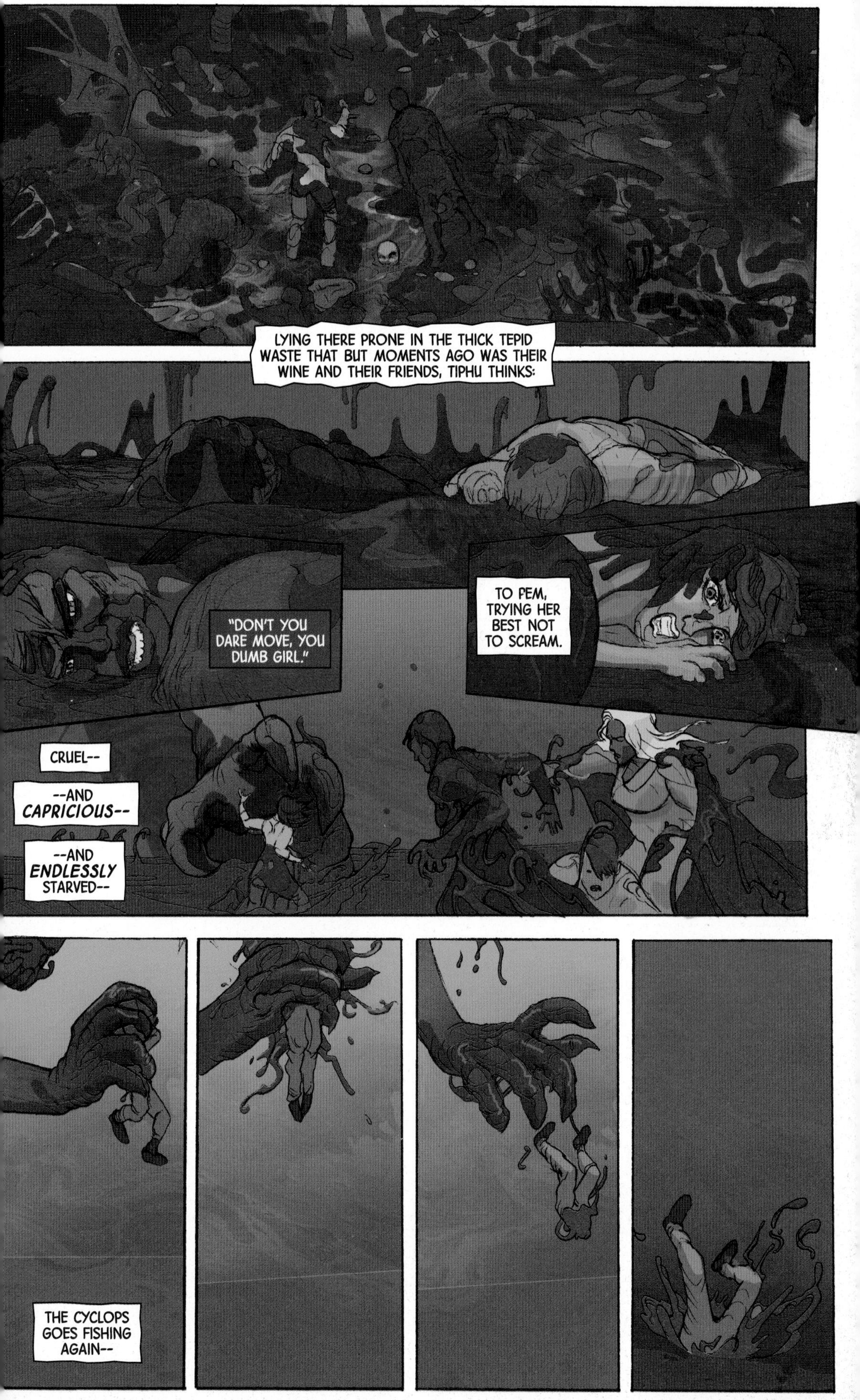
LYING THERE PRONE IN THE THICK TEPID WASTE THAT BUT MOMENTS AGO WAS THEIR WINE AND THEIR FRIENDS, TIPHU THINKS:
"DON'T YOU DARE MOVE, YOU DUMB GIRL."
TO PEM, TRYING HER BEST NOT TO SCREAM.
CRUEL--
--AND CAPRICIOUS--
--AND ENDLESSLY STARVED--
THE CYCLOPS GOES FISHING AGAIN--

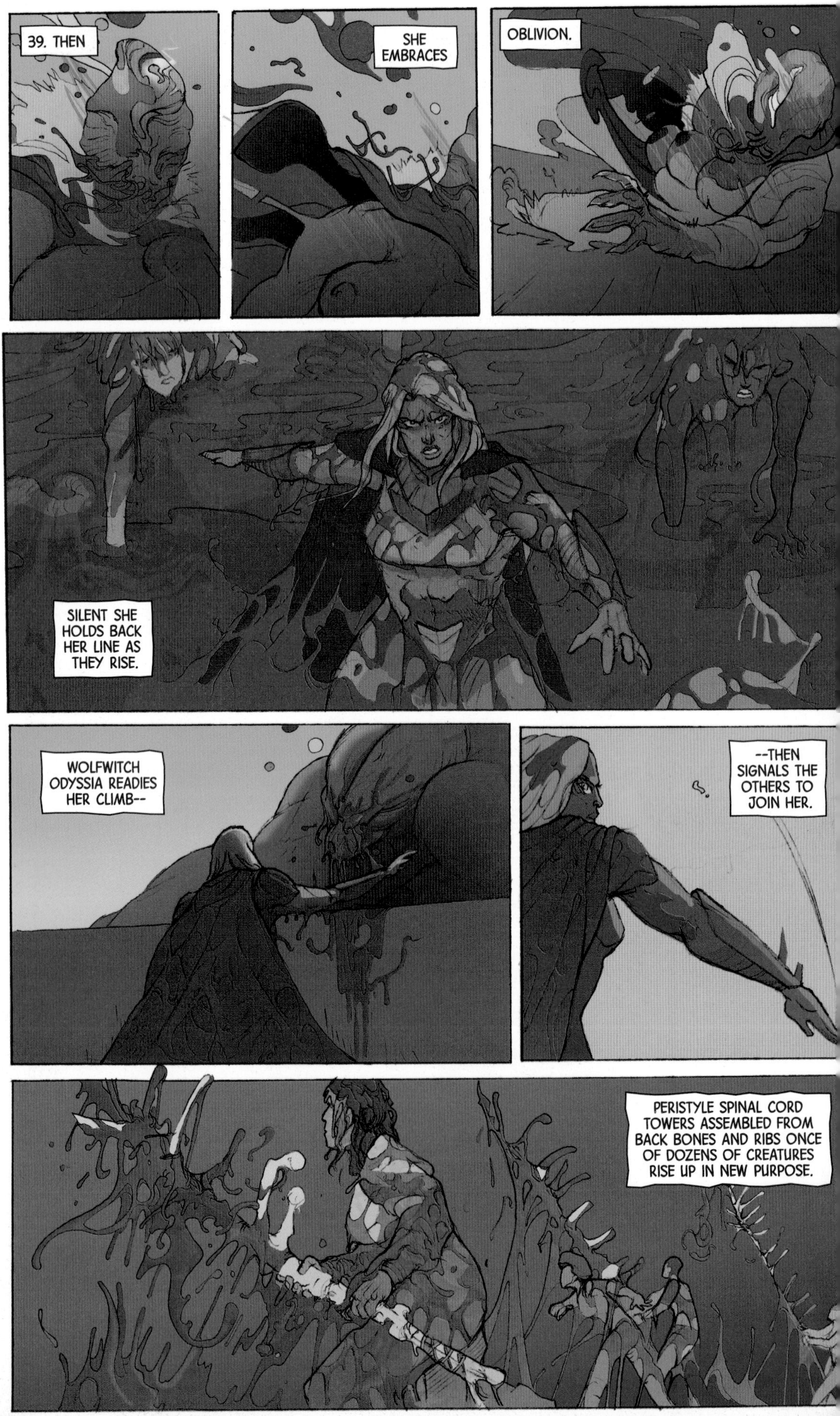
39. THEN
SHE EMBRACES
OBLIVION.
SILENT SHE HOLDS BACK HER LINE AS THEY RISE.
WOLFWITCH ODYSSIA READIES HER CLIMB--
--THEN SIGNALS THE OTHERS TO JOIN HER.
PERISTYLE SPINAL CORD TOWERS ASSEMBLED FROM BACK BONES AND RIBS ONCE OF DOZENS OF CREATURES RISE UP IN NEW PURPOSE.

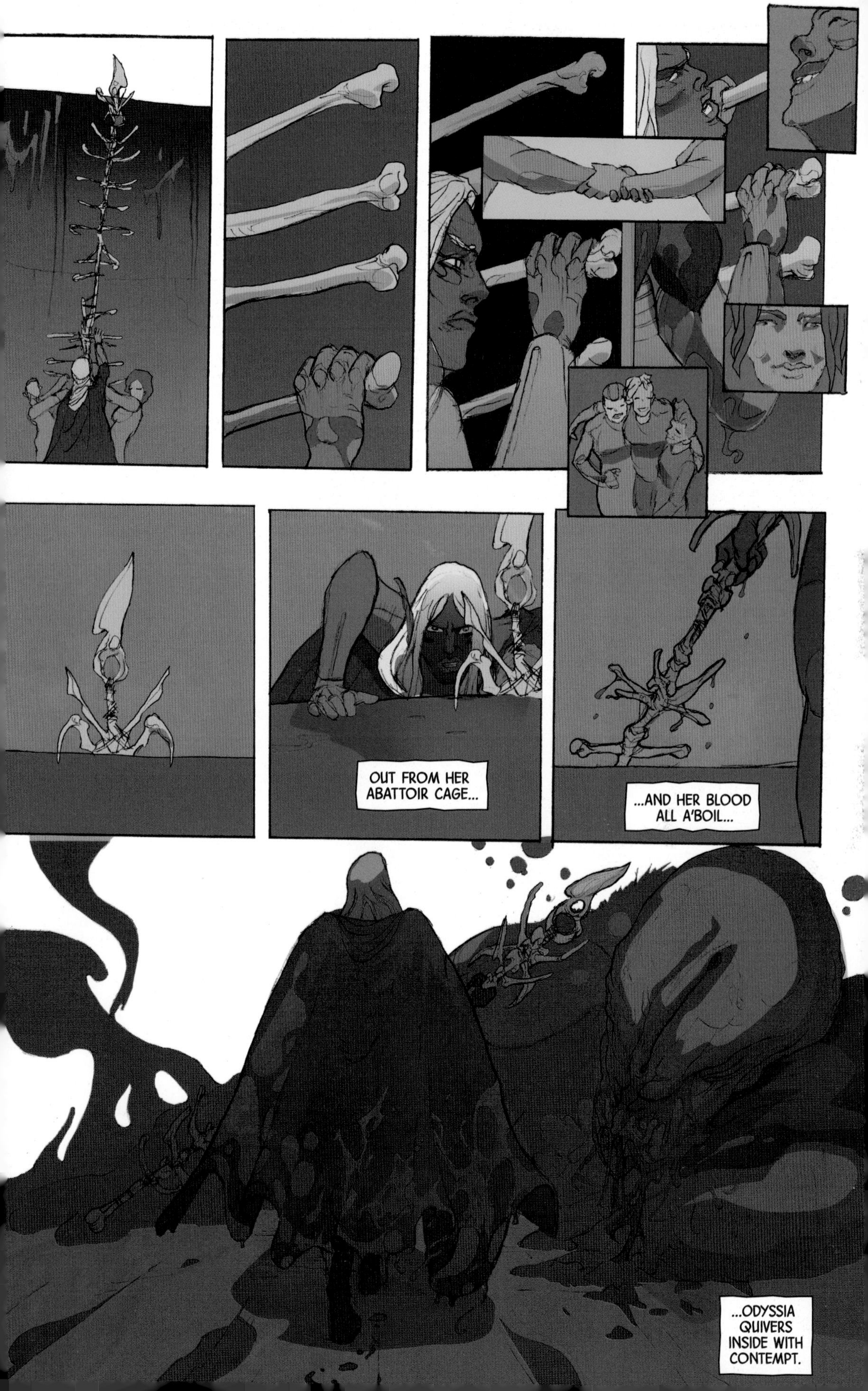

OUT FROM HER ABATTOIR CAGE...
...AND HER BLOOD ALL A'BOIL...
...ODYSSIA QUIVERS INSIDE WITH CONTEMPT.

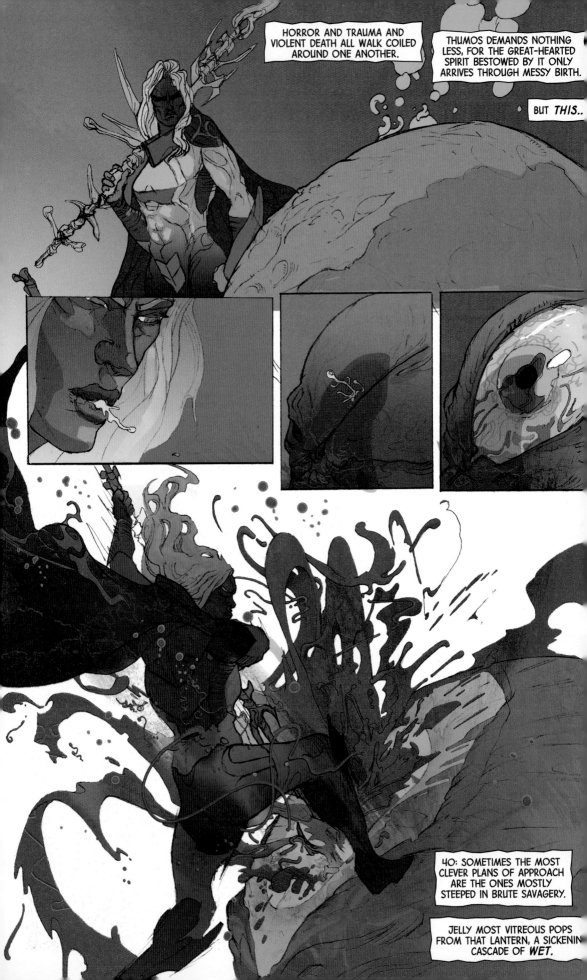

HORROR AND TRAUMA AND VIOLENT DEATH ALL WALK COILED AROUND ONE ANOTHER.

THUMOS DEMANDS NOTHING LESS, FOR THE GREAT-HEARTED SPIRIT BESTOWED BY IT ONLY ARRIVES THROUGH MESSY BIRTH.

BUT *THIS*..

40: SOMETIMES THE MOST CLEVER PLANS OF APPROACH ARE THE ONES MOSTLY STEEPED IN BRUTE SAVAGERY.

JELLY MOST VITREOUS POPS FROM THAT LANTERN, A SICKENIN' CASCADE OF *WET.*

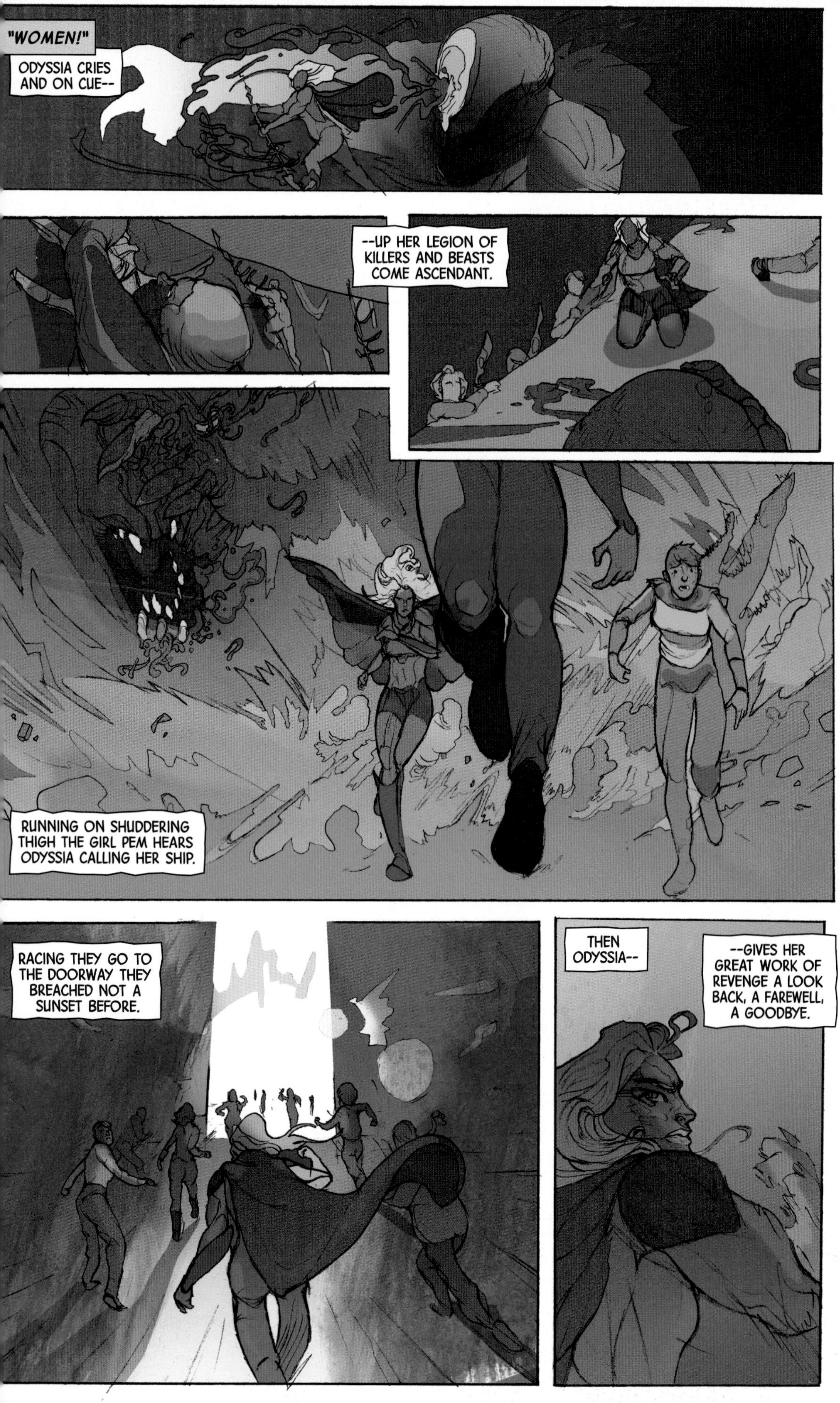
"WOMEN!"
ODYSSIA CRIES AND ON CUE--
--UP HER LEGION OF KILLERS AND BEASTS COME ASCENDANT.
RUNNING ON SHUDDERING THIGH THE GIRL PEM HEARS ODYSSIA CALLING HER SHIP.
RACING THEY GO TO THE DOORWAY THEY BREACHED NOT A SUNSET BEFORE.
THEN ODYSSIA--
--GIVES HER GREAT WORK OF REVENGE A LOOK BACK, A FAREWELL, A GOODBYE.

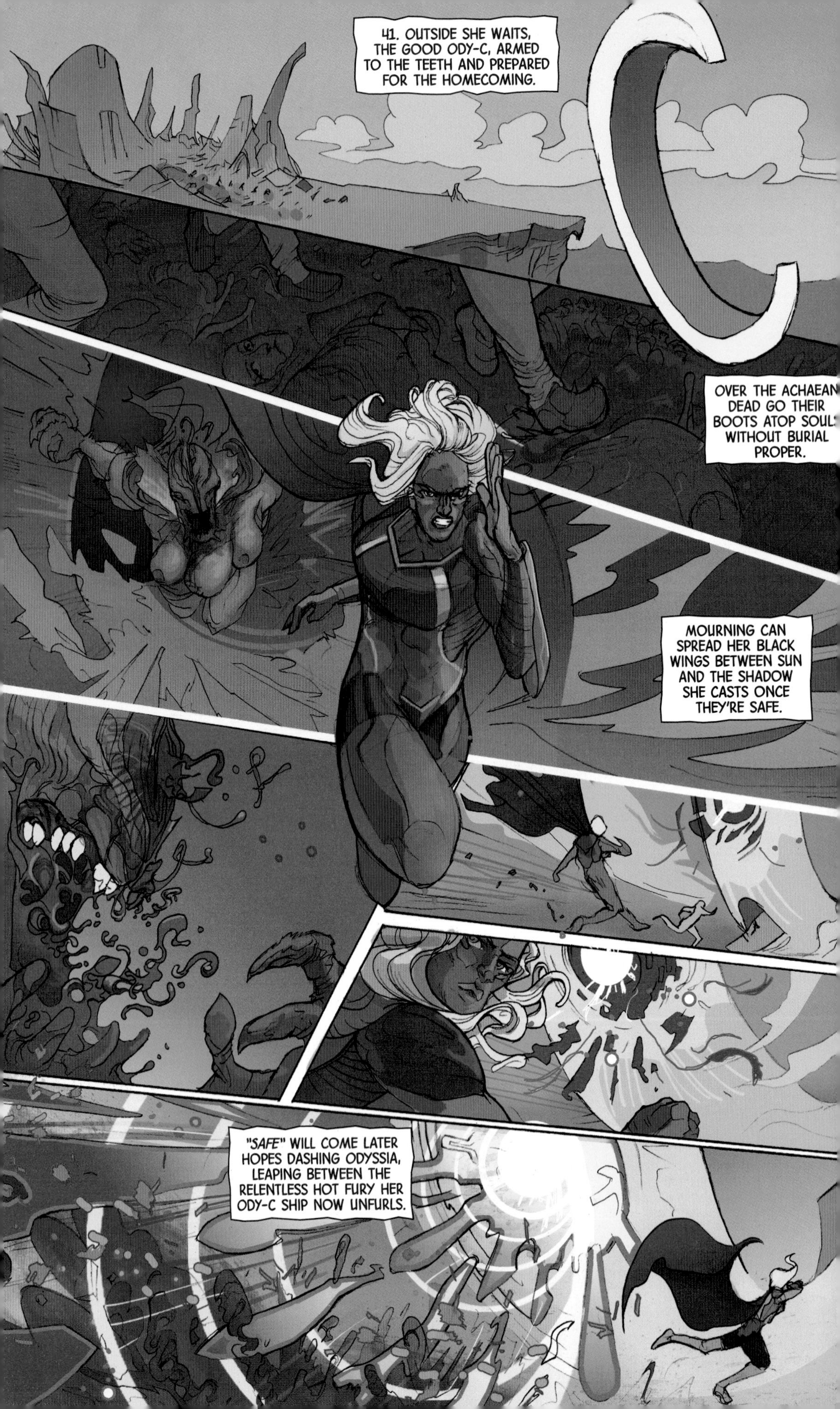
41. OUTSIDE SHE WAITS, THE GOOD ODY-C, ARMED TO THE TEETH AND PREPARED FOR THE HOMECOMING.
OVER THE ACHAEAN DEAD GO THEIR BOOTS ATOP SOULS WITHOUT BURIAL PROPER.
MOURNING CAN SPREAD HER BLACK WINGS BETWEEN SUN AND THE SHADOW SHE CASTS ONCE THEY'RE SAFE.
"SAFE" WILL COME LATER HOPES DASHING ODYSSIA, LEAPING BETWEEN THE RELENTLESS HOT FURY HER ODY-C SHIP NOW UNFURLS.

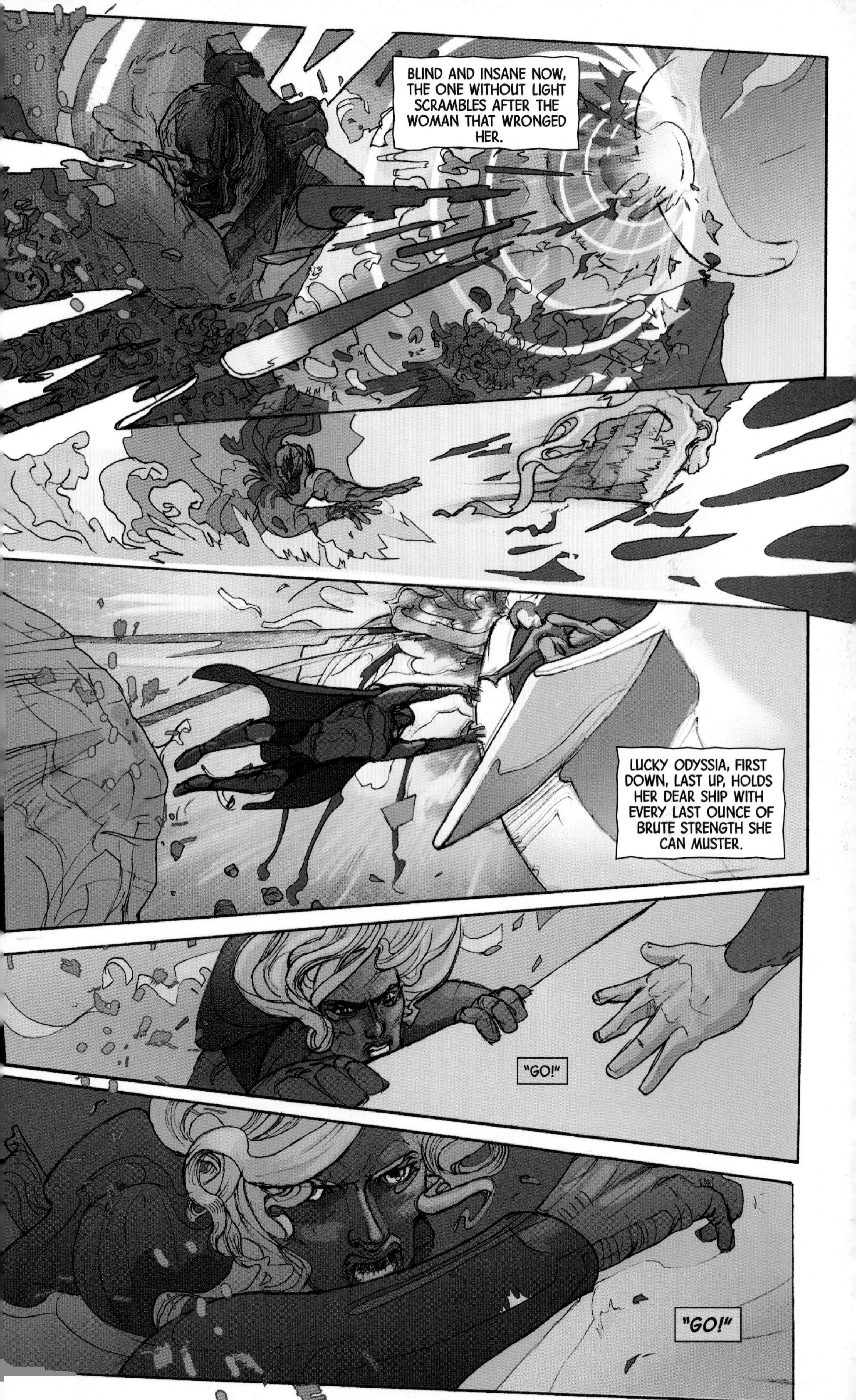
BLIND AND INSANE NOW, THE ONE WITHOUT LIGHT SCRAMBLES AFTER THE WOMAN THAT WRONGED HER.
LUCKY ODYSSIA, FIRST DOWN, LAST UP, HOLDS HER DEAR SHIP WITH EVERY LAST OUNCE OF BRUTE STRENGTH SHE CAN MUSTER.
"GO!"
"GO!"

42. RAGE ATOP RAGE RISES UP FROM WITHIN THE BLIND CYCLOPS WHO HURLS WITHOUT AIM ANY SCRAP SHE CAN SEIZE.

FINDING HER TARGET BUT LEFT ALONE, DARKENED, SHE BELLOWS TO MOTHER POSEIDON:

"HELP YOUR POOR DAUGHTER!

"AVENGE SHE THAT SUFFERS THIS VIOLENCE AT ALL-MEN'S BLACK HAND!

"RETRIBU... SHE FOULED ALL-MEN... GRIM CRIM...

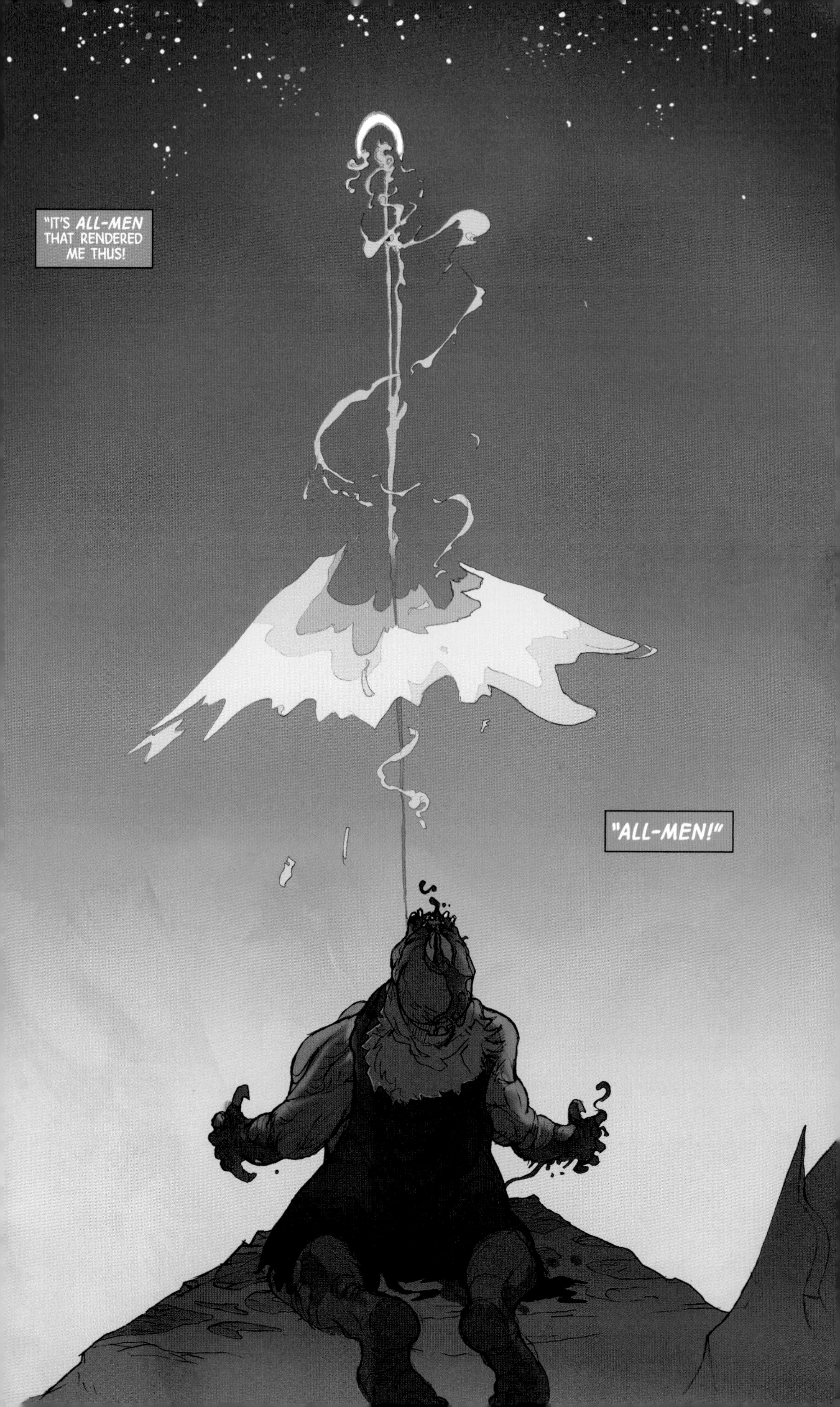
"IT'S ALL-MEN THAT RENDERED ME THUS!
"ALL-MEN!"

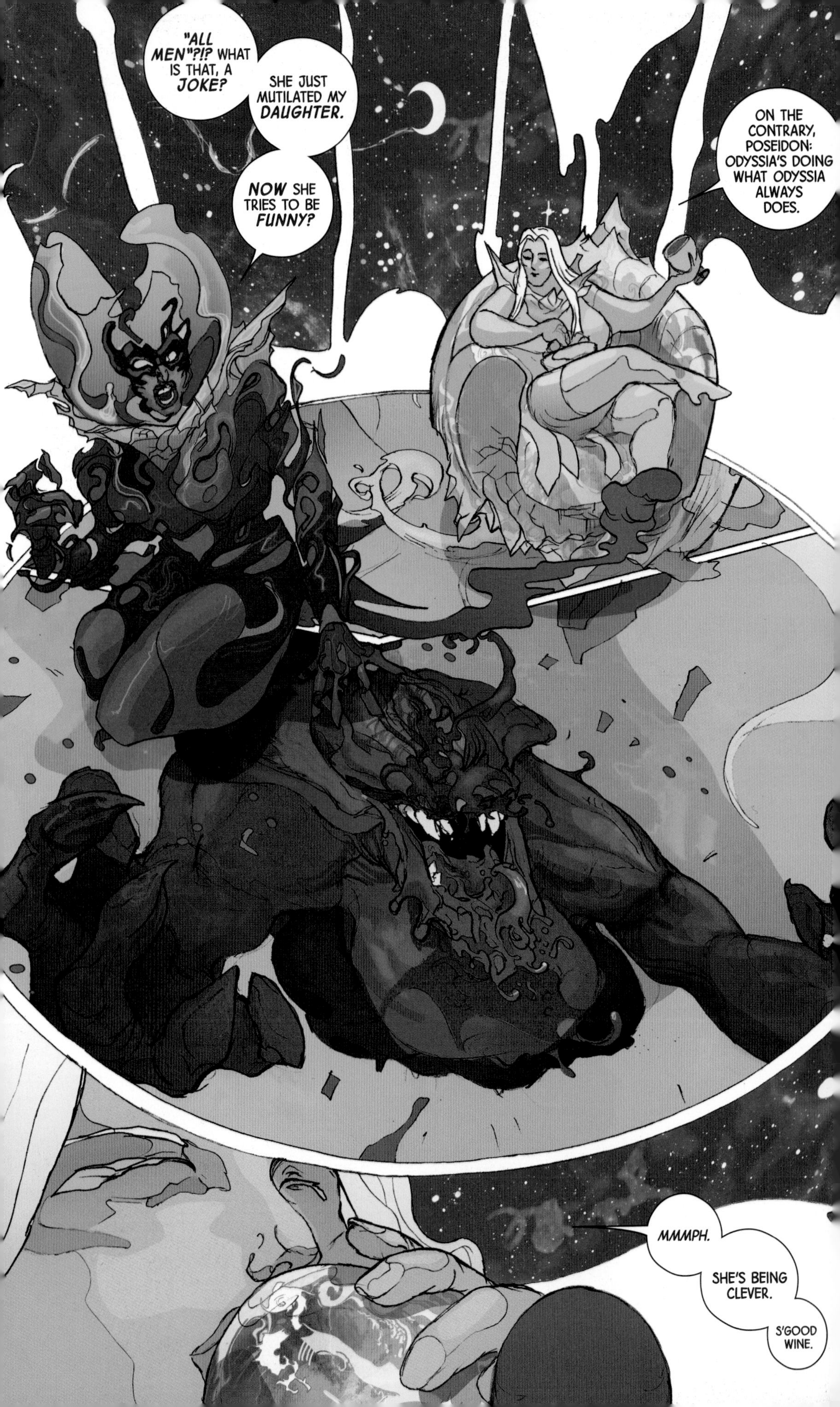
"ALL MEN"?!? WHAT IS THAT, A JOKE?
SHE JUST MUTILATED MY DAUGHTER.
NOW SHE TRIES TO BE FUNNY?
ON THE CONTRARY, POSEIDON: ODYSSIA'S DOING WHAT ODYSSIA ALWAYS DOES.
MMMPH.
SHE'S BEING CLEVER.
S'GOOD WINE.

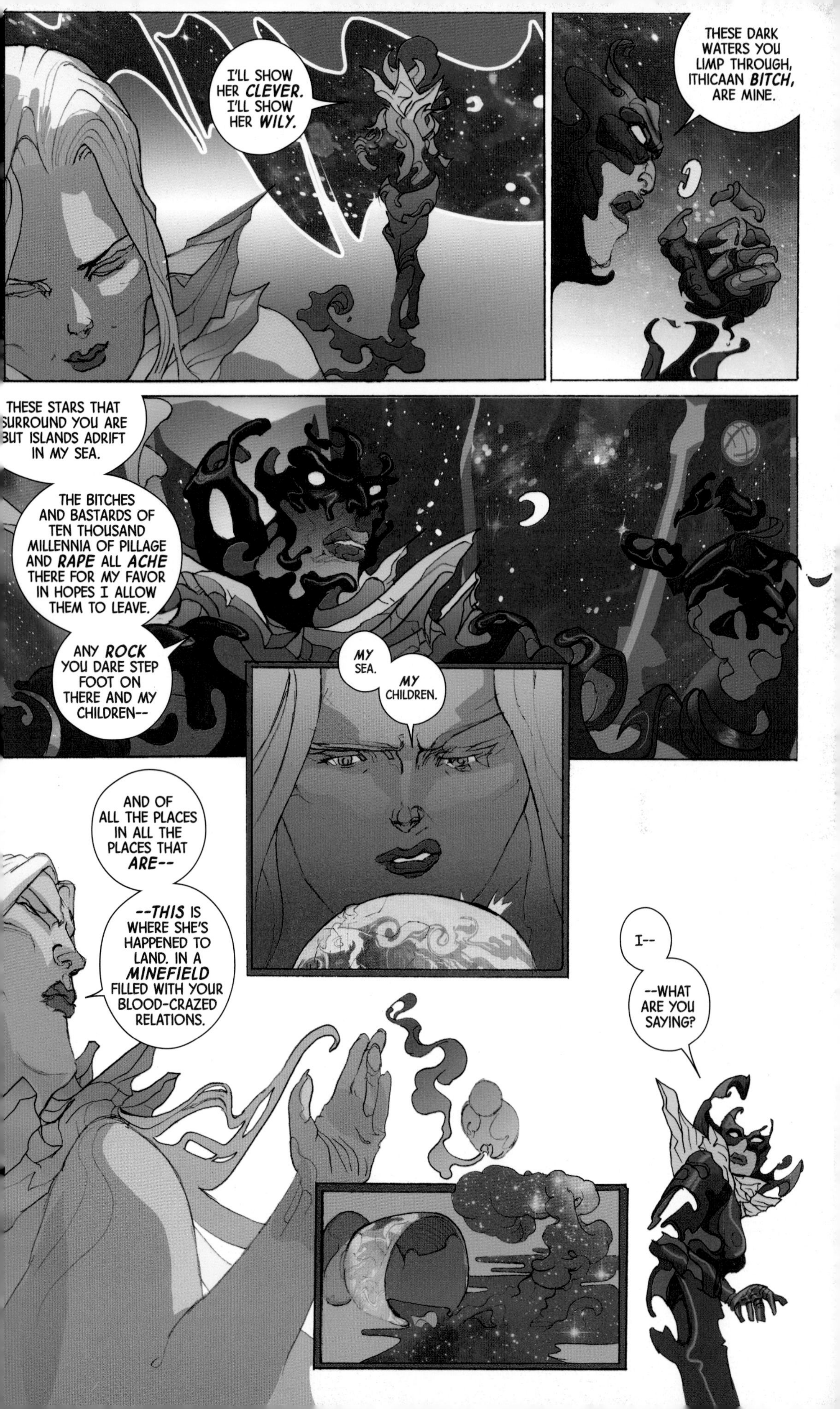

I'LL SHOW HER CLEVER. I'LL SHOW HER WILY.
THESE DARK WATERS YOU LIMP THROUGH, ITHICAAN BITCH, ARE MINE.
THESE STARS THAT SURROUND YOU ARE BUT ISLANDS ADRIFT IN MY SEA.
THE BITCHES AND BASTARDS OF TEN THOUSAND MILLENNIA OF PILLAGE AND RAPE ALL ACHE THERE FOR MY FAVOR IN HOPES I ALLOW THEM TO LEAVE.
ANY ROCK YOU DARE STEP FOOT ON THERE AND MY CHILDREN--
MY SEA.
MY CHILDREN.
AND OF ALL THE PLACES IN ALL THE PLACES THAT ARE--
--THIS IS WHERE SHE'S HAPPENED TO LAND. IN A MINEFIELD FILLED WITH YOUR BLOOD-CRAZED RELATIONS.
I--
--WHAT ARE YOU SAYING?

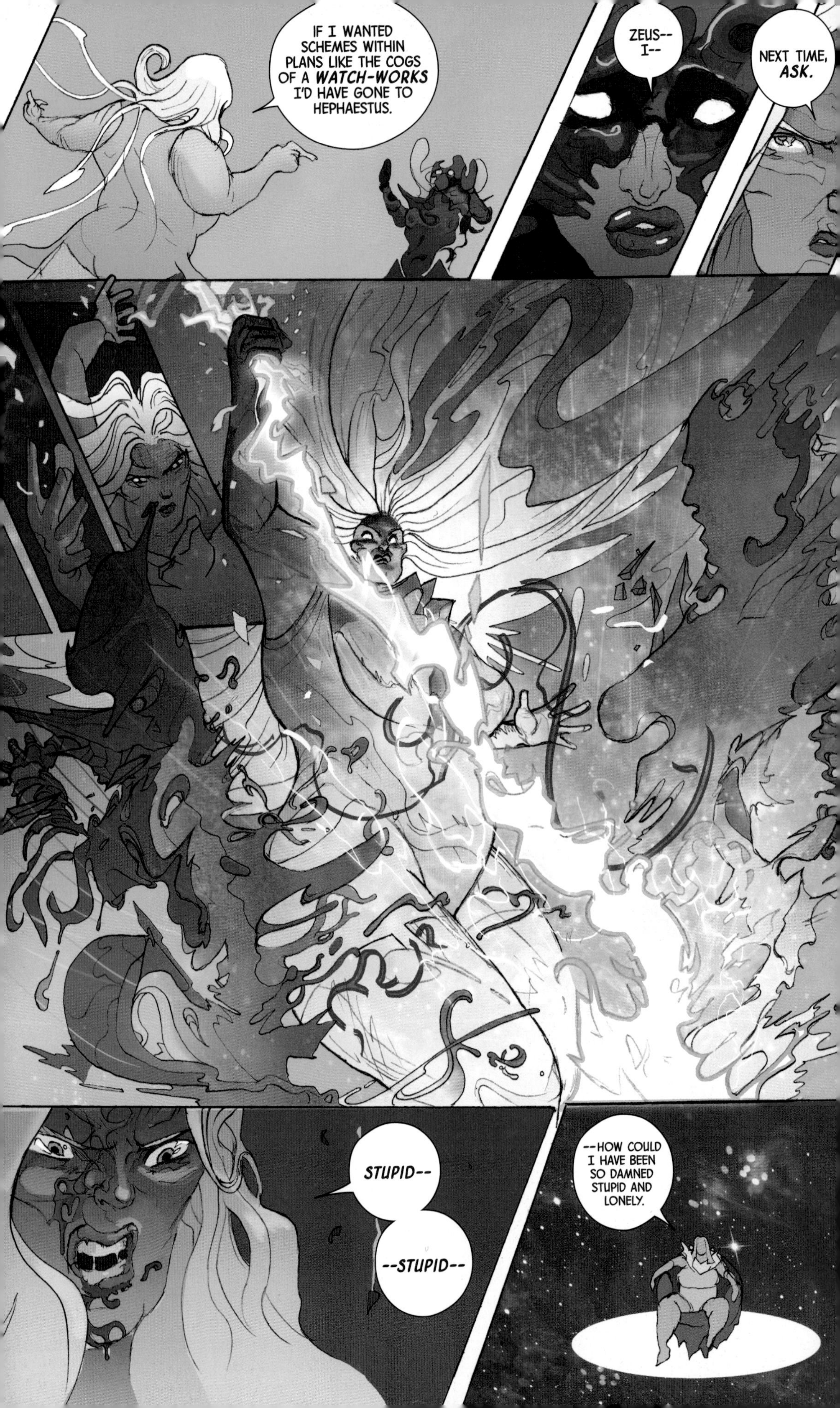
IF I WANTED SCHEMES WITHIN PLANS LIKE THE COGS OF A **WATCH-WORKS** I'D HAVE GONE TO HEPHAESTUS.
ZEUS-- I--
NEXT TIME, **ASK.**
STUPID--
--STUPID--
--HOW COULD I HAVE BEEN SO DAMNED STUPID AND LONELY.

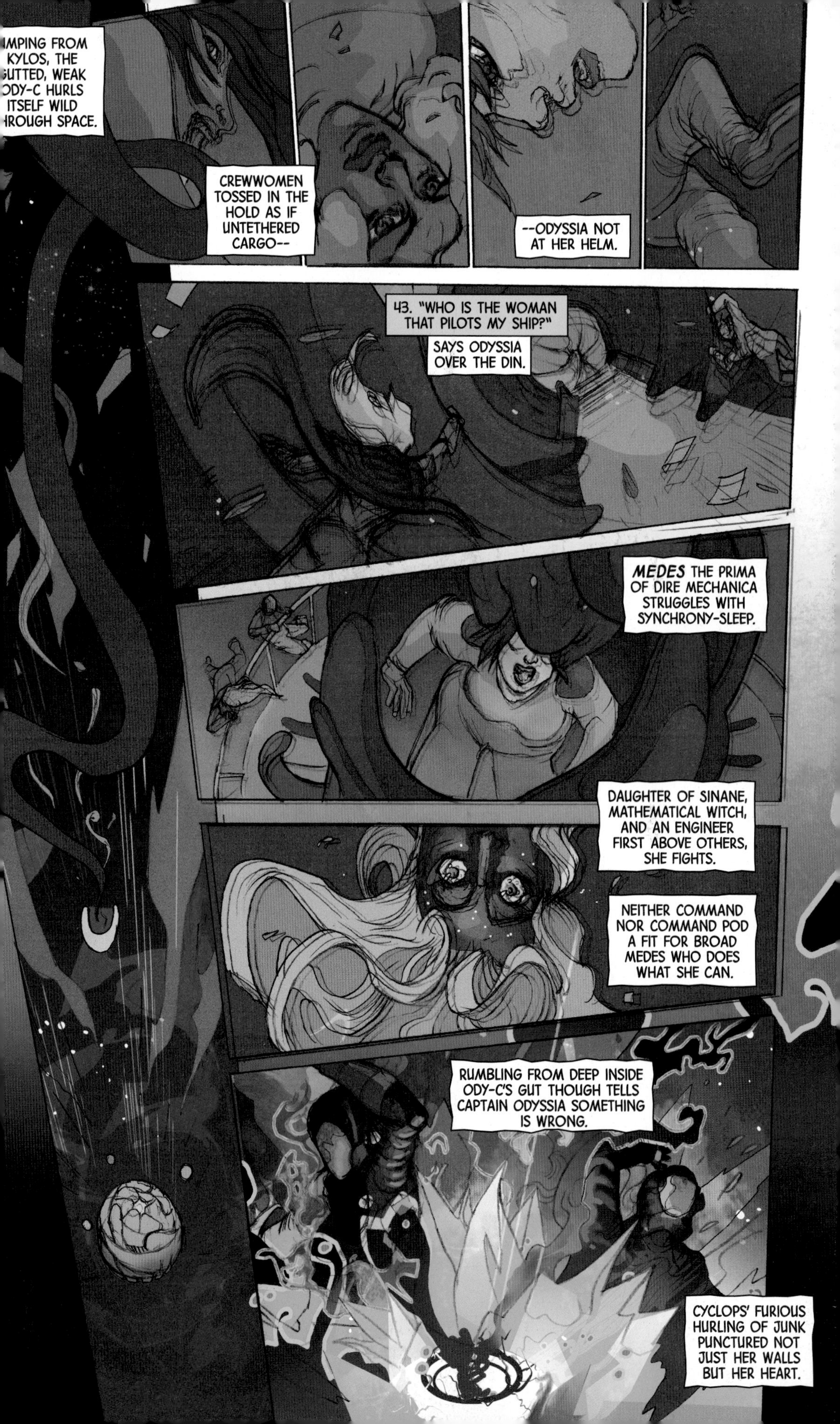

MPING FROM KYLOS, THE GUTTED, WEAK ODY-C HURLS ITSELF WILD THROUGH SPACE.
CREWWOMEN TOSSED IN THE HOLD AS IF UNTETHERED CARGO--
--ODYSSIA NOT AT HER HELM.
43. "WHO IS THE WOMAN THAT PILOTS MY SHIP?"
SAYS ODYSSIA OVER THE DIN.
MEDES THE PRIMA OF DIRE MECHANICA STRUGGLES WITH SYNCHRONY-SLEEP.
DAUGHTER OF SINANE, MATHEMATICAL WITCH, AND AN ENGINEER FIRST ABOVE OTHERS, SHE FIGHTS.
NEITHER COMMAND NOR COMMAND POD A FIT FOR BROAD MEDES WHO DOES WHAT SHE CAN.
RUMBLING FROM DEEP INSIDE ODY-C'S GUT THOUGH TELLS CAPTAIN ODYSSIA SOMETHING IS WRONG.
CYCLOPS' FURIOUS HURLING OF JUNK PUNCTURED NOT JUST HER WALLS BUT HER HEART.

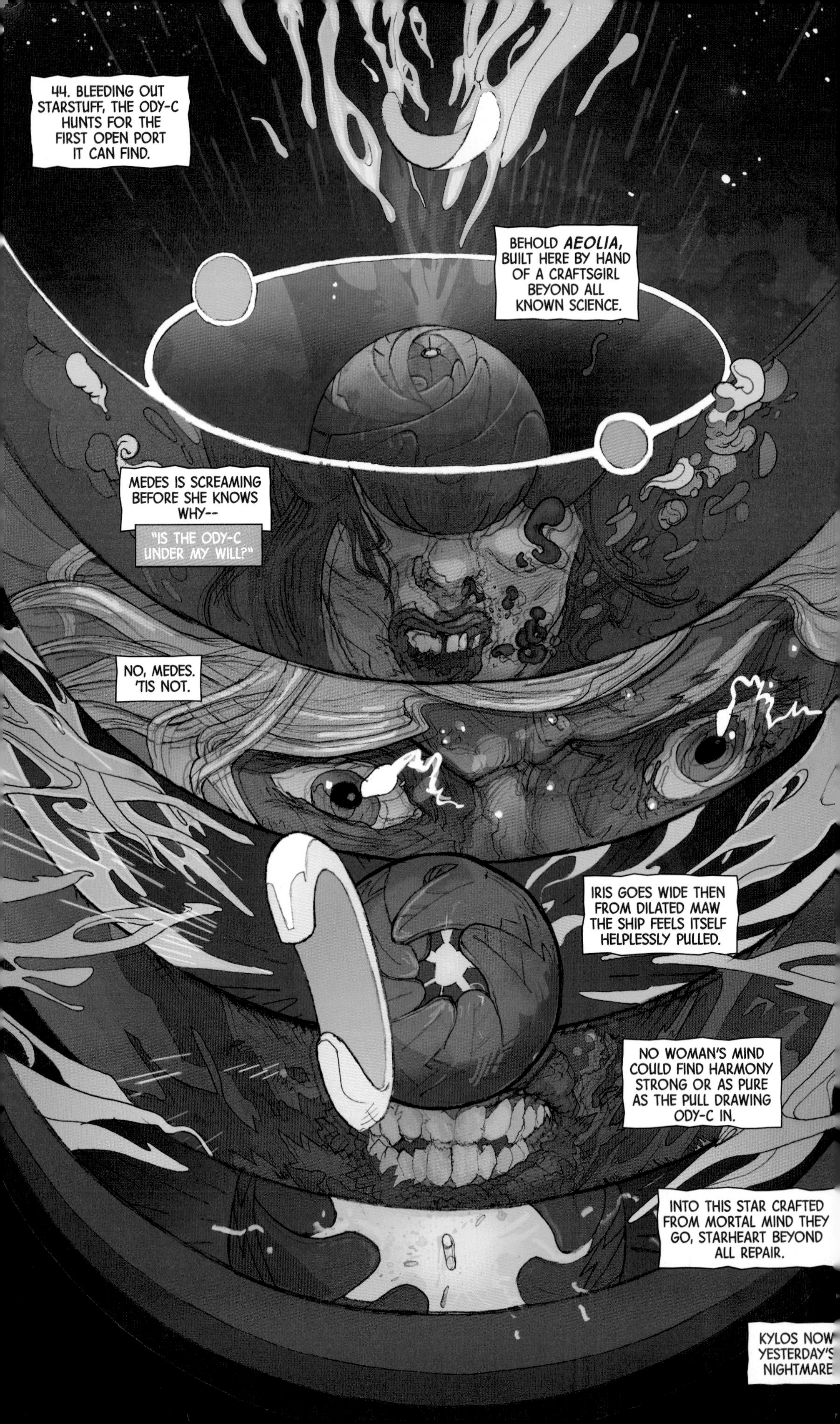
44. BLEEDING OUT STARSTUFF, THE ODY-C HUNTS FOR THE FIRST OPEN PORT IT CAN FIND.
BEHOLD AEOLIA, BUILT HERE BY HAND OF A CRAFTSGIRL BEYOND ALL KNOWN SCIENCE.
MEDES IS SCREAMING BEFORE SHE KNOWS WHY--
"IS THE ODY-C UNDER MY WILL?"
NO, MEDES. 'TIS NOT.
IRIS GOES WIDE THEN FROM DILATED MAW THE SHIP FEELS ITSELF HELPLESSLY PULLED.
NO WOMAN'S MIND COULD FIND HARMONY STRONG OR AS PURE AS THE PULL DRAWING ODY-C IN.
INTO THIS STAR CRAFTED FROM MORTAL MIND THEY GO, STARHEART BEYOND ALL REPAIR.
KYLOS NOW YESTERDAY'S NIGHTMARE

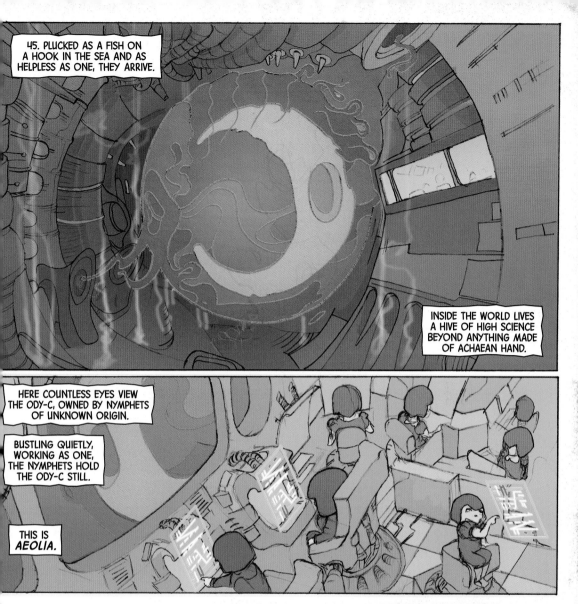

45. PLUCKED AS A FISH ON A HOOK IN THE SEA AND AS HELPLESS AS ONE, THEY ARRIVE.

INSIDE THE WORLD LIVES A HIVE OF HIGH SCIENCE BEYOND ANYTHING MADE OF ACHAEAN HAND.

HERE COUNTLESS EYES VIEW THE ODY-C, OWNED BY NYMPHETS OF UNKNOWN ORIGIN.

BUSTLING QUIETLY, WORKING AS ONE, THE NYMPHETS HOLD THE ODY-C STILL.

THIS IS *AEOLIA*.

POSEIDON'S GRANDDAUGHTERS, SAVIORS AT SEA, NEVER-YET MET BY OUTSIDERS, THESE.

"AEOLUS..."

SAYS THE NYMPHET THAT SEEMS MOST IN CHARGE.

"TELL US, WHAT DO YOU COMMAND?"

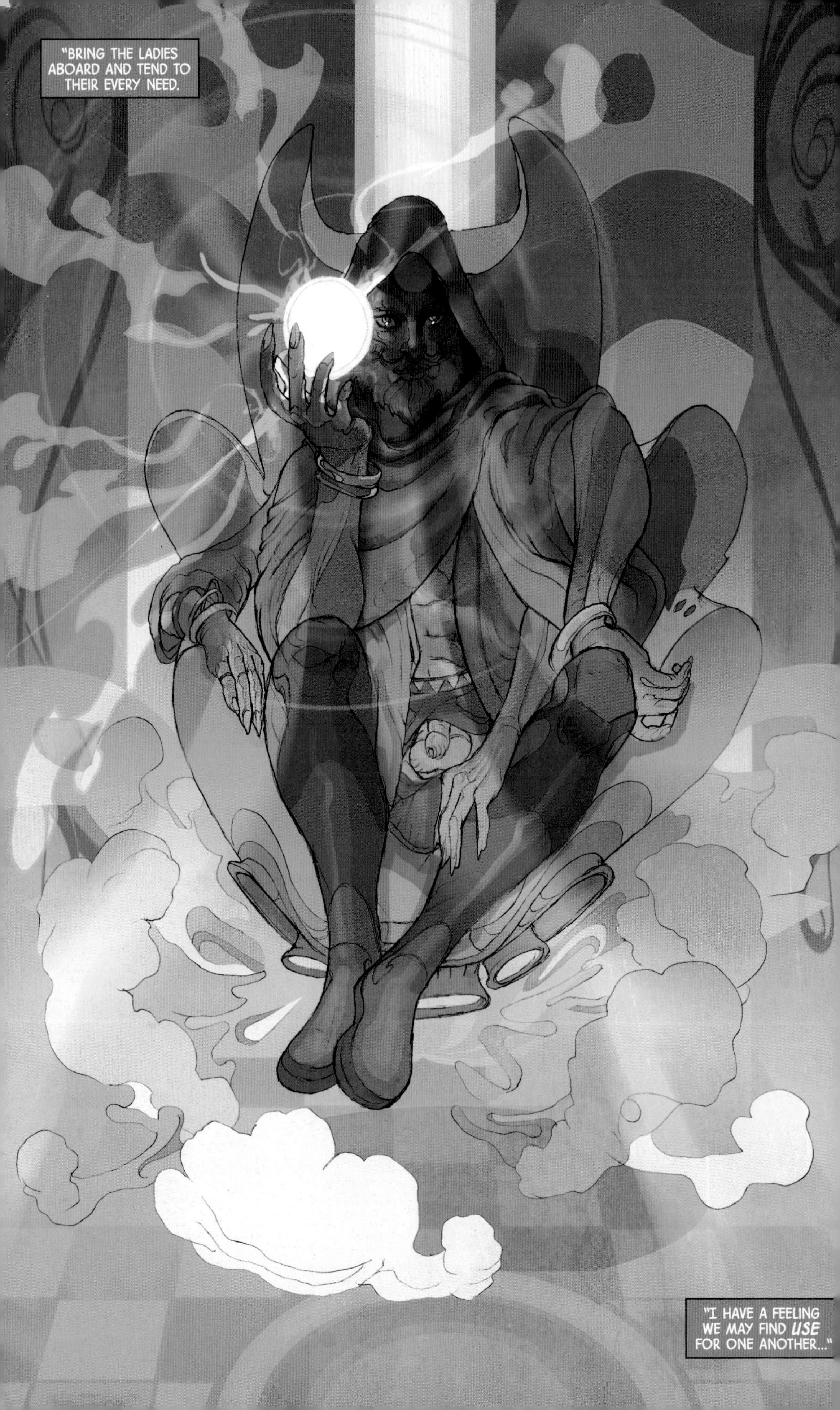
"BRING THE LADIES ABOARD AND TEND TO THEIR EVERY NEED.
"I HAVE A FEELING WE MAY FIND USE FOR ONE ANOTHER..."

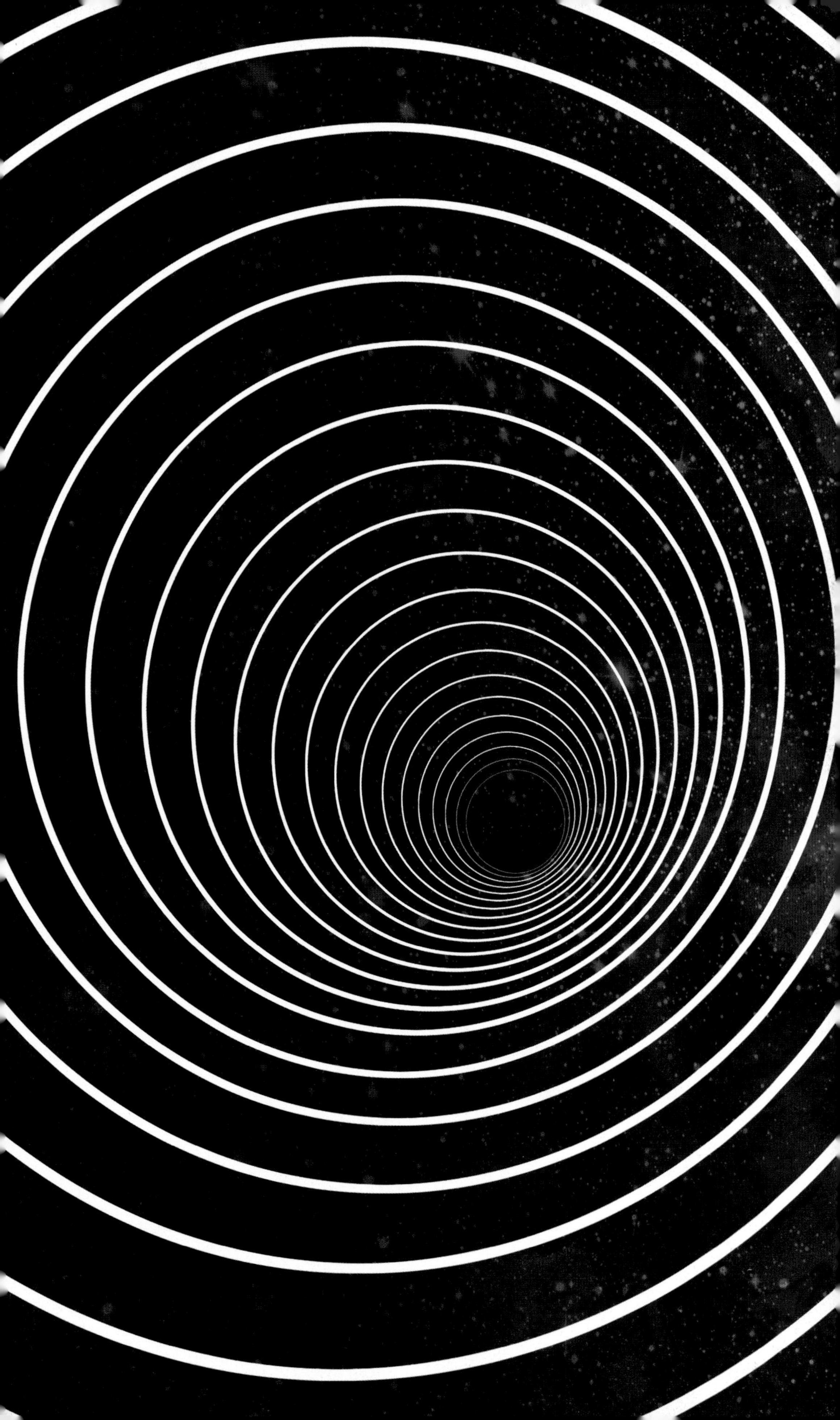

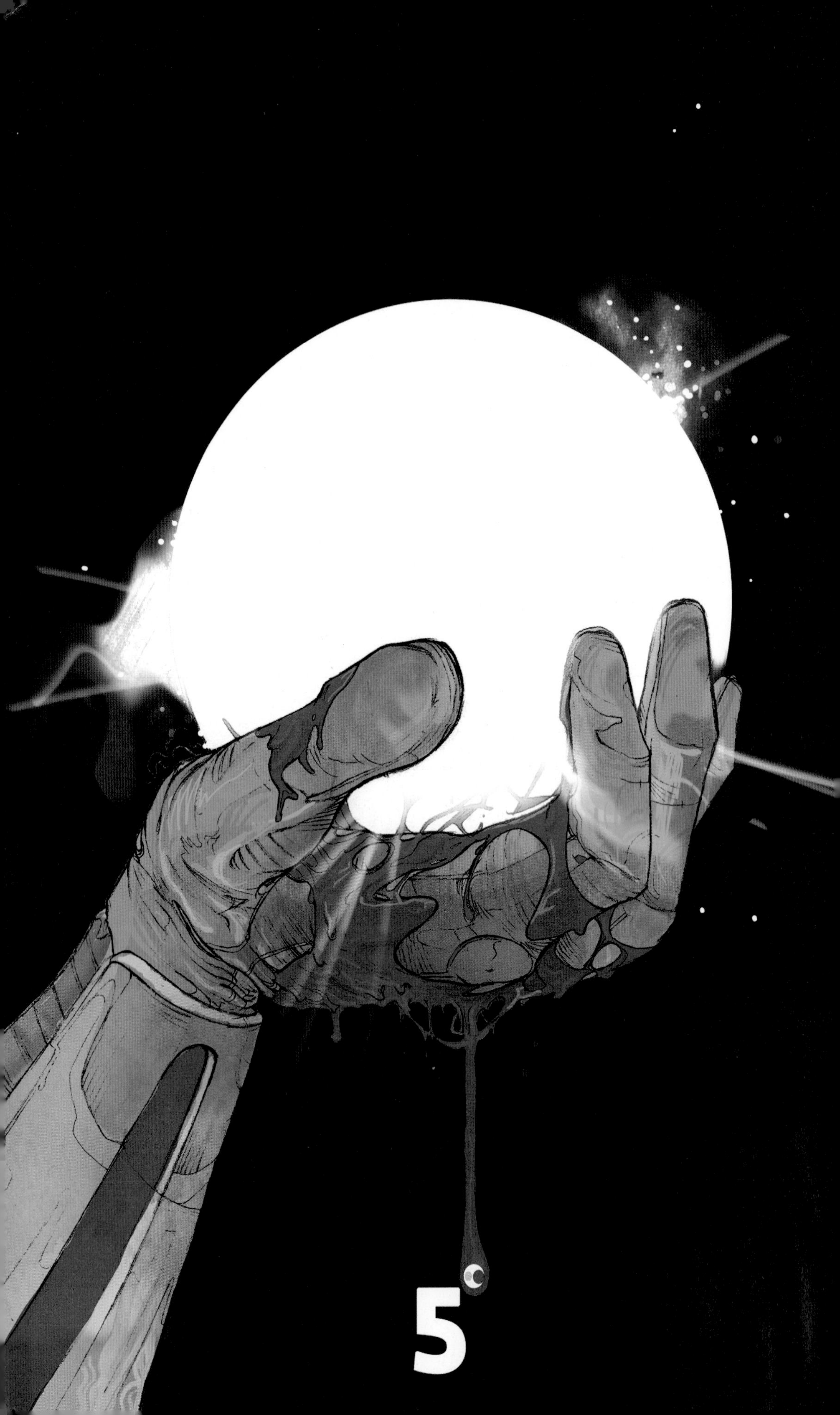
5

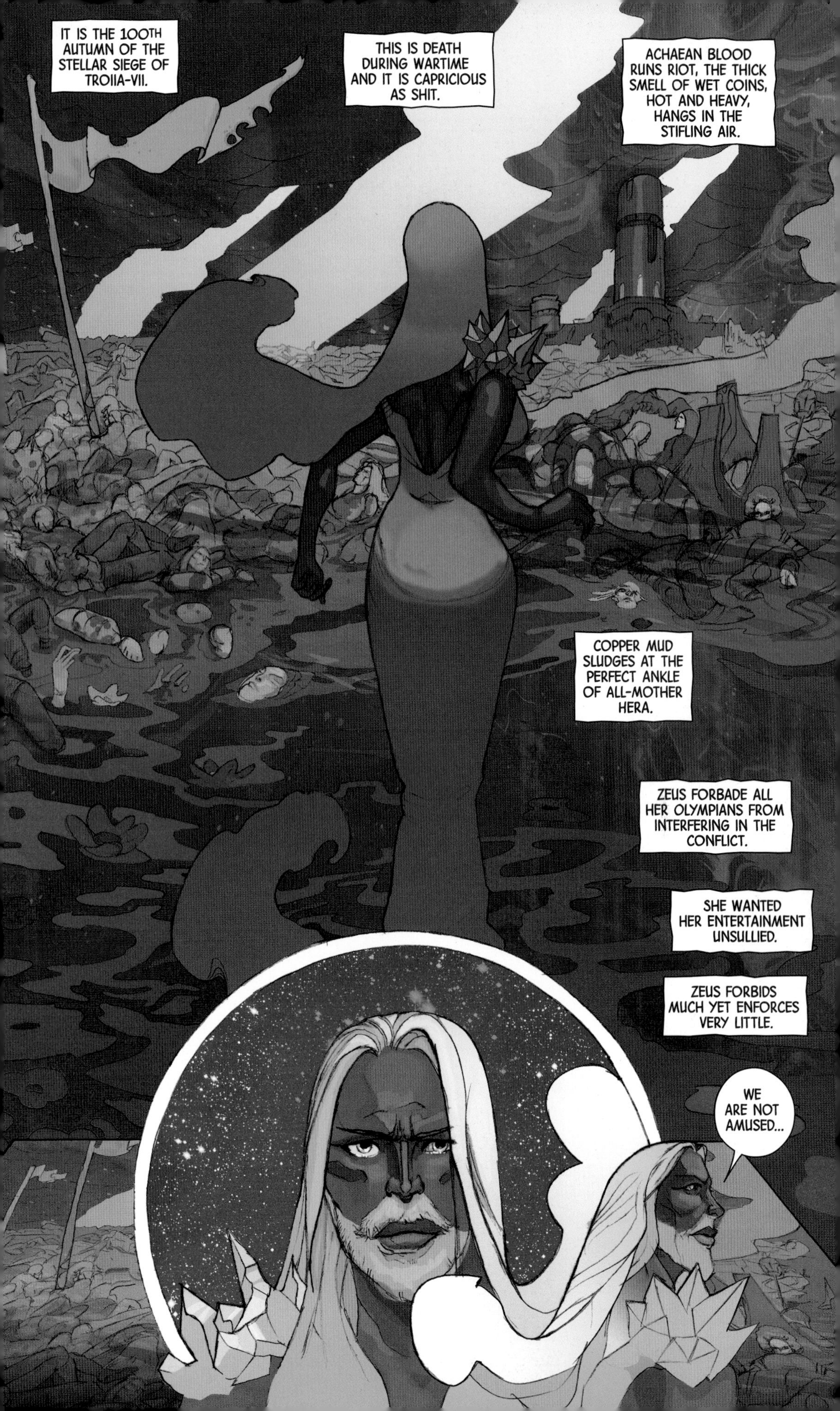

IT IS THE 100TH AUTUMN OF THE STELLAR SIEGE OF TROIIA-VII.
THIS IS DEATH DURING WARTIME AND IT IS CAPRICIOUS AS SHIT.
ACHAEAN BLOOD RUNS RIOT, THE THICK SMELL OF WET COINS, HOT AND HEAVY, HANGS IN THE STIFLING AIR.
COPPER MUD SLUDGES AT THE PERFECT ANKLE OF ALL-MOTHER HERA.
ZEUS FORBADE ALL HER OLYMPIANS FROM INTERFERING IN THE CONFLICT.
SHE WANTED HER ENTERTAINMENT UNSULLIED.
ZEUS FORBIDS MUCH YET ENFORCES VERY LITTLE.
WE ARE NOT AMUSED...

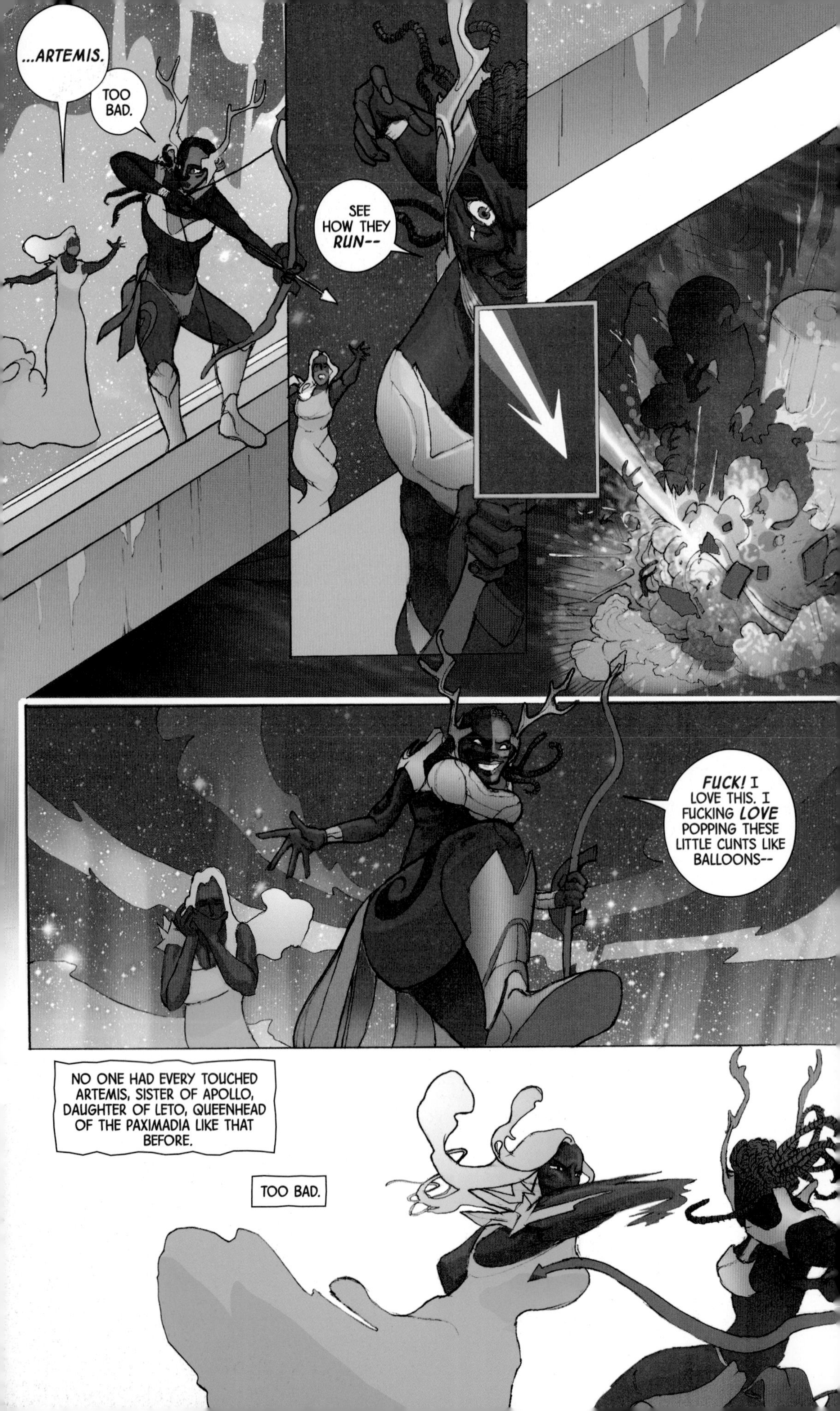

...ARTEMIS.
TOO BAD.
SEE HOW THEY RUN--
FUCK! I LOVE THIS. I FUCKING LOVE POPPING THESE LITTLE CUNTS LIKE BALLOONS--
NO ONE HAD EVERY TOUCHED ARTEMIS, SISTER OF APOLLO, DAUGHTER OF LETO, QUEENHEAD OF THE PAXIMADIA LIKE THAT BEFORE.
TOO BAD.

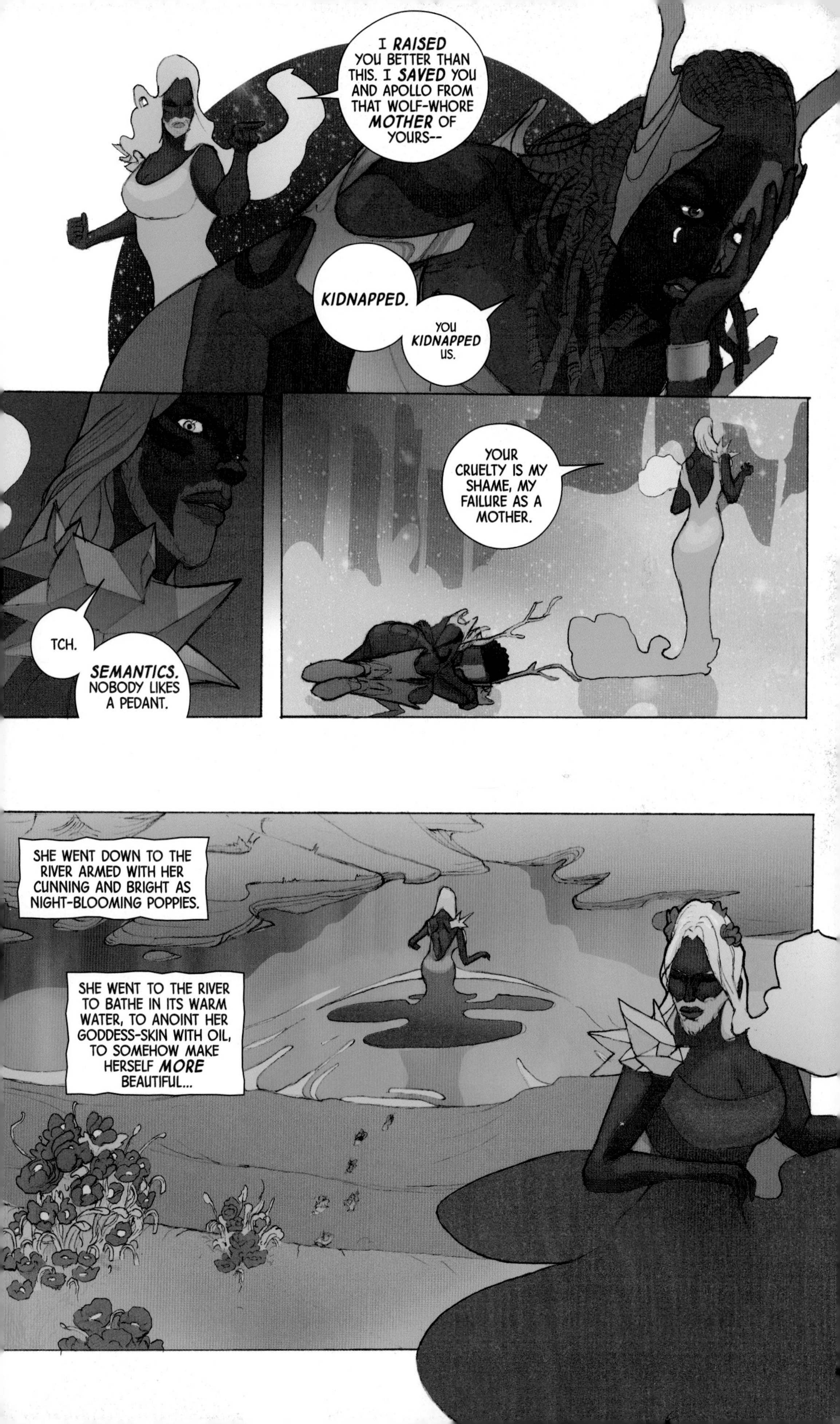
I RAISED YOU BETTER THAN THIS. I SAVED YOU AND APOLLO FROM THAT WOLF-WHORE MOTHER OF YOURS--
KIDNAPPED.
YOU KIDNAPPED US.
TCH.
SEMANTICS. NOBODY LIKES A PEDANT.
YOUR CRUELTY IS MY SHAME, MY FAILURE AS A MOTHER.
SHE WENT DOWN TO THE RIVER ARMED WITH HER CUNNING AND BRIGHT AS NIGHT-BLOOMING POPPIES.
SHE WENT TO THE RIVER TO BATHE IN ITS WARM WATER, TO ANOINT HER GODDESS-SKIN WITH OIL, TO SOMEHOW MAKE HERSELF MORE BEAUTIFUL...

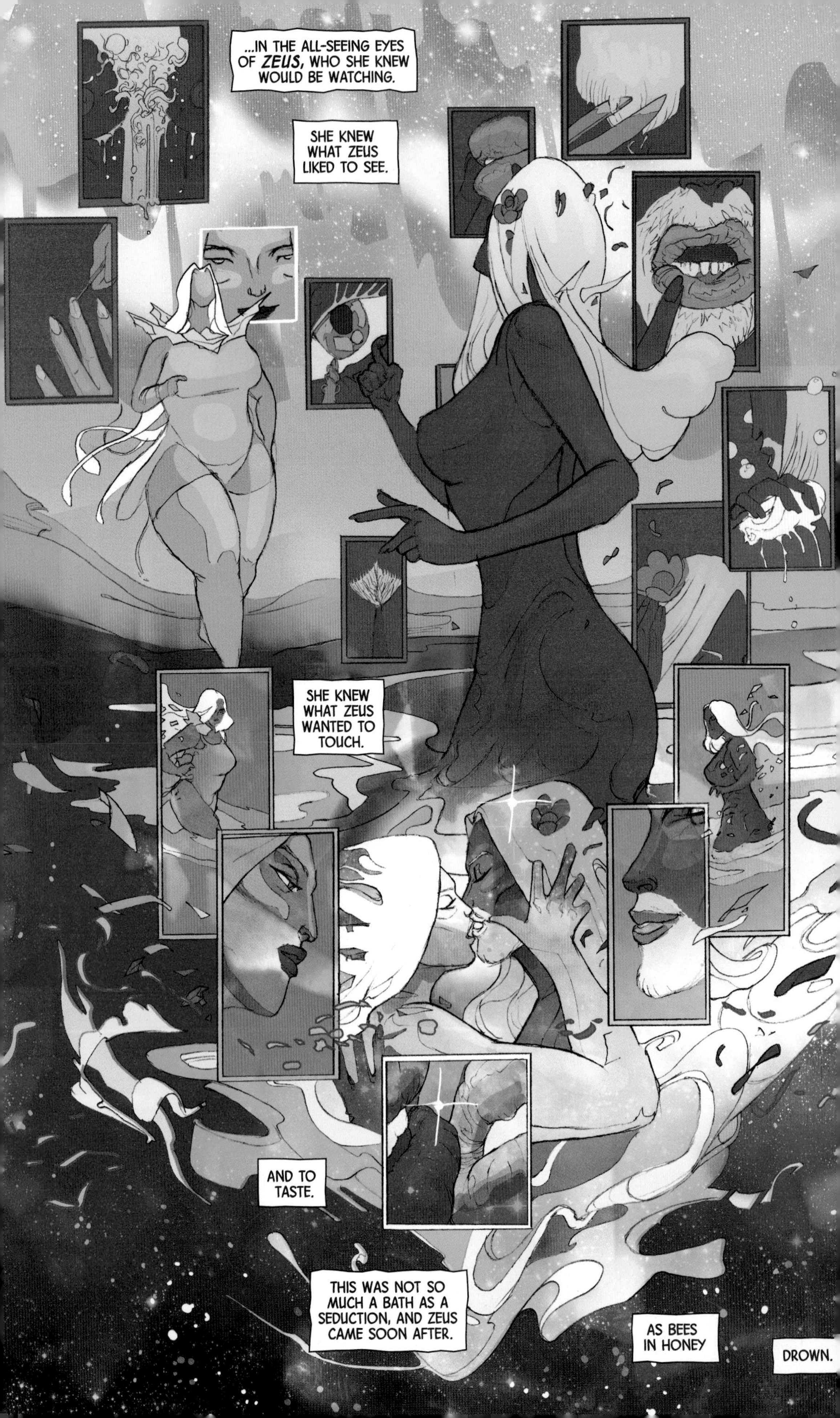
...IN THE ALL-SEEING EYES OF ZEUS, WHO SHE KNEW WOULD BE WATCHING.
SHE KNEW WHAT ZEUS LIKED TO SEE.
SHE KNEW WHAT ZEUS WANTED TO TOUCH.
AND TO TASTE.
THIS WAS NOT SO MUCH A BATH AS A SEDUCTION, AND ZEUS CAME SOON AFTER.
AS BEES IN HONEY
DROWN.

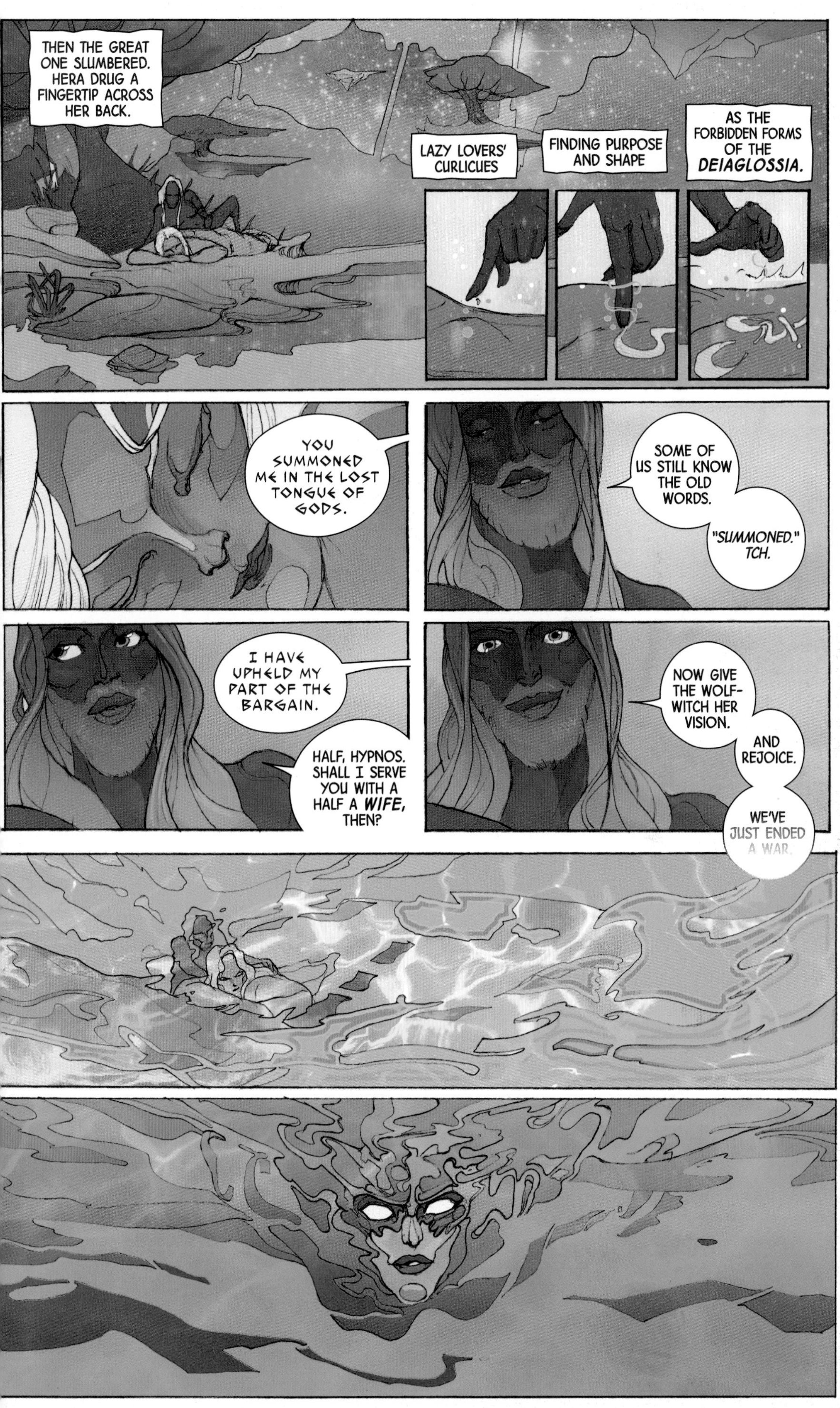
THEN THE GREAT ONE SLUMBERED. HERA DRUG A FINGERTIP ACROSS HER BACK.
LAZY LOVERS' CURLICUES
FINDING PURPOSE AND SHAPE
AS THE FORBIDDEN FORMS OF THE *DEIAGLOSSIA.*
YOU SUMMONED ME IN THE LOST TONGUE OF GODS.
SOME OF US STILL KNOW THE OLD WORDS.
"*SUMMONED.*" *TCH.*
I HAVE UPHELD MY PART OF THE BARGAIN.
HALF, HYPNOS. SHALL I SERVE YOU WITH A HALF A *WIFE,* THEN?
NOW GIVE THE WOLF-WITCH HER VISION.
AND REJOICE.
WE'VE JUST ENDED A WAR.

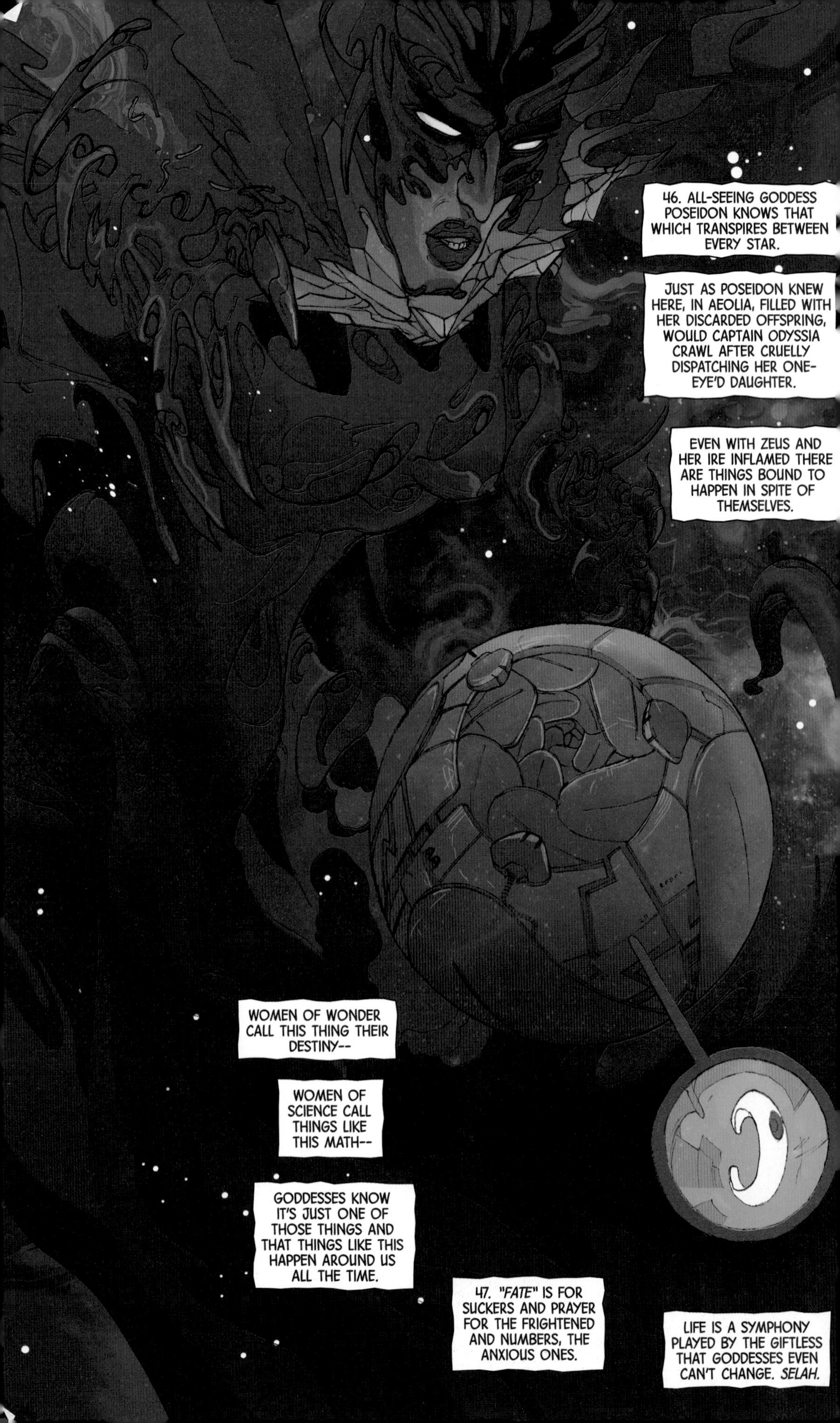
46. ALL-SEEING GODDESS POSEIDON KNOWS THAT WHICH TRANSPIRES BETWEEN EVERY STAR.
JUST AS POSEIDON KNEW HERE, IN AEOLIA, FILLED WITH HER DISCARDED OFFSPRING, WOULD CAPTAIN ODYSSIA CRAWL AFTER CRUELLY DISPATCHING HER ONE-EYE'D DAUGHTER.
EVEN WITH ZEUS AND HER IRE INFLAMED THERE ARE THINGS BOUND TO HAPPEN IN SPITE OF THEMSELVES.
WOMEN OF WONDER CALL THIS THING THEIR DESTINY--
WOMEN OF SCIENCE CALL THINGS LIKE THIS MATH--
GODDESSES KNOW IT'S JUST ONE OF THOSE THINGS AND THAT THINGS LIKE THIS HAPPEN AROUND US ALL THE TIME.
47. "*FATE*" IS FOR SUCKERS AND PRAYER FOR THE FRIGHTENED AND NUMBERS, THE ANXIOUS ONES.
LIFE IS A SYMPHONY PLAYED BY THE GIFTLESS THAT GODDESSES EVEN CAN'T CHANGE. *SELAH.*

AEOLUS, LORD OF AEOLIA, WELCOMES HIS GUESTS TO HIS HOME IN THESE STARS, OFFERING THEM ALL WHAT HE'S MADE--

ANIMA ASTRA, THE STARHEART SUPREMA, THE SOUL OF A SWIFTSHIP IN WANT OF A HOME.

HERE HE HAS BUILT, TELLS THIS MAN WITHOUT PEER, IN HIS FOUR-HANDED WAY, A MACHINE BEYOND EVERYTHING ACHAEANS THINK CAN BE DONE WITH THE LAWS OF IMMUTABLE SCIENCE.

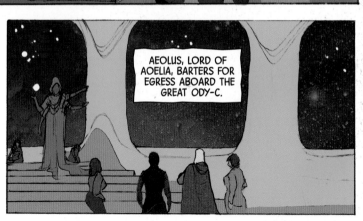

48. HERE HE HAS BUILT A MACHINE TO MAKE DISTANCE AN AFTERTHOUGHT, INCONSEQUENTIAL.

HERE HE HAS MADE FOR HER SHIP A NEW SOUL THAT WILL TAKE HER TO ITHICAA IN TEN DAYS TIME.

HERE HE HAS WAITED, FORBIDDEN TO BUILD FOR HIMSELF HIS OWN SHIP, AND NOW FORTUNE HAS SMILED UPON HIM.

"WHAT WILL IT COST ME,"

ODYSSIA ASKS HIM AND

"HOW COULD A WONDER AS THIS BE CONTAINED BY A CONCEPT LIKE *'VALUE'?*"

THE OLD MAN REPLIES.

AEOLUS, LORD OF AOELIA, BARTERS FOR EGRESS ABOARD THE GREAT ODY-C.

"I AM READY TO LEAVE PARADISE."

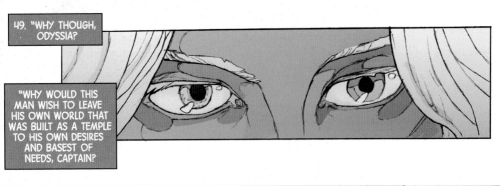

49. "WHY THOUGH, ODYSSIA?

"WHY WOULD THIS MAN WISH TO LEAVE HIS OWN WORLD THAT WAS BUILT AS A TEMPLE TO HIS OWN DESIRES AND BASEST OF NEEDS, CAPTAIN?

"SCADS OF NYMPHETTES WAITING ONLY FOR AEOLUS, BENT OF THE KNEE AND BOWED OF THE HEAD,"

SAYS EURY.

MEDES SAYS:

"THINK OF IT: AEOLUS, HERE AND ALONE, THE SOLE MAN AMONG THOUSANDS AND THOUSANDS OF STARS.

AND CONTINUES:

"MY CAPTAIN, THESE STARLOST YOUNG WOMEN NOW BOW AT HIS FEET AS THOUGH HE WERE SOME SORT OF GOD."

"AND WHY NOT?"

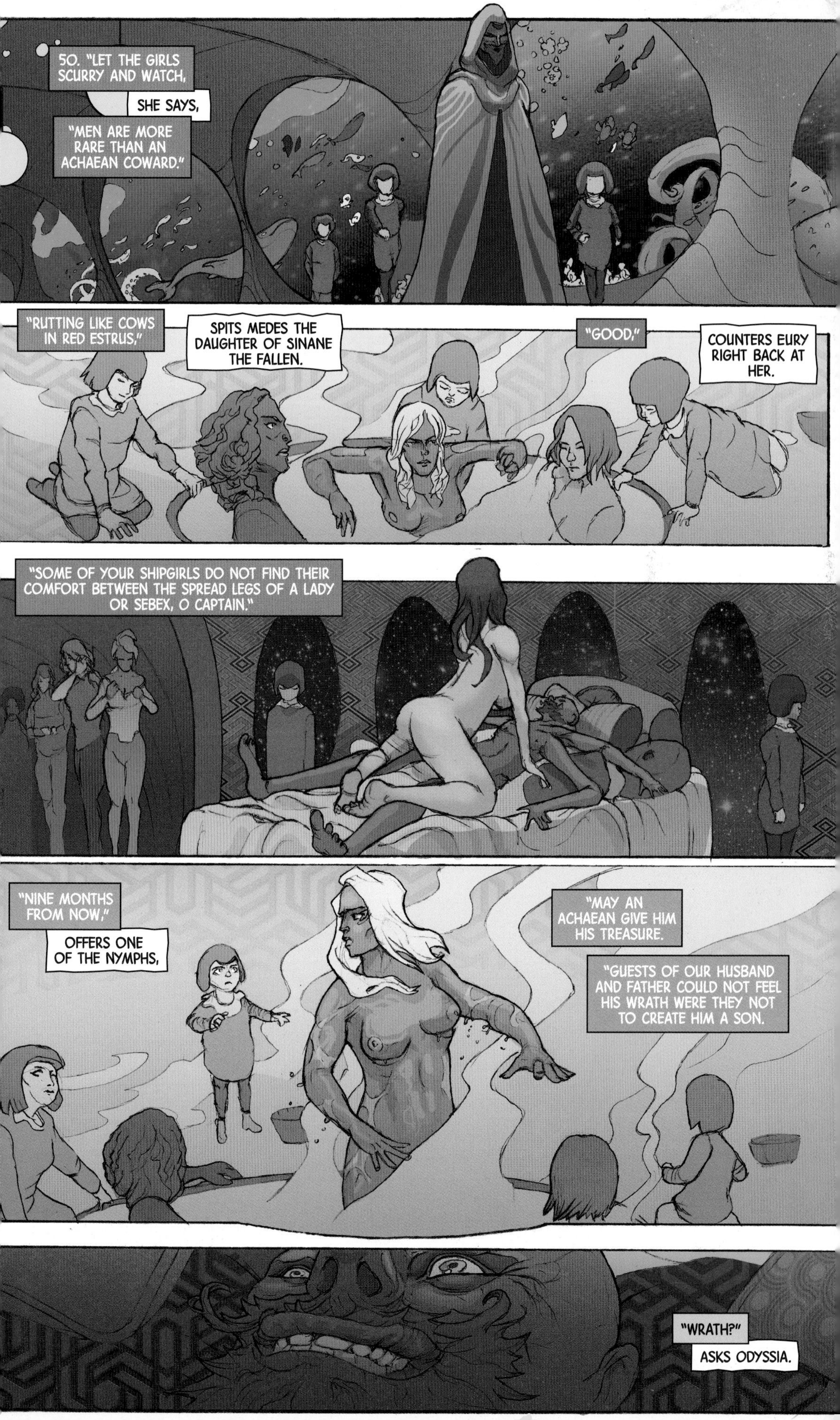
50. "LET THE GIRLS SCURRY AND WATCH,
SHE SAYS,
"MEN ARE MORE RARE THAN AN ACHAEAN COWARD."
"RUTTING LIKE COWS IN RED ESTRUS,"
SPITS MEDES THE DAUGHTER OF SINANE THE FALLEN.
"GOOD,"
COUNTERS EURY RIGHT BACK AT HER.
"SOME OF YOUR SHIPGIRLS DO NOT FIND THEIR COMFORT BETWEEN THE SPREAD LEGS OF A LADY OR SEBEX, O CAPTAIN."
"NINE MONTHS FROM NOW,"
OFFERS ONE OF THE NYMPHS,
"MAY AN ACHAEAN GIVE HIM HIS TREASURE.
"GUESTS OF OUR HUSBAND AND FATHER COULD NOT FEEL HIS WRATH WERE THEY NOT TO CREATE HIM A SON.
"WRATH?"
ASKS ODYSSIA.

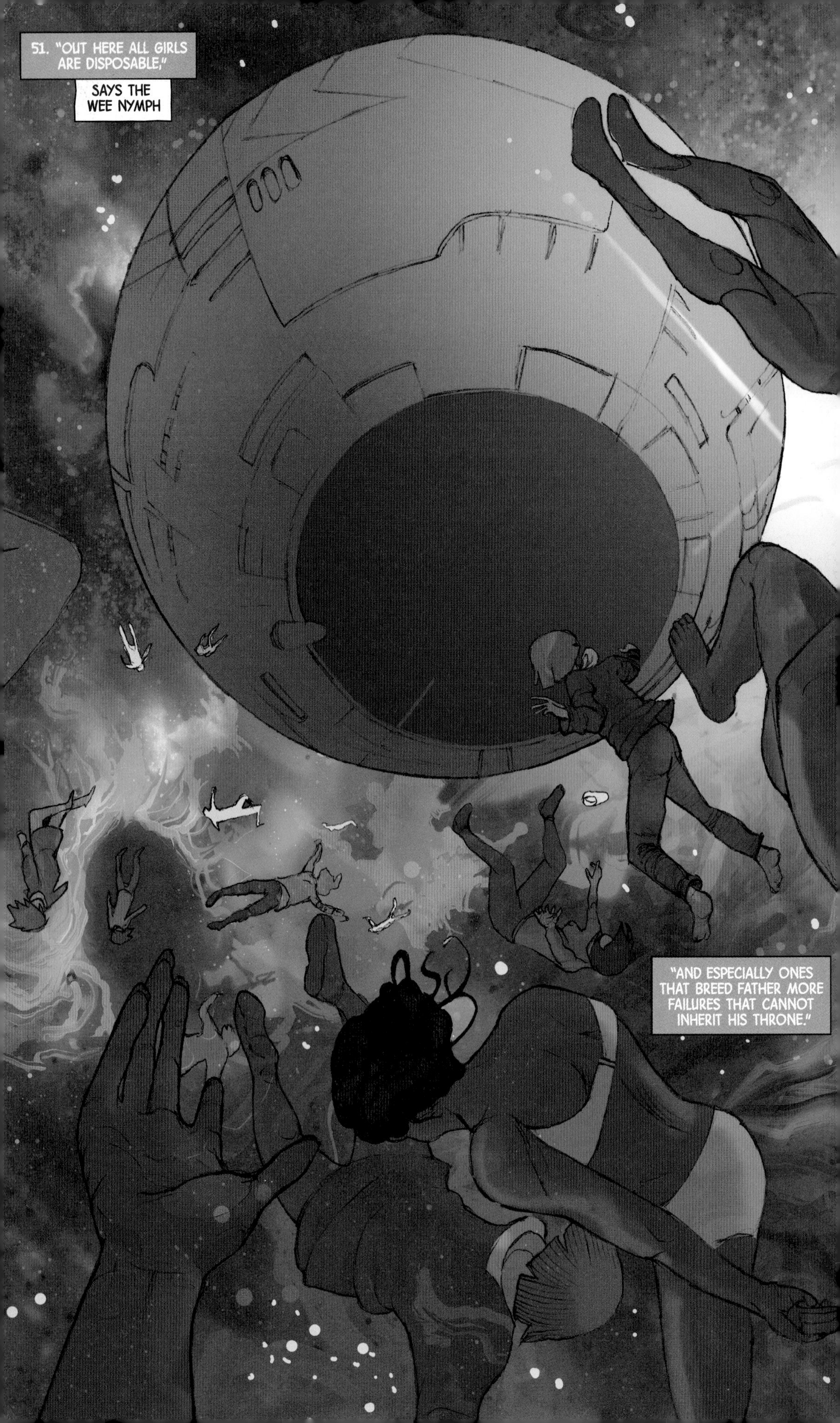
51. "OUT HERE ALL GIRLS ARE DISPOSABLE,"
SAYS THE WEE NYMPH
"AND ESPECIALLY ONES THAT BREED FATHER MORE FAILURES THAT CANNOT INHERIT HIS THRONE."

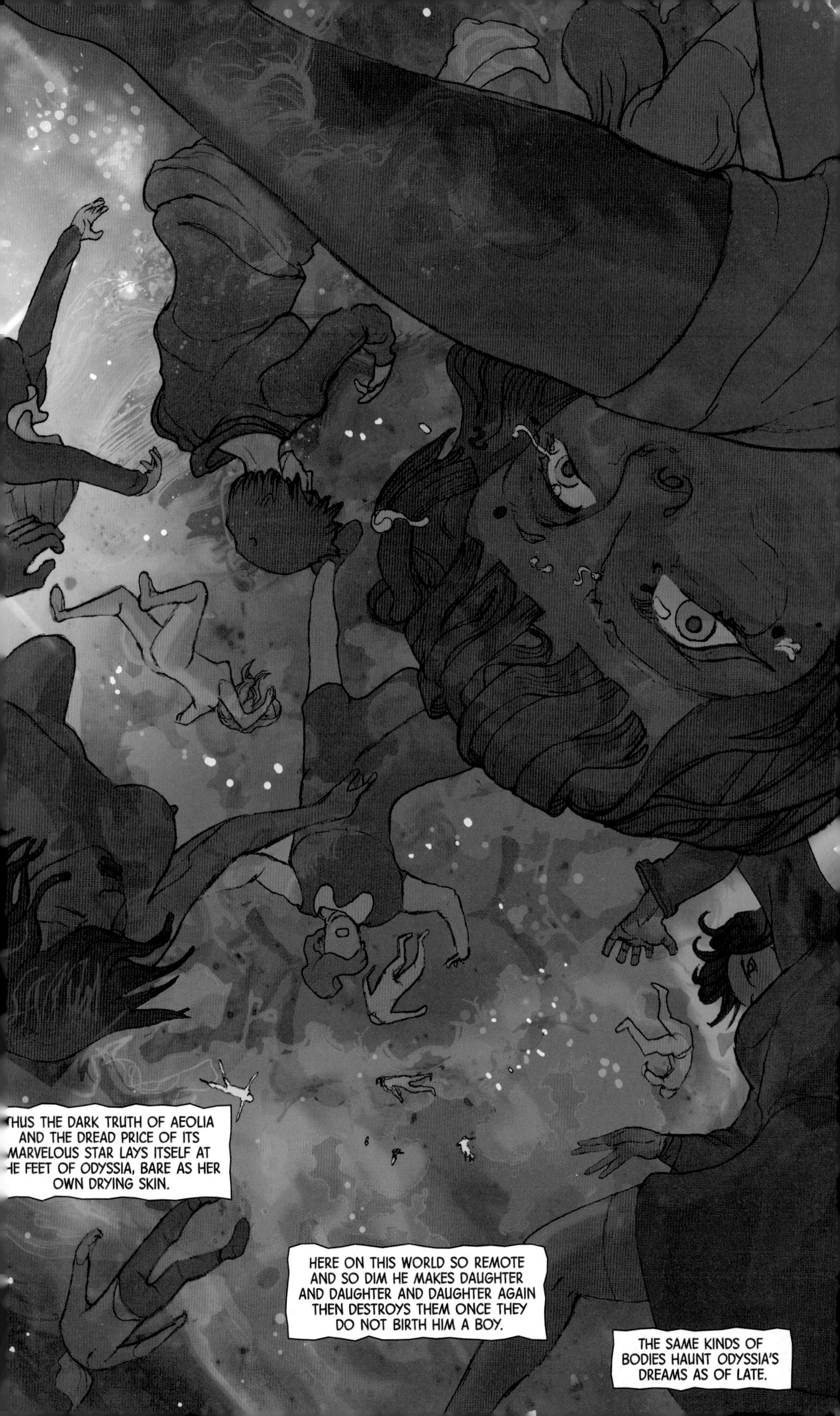

THUS THE DARK TRUTH OF AEOLIA AND THE DREAD PRICE OF ITS MARVELOUS STAR LAYS ITSELF AT HE FEET OF ODYSSIA, BARE AS HER OWN DRYING SKIN.
HERE ON THIS WORLD SO REMOTE AND SO DIM HE MAKES DAUGHTER AND DAUGHTER AND DAUGHTER AGAIN THEN DESTROYS THEM ONCE THEY DO NOT BIRTH HIM A BOY.
THE SAME KINDS OF BODIES HAUNT ODYSSIA'S DREAMS AS OF LATE.

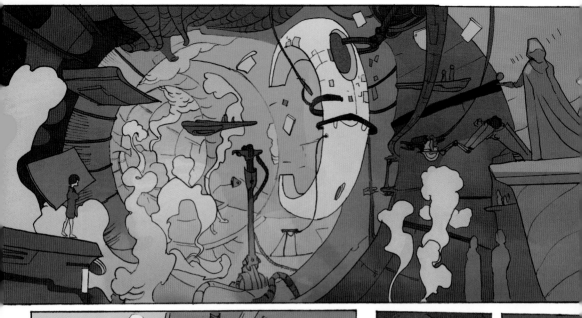

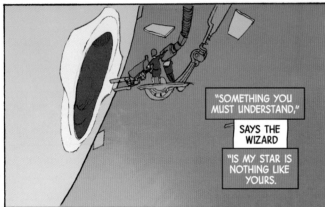

"SOMETHING YOU MUST UNDERSTAND,"

SAYS THE WIZARD

"IS MY STAR IS NOTHING LIKE YOURS.

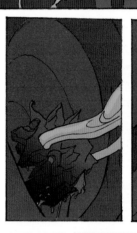

"THIS IS A THING MADE FOR WISHING BY MAGICKS THAT ONLY A TITAN AS I COULD CONCEIVE."

"WHAT DO YOU MEAN?"

ASKS ODYSSIA.

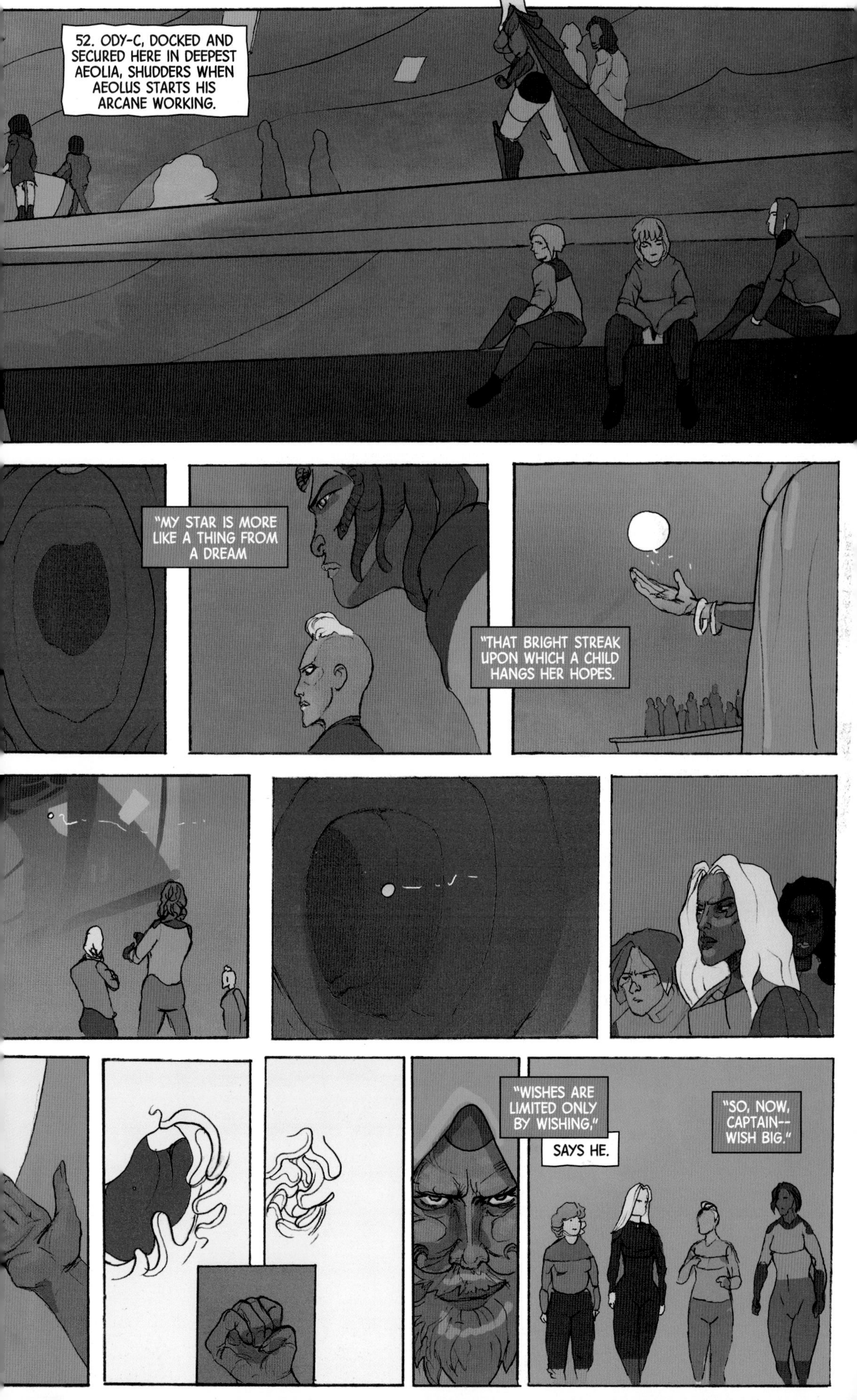

52. ODY-C, DOCKED AND SECURED HERE IN DEEPEST AEOLIA, SHUDDERS WHEN AEOLUS STARTS HIS ARCANE WORKING.
"MY STAR IS MORE LIKE A THING FROM A DREAM
"THAT BRIGHT STREAK UPON WHICH A CHILD HANGS HER HOPES.
"WISHES ARE LIMITED ONLY BY WISHING,"
SAYS HE.
"SO, NOW, CAPTAIN-- WISH BIG."

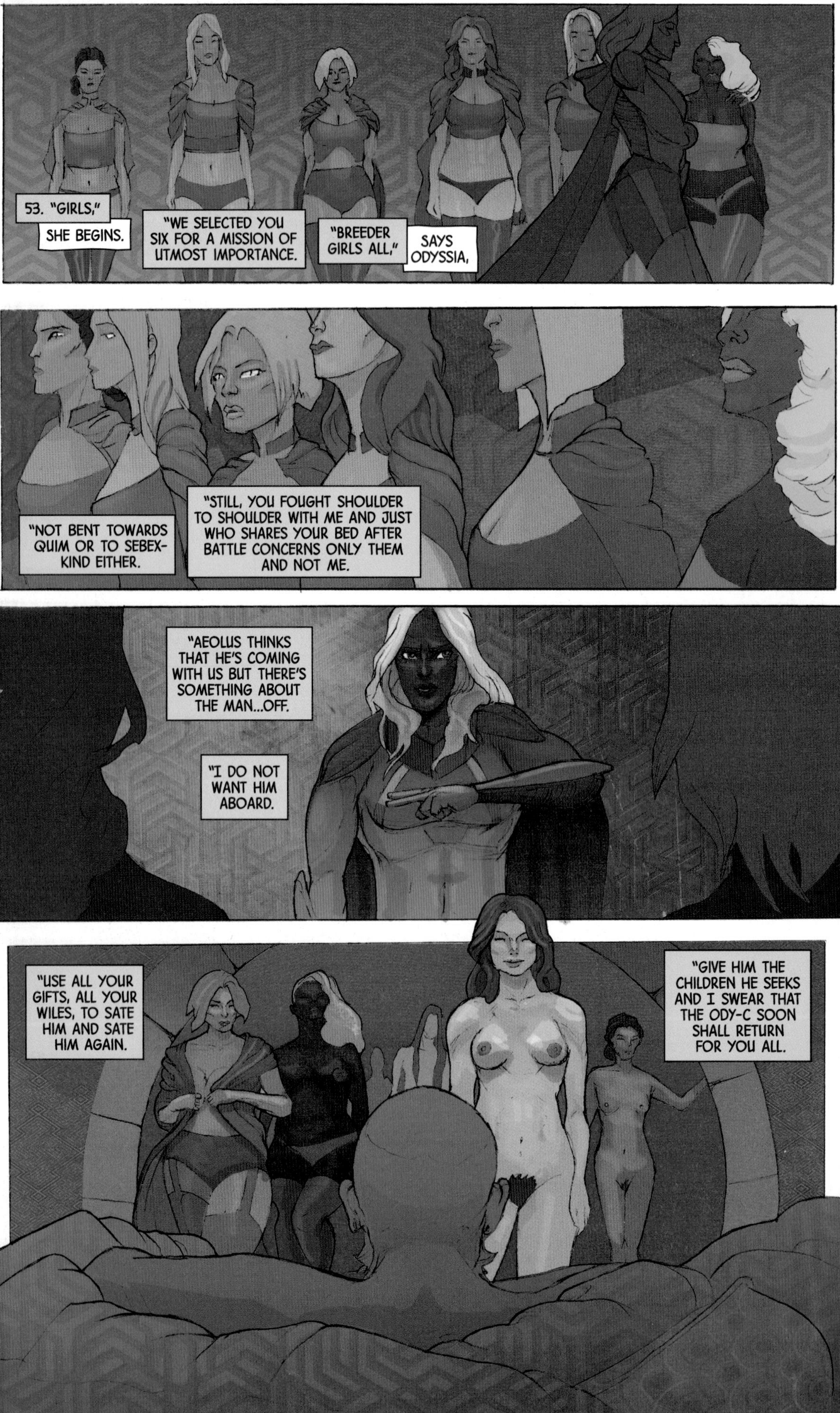
53. "GIRLS,"
SHE BEGINS.
"WE SELECTED YOU SIX FOR A MISSION OF UTMOST IMPORTANCE.
"BREEDER GIRLS ALL,"
SAYS ODYSSIA,
"NOT BENT TOWARDS QUIM OR TO SEBEX-KIND EITHER.
"STILL, YOU FOUGHT SHOULDER TO SHOULDER WITH ME AND JUST WHO SHARES YOUR BED AFTER BATTLE CONCERNS ONLY THEM AND NOT ME.
"AEOLUS THINKS THAT HE'S COMING WITH US BUT THERE'S SOMETHING ABOUT THE MAN...OFF.
"I DO NOT WANT HIM ABOARD.
"USE ALL YOUR GIFTS, ALL YOUR WILES, TO SATE HIM AND SATE HIM AGAIN.
"GIVE HIM THE CHILDREN HE SEEKS AND I SWEAR THAT THE ODY-C SOON SHALL RETURN FOR YOU ALL.

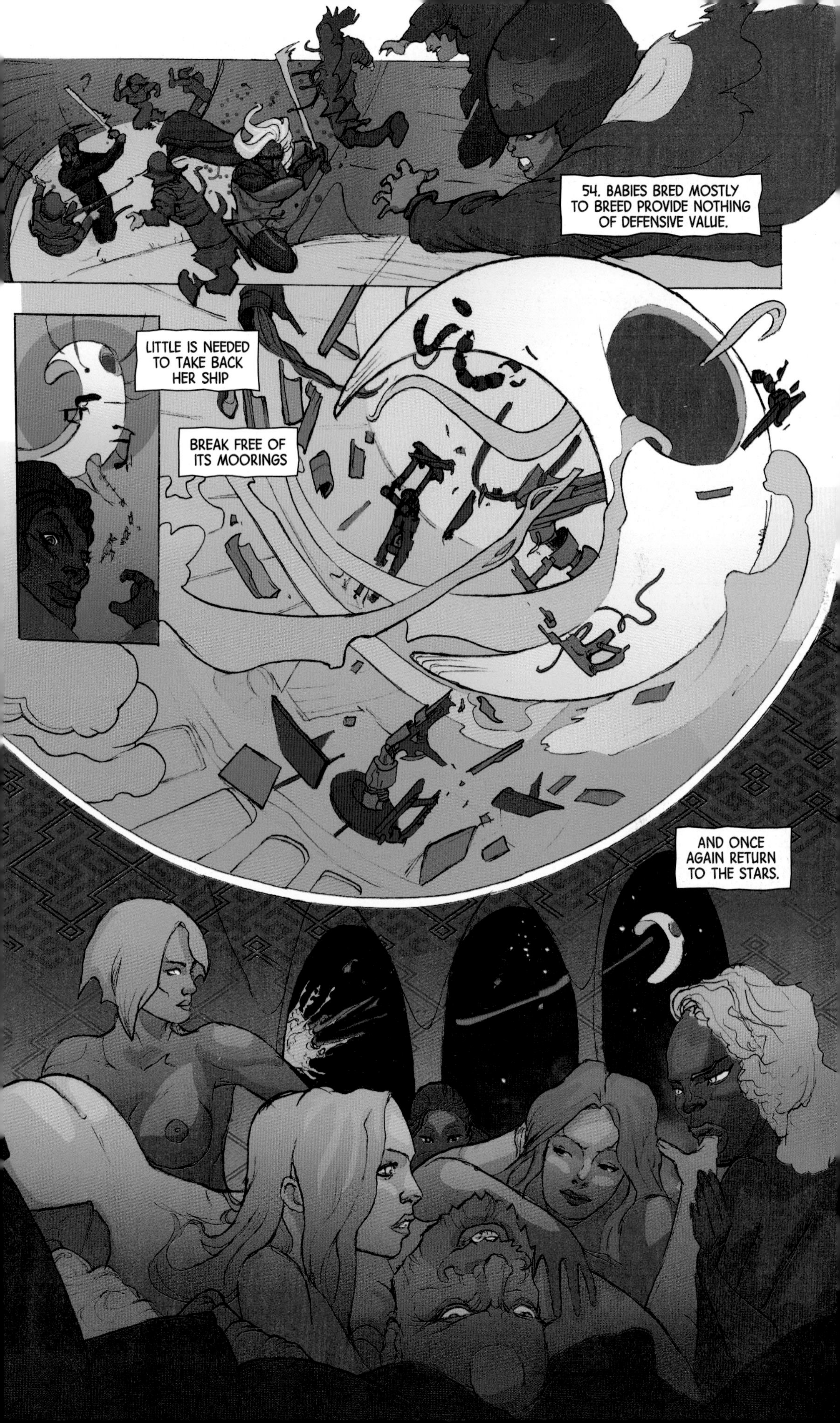
54. BABIES BRED MOSTLY TO BREED PROVIDE NOTHING OF DEFENSIVE VALUE.
LITTLE IS NEEDED TO TAKE BACK HER SHIP
BREAK FREE OF ITS MOORINGS
AND ONCE AGAIN RETURN TO THE STARS.

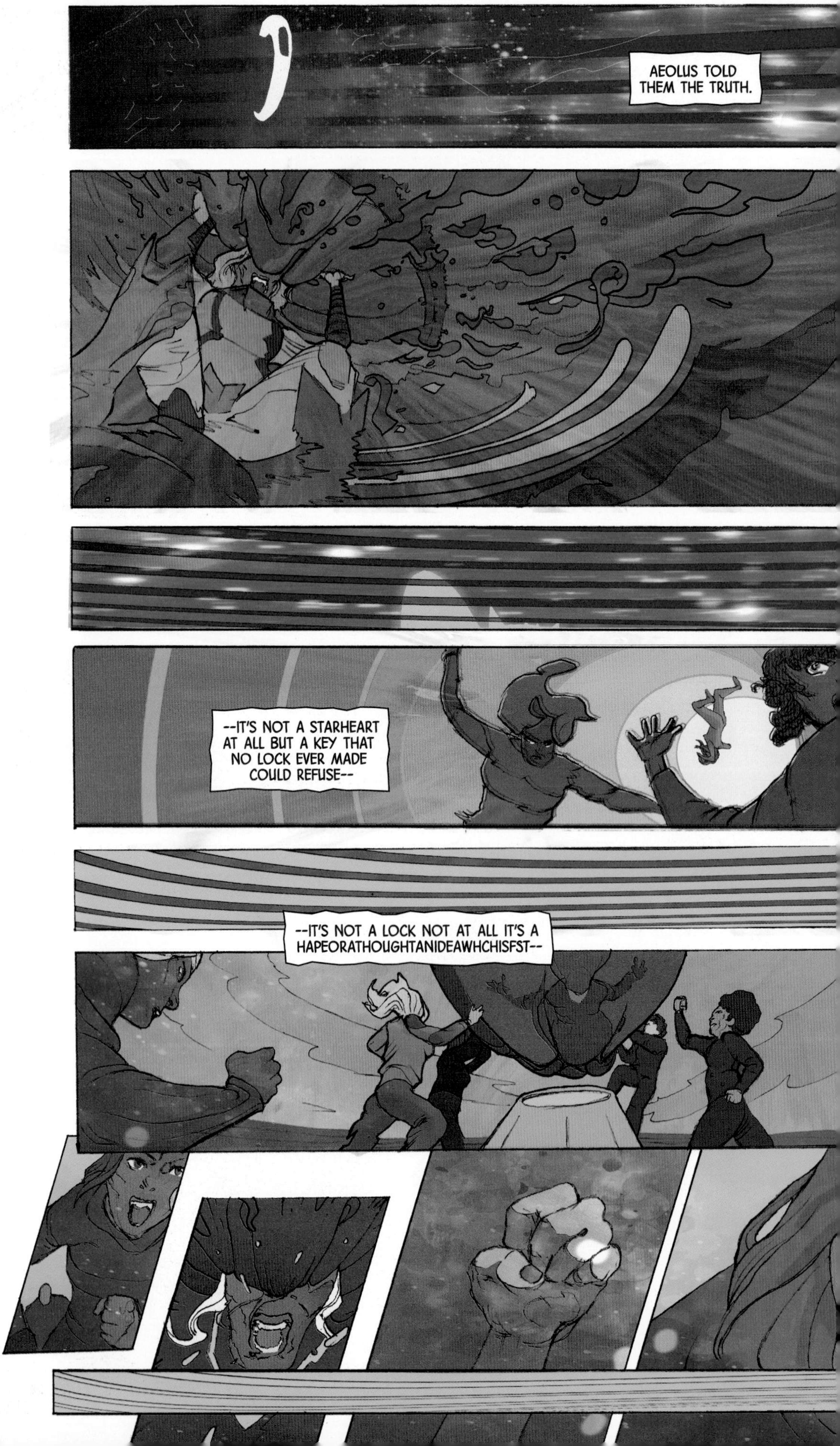
AEOLUS TOLD THEM THE TRUTH.
--IT'S NOT A STARHEART AT ALL BUT A KEY THAT NO LOCK EVER MADE COULD REFUSE--
--IT'S NOT A LOCK NOT AT ALL IT'S A HAPEORATHOUGHTANIDEAWHCHISFST--

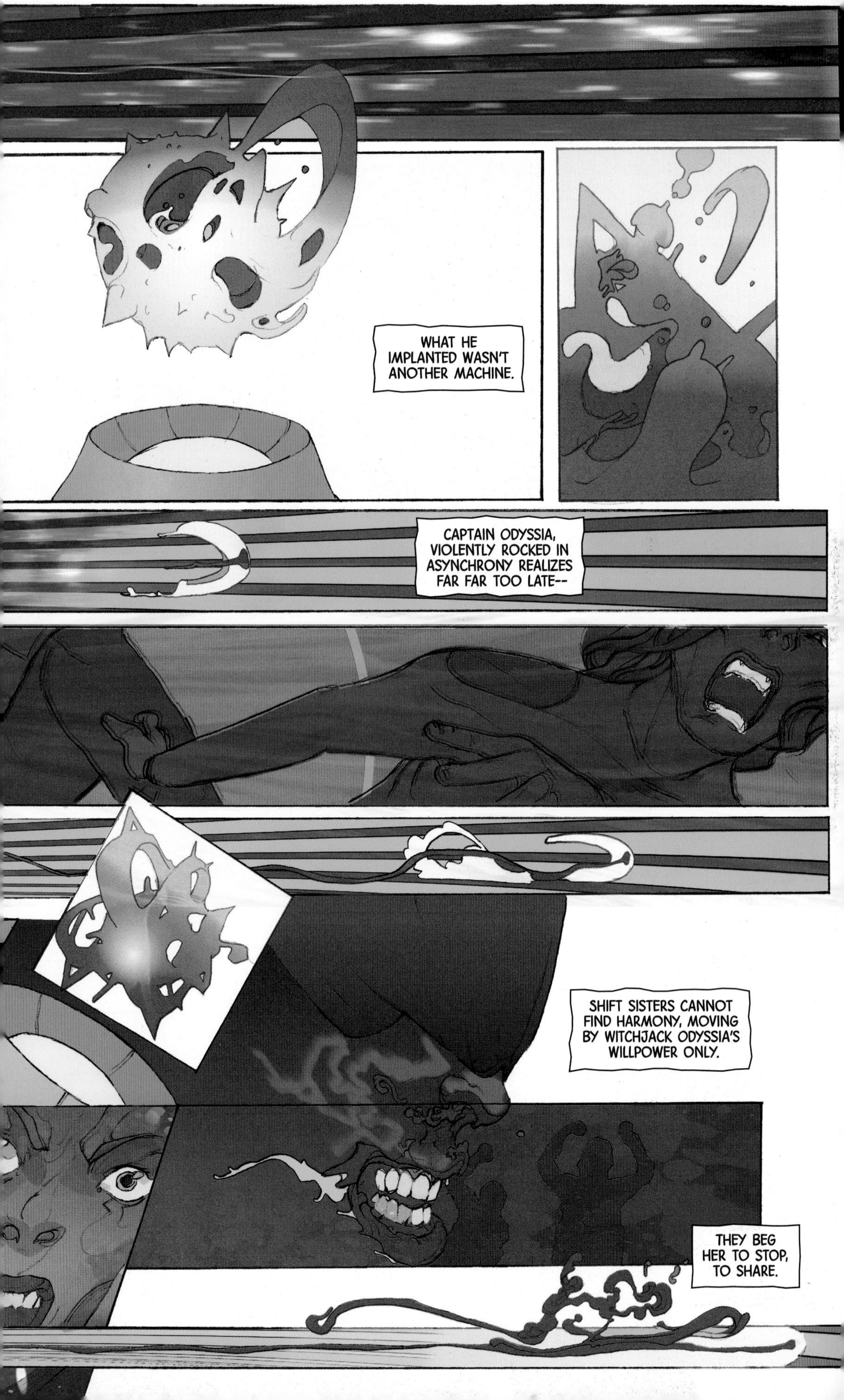
WHAT HE IMPLANTED WASN'T ANOTHER MACHINE.
CAPTAIN ODYSSIA, VIOLENTLY ROCKED IN ASYNCHRONY REALIZES FAR FAR TOO LATE--
SHIFT SISTERS CANNOT FIND HARMONY, MOVING BY WITCHJACK ODYSSIA'S WILLPOWER ONLY.
THEY BEG HER TO STOP, TO SHARE.

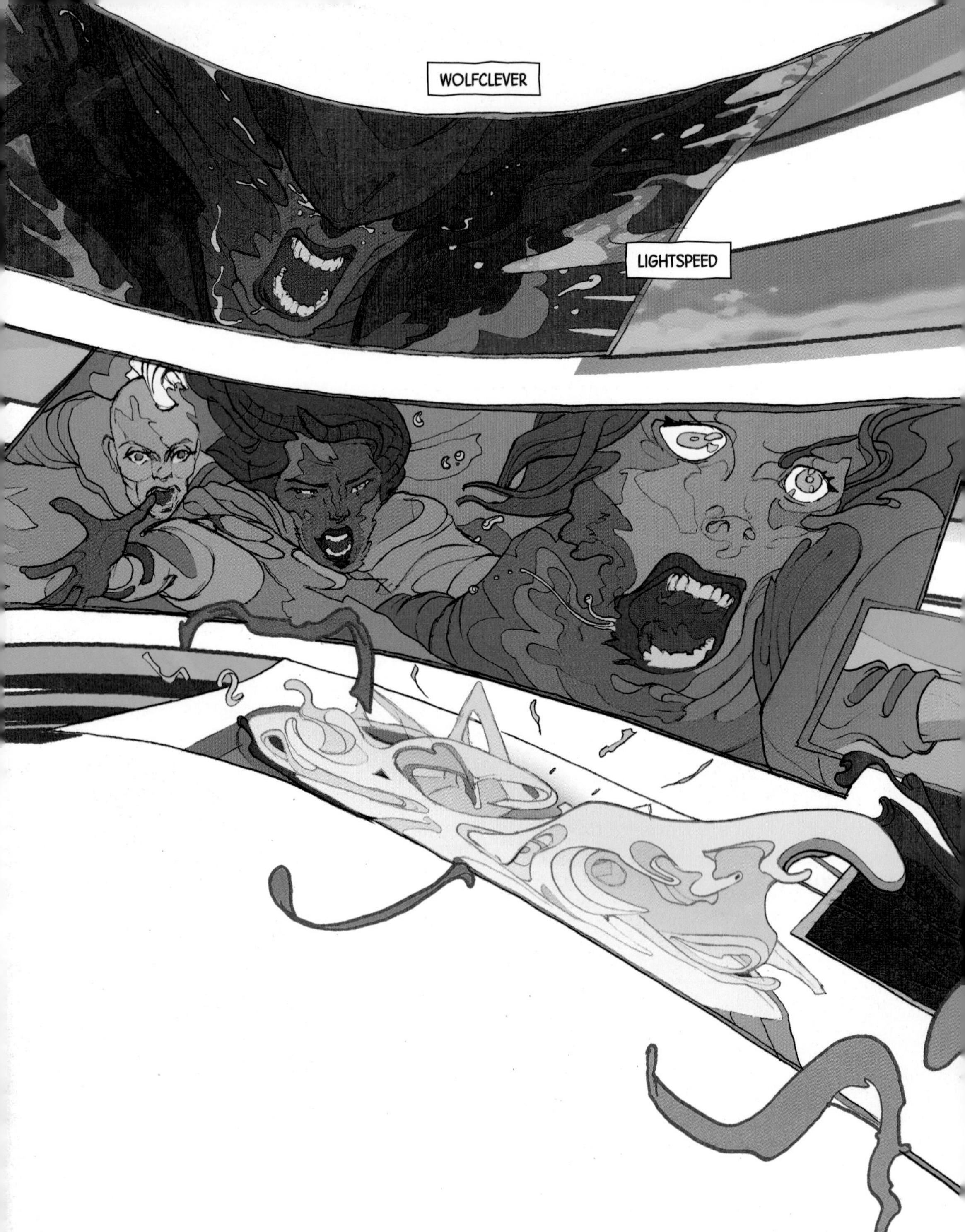
WOLFCLEVER
LIGHTSPEED

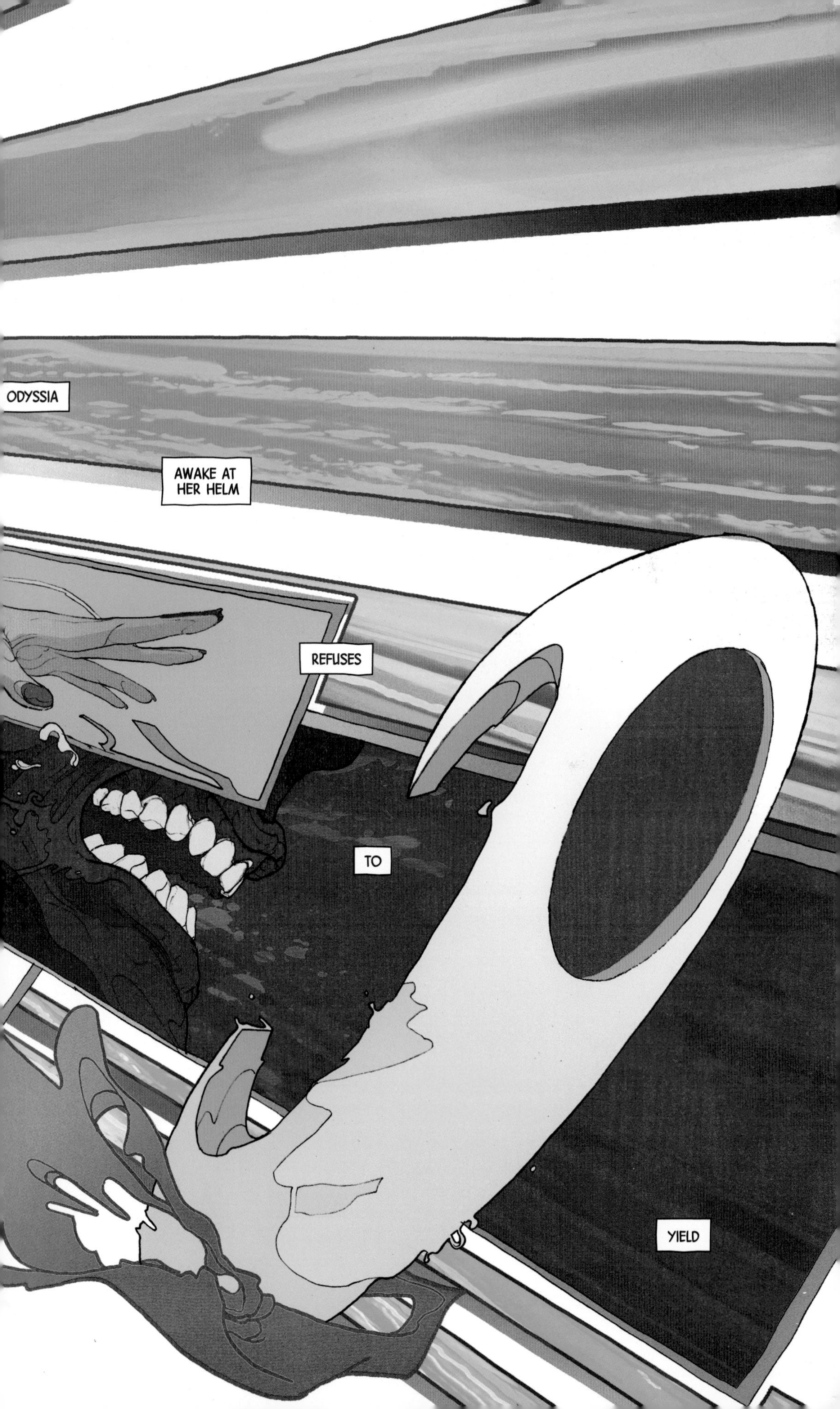
ODYSSIA
AWAKE AT HER HELM
REFUSES
TO
YIELD

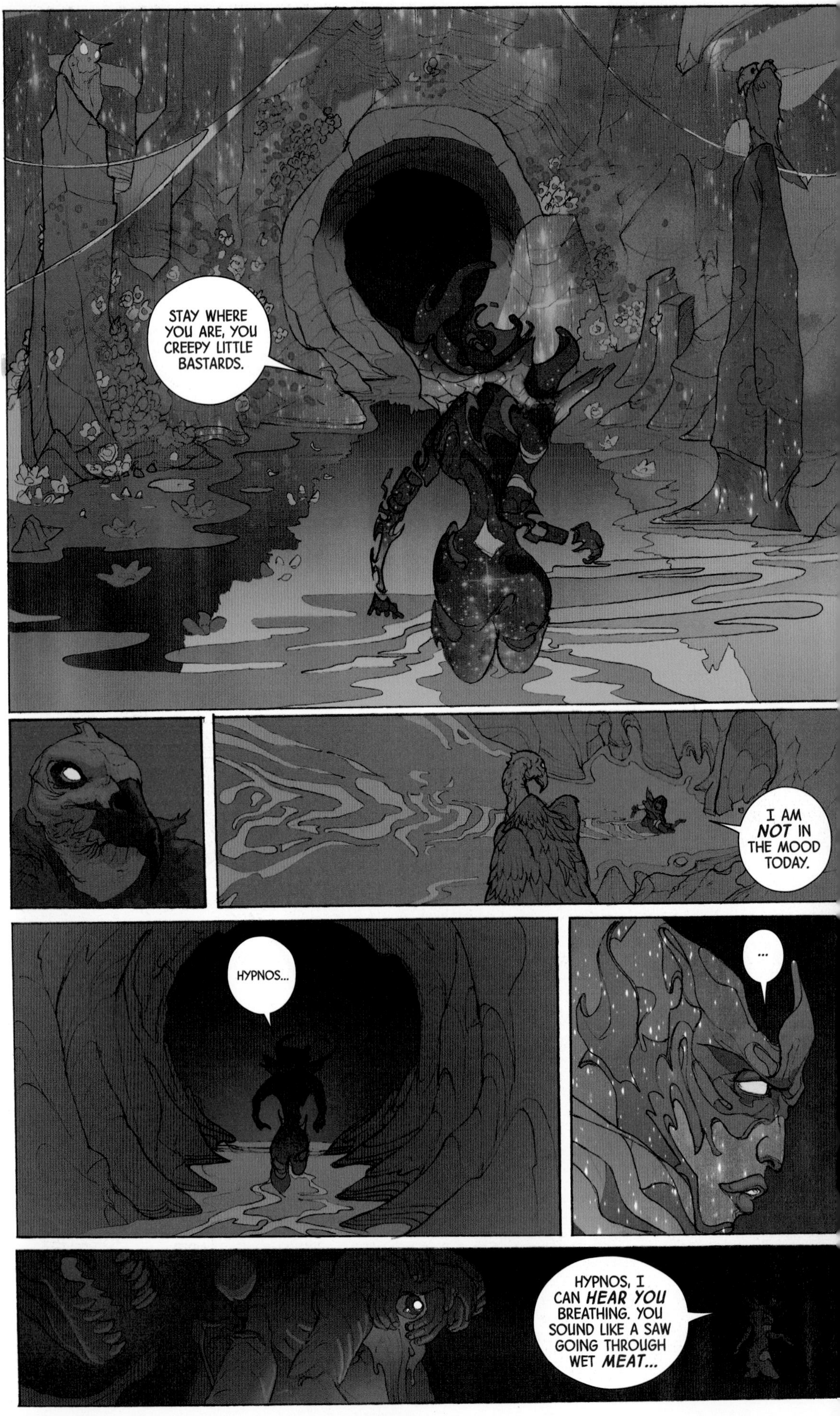
STAY WHERE YOU ARE, YOU CREEPY LITTLE BASTARDS.
I AM *NOT* IN THE MOOD TODAY.
HYPNOS...
...
HYPNOS, I CAN *HEAR YOU* BREATHING. YOU SOUND LIKE A SAW GOING THROUGH WET *MEAT*...

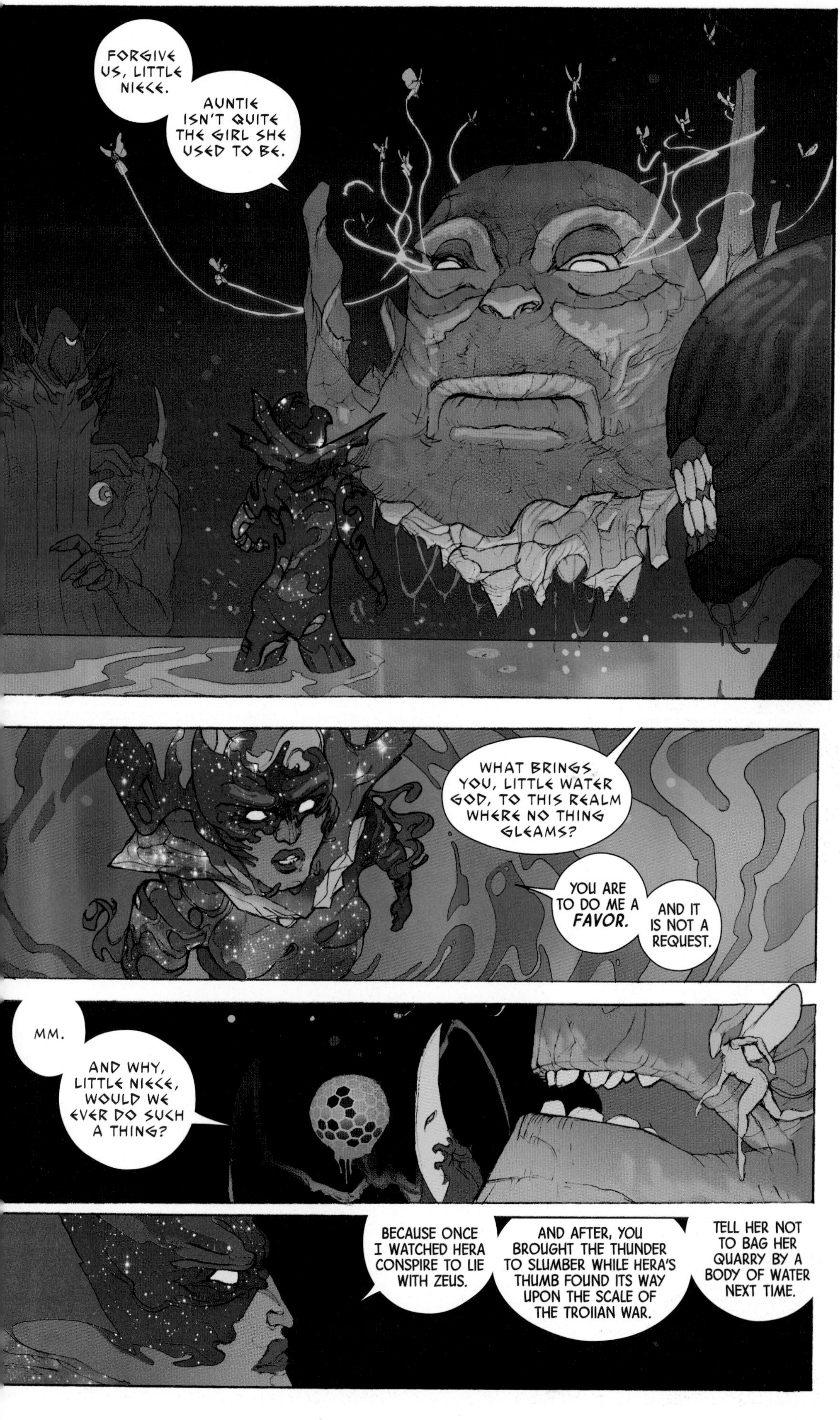
FORGIVE US, LITTLE NIECE.
AUNTIE ISN'T QUITE THE GIRL SHE USED TO BE.
WHAT BRINGS YOU, LITTLE WATER GOD, TO THIS REALM WHERE NO THING GLEAMS?
YOU ARE TO DO ME A *FAVOR.*
AND IT IS NOT A REQUEST.
MM.
AND WHY, LITTLE NIECE, WOULD WE EVER DO SUCH A THING?
BECAUSE ONCE I WATCHED HERA CONSPIRE TO LIE WITH ZEUS.
AND AFTER, YOU BROUGHT THE THUNDER TO SLUMBER WHILE HERA'S THUMB FOUND ITS WAY UPON THE SCALE OF THE TROJIAN WAR.
TELL HER NOT TO BAG HER QUARRY BY A BODY OF WATER NEXT TIME.

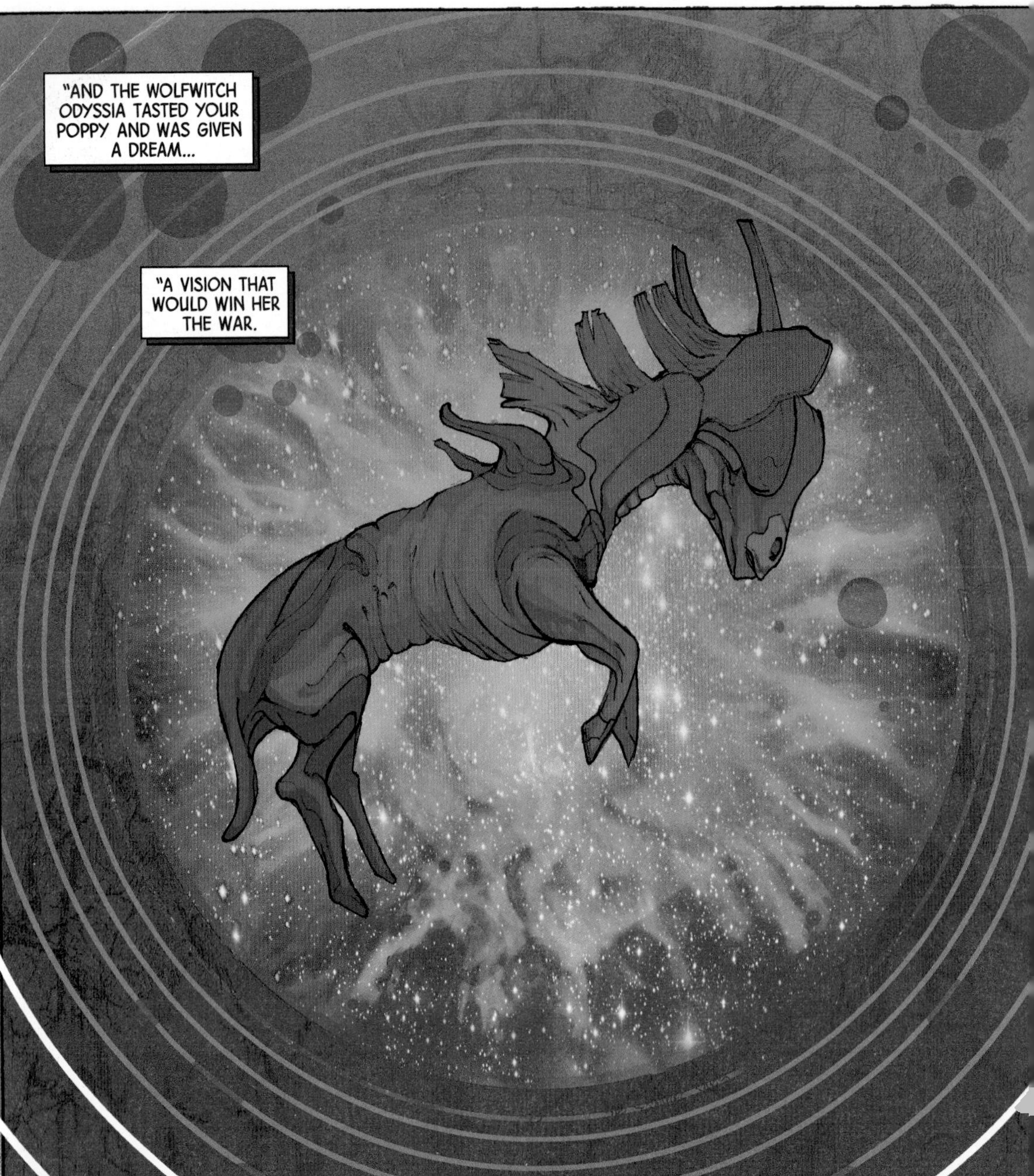
"AND THE WOLFWITCH ODYSSIA TASTED YOUR POPPY AND WAS GIVEN A DREAM...
"A VISION THAT WOULD WIN HER THE WAR.

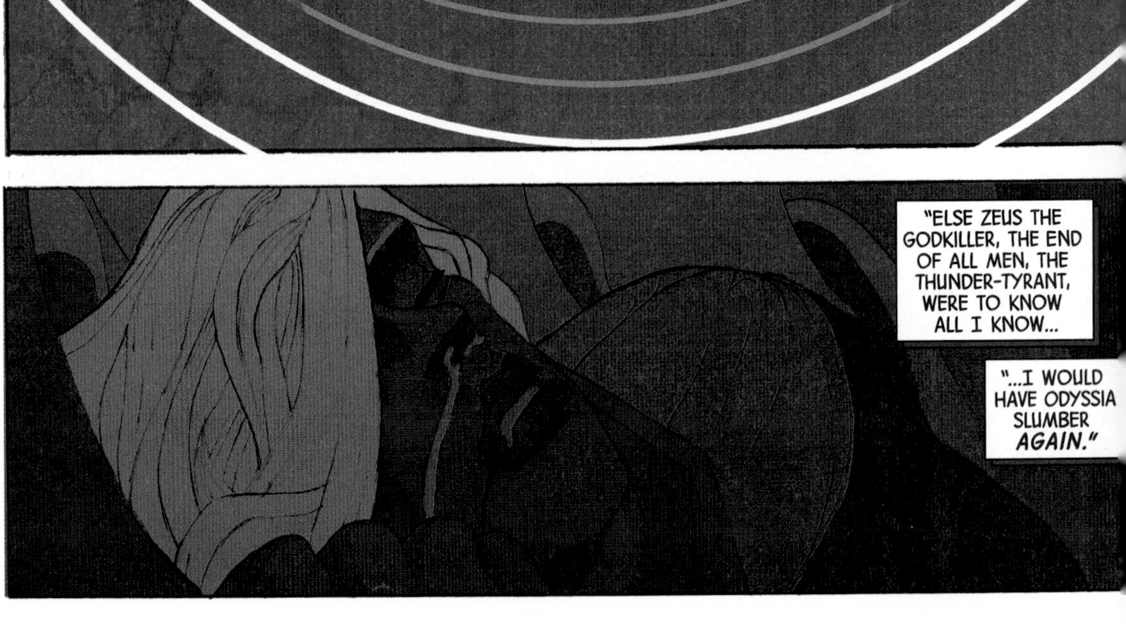
"ELSE ZEUS THE GODKILLER, THE END OF ALL MEN, THE THUNDER-TYRANT, WERE TO KNOW ALL I KNOW...
"...I WOULD HAVE ODYSSIA SLUMBER *AGAIN.*"

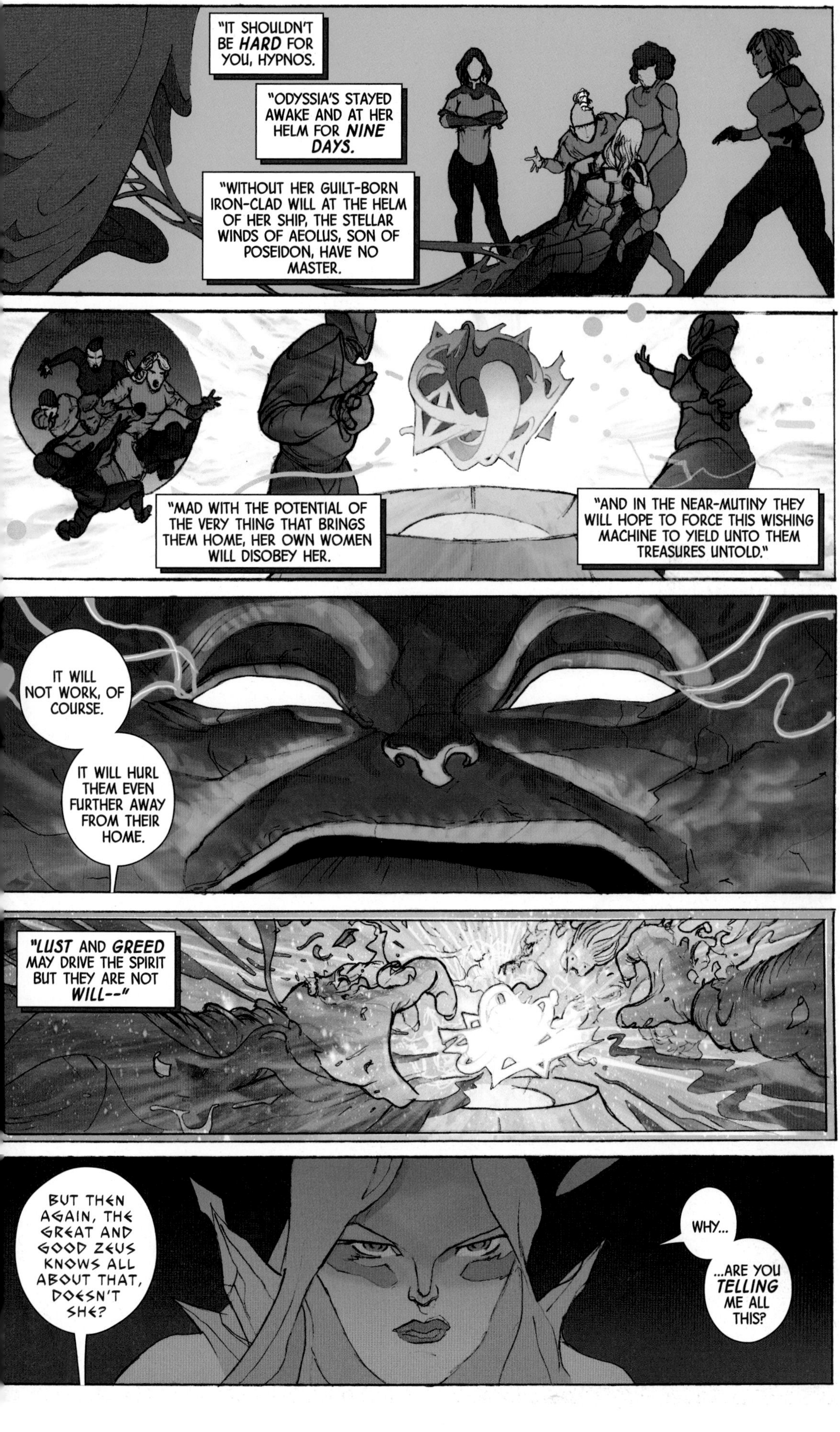
"IT SHOULDN'T BE HARD FOR YOU, HYPNOS.
"ODYSSIA'S STAYED AWAKE AND AT HER HELM FOR NINE DAYS.
"WITHOUT HER GUILT-BORN IRON-CLAD WILL AT THE HELM OF HER SHIP, THE STELLAR WINDS OF AEOLUS, SON OF POSEIDON, HAVE NO MASTER.
"MAD WITH THE POTENTIAL OF THE VERY THING THAT BRINGS THEM HOME, HER OWN WOMEN WILL DISOBEY HER.
"AND IN THE NEAR-MUTINY THEY WILL HOPE TO FORCE THIS WISHING MACHINE TO YIELD UNTO THEM TREASURES UNTOLD."
IT WILL NOT WORK, OF COURSE.
IT WILL HURL THEM EVEN FURTHER AWAY FROM THEIR HOME.
"LUST AND GREED MAY DRIVE THE SPIRIT BUT THEY ARE NOT WILL--"
BUT THEN AGAIN, THE GREAT AND GOOD ZEUS KNOWS ALL ABOUT THAT, DOESN'T SHE?
WHY...
...ARE YOU TELLING ME ALL THIS?

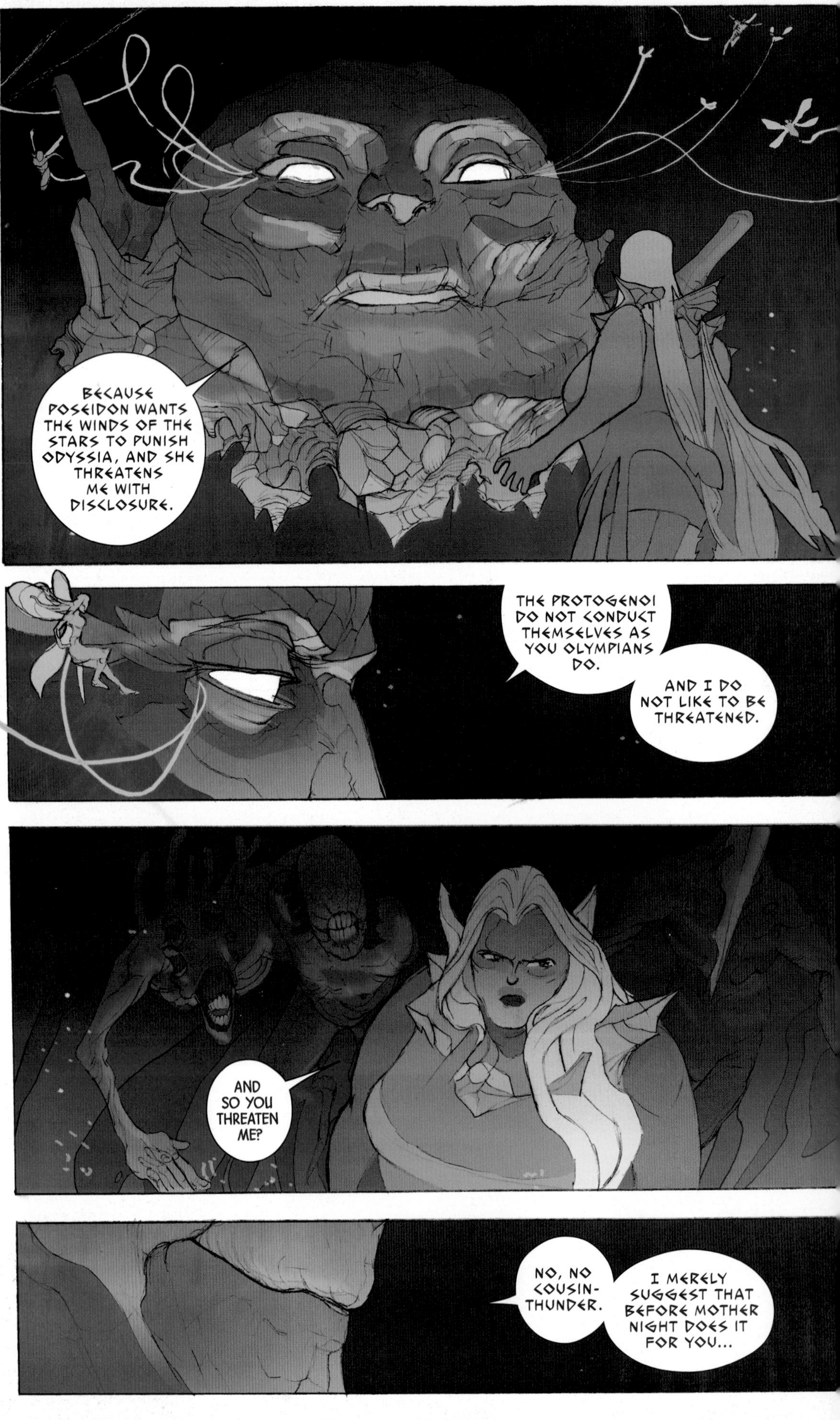

BECAUSE POSEIDON WANTS THE WINDS OF THE STARS TO PUNISH ODYSSIA, AND SHE THREATENS ME WITH DISCLOSURE.
THE PROTOGENOI DO NOT CONDUCT THEMSELVES AS YOU OLYMPIANS DO.
AND I DO NOT LIKE TO BE THREATENED.
AND SO YOU THREATEN ME?
NO, NO COUSIN-THUNDER.
I MERELY SUGGEST THAT BEFORE MOTHER NIGHT DOES IT FOR YOU...

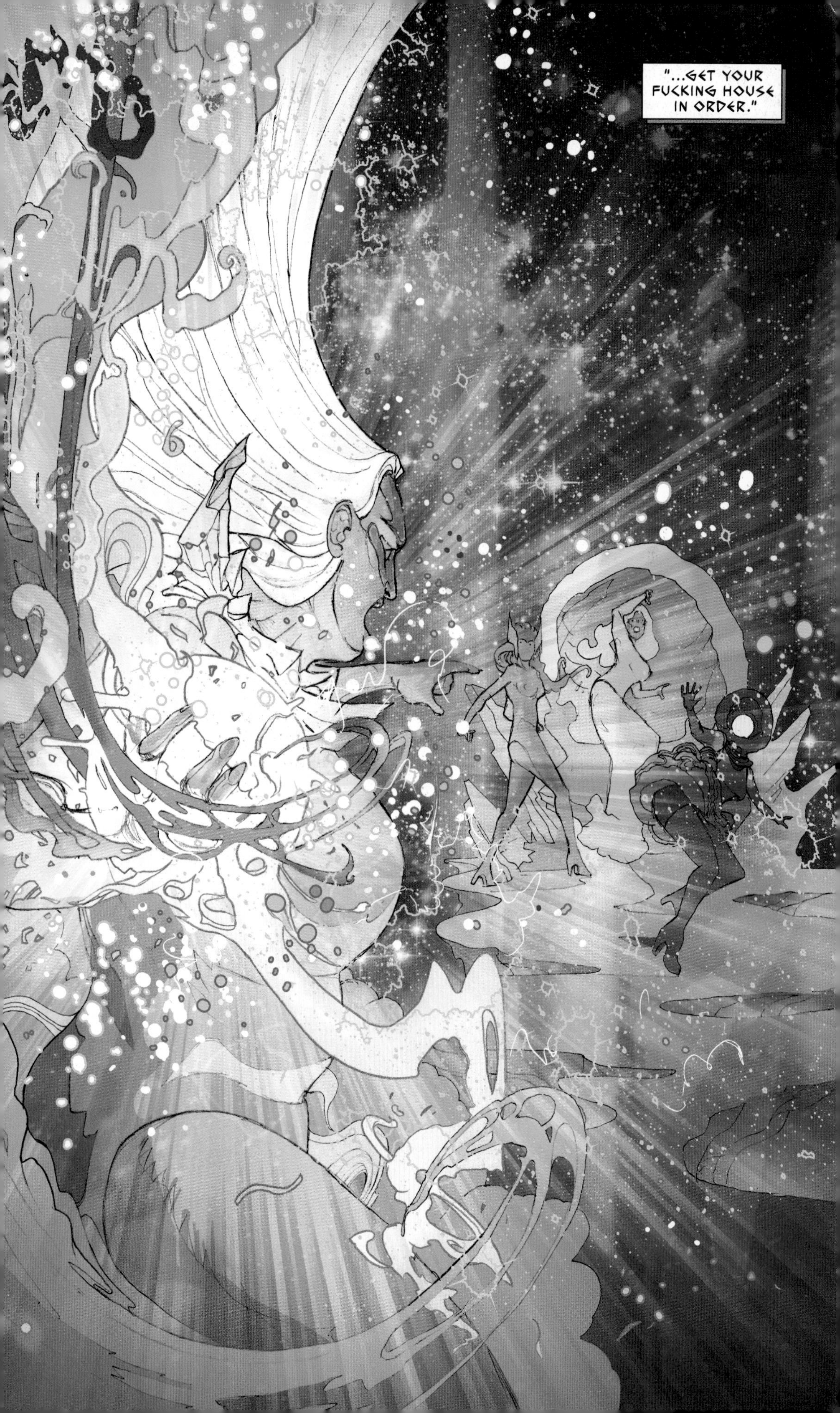
"...GET YOUR FUCKING HOUSE IN ORDER."

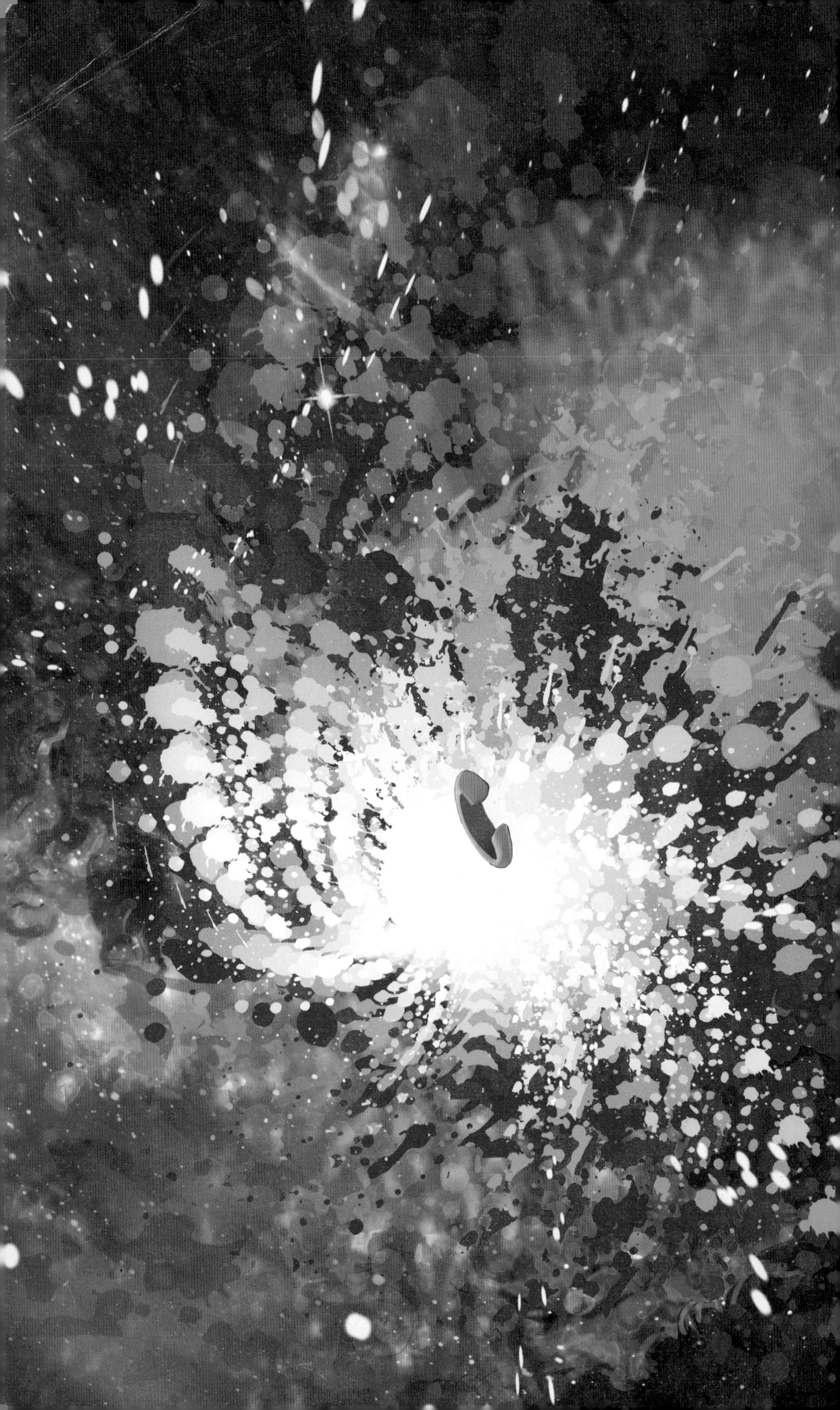